the Perfume Garden

Kate Lord Brown has worked as an art
consultant, curating collections for palaces
and embassies in Europe and the Middle East.
She was a finalist in ITV's The People's Author
competition in 2009. Visit her website at
www.katelordbrown.com.

Also by Kate Lord Brown

The Beauty Chorus

the Perfume Garden

KATE LORD BROWN

CORVUS

First published in trade paperback in Great Britain in 2012 by Corvus, an imprint of
Atlantic Books Ltd.

This paperback edition published in Great Britain in 2013 by Corvus, an imprint of
Atlantic Books Ltd.

10 9 8 7 6 5 4 3 2

A CIP catalogue record for this book is available from the British Library.

Paperback ISBN: 978 1 84887 934 8
E-book ISBN: 978 0 85789 675 9

Printed and bound by CPI Group (UK) Ltd, Croydon, CR0 4YY

Corvus
An imprint of Atlantic Books Ltd
Ormond House
26–27 Boswell Street
London
WC1N 3JZ

www.corvus-books.co.uk

For VL and KL, PB and DB

I have had worse partings, but none that so
Gnaws at my mind still. Perhaps it is roughly
Saying what God alone could perfectly show –
How selfhood begins with a walking away,
And love is proved in the letting go.

—Cecil Day Lewis

You can go proudly. You are history. You are legend.

—La Pasionaria
Final speech to the International Brigades
Barcelona, October 1938

1

SPAIN, SEPTEMBER 1936

In the last autumn of her life, the girl lay on her back nestled in the pale whispering grass beneath the Andalusian sun. Clouds idled overhead, and her gaze followed a solitary white butterfly, flying low with the breeze. She rolled over, wound on the film in her Rolleiflex, and held the camera to her eye.

'There you are,' Capa said, stretching out at her side. He squinted, gazed up the hillside. Three militiamen were standing there, rifles cocked, aiming out across the plain towards the mountains. 'I've been looking all over for you. I thought I'd lost my *pequeña rubia*, my little blonde ...' He kissed her shoulder, swung his Leica around. 'You look like a vixen hiding out in the grass here.' Side by side, sun glinting on the camera lenses, they began to shoot.

'I was bored. It looked like you were set playing cards for the afternoon.' Gerda focussed on the men. The lens turned smoothly beneath her fingertips as she framed her shot, first the stalks of grass, then the sweat-streaked faces of the men swimming into focus. The harsh sun beat down relentlessly on them, cicadas singing on the hillside.

'There's nothing going on here, just crowds of guys

parading and eating the best hams in town.' Capa edged forwards, his elbows stirring the dry earth. She could taste the dust, the salt on her skin as she licked her lips. She was hungry, she realised suddenly, but the light had been so good and clear this morning she hadn't wanted to miss the chance of capturing the perfect shot.

'We need something good to send to *Vu* magazine, André. It's time to get back to Madrid. Where are we anyway? Near Espejo?'

'Yeah, somewhere near Cordoba. I think we're heading to Cerro Muriano ...' Capa eased the lens around.

She sensed he was distracted, on to something. He was often like this when he was working, caught up in the moment of the photograph. Gerda remembered chasing a butterfly as a child in Germany, trying to catch it in her cupped hands. Sometimes photography felt like that to her – a luminous, perfect flash of colour and light just out of her grasp. They were both hunters, she realised, hunters of light. She noticed Capa had his camera trained on a militiaman who stood alone on the hillside, his rifle in his right hand. The soldier's white shirt was tucked into a leather cartridge belt, but he looked like a civilian, more like a young guy out shooting rabbits than a man at war. 'We're too far away from them.' He began to inch forward on his stomach. 'What am I always telling you?'

'If the photo's no good, you're not close enough.' Gerda pushed her red-blonde hair away from her face.

Capa grinned, a soft, purring laugh bubbling up. 'You're learning.' He clenched his fist, and pushed it into the air. 'Forward!' They scrambled up the hill, laughing like children, her rope-soled shoes slipping silently on the dry grass.

'There,' she said, raising her camera to her eye. She fired off a couple of shots, capturing two soldiers whose rifles pierced the sky like the blades of grass beneath their feet, their tanned faces the colour of the earth below.

Capa leapt to his feet, and strode over to the soldiers. '*Salud*!'

At the crest of the hill, Gerda sat back on her haunches to check her film. As she stood and caught her breath, she scanned the groups of Republican soldiers in the distance; thin, ragtag figures crouching low in the grass, dotted across the hillside like grazing sheep, a vast El Greco sky of billowing clouds above them. Gerda tightened the thick leather belt around her blue *mono* boilersuit, and felt for the pistol tucked there. For once, they were not in the thick of the action, but she knew that time would come again soon. She shielded her eyes, gazed warily across the plain to the distant, lavender haze of the mountains. Even here, away from the front, there was always the risk of snipers. From her breast pocket she slipped a compact and reapplied scarlet lipstick. She slicked the high arch of her brow, brushed some dirt from her cheek. At Capa's laugh, she looked up and smiled at him.

'I just spoke to the guys. We're moving on,' he said. As he walked towards her, she felt the familiar quickening of desire. It was always the same, ever since the moment she first saw him in Paris. 'Let's get a couple more shots and head back to Madrid.'

She ran her hand through his thick, dark hair, cupped his stubbled jaw. 'Let's get to the hotel ...'

'Now that,' he said, slipping his arm around her waist, 'is the best idea I have heard all day, Miss Taro.'

'Frankly, all I need is a hot bath and a clean bed, Mr

Robert Capa.' She flashed him a quick glance as she shrugged off his embrace.

'André,' he called as she walked ahead. 'Not Capa, with you. I will always be your André.'

'Always,' she said, laughing. She glanced up at the sky, shielded her eyes from the sun. 'Anyway, Robert Capa is as much me as you.' Gerda turned to him. 'We created him. The greatest American war photographer in the world.'

'You called?' He raised an eyebrow, grinned up at her as he swung his camera round. 'One of these days, I'm going to make an honest woman of you,' he said, stopping to roll on the film in his camera.

Gerda glanced over her shoulder at him as she skipped nimbly down the hillside. 'We'll see, André. Let's make a legend of Robert Capa first, shall we?' She saw him run back up the hill a little way, raise his Leica, focus on one of the militiamen. The shutter clicked, a trigger was pulled somewhere, and as the soldier fell, he was caught by the camera, frozen between heaven and earth, caught in history.

2

LONDON, SEPTEMBER 11, 2001

You see, Em, the trouble is they – the doctors that is – said it will give me ' closure ' (what a ghastly word), to leave a letter for you. I said ' do you really think I can distil a lifetime's worth of experience into a single letter? Can I say everything I want to my daughter on a few sheets of paper?' I cannot. You know me, I never did stop rabbiting on, did I, darling?

An image of Liberty came to Emma then – her mother sitting on the kitchen table in her grandmother Freya's house. It must have been the late seventies, because, against the morning sun, Liberty's hair was a chestnut halo of Kate Bush crimping and Blondie was on the radio. She was flapping her arms as she talked, and Freya was doubled over laughing. Emma was curled up in the dog basket by the stove, eating toast as she cuddled Charles's new pug puppy. That's what she remembered – the certain smell of home, of coffee percolating, fresh toast, the dry biscuit smell of the dog as he pawed at the green enamel 'Head Girl' badge pinned to her woollen jumper. Some people's memories lie in images or songs, but for Emma it was always fragrance. Liberty had taught her well, and even as a child she instinctively detected the harmonious notes of the scent accord that to her conjured 'home'.

'Emma, do get up, darling,' Freya had said. 'Look at you, your school uniform is covered with hair.' Emma remembered the warmth of the dog, the delicious fawn belly wriggling in her small hands. She remembered how Liberty had tickled her until they were both on the floor giggling, the puppy leaping around them. As her mother hugged her, Emma breathed in the scent of her perfume. Roses – Liberty always smelt like a rose garden in full bloom to her; warm, sunlit, a pure *soliflore*.

> *As you'll see, I got a bit carried away. I've left*
> *you a whole box of letters, one for every occasion*
> *I can think of. And I've enclosed my last notebook.*
> *I like to think of you picking up where I left off,*
> *Em. Promise me you'll carry on. Use it. Fill it with*
> *wonderful things.*

Emma leant her elbow on the suitcase at her side. She had been travelling for months, but as the Number 22 Routemaster bus lurched through the lunchtime traffic along the King's Road, she felt the days fall away. It was a typical cool, grey London day, a light autumn breeze scurrying leaves along the pavements. Nothing had changed, except her. The nausea that had dogged her for months welled up again, and she rummaged through her pocket for a mint. The lining had torn, and as she read Liberty's note, she wriggled her index finger down to the hem, searching in vain.

She had turned to the last page in her mother's notebook a hundred times, pen poised, and frozen, unable to pick up where Liberty had left off. Nothing seemed wonderful enough. Emma scanned the note one last time. It was the only one she had taken with her on her travels, and she had read it so many times the paper was falling apart along the folds. The letters were waiting for her, unopened, in a black lacquer box in Liberty's studio. After her mother's will had been read, and Joe had left, Emma had sat looking at the box for hours as dawn light filtered through the sloping glass roof. She had placed it in the middle of Liberty's desk – a specially built perfumer's 'organ' surrounded by tiered shelves of bottles, each one containing a note of fragrance. That was how Liberty had taught her their craft – to think of each essence as a musical note, each bottle on the organ as a key. This was where Liberty had composed all of her masterpieces, where Emma had played as a child. It was the place she still felt her mother's presence most.

The sound of milk bottles being delivered on the street below had roused her finally, and she had lifted off the lid of the box. She wasn't quite sure what she was expecting from Liberty – an explosion of confetti, a coiled paper snake to leap out. She laughed with relief when she saw her mother had simply painted the interior bright orange – her favourite colour. Her hand trembled as she lifted the loose sheet of paper on top. Beneath was a parcel of letters tied with cerise velvet ribbon, and the small black notebook. The first envelope was marked 'On Family'. As Emma read her mother's accompanying note, tears filled her eyes.

I love you, Em. I am so terribly proud of the woman you have become. I can't bear the thought of leaving you, but know my love goes with you, will always be with you. I know that love lives on.

Mum x

She had been tempted to rip open all the envelopes that morning, to gorge hungrily on Liberty's words. Just reading the note over and over brought her closer. But she waited. When she told Freya she had decided to leave the letters in London while she travelled, Freya had laughed.

'It's up to you, Em,' she said. 'You always did save your treats, even as a child. I've never known anyone who could make a bar of chocolate last so long.'

Emma took a deep breath, and gazed out of the window. It was almost her stop. *Perhaps it's time to stop saving the best till last*, she thought. She folded the note and slipped it into her mother's Moleskine notebook on her lap, flicking on through the pages illuminated with Liberty's flamboyant handwriting. Words leapt out at her – 'neroli', '*duende*', 'passion'. Her mother had pasted in cuttings alongside the notes and formulas for the new perfume she had been working on – pictures of orange groves, searing blue skies, a yellowed newspaper advert for a Robert Capa exhibition. It was the famous 'falling soldier' picture. Emma traced her finger over the soldier's face, wondered what he was thinking at the moment when death caught him running down that hill. She wondered what he saw as he fell. As she touched the paper, she felt the contours of something beneath. She flipped to the next page, and laid her hand on the smallest envelope Liberty had left in the box with the letters. On it, her mother had written an address: Villa del Valle, La Pobla, Valencia, Spain. Inside, there was just an old key. *I must ask Freya if she knows anything about it*, she thought. Emma had lain awake the night she opened that envelope, turning the key over in her hand, her mind full of possibilities. *Typical Mum*, she thought, remembering all the magical mystery tours Liberty had taken her on as a child, the trails of clues she had laid for Emma to follow to hidden presents. The chase, the anticipation, was always more fun than the present itself. Emma smiled sadly as she tucked the envelope safely back inside the notebook.

Emma turned the pages, glimpsed the melancholy, serene face of a madonna, a photo of a whitewashed wall with flaming bougainvillea spilling over it. The notes became sparser, the hand less sure towards the end. She sensed Liberty had been looking back, as well as forwards. Next to a pasted label from 'Chérie Farouche', the perfume Liberty had created for Emma on her eighteenth birthday, she had written: 'Some perfumes are, like children, innocent, as sweet as oboes, green as meadow sward – Baudelaire'. It was still Emma's signature scent. On her it smelt like rain in a garden at first, fresh and intoxicating, then as the green top notes evaporated Emma always thought of the earth, of picking flowers in a forest with her mother. The heart note of lily of the valley and jasmine melded perfectly with the base of sandalwood and musk. Liberty always said the scent was like her – shy but surprisingly fierce. A photograph of Liberty with Emma as a baby was tucked into that page. She flicked on, unbearable longing piercing her as she looked at her mother's beautiful, open smile. Emma paused at her mother's final sketch of a new Liberty Temple perfume bottle, her hurried scrawl: *'Jasmine? Orange blossom, yes!'*

Then came the poignant empty spaces. The blank pages her mother had left her to fill. Emma blinked quickly as she touched the gold filigree locket around her neck. She hadn't expected to feel so upset returning home. For months, she had convinced herself that she was coping as she sleepwalked through endless meetings. Countries and hotel rooms kaleidoscoped in her mind. Her hand instinctively fell to the gentle swell of her stomach. *Something wonderful,* she thought. She pulled a pen from her bag, smoothed her hand over the first clean page, then wrote: 'Spain'.

3

CAMBRIDGE, SEPTEMBER 1936

The last punts of the year drifted along the Backs on the River Cam, autumn leaves swirling in their wake. Charles tucked the letter from his sister Freya into the breast pocket of his tweed jacket, and settled back, his hands laced behind his head.

'How is she?' the fair-haired boy at the stern asked, heaving down on the pole.

'Freya? It sounds ghastly in Spain, to be honest.'

'Shall we go or not?'

Charles thought of the copy of *Vu* he had seen the night before, of Robert Capa's photographs of the war. One of the students from King's had stood on a chair in the pub, thrust the magazine into the air, shouting above the noise of the bar that anyone in their right mind had to join the International Brigades and fight fascism in Spain. Charles was haunted by the photograph of the falling soldier he had seen, could almost feel the impact of the bullet, the thud of the body as it hit the ground.

'Charles!'

'Sorry, Hugo. I was just thinking.'

'I heard there's a chap in Paris sneaking people down

on the railway, or over the Pyrenees. I have an address on the Rue Lafayette that we can go to. There's a train of volunteers leaving in a couple of days from the Gare d'Austerlitz. Your friend Cornford said we could be at the training camp in Albacete in a few days.'

Charles thought of the Movietone news headline he had seen the night before as the fug of cigarette smoke in the cinema joined the leaping black-and-white flames on the screen: *'Civil War follows fascist revolt in unhappy country. All is turmoil.'*

'I don't know. I haven't squared everything with Crozier at the *Manchester Guardian* yet. If there's no job for us ...'

'Then we shall just be common soldiers like the rest of them,' Hugo said, laughing. 'It would serve you right for spending your savings on that ridiculously expensive camera. You could have bought a car, Charles. Personally I shall just be taking a pencil and notebook.'

'Photography is the future, Hugo. If people see a photo, or a film, they believe it, mark my words.' He paused. 'Still, perhaps it was a bit rash. If we don't get this job I can't afford my ticket down.'

'You could always take portraits.'

Charles scowled at him as he stood and took the pole. 'I've always fancied being a war reporter.'

Hugo stepped back into the punt, the water lapping the boat around them. 'Butterflies not exciting enough for you?'

'I can always come back to my PhD in a couple of months, once the war is over.' Charles exhaled as the punt skimmed along. 'Though very few of my mentors even have doctorates.'

'Lepidoptery is full of gentlemen amateurs.'

'Oh, shut up, Hugo. For goodness sake, sit down. You'll tip the ruddy thing over.' Charles glared ahead. Clouds scudded across the sky, reflected in the windows of King's Chapel like a bridal train sweeping by. Rain began to pepper the smooth surface of the river. 'At least in Spain we might make a difference.'

'Exactly. Look at what is going on in my country, what Hitler is doing.' Hugo's face fell for a moment. 'I can't just hide away here in an ivory tower, much as it would please my parents. It's the first chance we've had to fight back. If we don't, Hitler, Mussolini, Franco ... well, they'll take the whole of Europe.' He lit a cigarette, flicked the match into the river. 'Besides, it's a beautiful country. I can't bear to think of it being torn to pieces.'

'I told you we came back too soon,' Charles said. As the rain pattered down on his face, Charles remembered the shimmering summer heat of the hillsides near his friend's old house in Yegen, the swish of the dry long grass against his legs, the scent of rosemary and lavender crushed underfoot as he hunted down butterflies. He thought of the snow on the Sierra Nevada, the stars that seemed to glow with unusual brilliance there. 'Do you remember how beautiful it is? I can't believe the country is eating itself alive.'

'Well, that's civil war.' Hugo exhaled a plume of smoke. 'The Spanish are a bloodthirsty lot. Bullfights and flamenco, peasants on mules – it's like the Middle Ages still.'

'Perhaps it's better than all this,' Charles said, idly watching a woman in a beige gaberdine mackintosh who was walking a wheezing labrador along the bank.

13

'There's still passion. They look death square in the eye, see it as the ultimate, culminating moment of existence.' He leant towards Hugo. 'The cemetery is the *tierra de la verdad*, their moment of truth. To the Spanish, all life is an illusion.'

'I still say they are backward.'

'No, they are in touch with the earth. They still believe in *hechiceras*, white witches, you know. They think they fly in the moonlight and meet on the threshing room floors. You have to watch out for the *brujas*, though, the black witches …'

'Don't be ridiculous,' Hugo said, laughing. 'You are a romantic, Charles – perhaps the last of a dying breed.' He held out his hand to his friend. 'So, we shall go. Agreed? The world hardly needs another second-rate German artist, and for you there will always be butterflies.'

Charles shook Hugo's hand, then settled back and laid his fingertips against the rough wool of his jacket, felt Freya's letter crinkle in his pocket. 'It's our chance. What's being played out in Spain is a miniature version of what could happen across the world. If we don't fight the fascists on the roads to Madrid, we'll be fighting them on the King's Road or the Fosse Way next thing you know.'

Freya huddled in the back of the truck as it bumped along the road towards Madrid, a purple dressing gown tied over her head against the cold.

'Damn,' she said under her breath as they hit another pothole and her pen skittered across the page. Her hands were freezing, and she hunched over her dog-eared copy of *Gone With the Wind*, the pages flapping in the breeze.

Spain is quite beautiful as you know, Charles.

she wrote on the blank back page.

You simply must come. Thank you for the fruit cake by the way. It is a boost to get your letters. It seems like a lifetime since people showered us with flowers at Victoria Station as we left - was it only last month? The drive down from the Spanish border was exhilarating. We had the truck loaded up with toffees and liquorice for the children. At every village we passed, they would come running to us. Women pressed oranges and melons on us - Charles you would not believe the bliss of cold melon when your throat is tight and dry from hours on the road.

We are desperately short of everything in the hospitals. The nurses are exhausted and hungry all the time, and the winter will be worse, but we mustn't grumble. You would not believe how brave and marvellous the people I am working with are. This poor country. I cannot bear it that this sickness, this civil war, is tearing it in two.

Come, as soon as you can. For the first time, there is only one choice for us. Good must win over evil. We cannot let them crush democracy here. This is our war too, dear brother.

The truck shuddered to a halt at the first checkpoint outside the city, and Freya looked up. Vehicles streamed past, and she heard a babble of voices, a phone ringing non-stop in the guard house. Freya signed the note quickly and tore out the page, stuffing it in an envelope she had ready to send. She untied the arms of the dressing gown from under her chin, and shook out her bobbed blonde hair.

'*Salud, compañero*!' she called to one of the guards. 'The post?'

'He comes soon.' The soldier motioned for her to pass him the letter. As the truck pulled away, she thrust it into his outstretched hand.

'*Gracias*!'

'*De nada*. No problem.'

Freya sat back among the other nurses, and looked towards Madrid as they drove on towards the city. She had heard that fifty churches had been set ablaze, and acrid smoke still hung in the sky, dark and sulphurous. *This is it*, she thought, suddenly aware that they were driving right into the heart of the battle. Freya glanced at the pale faces of the nurses around her, and saw her fear reflected there. *Pull yourself together*, she told herself. Her eyes smarted with the dusty wind buffeting her face. Freya's guts coiled with adrenalin as beyond the crashing noise of the trucks she heard in the distance the first thunderous boom and explosion of war.

4

LONDON, SEPTEMBER 11, 2001

Emma leapt down onto the pavement from the bus, rose petals and golden Ash leaves drifting at the steps of Chelsea Registry Office like hearts and bones. Her black coat swirled around her as she strode through the crowd, the heels of her polished tan boots clicking as she dragged her silver suitcase behind her, airline tags fluttering. She paused, looked up at the newly married couple embracing in the doorway. As their friends cheered, she walked on. *It could have been us*, she thought, searching through her bag as her phone rang.

'Hello. Emma Temple,' she said, crooking the mobile against her shoulder as she turned into Flood Street.

'Thank God. I've been worried sick. Are you home yet?' Freya asked.

'Just.' She smiled as she stopped outside Chelsea Manor Studios. A group of young Dutch tourists were taking photographs by the entrance. They stepped aside to let her pass, and one of the boys heaved her case up to the door. 'Thank you,' she said.

'Is Sergeant Pepper, yes?' the boy said. 'The Beatles?'

'Yes, that's right. They took the cover photo in my

Mum's studio.' Emma was dizzy with jet lag, her eyes red and raw. All she wanted to do was collapse into bed, but their young faces touched her. 'Here, let me.' She beckoned for him to hand over the camera, and took a picture of the teenagers. As they walked away, she leant against the doorway and shifted the phone. 'Sorry. I've just arrived. The flight was delayed.'

'We've moved all your things in. It's a bit of a mess I'm afraid, but then the studio always was, even when your mother was alive.' Freya paused. 'I haven't unpacked the boxes. I thought you might want to clear out some of Liberty's things before you settle in?'

'There's no hurry. Thanks for taking care of everything. I couldn't bear to go back to the house.' She frowned. 'So she's moved in, then?'

'Delilah?' Freya's voice hardened. 'Yes. Our Ms Stafford didn't waste any time, though I wouldn't be surprised if she forced Joe to sell up and move to the States—'

'How is he?' Emma interrupted.

'Fine, he's fine. It's you I'm worried about. Have you seen the doctor yet?'

'Freya …'

'Don't worry, there's nobody here. They're all at lunch. I haven't told a soul, I promise.'

'Let's keep it that way, at least until I speak to Joe.'

'What a bloody mess,' Freya said. 'I could kill her, honestly. Delilah always was a cuckoo in the nest. I haven't spoken a word to her for weeks, not since you left. The atmosphere in the office has been hideous.'

'I can imagine. I'm sorry everyone is caught up in this.'

'What are you apologising for? None of this is your fault, Emma. As I'm always telling you, you are too damn nice. When I think what she has done to you. That woman pushed her way into the company, and then …'

'She didn't force him to choose her, you know. It was Joe's decision.'

'I know it's un-Christian of me, but I can't wait to see the look on her face when she finds out you are carrying his child.'

Emma perched on her suitcase, rested her head wearily against the wall. 'I'm thrilled about the baby, of course, but I can't say I feel proud about it. We had already separated when we …' Emma thought back to the day her mother's will was read.

'Only just. It's perfectly understandable that you needed each other. I hope— Well, let's hope he sees sense.'

'It's too late, Freya. I thought, when he came to me that night he'd chosen me.' Emma paused. 'That's why I had to get away. I feel like a complete fool.'

'No. You're far from that. Oh, it breaks my heart. You two were practically children when you met.'

'Maybe it would have made a difference if I'd agreed to marry him.'

'Nonsense.'

'Joe's always been more traditional than us.'

'No, Delilah has been after him for years.' Freya clicked her tongue in annoyance. 'You know, she had the nerve to say to me that she saw him first, that you took him from her!'

'I hope she hasn't been giving you a hard time while I've been away?'

'Don't worry about me, darling. I can handle Ms Stafford – my cat has more attitude than her.'

'Anyway, they were just friends when I met them at

Columbia.' Emma frowned. She had always wondered if that was true. 'You know what he said, last time I saw him? He was confused. He said he loves us both.'

Freya muttered something under her breath, and said 'Joe's not cut out for complicated affairs of the heart. He doesn't know what he's doing, he's still upset about your mother.'

Emma rubbed the bridge of her nose. 'He was as devastated as us when Mum finally died.'

'They were very close. In some ways I'm glad Liberty's not here to see all this, though she would have loved being a grandmother. I feel positively ancient at the thought of being a great-grandmother ...' Freya's voice became muffled as she covered the receiver to speak to someone. 'Listen, the office is filling up again. Are you coming over?'

'In a while. I'm going to grab a shower.' She paused. 'I guess I should call Joe.'

'He's in New York. Well, they are in New York.'

'Delilah went with him?'

'Of course,' Freya said. 'She couldn't risk the deal folding, could she? Not now she can smell the money. I hope you're not rushing into this. You don't have to sell the company, you know.'

Emma sighed. 'Yes I do. There's nothing here for me now. We've spent years building the business, but the Americans' offer is too good to pass up. It's a clean break.'

'Your mother would hate it. She always wanted it to be a family business, for the three of you to carry on. She would never, never have split the company between you all in her will if she had known what Delilah was up to.'

'What can I do? It seemed best she didn't know about

20

their affair.' Emma closed her eyes. 'I'm glad she didn't know. Anyway, now Joe and Delilah have a controlling interest together. There's nothing we can do. Once we've sold, I can move on.'

'Do you think so? You know the Americans will want you to stay – Liberty groomed you to be the face of the company.'

'I was just the window dressing. We all built the brand together.' Her face fell as she glanced along the street. A crocodile of five-year-olds from Hill House walked past. How many times had she and Liberty walked hand in hand, coming home from school? *All those precious, unremarked moments, gone.* Emma's throat tightened, tears pricked her eyes. No matter how hard she was working, Liberty was always there to pick her up – often late, but she always came. It was their time, after school and in the early mornings, the only times Emma ever had her mother to herself. *Backwards and forwards, hundreds of times, and I can only remember a handful of moments.*

'It just seems a damn shame, after everything we've worked for.'

'Hm? No, it's time for a new start. Hey – you can retire at last,' Emma teased as she rifled through her beaten-up tan Mulberry handbag for her keys.

'Me?' Freya let out a short, deep laugh. 'That's what Charles said. It will never happen. Work keeps me going. If I wasn't pottering around the office getting under everyone's feet, what would I do?'

Emma smiled. Liberty had never had the heart to force Freya to retire. 'How is Charles?'

'Same as ever.'

'I am sorry I missed your birthday last month.'

21

'I'd rather forget I am eighty-four, darling. Why don't you come over and have a bite with us?'

'Thanks, but I'll grab a sandwich from the café. I just want to sort everything out here as quickly as possible, and head off to Spain. I need a new start.'

'Yes,' Freya said, drawing out the word. 'We really need to talk about that.'

'Please don't start,' Emma said, her brow knitting. 'I know you hate the idea, but it's just what I need. I had no idea Mum had bought a house down there.'

'Darling, it's not at all what you think. I know you – you're picturing some divine little finca with jasmine spilling over the walls.'

'I am not.' She was, of course.

'Spain ...' Freya paused. 'Well, I was surprised when your mother told me she had bought the house.'

'Why don't you come with me? It's about time you took a break.'

'No,' Freya said firmly. 'Charles and I swore we'd never set foot in Spain again, not after everything that happened.'

'What did happen? Neither of you have ever talked—'

'It doesn't matter now,' Freya interrupted. 'It's a lifetime ago.'

'Do you have any idea why Mum picked Valencia, though? That is where you were nursing, wasn't it?'

'Valencia, Madrid ...' Freya cleared her throat. 'We moved around a lot, wherever we were needed.'

'Well it sounds beautiful. I've been reading about it online. You know, they call it the Spanish Eden.' Emma's thoughts filled with neroli-scented orange groves, gardens rich with jasmine and cool churches infused with heady incense.

'Of course I know,' Freya snapped. 'It's a ridiculous idea. I don't know what Liberty was thinking of. From what she said, no one has done a thing to the house for decades. It's probably a deathtrap, and you will have your hands full with the baby. You're mad! You have no idea the amount of work a child is. You need family around you.'

'I need,' Emma paused, 'to do this.' She heard Freya take a deep breath.

'You're as wilful as your mother.'

'I know.' Emma glanced down the street as the last of the schoolchildren disappeared. 'I know I can make a go of it. I've worked my whole life, and thanks to Mum I've always saved. I can afford to take a few months off, get help to sort out the house, maybe even someone to help with the baby.'

'I know, I know. You're a sensible girl, you always were.'

'I promise I'll be back and forth. I'm just going to use it for holidays, so it's not like I'm taking your grandchild away from you.'

Freya fell silent. 'Of course. Look, I don't want to argue the moment you're home. Come over once you've settled in.'

'I will.'

'Love you, Em,' Freya said.

'You too, Gammy.'

Freya paused. 'You haven't called me that for years.'

'Thanks, for everything,' Emma said, twisting the gold locket at her neck, winding the chain around her finger. 'I couldn't have got through all this without you, but what I need now is a new beginning.'

5

MADRID, SEPTEMBER 1936

'*Qué pasa*? How was the meeting?' Rosa strolled up to the café, her hand on the gun at her belt. She was dressed like a Republican militia, but her movements had the rhythm and precision of a flamenco dancer, and her tightly belted *mono* revealed a waist as tiny as a child's. She glanced down the cobbled alleyway to the barricades, saw three men crouched over a single plate of food as the red, yellow and purple Republican flag fluttered overhead. The walls of the street were lined with bright revolutionary posters. '*Defendeos Contra Fascismo!*' one cried beneath bones in the shape of a swastika. Rosa adjusted her beret, smoothed her cropped black hair against the nape of her neck. Jordi sat on the bonnet of the old bus, waiting in the sunshine for her. He was watching a flock of sheep being herded through the city, escaping the battlefields and heading for Valencia. He turned at the sound of her voice, his dark brilliantined hair gleaming. When he saw her, he leapt down and raised his fist in greeting.

'*Señorita Montez. Mi compañero.*' He grinned, pulled her into his arms. '*Mi amor,*' he murmured, and kissed her. 'You didn't miss much. Some anarchist from Valencia has annoyed the communists,' he said as his lips grazed her neck. 'He doesn't want the Russians involved – Spanish affairs concern only the Spanish, that's what he said in his speech.' Jordi shook his head. 'Tell that to Hitler and Mussolini. They are arming Franco's troops – without the Russians, what hope do we Republicans have?'

They walked down stone steps into the shade of the basement café, and behind the bar, a record played: '… the music goes round and round and it comes out here …' Jordi slipped his hand over her eyes.

'What are you doing?' she asked, smiling.

'I have something for you.' From his pocket, Jordi pulled a long gold chain, and clasped it around her throat. 'Happy Birthday.' He kissed the soft curls at the nape of her neck.

'I thought you had forgotten!' Rosa looked down at the gold locket and gasped. 'Oh, Jordi, it's beautiful. How could you afford this?'

'It was my mother's. I took it last summer in Valencia when Vicente wasn't looking. Oof …' He doubled over as she punched him on the arm. 'He won't notice! All my brother cares about is money – if he had seen it he would have sold it. Mamá always thought it was too good to wear.' He carefully opened the filigree cage. 'I think people used it for perfume in the old days.' Rosa inhaled, caught the ghost of a fragrance. 'But I put our photographs inside.'

Rosa recognised the studio portraits they had had taken a few months ago, carefully trimmed to fit the gold frame. 'I love it.' She kissed him, lingering, tasted the hot salt on his lips, his skin.

'Promise you'll wear it always,' he said quietly.

'Whatever happens, we will always be together then.'

'Nothing can keep us apart, Jordi.'

'No,' he said, his hand falling to her stomach. 'I won't have you fighting with us any more. Just as soon as I can I am taking you to Valencia. Vicente will take care of you.' He took one of the last of the wild roses from a jam jar on the bar, and threaded it through the buttonhole of her suit.

'I won't go.' Rosa dug her hands into the pockets of her *mono*. 'I can still fight. We are together. That is enough.'

Jordi turned to embrace his friend Marco, who was standing near the bar. Rosa listened to the snatches of conversation drifting from the packed lunchtime tables, watched as the waitress twisted skilfully through the sea of soldiers' hopeful, lonely hands.

'Valencia is safe for now,' one of the soldiers was saying. 'The city is full of dockers loyal to the CNT trade union, and the Huerta is full of rich peasants who will keep their heads down and quietly continue to grow rice and oranges in their smallholdings.'

'Rice and oranges!' Marco laughed, nudged Jordi. 'You should know all about that.'

'I am not a farmer! I am a *recortadore*.' Jordi leapt with the grace of a cat onto the bar, and the people at the tables nearby cheered and clapped. 'I am the greatest bull leaper in all of Spain!' Rosa tugged him down, laughing. Jordi swept the hair from his eyes. 'It is my father who was the farmer.' He put his arm around Rosa. 'He was a landowner who lost his land. He poured his dissatisfaction down his throat with his cognac, and spoiled my brother for life. Vicente is a failed matador, an unhappy butcher who thinks he should be an aristocrat. He drinks in the café till three or four, sleeps a few hours, serves the women of the village with pork bellies—'

'And more, from what I hear,' Marco murmured.

'You want me to stay with this man?' Rosa laughed awkwardly.

Jordi shrugged. 'It will be safer than here. Vicente is no *político* – he is firmly on the fence. But he is my brother, and I love him. Me, I was a little surprise for my parents – they thought after what my mother went through with Vicente's birth she couldn't have more children. To me, growing up, he was a god.' Jordi turned to her. 'You should see him. Yes, he is bald now, and his beard and chest hair are grey, but when he goes down to the lake each day to swim after siesta, and takes off his pink dressing gown, there is still something of the arena, the roar of the crowd ...' He leant closer to her, whispering in her ear. 'I remember the day Marco and I spied on him. He had the postmaster's wife up on the glass counter, his head lowered like a bull, his trousers around his ankles. His hands were dark against her dimply thighs ...'

Rosa giggled. 'You're teasing me!'

'No! You wait till you see him at the lake. Vicente stands like this ...' Jordi puffed his chest out, planted his thighs firmly apart, put his hands on his hips and looked slowly from left to right. 'All the women adore him. He keeps them mesmerised with his stories of the *toros*. The way he drops his dressing gown like a silk cape ...' Jordi mimed tossing it aside. 'When he sniffs the air like a bull, he is still Vicente the Magnificent.'

'It is true,' Marco said. 'He has had half the women in the village.'

'Why hasn't he been shot by an angry husband?' Rosa asked.

'The men are either afraid of him, or admire him.' Marco sipped his drink. 'I think the mark of Vicente's gold incisors on your wife's body is like a brand of quality to some men!' As the old friends swapped stories about Jordi's elder brother, Rosa frowned, tuned in to the conversations around them again.

'At least now they will not advance on Madrid from the east,' a soldier said. Rosa thought of the west, the noise of the battle. The blood still rang in her ears, a shrill whine like the aftershock of the explosions.

'We shall hold them back on the other fronts, and the Valencia road is clear.'

'They are evacuating the pictures from the Prado, you know?'

'You know what the right are saying? Reds are raping nuns …'

'Well, what about General Queipo de Llano's broadcasts from Seville, eh? Did you not hear he offered up the women of Madrid to his troops as a reward if they sack the city?'

Rosa's gaze fell to the polished wood of the bar as the conversations overlapped. She leant against it as Jordi ordered three more goblets of sherry. The tiles were wet in the café, freshly washed, and Rosa breathed in the tang of wine-soaked wood, the salt air clinging to the shellfish. The display was pitiful, she thought, her stomach grumbling for the days when crabs and oysters spilled across the crushed ice. *It is always the women and children*, she thought, remembering the wife of a friend in the south, raped by an entire firing squad before they shot her.

'Queipo de Llano said for every man we kill, he will kill at least ten.'

Jordi spun around to interrupt their conversation. 'This is why we cannot let them win, *compañero*. Yes, there are atrocities on both sides – this is war – but Franco will destroy half of Spain if he has to. They are throwing entire villages from cliff faces.'

'I heard the Falangists are organising peasant hunts on horseback,' someone called over to Jordi.

'That I can believe,' he said. 'All I hear is reports of those fascists "clearing up" towns after the troops have passed through, careering around in their parents' cars, with their girlfriends, firing pistols like it is some game.'

The game of life, Rosa thought. She remembered the early days in the summer after the rebel Nationalist uprising. People would ride out to Toledo like tourists of war, like they were going on a picnic to take a few shots at the Nationalists in the name of democracy. They would drive out to the front like they were heading to a party, armed with guns, tortillas and bottles of wine – then go home to sleep and make love. There was singing everywhere in the early days, she remembered; she had never heard so much singing. She remembered the excitement when the grand hotels threw open their doors – where aristocrats had dined, ordinary men and women now ate in the new working men's clubs on bone china. All was equal – but already things had changed. There had been so much loss, so quickly, so violently. Prisons were emptied, criminals avenged themselves. It was the criminals responsible for the worst of the atrocities, not the Republicans, she was sure. The war was suddenly too close to home.

'It isn't a game!' she cried. 'Let them come, but fight me face to face on level ground.'

As the café erupted in cheers, Rosa turned away. She felt Jordi watching her. 'Jordi, I can't bear the cruelty,' she said. 'What kind of a world are we bringing a child into?'

He took her face in his hands. 'A good world. We will make a free Spain, a better Spain for our child. Don't be afraid. The Nationalists have to terrify the workers – that is the only way they will win, through fear. This is why they display corpses, why they allow people to set up snack bars at the site of executions. To them it is a holy crusade and they want to put the fear of God into us. But they are only men, and we will win.'

Rosa glanced up as a group of men jogged down the stairs, greeted by cheers and fists shooting into the air. The first man raised his arm, silhouetted against the light.

'Viva la República! Viva la Libertad!' Robert Capa shouted.

'Eh, Capa!' Jordi called, embracing him when he walked over. 'Congratulations! Everyone is talking about the photograph of the falling soldier. Now the world will sit up and take notice of Spain.'

Capa shrugged. 'It was a lucky shot.'

'Have you met my girl? This is Rosa.' Jordi turned to the barman. 'Drinks for my friends.'

'No, let me.' Capa threw a roll of money onto the bar.

'Who are these people?' Rosa whispered to Jordi.

'Photographers, journalists,' Jordi said. 'Capa took photos of me a while ago. They are going to tell the world the truth about Spain.'

'Damn right we are,' Capa said. He turned to Rosa,

kissed her hand, raised his gaze to hers. 'You are a lucky man, Jordi. I would like to photograph your girl.'

'No, I don't think so,' she said.

'Why, are you afraid I might steal your soul?'

'I don't think it is my soul you are interested in.'

Capa's laugh reminded her of a cat purring. He winked at Jordi. 'Like I said, you are a lucky man.'

'I am.' Jordi put his arm around Rosa. 'And right now, Capa, we need all the luck we can get.'

6

LONDON, SEPTEMBER 11, 2001

The door of the Picasso Café swung closed behind her, and Emma pulled the collar of her coat up. A few locals were lingering over a late lunch at the pavement tables, and one of the market traders from Antiquarius called over to her in greeting. She waved back, sipped at her Styrofoam cup of tea as she waited for a break in the traffic. The smoky, rich smell of the bacon sandwich she was carrying in a paper bag made her stomach grumble with hunger. A taxi slowed to let her cross, she nodded in thanks, and ran across towards the cinema.

Every cracked flagstone was familiar to her, every face it seemed. The crisp autumn air, the smells of exhaust fumes and coffee – she knew and loved them all. Sometimes she daydreamed about creating fragrances that captured cities in a bottle. *London would be coal fires, tea, petrol*, she thought. This was her home, her corner of the world, and yet it would never be the same again. She had taken one look at the silent studio piled high with packing crates, showered and left. The lacquer box had been exactly where she'd left it months before, surrounded by the fragrances on Liberty's desk like a conductor at the heart of an orchestra.

Emma ate ravenously as she skirted the side of Habitat and strode towards St Luke's Gardens. She tossed the paper bag into a bin, and drained her tea. The garden was almost empty, the office workers returned to their desks. A few mothers were pushing children in buggies towards the playground as Emma walked towards what she had always thought of as their bench, hers and Liberty's. She had come here with Freya, Charles and Joe after the funeral, and scattered Liberty's ashes on the rose border. The thought of the flowers to come in the summer reminded her of one of the first trips her mother had taken her on, to their suppliers in Turkey. Men had stood waist deep in roses, and Emma had plunged her small hand into a sack of petals, silken and perfumed. The fragrance was so intense, it seemed to have a texture to her, a powdery voluptuousness. Emma had missed these roses' single flowering. Now the earth stood bare again, the bushes cut back for the winter.

'Hello, Mum,' she said quietly as she sat down. In her mind, as she looked at the garden, she played out their conversation, told her mother how she missed her, how she was going to be a grandmother at last. *'Roots and wings, Em,'* she remembered her mother saying. *'That's what you give your children.'*

Emma's face fell as a bus trundled by emblazoned with an advertisement for the new Liberty Temple fragrance. The marketing department had gone into overdrive to prepare for the launch, introducing Emma as Liberty's successor. Emma thought back to the final interview with *ES Magazine*, how Joe had shown the journalist around their new house, pointing out all the toys he had installed – the home cinema, the statement artworks by Hirst, the furnishings that read like a Design Museum catalogue. The photographer, meanwhile, had asked Emma to sniff the orchids on the mantelpiece.

'But they have no scent,' she said.

'Well, stroke them, lovey. Look inspired.' He circled his hand in the air without bothering to look up from his viewfinder.

While she was dutifully caressing the orchids, Joe's mobile had beeped in the kitchen. They were waiting for news from Liberty at the hospital, so she decided to check the message. A hundred times she wondered what would have happened if she hadn't. *'Miss you,'* it said. *'Tonight x.'* Emma heard Joe's footsteps echoing down the new wenge staircase. She quickly turned the phone upside down as she had found it, and poured a glass of champagne for everyone.

'This place is fabulous!' the journalist said, settling onto a stool beside the gleaming Corian countertop. 'How long have you been here?'

'Not long,' Emma said. She was trying to think clearly. 'It's all Joe's hard work, really.'

'Nonsense!' Joe settled back on the Eames lounger by the fireplace, and put his hands behind his head. 'I took care of the bricks-and-mortar stuff, but Em has a great eye. She was emailing me orders from all over the place.'

'I travel a lot for work.' The pieces were beginning to fall into place. 'Our biggest markets are Japan and the US.'

'Em's mum ran a cosmetics company for years, but then in the late eighties we got involved and the Liberty Temple perfume brand just exploded. Emma is the creative brains now – the nose – aren't you?'

'Sorry?' She glanced at him, his familiar face suddenly

strange to her. Was that a new shirt from Pinks he was wearing? He was immaculate as always. Though he hadn't followed his father into the American armed forces, there was something military in his bearing and precision. His hair had been freshly trimmed at Trumpers that morning, his nails buffed. Emma looked down at her hands – she hadn't had time for a manicure for weeks. She forced herself to concentrate, and began the story she had recounted a thousand times at different press conferences, how a family business started on a kitchen table had grown to become one of the world's leading independent perfumers.

'My mother always wore Calèche,' the journalist said. 'You know, sometimes I pass a woman in the street wearing it, and I think it's her.'

'Exactly. I love the emotions fragrance evokes in us.' There was a tight knot in Emma's throat. 'I'd love to make a truly classic fragrance like Chanel No 5.'

'Yeah, I'm sure the accountants would be over the moon too,' Joe said, laughing.

Emma's hand was shaking as she put down her glass. 'Did you know, in some parts of the world the word "kiss" means "smell". Isn't that amazing, the link between scent and sensuality.' She was staring hard at Joe.

'Maybe that's my title,' the journalist mused. '"Scent and Sensuality", you know, like *Sense and Sensibility*. Everyone loves Jane Austen.'

'I'm sorry,' Emma stood and shook her hand. 'You must excuse me. I'm not feeling well.'

Emma settled back on the bench. For a moment, she allowed herself to imagine a perfect life where she and Joe were still together. Longing spread through her. In spite of everything that had happened, she loved him. It would never be the same, she was old enough to realise that. The simple, open trust had gone, but she had loved Joe too long for these feelings just to disappear neatly. Emma glanced at her watch, turned the heavy-duty, man's Patek Philippe over. It was nearly two.

Emma walked on towards Chelsea Green, took a deep breath as she pulled out her phone, and speed-dialled 1.

'Em?' He answered instantly. 'I've been trying to call you for weeks.'

'Hey, Joe,' she said, just like always. She blinked slowly as she remembered him looking up from his MBA books in Columbia University library, his blonde fringe falling over his indigo eyes. *Hey, Joe.* Rolling over towards her in the dawn light of their curtainless first flat together in Battersea. *Hey, Joe.*

'Where the hell have you been? You just dropped off the radar after Tokyo.'

'I stopped off in Vancouver to see Dad.'

'Your dad?' Joe sounded surprised. 'You haven't seen him for years.'

Emma frowned. 'It felt like it was about time. I just wanted ... I don't know what I was hoping ...' She took a deep breath.

'Sure, I understand, after your mum ...' His voice trailed off. 'Are you in London?'

'Just back.' She hoped she sounded calm, offhand. She recalled the last time she had seen him, after Liberty's will was read, when he'd left with tears of regret, and loss in his eyes. *Hey, Joe.*

'Well done. The guys in Japan were over the moon.' He

paused. 'I've been worried about you. You OK?'

'Sure. You sound tired.' *You sound guilty*, she thought.

'Yeah, hell ...' She heard him sigh. 'You know what it's like.'

What what's like? She kicked angrily at a Coke can in the gutter. *The business? Being with Delilah?* Just the sound of his voice, his easy East Coast accent killed her. The night she confronted him, they had held one another in the gleaming kitchen of their new house, weeping like children for everything that was broken and lost. It was like something she had carried within her tore free. *Love?* Now, that space was a wound, a hole that ached for him, for them, for everything they had been. She thought of the email Charles had sent her at her lowest point: *'Hemingway used to say the world breaks us all. Afterwards some are stronger at the broken places. I like the idea that what breaks us makes us stronger. Hold on to that, Em. It will get better.'* She cleared her throat. 'So, is it good to be home?'

'New York? Yeah, it's always good to be back. Mom and Dad send their best,' he said awkwardly.

Emma winced. 'Are you going to stay?'

'Maybe. Lila is going on about moving out here.' He sighed. 'D'you get the papers?'

Emma glanced left and right as she crossed the road. 'Aha.'

'Sign them, Em. It's what we've worked for.'

'To sell out?'

'No, to make a fortune, to do what we want with our future.'

'What future, Joe? We have no future.' She hesitated. 'Oh God, you mean with her, don't you?'

'I don't know what I mean.' She imagined him raking his hand through his hair. 'You're the one who left.'

'What was I supposed to do? You were sleeping with my friend, our friend—' A businessman glanced up at her as she walked past. She turned away, cupped the phone. 'It's such a cliché, Joe. I would have thought you'd have more imagination.'

'You were always so tired. You were away so much …'

'I was working for *us*! For *our* future.' She hesitated, almost told him then.

'Anyway, we had to go ahead with the winter launch without you. Lila stood in for you at the press conferences.'

'She's obviously very good at standing in for me.'

'Don't, Em. She was useless, too full on. We've argued. Emma, I need to see you. I've made a dumb mistake. I don't know what I'm doing any more.'

'You're right, Joe,' she said. 'Let's quit on a high. We've all put years into Liberty Temple.'

'I'm not talking about the business.'

'Lila wants the money, Joe – that's all she's ever been interested in.'

'*She's* nagging me to sell, you disappeared, Freya's telling me we should hang on to the company. Between all of you I just feel like disappearing too.'

'Well why don't you then?' she snapped. 'Anyway, I didn't disappear. I've been on the road for months making sure the brand survives.'

'I miss you.'

'Don't say that.' She angrily wiped away a tear. 'You have no right.'

'It's not too late. We can work this out.'

'I have to go.'

'OK, OK. We'll speak later.' She heard him whistle for a cab, pictured him standing on the kerb beneath the skyscrapers of New York, traffic streaming towards him. 'I've got to get across to the World Trade Centre. I'm meeting the guys in Windows on the World for breakfast.'

Eggs Benedict, she thought. *Double espresso, two sugars.*

'I'm not going to let them leave until we get everything hammered out. Will you fax the papers over once you're in the office?'

Emma scowled. 'Yes.'

'Thanks, for everything. Em …' He paused. 'I'm sorry. I'm an idiot. I love you. You know I'll always love you.'

'Right.'

'Tell me you still love me.'

'No.'

'Give me a chance. I can make it right.'

'No,' she said again, angry this time. 'Nothing is ever going to be the same.'

'I'll call you.'

'You do that.' As she stopped by the door of the Pond Place offices, Emma punched in a final text message. *'Love? Show me. We're having a baby.'*

She reached for the brushed-steel door handle, and hesitated. Instead, she went next door and knocked on the bright red door. As she waited, she imagined Freya walking stiffly through the cottage, her silver-topped ebony cane tapping on the creaking boards. Emma heard the chain slide back, and as the door opened an Ella Fitzgerald tune drifted out.

'Oh no you don't, Ming,' Freya muttered, blocking the path of a Siamese cat with her cane. She glanced up. 'Em!'

Emma hugged her grandmother. She seemed thinner, her bones more angular beneath the soft black cashmere roll-neck she was wearing. 'I've missed you,' she said, her words muffled.

'Let me look at you.' Freya held her at arm's length. 'I love your hair.'

'Thanks.' Emma ran her hand through her dark, shoulder-length hair. 'I had it chopped in Tokyo. Thought I'd go back to my natural colour.'

'Just as well. No hair dye for a few months now for you,' Freya whispered, squeezing Emma's hand.

'So, do I pass?'

Freya pursed her lips. 'Well, you look a bit peaky, but I'm not going to start nagging you the moment you get home. Come on, come in,' she said, ushering her inside. 'Charles is in the conservatory.'

'It is good to see you,' Emma said, taking her arm as they walked through the cottage. *At least nothing has changed here*, she thought, comforted by the familiar chaos of Freya and Charles's home. The yellow living room lined with books and bright abstract paintings fronted the street, and a constant stream of pedestrians and cars passed in front of the sash windows. Worn kelims flanked the sagging sofas, and a large tuberose candle on the Ottoman perfumed the air. A fire glowed in the hearth, and from upstairs the sound of vacuuming drifted down. In the small kitchen, a Welsh dresser piled with blue-and-white crockery and old postcards leant companionably by a scrubbed table, and Ming lolled on an old red armchair in the sunlight, turquoise eyes watching the women.

'Charles!' Freya called, shuffling into the conservatory,

her cane tapping on the terracotta floor. Among the plants the wings of iridescent blue butterflies beat slowly in the hot, liquid air, tongues unfurled to nectar. Condensation dripped from leaves, and a swallowtail settled, unnoticed, on Emma's hair. 'Charles!' Freya shook her head. 'He must be in his study.' She swept aside a curtain of fine chains, opened the back door and leant against Emma as she negotiated the low step to the garden. Freya walked gingerly along the uneven paving stones to a sky-blue shed, and pushed open the door. They found Charles bent over his roll-topped desk, pinning a fritillary onto a cork board.

Emma smiled. She had spent hours in here with Charles as a child, helping her great-uncle catalogue his specimens. The walls were lined with cases of butterflies, a Technicolor mural of wings. A grizzled pug snored softly at his feet while a longcase Mora clock ticked away the minutes. 'Hello ...'

'He won't hear you.' Freya nudged his back with the cane. 'Charles! We have a visitor.'

'What the ruddy hell?' He spun around, pushed his half-moon glasses back on his mane of thick white hair. His empty left sleeve, pinned at the elbow, swung against his side. 'Do you want to give me a heart attack, woman?' He smiled, shuffled forward as he noticed Emma. 'Em!' He embraced her with his right arm, and she kissed his dry, smooth cheek.

'Turn it on.' Freya motioned to him.

Charles flicked on his hearing aid. 'Only way a chap can get a moment's peace in this madhouse, people coming and going all day,' he grumbled to Emma.

'Stop moaning,' Freya said. 'You'll miss them when they're gone.'

'It is good to see you. You look well,' Emma said.

'Do I? At our age you're just glad to be alive. All our friends are dropping like flies.' He sighed. 'Every year there are a few less of us at the Brigades' commemoration in Jubilee Gardens.'

'You know what he's like.' Freya folded her arms. 'Always turns to the obituaries first to see if he knows anyone.'

'I do not. Ah, you have a passenger, Em.' Charles caught the butterfly on her hair in a small net box and closed the lid.

Face to face, Emma thought the similarity between the siblings was unmistakeable even in age – both had tall, slender bodies, rather stooped now, the same high cheekbones, aquiline noses. Whereas Freya was a picture of understated, monochrome chic, Charles's umber cords were flecked with scorch marks from years of log fires and cigarettes, and hung loose from his hips. As he turned to the desk and slid a sheet of glass into the frame, Freya sighed.

'Look at the state of you, Charles. I do wish you'd let me buy you some new clothes.'

'Why?' He dug his hands into the stretched pockets of his navy cardigan, and pulled out a tobacco tin. 'What do I need with new clothes?' he muttered as he lit a roll-up.

Freya narrowed her eyes in irritation, and brushed some dog hair from his sleeve.

'Bugger off, stop fussing, woman!' he said, batting her hand away.

She smoothed down her immaculate grey bob. 'Fine.' Freya bit her lip. 'Well, everyone is dying to see you, Emma. Shall we go through?'

From the chaotic mews house that had been the family home for nearly seventy years, Freya, Charles and Emma stepped onto the pavement, and through the door into the adjoining house. The Liberty Temple office was bustling. As Emma pushed the front door open the breeze made the orchids on the white reception desk dance. The open-plan back offices were buzzing with elegant young women and languid men; snatches of French, English, Japanese and the scent of roses drifted on the air.

'Welcome home, Em,' the receptionist said.

'Thank you,' she replied as she strode into the office area. 'Hello everyone.'

Freya and Charles waited in reception as the team crowded around to greet Emma. 'I hope she's doing the right thing,' Freya said quietly. 'This is the closest thing she has to a family right now. Once the company is sold ...'

'Are you talking about Emma, or yourself?'

Freya dug him in the ribs.

'Ow, not so ruddy hard,' he winced.

'I'll be fine, don't you worry.' Freya tucked her chin down into her black polo neck, and crossed her arms over her narrow ribcage. 'I've spent my life looking after Liberty, and Emma, and the company ...'

'Exactly. The girls have kept you young.'

'Unlike you.'

Charles pulled a face at her. 'I shall choose to ignore that remark.' He glanced at her out of the corner of his eye. 'Will you move to the Cornish house permanently?'

Freya shook her head. 'You won't get rid of me that easily.'

'You do love it down there, and there will be no need for—' Charles's breath caught in his throat as he glanced over at the flat-screen television above the fireplace. He shuffled over and turned up the volume. 'Be quiet!' he shouted, the newsreel footage on the BBC glimmering in his glasses.

'What's going on?' Freya was the first at his side. She gazed in horror as smoke plumed from the World Trade Center. 'Oh God, no!' Her hands flew to her mouth as another plane ploughed into the second tower.

Emma ran over. 'I don't understand. What's happening?' She put her arm around Freya. 'Joe's there,' she said, her voice breaking. 'I just spoke to him half an hour ago. He's in the North Tower.'

7

MADRID, NOVEMBER 1936

'Hugo!' Charles called, and jogged to catch up. The 11th International Brigade were marching along Gran Via, and Charles fell in with the British machine-gunners and Germans of the Edgar André Battalion. Neon signs, vivid in the winter light, flickered along the road as the Madrileños cheered them on. 'How was lunch?'

'Nothing like a few pre-prandial artillery shells to get your appetite working.' He turned his pale, tired face to Charles. 'Did you get any photos?'

Charles shook his head. 'I thought perhaps the paper might like a few shots of ordinary men and women ...'

'Couldn't find any?' Hugo smiled.

'What's the latest?'

'The fascists are advancing into the university,' Hugo said, marching at Charles's side.

'Just as well the Brigades are here then,' Charles said, shifting the old Soviet rifle slung over his shoulder. 'The 11th should drive them out.' Nearby he could hear the sound of marching feet, shouting, singing, the noise of motor horns. But beyond that was the sound of battle –

rifles, machine guns, mortars. They were getting closer and closer to the front.

'Do you have plenty of film?'

Charles gazed at the square, dignified forms of the new university buildings ahead of them, yellow and russet against the distant sky, already swirling with the smoke of battle. 'I hope I have enough.' It seemed to him the whole city was blazing, light flaring into the sky. They worked their way through smoke-filled streets. Splinters of rafters snagged the sky like broken ribs, and empty, stained stretchers scattered with flowers littered the pavement. His hair was thick with dust as he ran his hand through it, his ears ringing from the continual, deafening bombardment.

'Wait,' he said to Hugo. As the men marched on to the front, Charles rolled the film in his camera on, and focussed on the vacant, mask-like faces of a dead mother and child laid out side by side on the edge of the road.

'What are you doing?' A Spanish militiaman grabbed him by the collar. 'You vulture! You make me sick, you newsmen.' He spat on him.

Charles looked at him with unseeing eyes as Hugo grabbed his arm and dragged him forwards. 'My job,' he said. 'I'm doing my job.'

At sunset, the shadows of pigeons wheeled over the tangled bodies of men. Charles felt like the mouth of hell had opened up. In the frenzy of the battle, he had lost Hugo. He knew he had to get out of here, that the Press cars would be leaving soon for the night. He ran blindly for the shelter of a doorway, heard bullets ricocheting behind him. He crouched down, sweat and smoke stinging his eyes, his heart pounding. He gripped the hot shaft of his rifle, checked his ammunition and shouldered open the door. He ran through an abandoned lecture hall, blackboards cracked and broken, the benches smashed like matchsticks. Water rained down from shattered pipes. He scrambled down a ruined staircase into the darkness, his feet splashing through black puddles, feeling his way, desperately hoping he would not discover a body there. Charles pushed his back flat against the wall by a broken window, peered cautiously around, wary of snipers. He looked out across the campus, saw Moroccan troops moving through the mist in the distance. He had to make a run for it.

Terror gripped his stomach as he sprinted for safety, keeping low, diving from cover to cover. He flung himself head first into the nearest dugout just as there was a massive explosion nearby. The earth fountained up around him, and the force of the blast hit him like a punch in the chest. He cowered, burying his head against his knees. 'Christ!' he cried out, his bowels loosening with terror.

Charles lay shivering as night fell, thinking back to the day Comrade Marty's voice had drifted over the crowd of new recruits packed into the Albacete parade ground like candles in a box. The woollen cap he had been given was itching, and his boots were bad. They had already worn blisters on his heels during drills that morning, but when he looked around at the eccentric rags worn by many of the soldiers, he realised he had been lucky. Some were dressed in Great War surplus, some in pantomime costume it seemed. The commander, however, wore a black leather jacket and a dark beret, and on his Sam Browne belt hung a 9mm automatic pistol.

'You will be sent from here to the training centre at Madrigueras,' the commander had shouted.

'How come he gets a pistol?' Charles murmured.

'He's the boss,' Hugo whispered. 'Broom handles are fine for the rest of us. It looks to me like those sentries are handling rifles for the first time.' He looked across at a boy leaning against the wall. 'For God's sake stop smoking, man!' he hissed, and pointed at the boxes of dynamite stacked beside the boy.

'I'm not sure about this,' Charles said. 'You'd have thought they'd have enough guns to go round.'

'Yes, it would have been nice.'

'I know what we are fighting for, but I'm not quite sure how.'

'It's too late to back out now, Charles,' Hugo said. 'They took our passports at Figueras.'

Charles recalled the sallow, prawn-faced man in the glass box at the entrance to the old castle. He had taken their details, tossed their passports into a box spilling over with others from a multitude of nations. 'Here,' he had said, thrusting a 100 peseta note, condoms and a tasselled forage cap into his hand. 'You are now part of the Republican Army.' He had raised his fist, and Charles and Hugo followed suit, hesitantly.

Marty raised his voice. 'Who can drive a truck?' A few men put up their hands. 'Right, line up over there. Who can ride a motorcycle? Anyone with medical training?' As the last men shuffled away, he looked out across those who remained. 'The rest of you are infantry. You will make history.'

'Even maps would be nice,' Charles said under his breath. He blew on his hands as he gazed around the ragged group of dockers, miners, ex-cons and dreamy undergraduates. 'Surely someone must have a Michelin map at least, somewhere?'

'No maps, no compasses,' Hugo said cheerfully. 'It will be chaos blundering around in the sleet and dark.' He shivered. 'I have a feeling we should be getting more than 10 pesetas a day.'

'You! Temple!' Marty pointed at him. 'You are reporters, yes?'

'We are with the *Manchester Guardian*, sir.' Charles stood to attention. 'But we wish to fight alongside the Brigades, sir, if we can.'

'Good. There are too many reporters and photographers along for the ride.'

Marty sorted through a file. 'Make Madrid your base. Report to Brigade headquarters there.' He scribbled his signature on a piece of paper. 'Here is a Safe Conduct pass for you both. Fight if you will, but I want you to report from all over the country. Tell the British what is going on here. We will make a car available for you.'

'Thank you, sir.' Charles raised his fist.

Thank you, sir, Charles thought as he hunkered down. The night air was bitingly cold, and his clothes were wet and foul. *Right now I wish I was along for the ride.* He thought longingly of his hotel bedroom. He remembered complaining to Hugo about the lice-infested straw mattresses they had to sleep on in Albacete, and the overflowing latrines. At this moment he would be glad of either.

'The smell of war is rotting food and shit,' he had said, throwing himself down on his bed in the barracks.

'There you go. To think you were struggling for an opening line for your first article,' Hugo said.

'Very droll.' He leant over, lit the wick of a tin full of olive oil. The flame danced, weak light spreading in the darkness. 'These ruddy lice are driving me insane,' he said, scratching at his crotch.

'It's the rats you have to watch out for. Haven't you heard the song? "There are rats, rats, rats as big as cats ..."' Hugo frowned. 'Are you sure we're cut out for all this?'

'Of course we are.' Charles looked at Hugo. 'We can write, and we can see the truth. When you look at the rubbish the newspapers at home are printing against the Republicans, it makes me furious.' He thought of the scarred, exhausted faces of the Brigaders who had returned from Aragon. They were half mad with bitterness, it seemed to him. 'A cock-up', they said – no artillery, no planes. They spoke of the quiet savagery of the Moroccans, of friends whose throats had been slit, then casually tossed over a bridge.

Now Charles understood what they had seen. He screwed his eyes tight shut. He thought how full of hope they had been as they headed to Madrid. He recalled the singing on the train as he and Hugo sat among women with chickens on their laps in third class. At every station the crowds had cheered the soldiers: '*Salud*!' '*No pasarán! They shall not pass!*' They had sung the 'Internationale' with peasants who pressed oranges, screws of olives and wine on them. Each platform was a sea of clenched fists as the train chugged out, carriages jerking and clattering. He remembered a dark-eyed girl who blew kisses to him, crying out '*Chico*, your wife is not here to kiss you goodbye!'

50

'Wife! That would be a fine thing,' Charles said under his breath as he rolled over onto his side, his teeth chattering. A macabre babble of tongues echoed around him between explosions.

'Charles?' Hugo scrambled down to him. 'Are you all right? I lost sight of you in there.'

Charles could see Hugo's lips moving, but his words were muffled, seemed to be coming from underwater. 'Thank God, I thought you ...'

'What happened?'

'A shell nearly got me. I'm afraid I'm rather a mess.'

Hugo took him gently by the arm. 'Let's get out of here. I want to write up my report while my memory is still fresh. God it was hellish, we were fighting room by room at the end.' He grimaced. 'Come on, we'd better get you cleaned up.' He guided Charles past barricades bristling with chair legs, padded with mattresses. Faceless figures pushed past them in the darkness. They staggered to the Press car, along a road marked with bloody footprints. An alarm clock was ringing somewhere in the night.

'Let's go,' Charles said to Hugo as he slumped back in the seat. The car door slammed and he closed his eyes as the gears crashed into reverse.

8

LONDON, SEPTEMBER 11, 2001

'Open your eyes.' Emma remembered Joe's voice, full of laughter, the warmth of his breath against her ear. She had felt the weight of his hip against hers, their thighs touching.

'I can't!' Emma had frozen to the spot, stretched out across the cool glass of the World Trade Center observation deck window, unable to move. She jammed the soles of her Converse Hi-tops against the ledge, tried to inch backwards.

Joe squeezed her hand. 'Trust me. Open your eyes.'

She opened one eye, flinching.

'Look at it.' He laughed. 'It's beautiful.' They turned their faces towards the earth, gazed out across New York. 'I feel like we're flying.' Beneath them, the city was dazzling, spring sunlight dancing across the water, illuminating thousands of windows, warming the fresh green of Central Park.

Emma had felt the world spin as vertigo swept over her, and her mouth dried. All she could think of was what would happen if the glass gave way. She inched backwards, turned to Joe. 'Are you happy now? I accepted the dare.'

'Look at you, you're shaking like a leaf!' He pulled her to her feet, laughing. 'I've got you now and I'll never let you go.'

Emma buried her head against his chest, slipped her arms beneath his Puffa waistcoat. The feel of him was still intoxicating then. That morning they had kissed for hours. When they were together it felt as though they were one, not two, their bodies lean and hungry, new.

'Hey,' he said. 'You weren't kidding, were you? Are you OK?'

Emma punched him gently in the stomach. 'Let that be a lesson for you. Never dare a Temple woman. You owe me lunch.'

He grinned, an even, white smile breaking across his tanned face. 'You've got a deal.' He slung his arm over Emma's shoulders as they walked to the lift. 'Anyway, we'd better get a move on, Delilah's waiting for us.'

Emma groaned. 'Again? When am I ever going to get you alone?'

'Now *that* I like the sound of,' he said as they squeezed into the lift. 'Lila's my friend, honey. Her nose is kind of out of joint since we got together – you don't mind if she tags along, do you? She's still getting used to the idea that some beautiful Brit has swept me off my feet.' As the lift plummeted down, he slipped his hand around Emma's waist, searching for the band of her Levi's 501s. She felt his fingertips, warm and firm, tracing the indentation of her spine.

'No, of course I don't mind.' She laid her head against him, his collarbone jutting against her hairline.

The lift doors opened, and he kissed the top of her head. 'We can be together later, I promise. I've got a late tutorial, but I'll pick you up around seven, OK?'

'Sure,' she said, forcing a bright smile as they walked through the lobby. '*Smile, Emma.*' She thought of her mother's advice. '*I think it's charming if his best friend is a girl – shows he has a sensitive side. Delilah is part of the package, and you're just going to have to get used to it. Befriend her. Boys hate it if you're clingy and jealous. If Delilah is upsetting you, smile, darling. She'll soon get bored and give up.*' Emma spotted Delilah immediately, sitting in the square waiting for them, her blonde hair shining in the sunlight, and her seemingly endless legs stretched out across the bench. *Right, Mum! She doesn't look as if she's ever given up on anything in her life.* As they walked towards her, Delilah unfurled herself. The light glinted on the large gold hoops in her ears.

'Hello, children,' Delilah drawled. She stood with the easy grace of a girl who has taken dance lessons her whole life, and the shoulder pads of her linen jacket accentuated her tiny waist. Emma felt awkward as she looked down at her jeans and sneakers. Delilah was a native New Yorker, and the confidence of the city seemed to course through her veins.

Joe slung his free arm over Delilah's shoulder. 'Hey, Lila, how was the class?'

'Dull, dull, dull. But I aced that final paper,' she said.

'Don't you mean "we" aced it?' Joe laughed.

'Whatever. I've helped you out enough over the years.'

Emma flinched. It felt like Delilah was constantly reminding her how well she knew Joe, how long they had been friends. She glanced uncertainly at them.

'At least we graduate in a week, then it's so long to all the textbooks and hello expense account.' Delilah tossed her hair.

'What will you do?' Emma asked.

'I have a few options.'

'I wanted to talk to you both about that,' Joe said as he guided them towards the crossing. 'I had an interesting conversation with Liberty yesterday. Let me take my two favourite girls to lunch, and we can discuss it.'

As Emma looked at the Twin Towers on television now, she recalled every detail of that day over ten years before. She had forced herself to look calm, smile warmly, as Joe talked about the three of them building a new company with Liberty, something to replace her collapsed first venture, 'Senso'. Liberty had loved Joe the moment they met – Emma always thought he was the son she had never had. Naturally, where Joe went, Delilah went too and as Liberty Temple took shape they became the business and marketing brute force that Liberty needed to push the new company forward. Emma was the creative brain, Liberty's successor, the 'nose' who would shape the future. Liberty had insisted she did a short business course at Columbia after studying perfumery in Grasse, hoped a spell in New York would toughen her up. Emma remembered the late nights sitting around Freya's kitchen table as Liberty paced, talking endlessly about how she worried her daughter was too cloistered, too unworldly to cope with running a business alone.

'You're an artist, darling, like me,' she had said. 'An artist of fragrance. You're too fragile to cope with the business side of things. Look at how the investors have shafted me! Business is tough, Em. It's a different world from when I started Senso, making soap and face cream on this kitchen table while you played with your bricks underneath.' The glasses jumped as she slammed down her hand. 'You need help.' That was how Joe and Delilah came to join them in London.

Emma's head swirled now, and she reached out to steady herself. She couldn't grasp that the images on the screen were real. 'I spoke to him, just a few minutes ago,' she said, fumbling for her bag. She dialled his number. The line was engaged.

Three missed calls and a voicemail flashed up from Joe: 'Em! You're kidding! A baby?' She heard him laugh. 'My God, you always were good at surprising me. I don't know what to do … I've done something really stupid. Listen, I'm going to make this right. Em, I've got to go in now. I'll call you after the meeting. Love you.'

'Oh God,' she cried. 'He can't be in there …'

Freya put her arm around her, gripped her shoulder. They watched in stunned silence as the headlines scrolled: *'Breaking News. Plane has crashed into the World Trade Center Tower in New York.'*

'It's not possible,' Emma whispered, her gaze fixed on the top of the tower. She imagined him sitting at the table across from the buyers, a fresh white shirt, his lucky blue tie that brought out the colour of his eyes. She heard the chink of china, of cutlery, the hiss of the coffee machine, the swift, efficient steps of the waiters. And then the impact, the still moment before all hell broke loose. Emma gasped for breath. All the anger and pain she had felt fell away. 'Joe, oh God, Joe …' She saw the smoke billowing upwards, knew he would be fighting for a way out, taking charge, getting people together. That's what Joe did. That's what he always did. She imagined him looking out across that terrible, beautiful clear sky.

'He'll get out,' Freya said quietly. 'If anyone can get out, Joe will.'

The shrill sound of the telephone cut through the air. The receptionist ran to the desk. 'Good morning, Liberty Temple,' she said automatically. 'Yes, Ms Stafford—'

'Is that Delilah?' Freya called. 'Put her on the conference phone.' The sound of sirens crackled from the speakers as everyone crowded to the meeting room table. 'Delilah. It's Freya. Are you all right?'

'Freya?'

'Where are you?'

'I'm on the street, near the South Tower. Oh God, Freya, what's happening?'

Emma leant towards the speaker. 'Is Joe with you?'

'Emma? Christ, I don't know! I—'

'Where is he, damn it?'

'Both of you, calm down!' Freya snapped. 'We need to think clearly. Delilah, where is Joe?'

'He was at the meeting. I was meant to be with him, but the heel broke on my shoe and I had to stop off.'

In the background, they heard a woman shrieking, 'People are falling! God, save their souls! They're jumping, oh please God!'

Delilah's voice was choked, it sounded like she was running. 'They're telling us to clear the area ...' she gasped. 'There are people falling, falling ...' The line cut out.

Freya turned to the receptionist. 'Keep trying their phones, Joe's and Delilah's.' In silence, they gathered once more in front of the television.

9

VALENCIA, NOVEMBER 1936

Rudolph Valentino's profile flickered on the white sheet hung in La Pobla's market square, the light of the projector cutting through the darkness, moths casting shadows as they danced in its beams. Rosa looked up at the clear night sky, at the blanket of stars above them, and curled up closer to Jordi, her feet resting in his lap. He pulled his coat around them, held her warm in his arms.

'You don't like the film?' he whispered. The villagers were watching *Blood and Sand* in rapt attention, only the whir of the projector breaking the silence, distant dogs barking. At the side of the square, children were playing. A small boy – feet close together, chest out, buttocks in, chin lowered – raised his arms. 'Ha-da!' he cried, and stamped his foot. The other boy lowered his horns, charged.

'No, the film is fine,' she said, frowning. 'It is this place I don't like.'

'You've only been here a day. Give it a chance.'

Rosa couldn't stop thinking of the great swathe of vehicles that had covered the highway to Valencia as the Republican government fled Madrid. She felt ashamed that they had been among them. As they'd passed through

Tarancón, she had cringed with embarrassment as a group of anarchists had held up the car full of politicians in front. 'Cowards!' she heard them screaming. 'We should shoot you now for abandoning Madrid.' With his papers, Jordi had managed to drive on through the blockade, but their words rang in her ears.

Jordi stood, and took her hand. People behind them grumbled, craned their necks to see the film. Jordi ushered her away to the side of the square. 'Rosa, we have talked about this. I grew up in La Pobla, you will be safe here.' He checked his watch. 'Vicente will have finished work by now. Come, I said we would meet him in the bar, then I must get back to Madrid.'

Vicente, she thought. Their first meeting had not been a success. Jordi had parked the car beside a whitewashed wall on the outskirts of the village, and taken her hand as they walked. 'This is the Villa del Valle, our family home,' he said, pointing at the closed metal gates, 'and this is Vicente's shop.' The smell of cold blood on the air turned her stomach. Jordi pushed open the door, and a bell chimed. In the shadows at the back of the shop, a man was concentrating on the knife he was sharpening.

'Vicente!' Jordi cried. Rosa's eyes adjusted to the dim light. In profile, Jordi's elder brother was handsome. But then he turned, and smiled. Rosa fought hard not to recoil. His mouth was twisted and scarred, his teeth gleamed gold. Jordi put his arm around her, steered her forward. 'This is my girl, Rosa.' He leant down to her ear. 'Don't let Vicente scare you. He lost an argument with a bull once.'

Vicente laughed, wiped his hands on a cloth streaked with blood. 'But now people are eating the fighting bulls, so maybe I win the argument after all.' He stepped forward, inspected Rosa with a practised eye. 'Very beautiful. Congratulations, little brother.' He held Rosa's gaze. 'Jordi tells me you are a dancer.'

'Rosa is many things,' Jordi said proudly. 'Her ancestors are from Sacromonte – they are dancers, healers.'

'So, a little gypsy, eh?' He stepped closer, his eyes black pools. 'Jordi tells me you knew Lorca. Too bad they took him for a ride.'

Dar un paseo. Rosa flinched as she remembered him. Such an innocent phrase before all this. *How many more will be forced to 'take a ride' and dig their own grave?* 'I still don't understand why they are killing poets,' she had said to Jordi one night as they lay in bed. 'He wasn't a politician, or a soldier.'

'Lorca wounded them more with his pen than he could have with a gun, that is why,' he said. 'He stood for everything they hate – love, freedom, justice, compassion. This is why our poets are being shot at the cemetery walls.'

Rosa had closed her eyes, thought of Lorca's beautiful 'Sleepwalking Ballad' as she drifted into sleep. It always made her feel like she was floating in clear emerald water, or flying through whispering green leaves. She always felt he wrote those lines about the little gypsy girl for her. The first time she met Lorca, she was just a child, pulling water from the well in Granada.

She remembered how Lorca's verse about two friends climbing into the rafters of a house came to her, and how she had jerked awake. With dazzling clarity she saw Jordi and Marco climbing, higher and higher, trailing blood. Rosa had tried to shake the image that flashed into her mind. She had seen these visions before, trusted them. Jordi turned now and smiled at her. She hoped she was wrong.

'My brother, the poetry lover?' Jordi laughed.

Rosa stared Vicente down. 'Yes, I knew Lorca. I danced for him,' she said proudly. 'I inspired him, the great poet. We met at the Concurso de Cante Jondo, the flamenco festival. I heard Caracol and Pavon sing, I danced with them.'

'You must have been a child!' Jordi said.

'I was.'

'Maybe, one day, you will dance for me, eh?' Vicente turned away. 'Meanwhile, you can help in the house, with the cleaning ...'

'I'm going to work,' she said clearly. 'If they won't let the women fight any more, I can help in the hospitals in town, at least until the baby is born.'

'How old are you?'

'Nineteen.' She raised her chin defiantly. 'Old enough.'

'Are you going to marry her?' he asked Jordi.

Jordi held up his hands. 'I've asked her, believe me.'

Vicente shrugged. 'As long as you pull your weight here, I don't care what you do.'

'Take me with you,' she begged Jordi. 'I can't stay here. It makes me sick to see the shops full of hams and cakes and sweets, people taking their evening *paseo* like there is no war. Don't they care what is happening in Madrid? Have they forgotten what happened in the summer? There is no distant front now against the fascist assault – Madrid *is* the front.' She buried her head in his chest. 'The wolves are at the gate. I should be there, fighting beside you.'

'No,' he said. 'I will not hear of it. If you love me, and

61

you love our child, stay here. I will come back to you, I promise.'

'But what if …?'

'Rosa.' He took her face in his hands. 'No fascist bullet can touch me, no bomb can keep me from you. I will come back. I swear.' He glanced over at the boys play-fighting. 'See? That little boy has it in him too. To fight the bull, you must have the courage to stand still. You must not run – you must conquer your fear.'

'That's what you want me to do? Stand still?' Rosa's dark, kohled eyes flashed as she looked up at him.

'Not stand still, be still.' He kissed her hairline. 'Rest, eat well. Make sure our son is strong.'

'Son?' Rosa laughed. 'What if it is a girl?'

'Then she will be as beautiful and stubborn as her mother.'

Jordi slung his arm over her shoulder, and she slipped hers around his waist as they walked. She wanted the air between them to disappear. Ever since the night they had first met, at a bar in Madrid where Rosa was dancing, she'd felt a hunger for him, an ache in the pit of her stomach. She looked down at their feet, walking in unison along the moonlit street. From the moment he had taken her in his arms, she had been unable to resist the rhythm their bodies created – when they danced, when they walked, they moved as one. She wanted him now, wanted to feel his body with hers one last time before he left. Rosa dragged him into an alleyway, a dark doorway, pressed her lips, her tongue to his. Music drifted from an open window above, a guitar, the liquid notes, the rhythm of drumming fingertips on the soundboard. She felt his fingers trace the darkness, reaching for her. The air between them felt phosphorescent, electrified, fresh against the warm skin of her thighs. She closed her eyes, heard the music, castanets clicking like oil-blue scarab beetles, the metallic clink of his belt.

'*Mi amor*,' he whispered in the crook of her neck, his hand at the base of her spine, lifting her to him. Rosa felt fresh longing rise in her like sap in a pine tree, rising up from the earth. As he touched her in the darkness, she felt his fingerprints mark her body like tracery, she felt the light break out in her like a sun-warmed fruit splitting open.

'*Te amo*,' she whispered, '*te quiero*. I love you, I want you ...'

'Always,' he said, the breath catching in his throat. 'Always.'

10

LONDON, SEPTEMBER 11, 2001

Just before three, Charles stepped out onto the empty street, and lit a cigarette. Freya joined him, reached across and took it from him.

'You haven't smoked for years,' he said.

'I can't believe it,' she said, exhaling. 'Not war, again.'

'This isn't war. This is terrorism. At least when we were at war you could see the face of your opponent. You knew where to hit back.'

'We *are* at war, don't you see?' Freya said, her voice breaking. 'Oh God, will no one ever learn?' Her face was pale as she looked at him. 'This is just the beginning. This is our war, just as much as the Americans'.' She turned to the office as she heard a collective gasp of 'No!'.

Charles tossed the cigarette into the gutter, and they pushed their way inside through the people crowded in front of the television. 'What's happened?'

'The South Tower has collapsed,' Emma said, her face drained of colour. They all watched as vast clouds of dust powered through the streets of New York.

'There's still a chance,' Freya said. 'They may have time to evacuate the North Tower.'

Emma shook her head. 'He's trapped. If he was in the restaurant, Joe's trapped.' She hugged herself, hooking her hands tightly around her elbows. 'Joe,' she whispered. *Hey, Joe.* Her Joe. Joe and Emma. And he was alone in there. She blinked back tears. 'Get out, Joe,' she murmured. She remembered him on the observation deck: *'I feel like I'm flying ...'*

In silence, they stood transfixed as minute by minute half an hour ticked away. 'I feel so helpless,' Charles said hoarsely.

'We all do,' Freya said. 'There's nothing—' She gasped, her hand flew to her face. 'Oh God, no ...' Her head shook in disbelief as the North Tower crumpled, and fell.

Emma stepped forward, touched the television screen. 'Joe,' she said under her breath as tears trickled down her cheeks. 'Go home, everyone,' she said quietly. 'Go home and be with your families.'

They stayed up late into the night, switching between CNN and the BBC, the light from the television and the fire in Freya's living room flickering. Gold light from the street lamps spilled through windows where they had not bothered to draw the curtains. Emma fell into exhausted sleep, curled up beside Freya on the old sofa.

'Terrorist attacks can shake the foundations of our biggest buildings, but they cannot touch the foundation of America,' they heard George W Bush saying. 'These acts shatter steel, but they cannot dent the steel of American resolve ...'

Freya reached up absentmindedly to stroke Ming where he lay, draped across her shoulders. 'What kind of world is this?'

'Same as it ever was,' Charles said as he heaved himself out of his armchair. He shuffled across the room and stoked the fire. 'Don't you remember, when the fascists used the bombers at Guernica, and in Madrid and Valencia for the first time, we said the same?'

'This is different,' Freya said angrily. 'This is cowardly. My heart breaks when I think of the thousands of men and women, the children whose parents aren't coming home tonight.' When she closed her eyes, she saw the image of the falling man.

'Why is it different? Just because it is a different sort of war?'

'The people who died weren't soldiers, Charles. They were ordinary, like Joe, just going about their day.'

'You're forgetting,' Charles said, his face hard. 'They weren't soldiers in Spain, not most of them. Remember the women, the children?'

'Of course I do. You don't need to remind me of what we saw.'

'They were innocents, just like our girl here.' He stroked Emma's hair as she slept. 'There's not a damn thing we can do about it. Joe's gone. I never trusted the smarmy chancer, playing them both along.'

'Charles!' Freya mimed at him to lower his voice.

'Emma has to think about herself now, herself and her child.' He offered Freya his hand, and they draped a blanket over Emma before going upstairs to their rooms.

Emma woke at dawn, curled up on Freya's sofa, the grey embers of the fire smouldering beside her. A muffled ringing forced her completely awake now, and she pushed back the blanket, searched for her bag. 'Hello,' she mumbled as she flicked open her phone. She rubbed her red, swollen eyes.

'Em? Emma? It's me.' The line crackled.

'Lila? Where are you?' Emma hesitated as she heard Freya's bedroom door open upstairs.

'Oh, God, Em ...' Her voice was choked with sobs.

Emma stood, the blanket tumbling to the floor. 'Have you found him? Have you heard anything about Joe?'

'No. Nothing. I thought you might have heard something at the office?'

'No one's called. We haven't heard a thing.'

'He's just ... They've all just disappeared. All those people. I ... I can't believe it,' Delilah said, weeping. 'He can't be gone. He can't be. It's not fair, I can't live without him. What am I going to do?'

Emma clenched her fist as Delilah's voice trailed off into a wail. 'Where are you?' She heard Delilah trying to compose herself, her breath catching.

'I'm back at the Paramount.'

'Why aren't you looking for him?' Emma cried out.

'I have been! I've been out for hours trying to find out if anyone has seen Joe. People are keeping vigil at Union Square Park. Everyone is wandering around with photographs of all the missing people ...'

Emma looked up as Freya's slim feet appeared at the top of the staircase, a silver kimono wrapping around them. 'I'm going to come out.'

Delilah paused. Her voice was cold, suddenly. 'Why? There's no need. Besides, all the flights are grounded.'

'I have to come out. I have to find Joe.' Emma followed Freya with her gaze as she walked downstairs, her pale bony hand gripping the banister.

'That's not necessary. I'm here now.' She could hear the defensive tone in Delilah's voice. 'I should have been with him. I can't … I can't be without him. If he's dead … I wish I'd died with him.'

'It's not finished, Lila,' Emma said, her voice cracking. 'I spoke to Joe, just before the meeting …' Freya walked towards her, shaking her head, her expression filled with compassion. 'He told me he'd made a mistake. He told me he loved me.'

'That's rubbish.'

'He said he'd always love me.'

'Yeah, but not like *that* any more.' Delilah laughed, her throaty, sexy laugh that Emma had seen reduce grown men to stammering fools. 'You lost, Emma. He chose me.'

'We were going to get back together.'

'That's what you think.' Delilah paused. 'So I guess Joe didn't tell you?'

Emma's heart clenched in her chest. 'Tell me what?'

'I think he wanted to tell you face to face.'

'Tell me what?'

'Hang up, Emma,' Freya whispered. When Emma shook her head, Freya reached for her hand. Emma snatched it away. 'Please hang up, don't let her upset you. Think of the baby.'

'We got married, Em. Last month.'

'No.' Emma felt a wave of nausea rise in her stomach. 'You're lying. He *married* you?' Emma could tell from Freya's stricken face that she had no idea either.

'You walked out on him. I love Joe, I always loved him. We would have been together years ago if it hadn't been for you.'

'He was having an affair with you, for God's sake! What

was I supposed to do?' Emma ran her hand through her hair. 'So you just bulldozed in and pushed him to marry you the minute I was gone?'

'You know how much Joe wanted to get married and have a family. You turned him down enough times.'

'Yes, well, a family is one thing you could never give him, isn't it?' Emma curled her arm protectively across her stomach.

'That's low,' Delilah growled.

'How many abortions did you have over the years, Lila?'

'We were going to adopt.'

'How lovely. A ready-made family, to go with the ready-made home I built with Joe.'

'You always hated that house! It was Joe who made it happen, while you were off travelling.'

'Building the business!' Emma broke down in tears. 'How could you? How could Joe?'

'Anyway, we weren't coming back,' Delilah said quietly. 'We'd found a place out here, near his parents. We were going to sell up in London. Don't worry, you'll get your cut.'

'As if I give a damn about the money!' Emma wiped angrily at her eyes with the heel of her hand. 'When I think you'd been sneaking around for months ...'

'We couldn't tell you when Liberty was dying!'

'I found out anyway, didn't I?' She rummaged under the sofa, pulled on her old pair of Uggs.

'We never wanted to hurt you.'

'You have, and you did.' Emma slung her bag on her shoulder. 'Well it's all yours now, Lila. If Joe's dead, it's yours – the house, two-thirds of the company. You're rich. I hope it makes you happy. It's all you ever wanted.'

'No … Maybe once. All I want is Joe.'

Emma shook her head as Freya reached out to her, flung open the front door. 'That's all we ever wanted, wasn't it?' she said before she hung up, and ran down the street.

'Emma!' Freya yelled, stumbling as she followed her onto the pavement. 'Come back!'

Charles padded down the stairs behind her, and pulled her gently indoors. 'Let her go. Em's a big girl now. We can't fight her battles for her. She knows we're here if she needs us.'

'But …'

'But nothing. You were always the same with Liberty. You can't protect them forever, Frey.'

'I know.' Freya's face was etched with grief. 'That poor girl. What will she do now?'

'She'll go off, lick her wounds. It's what she always does.' Charles kissed the top of Freya's head and sighed. 'Let her go.'

11

MADRID, NOVEMBER 1936

Charles staggered along the corridor of the Hotel Florida, his arm around Hugo's shoulders. The doors of the rooms stood open, and as he glanced through he saw men hunched over typewriters, typing their reports to cable home. One, a cigarette clamped in the corner of his mouth, smoke swirling about his fingers as they flew along the keys, swore quietly under his breath. 'Those bastards,' he muttered. 'They're still denying the Nazis are down here. If they're not, then what the hell has been bombing the crap out of us for the last three days, hey? You watch, I'm going to tell them what I saw, Junkers of the Condor Legion filling the sky. I bet you it won't make it to press ...'

'Hey! Capa!' Hugo cried.

'Where have you been?' A man in his early twenties with thick dark hair looked up from under strong brows. He was leaning against the doorjamb, smoking. Charles noticed his hands – strong, long fingers, strangely feminine.

'We've been up at the front. Charles's first visit. Do you have any spare trousers?'

Capa smiled and clapped Charles on the shoulder.

'Another one whose bowels are weaker than his feet? Come on, let's get you cleaned up.' As he staggered through to the bathroom, Charles glanced longingly over at the bed. All he wanted was to lie down, curl up in an embarrassed ball. 'Don't worry,' Capa said. 'I was a dreadful mess after my first outing. I'd defy any man's guts not to turn to water the first time he's under shell fire.'

Charles knew Capa's work – he had seen the 'Falling Soldier' in *Vu*, and he'd been dying to meet him, to talk about photography. *But not like this.* Charles cringed inwardly. His clothes stank to high heaven, stiff with blood, and worse. He tried desperately to think of something to say, something that might atone for the fact he was wearing dreadful, putrid clothes, something that might make him as heroic and laconic as this fellow. Capa's words washed over him – Charles felt like he was hearing them from the bottom of a swimming pool. Capa laughed, pointed at his ears, and mimed an explosion. Charles nodded awkwardly.

'You'll get used to it.' Capa ran the tub, and tossed a clean pair of trousers onto the rail. 'We'll be downstairs when you're done.'

Charles scrubbed himself clean before sinking gratefully into the steaming water. His limbs felt heavy with exhaustion, and he sank below the surface, his eyes closing. It came back to him, suddenly, the babble of languages, the screaming artillery. So this was war. Nothing had prepared him for this. He had held a boy's hand as he lay dying that afternoon. Charles grimaced as he remembered the boy's face, as pale as a marble tomb, completely unblemished while his guts spilled out onto the cold earth at his side. He stayed with him to the end, as the boy talked about his mother and sister, his eyes flickering, the light in them fading. The relentless day of fighting and carnage contracted into that single moment for him.

'Over here!' Hugo called across the crowded bar to Charles. As he pushed through he felt like he was swimming through the noise of a multitude of languages, the fug of smoke and the smell of the battlefield, sweat and cheap cologne.

Capa looked up. 'Ah! The Englishman!' He put his arm around Charles's shoulders. 'Feeling any better?'

'A little.'

'Hugo – a drink for our friend. Today, he has lost his virginity.'

The whisky burnt Charles's throat, and his hand shook as he leant against the bar to steady himself.

'It gets easier.' Capa offered him a cigarette. 'You came here with Hugo didn't you? Are you press?'

'Charles Temple. Yes, I'm meant to be reporting for the *Manchester Guardian*. I take ... well, I'm learning to take photographs.'

'What do you use?'

'A Contax.'

Capa let out a slow whistle. 'Nice camera. I use a Leica myself.' He raised his glass. 'Welcome on board. We're quite a motley crew as you can see.' Capa leant against the bar and sipped his drink as he scanned the room, and signalled to a bespectacled man playing chess. 'That's Chim.'

Chim wandered over and held out his hand to Charles. 'Pleased to meet you.'

'Hey, Capa, there's a call for you,' the barman shouted.

Capa switched his cigarette to his other hand, and hooked the phone under his jaw. 'To whom am I speaking?' His face creased into a flirtatious smile as he listened. 'I'm sorry. You'll have to remind me. Taro? Have we met?' He grinned, took a drag of his cigarette. 'Tell me, are you a brunette? Tall? Shapely legs?' He winked at Chim, and laughed. 'Ah, *that* Miss Taro. The little fox.'

God, I wish I could talk to girls like that, Charles thought. He turned to Chim. 'How long have you all been here?'

'A while. I've been photographing behind the scenes. I leave the dangerous stuff to him and Gerda,' he said, tilting his head towards Capa.

'Gerda?'

Chim smiled. 'You'll meet her. Everyone is crazy about Gerda.'

'Is she with Capa?'

'Yes. More's the pity for a lot of men.'

'I think I'm in love with you, Miss Taro.' Capa went to hang up the phone. 'Come soon. It hurts.'

As he rejoined them, Chim raised his glass. 'When's she coming?'

'Soon.'

'Is this your girl?' Charles tried to sound casual, worldly.

Capa nodded and flipped open his wallet. Charles looked at the photograph Capa handed him. Something kicked inside him. When he looked at her face, he felt he recognised her, knew her somehow. *You*, he thought, still and focussed on her smiling face.

'We're going to marry when this is over,' Capa said.

Charles blinked, returned the photograph. 'Congratulations.'

'Ah, love …' Hugo staggered as he reached for the bar stool and sat down, his whisky slopping in the glass. 'You know, the bishops are saying this war has been called by the Sacred Heart, and God's love has given power to Franco's soldiers.' His face contorted with anger. 'What kind of love is that? That is not my God.'

'Nor mine.' Charles's jaw set. The photograph had unsettled him. 'But no one wants to know the truth.'

'The papers don't want to upset my countrymen by printing the facts,' Hugo said.

'I bet you'll never hear about that Dornier that came down near Bilbao. The Nazi they pulled out had plucked eyebrows and was wearing lipstick and girl's pants. Bet that won't make the headlines, eh?' Charles glanced at Capa, pleased when he laughed.

Hugo knocked back his drink. 'Was that true? Typical Nazi.'

'You'd think from the press that the massacre of hundreds of Spanish children is less interesting than Mrs Simpson's shoes.' Charles forced down the whisky.

'I spoke to a guy who had been up in Aragon,' Chim said quietly. 'He saw a mother and son shot in place of the father. He said she held onto her child like she was rocking him to sleep.' They fell silent, the noise of the bar eddying around them.

'Come on. Who's up for cards?' Capa said finally, hooking his arms over their shoulders. 'Couldn't help noticing you had a bottle of schnapps upstairs, Charles. Shall we?'

At dawn, Charles woke on the floor of Hugo's room. It appeared to be spinning. Hugo was moving around, packing up his kitbag for the day. He kicked at Charles's feet.

'Come on, old boy. The jeeps will be leaving in ten minutes. Get a move on.'

Charles scrambled to his feet, and pulled on his boots. 'Where are we heading?'

Hugo shrugged. 'Who knows. Back out to the university, maybe? Wherever they think the action will be today. To be honest, most of the men seem to wait and see where Capa is heading – he has an uncanny ability to end up in the thick of it.'

Red-eyed, unshaven men were streaming downstairs from every room. Charles nodded at a reporter he had last seen in the bar a couple of hours earlier. Everywhere there was the sour smell of sweat and stale alcohol. Charles's head was thumping, his mouth dry. He longed for a cold glass of water, but in the lobby all he could see was thick black coffee being poured from tin kettles. He searched in his pocket for some change to buy a tortilla, then remembered, vaguely, losing all his cash to Capa the night before. Charles grabbed a tin mug, and gulped the coffee down too quickly, scalding his mouth.

Hugo pushed through the crowd. 'Right, we're all set.'

In the chill dawn light, the reporters and photojournalists streamed out onto the street and into the waiting trucks and jeeps. Charles watched as Capa loaded his cameras into the jeep in front of them. He thought of the photograph of the girl. He hadn't felt like this since he was a child. A boy in the year above him at school had a toy boat that he had wanted desperately. The boy was charismatic, admired – the kind of person people wanted to be around, to be seen with. This boat was the most wonderful thing Charles had ever seen, with its bright red lacquered hull and strong white sail. In the night someone – a rival presumably – had broken into the boy's tuck box and broken it, smashed the beautiful boat to pieces. All that was left were red splinters of wood on the floor.

12

ST IVES, SEPTEMBER 2001

Emma closed her eyes, raised her face to the clear sky, where gulls wheeled overhead. A cold wind blew in from the sea, and Bamaluz Beach was deserted. This had always been her favourite beach as a child – most of the visitors to St Ives didn't even know it existed, following the crowds instead to Porthmeor or Porthminster. Liberty had always brought her here. At this time of year, when all the emmets – as the locals called the tourists – had deserted Cornwall, Emma had the beach to herself. The tide was high, and the waves crashed beneath her as her footsteps crunched along the shoreline. The beach was a short walk from the old fisherman's cottage Charles and Freya had bought decades ago, before St Ives became fashionable. This beach had been her mother's playground, growing up, and to Emma it always meant summer holidays, surfing, sunkissed skin. It always made her feel safe.

She had driven non-stop to Cornwall the morning she left Freya's, pausing only to pick up her suitcase and Liberty's box of letters from the studio. By the time she arrived in St Ives, night was falling. She parked outside the cottage, listened to the hot engine ticking in the silence. The street was deserted, lamplight spilling onto the pavement from the pub, the muffled sound of someone's television drifting from across the road. Emma glanced up. Illuminated in a golden window she saw a family sitting down to their evening meal, the husband pecking his wife on the cheek as he sat at the head of the table. She had never felt so alone.

Her breath caught in her throat as she walked to the beach, her footsteps echoing. *Joe*, she thought, the same images playing again and again in her mind. She thought of the night she first guessed there was something wrong. It was Millennium Eve, a party in London. Familiar faces at the party had gone through the motions like a performance chess match, each living up to their usual role, and Emma was Emma, good old reliable Emma, as always.

'Will there be wedding bells this year then, Em?' the host had asked as she helped him clean up afterwards. 'It's about time Joe made an honest woman of you.'

'What's the point?' she had laughed. 'We're happy as we are.'

They were happy. She had answered that question with the same words so many times she felt like an automaton, but this time something did not ring true. Like a muffled bell, the words were dead on her lips. Happiness tasted of dust, of pressed flowers and yellowed photographs now. Nothing had changed on the surface, but something had sucked the life from their love.

No one would have known to look at them. Two pipers at the party led the procession down to the riverside at midnight, piping aside the crowds, clearing a path through the gardens. Although Emma began the walk arm in arm with Joe, by the time Big Ben began to strike, she found herself alone, holding back a friend's hair as she vomited in a flower bed. She missed the fireworks, the river of fire, in the crush, supporting the girl as her body heaved. Perhaps if she hadn't been walking so slowly, practically carrying the girl back to the party, she wouldn't have seen Joe. He didn't see her, she knew that. As the departing crowds drifted around them, she saw him in a doorway halfway down Lord North Street. He was talking to someone on his mobile. She didn't have to hear what he was saying to know that this was the beginning of the end. The sight of him was enough. He was talking how he used to talk to her when they were first together.

When he found her at the party later, Emma pretended nothing had happened. He had been looking for her, he said. They walked home at sunrise to their half-finished house on Old Church Street, and made love. Joe proclaimed a new beginning while Emma sensed a last goodbye. It took some time, more than a year. Joe was very careful. And then Liberty's cancer returned. Emma had been too young to know what was happening the first time, but now there was no mistaking that this was the end. Between work and caring for her mother, Emma felt herself pulled away from him, just when she needed him the most. She would wake at night in a hotel in Hong Kong or Sydney, tangled in the sheets, her chest heaving as she caught her breath from a dream that had scared her witless. She was always falling, a spiral staircase that went on and on, plunging down, gathering speed, calling for Joe to help her, but he was never there.

After ten years together there was no wedding dress to

weep over, no children, not even cats to fight for custody of. She waited for the formality of hard evidence because she knew he would deny it without proof. In her heart, she hoped that she would be proved wrong. Finally, he relaxed too much, left the key to his filing cabinet behind one day when he went to play squash. There it was, a neat paper trail of restaurant and hotel receipts, of one familiar number punctuating his phone bills too often. Emma told herself perhaps there was an innocent explanation – Joe often travelled for business too, and of course he had to call her for work. Then she saw Delilah's text.

Emma moved out, went to Liberty. Her mother was the one person she wanted to pour her heart out to, but couldn't. How could she destroy her mother's love and trust in Joe, now she was so close to the end? Emma said that Joe was being very understanding, that she wanted to be with her mother constantly, for whatever time they had left. *Which was true*, Emma thought as she walked on the beach. During the last weeks, as Liberty grew frailer, they kept up the pretence. Delilah came one last time to say goodbye, unable to look at Emma until the moment she left – when she shot her a single, triumphant glare.

After the funeral, Emma left Joe's life as she had arrived, with a single case, the years between them slipping away like sand between the cracks. He had denied everything at first, as she had expected, but eventually he caved in under her calm fury. She was not a vindictive woman. She toyed with the idea of slashing suits, or destroying future pleasure in his wine by turning up the heating. But she knew that for him to have to return to their life and find it complete, except for her, would be the best revenge. Joe hated change. He loved their life. He told her Delilah had caught him at a weak time – they could start again. He said their new home was a testament to their years of love. The ashtray on his desk was there because they had picked it out together in a little shop in Hamburg; every painting on their walls had been discussed and hunted out in tandem on their Sunday trips to Christie's in South Ken.

Emma thought of the night he came to the studio after Liberty's will was read, how they drowned their grief in the familiar comfort of one another's arms. He did not want her to go, he told her that much in their final conversation, his voice thick with regretful tears. It was insane, he loved her, this was just a fling. When he returned from his business trip, he said, they would start again. She mustn't do anything rash. He would break it off with Delilah. She remembered how her heart stood still.

'You mean you're still seeing her?' Emma had pushed him away, pulled the sheet protectively around her. 'Get out! How could you come here ...?'

'Emma, I love you,' he said.

'Get out!' She had thrown his clothes at him, bolted the door behind him as he stood in the hallway begging her to come home.

When Joe returned from New York, he found their house as clean, as perfect looking as a blown egg. He congratulated himself, thinking Emma had seen sense. He ignored Delilah's frantic messages, and cooked dinner for Emma – oysters and roast chicken, their favourite – and uncorked a bottle of Sancerre. As the night grew darker, Joe waited by candlelight for her to come home. He called her phone – it was switched off. The oysters grew dull, the chicken dry and burnt. Finally, he searched the house. He found only a few things had gone. Her favourite perfume – the others left half used on her dressing table. Her best knickers, old jeans and boots, the leather jacket they had both worn on and off, though it looked a hundred times more at home on her than him. He glanced at her bedside table. She had left behind the photograph of the two of them at the party on the night when they had first become lovers, but taken the one of her as a baby, in her mother's arms. A small rectangle of dark mahogany shone in the silvery dust. She had taken the best of her life and gone. She was travelling light.

The week in Cornwall had done her good. Emma felt more herself, she thought, as she scrambled up onto what she had always thought of as 'her' rock and looked out to sea. Beams of sunlight between the clouds illuminated the surf. The pain was less keen already, she realised, as she tucked the leather jacket around her. She felt the baby kick, push against her hand. She rubbed her stomach, thinking of the night she had arrived. That first night on the beach she had cried Joe's name into the wind again and again, her body convulsed with sobs as she let him go, let everything she had hoped for go. The salt air had lashed her face, mingled with her tears. 'Why?' she cried out. 'Why me? Why him? Why take Joe from me?' She had stumbled back to the cottage, searched for the key Freya left hidden beneath a stone beside the back door. On the doorstep she found a pint of milk and a pot of soup, still warm. Through her tears, she laughed. Freya had obviously called the neighbours and told them to keep an eye out for her.

Am I that predictable? she wondered now. She buried her face in her soft pink scarf, inhaled the warm, white floral scent of 'Chérie Farouche'. From her pocket, Emma pulled one of Liberty's letters. She had been saving this for her last morning. When she'd first arrived at the cottage she had laid the letters out on the old kitchen table, and sat looking at the titles, choosing which to open first. The seventh was marked 'In Case of Emergency' and her hand had hovered over it. *No. Better save that one.* She had smiled to herself, and picked this one instead. Her mother's handwriting looped across the envelope: 'On Family'. Emma turned it over in her hands, and tore it open.

Em, if I know you, you will have kept these letters unopened for some time. You always did prefer the anticipation of wrapped presents, always savoured every gift. You're not quite as bad as Freya, who still saves every sheet of wrapping paper to reuse, but I think she taught you the value of enjoying every moment, something I understood too late.

Do you remember that time when you were about seven years old, and you released a load of Charles's butterflies? I think you thought you were doing them a favour, giving them their freedom, but of course they were tropical and Charles lost his temper with you. You weren't a naughty child at all. In fact I remember being rather relieved that you had done something so uncharacteristically spontaneous. I said to you to learn from your mistake. I told you that you have to discover life's lessons yourself; no one can teach you.

You said, 'That's not fair, Mum. What are the lessons?' I still think you have to experience them for yourself, but as I won't be around to guide you, I'll try in these letters to tell you the lessons I've learnt.

I rather hope you might read this listening to Sister Sledge. 'We are Family ...' - do you remember, we used to dance to that all the time? We are a family of women - and Charles, of course. I've always regretted that your father chose 2.4 kids, a station wagon and a woman who wore drip-dry nylon over you and me, but what could I do? Trust me to choose the most traditional hippy on the west coast of America. My relationships were a disaster, but we made the best of it, I think, you and I, we made our family.

I wonder if Freya has talked to you about me, now that I have gone? I have had suspicions for years, but Freya always refuted them. I think she was trying to protect me, in some misguided way. I never quite felt like I belonged, Em, never really felt at home. It's like I was missing something that I had never known. Perhaps she will tell you more. Perhaps you will be able to solve the mystery of our family. I have run out of time. Maybe that's the first lesson - I suspect in life the families you create are not always tied by blood. I hope that you will discover the truth about ours. I love you.

Mum x

85

13

MORATA DE TAJUNA,
JARAMA, FEBRUARY 1937

The surgeons in the field station near the Jarama front worked bare-chested, their legs wrapped in white aprons and their feet in white boots. A rickety metal scaffold supported a weak spotlight above the patient, like a child's attempt in Meccano to create an operating table.

'What have we got coming in?' one of the surgeons called.

'Six abdominals and a couple of heads, Doctor,' Freya said.

'How is the last man doing?'

'He's stable, Doctor. The transfusion is helping.'

'Good. Scalpel.'

Freya groped around in the darkness behind her for the right instrument, candlelight flickering over the silver scalpels on the tray.

'How many bottles of blood have we left?' he asked.

'We just used the last one,' a nurse near the refrigerator replied.

'Damn. The delivery is late.' He wiped the sweat from his brow with the back of his hand. 'Get a message to the blood bank to send us everything they can.' He leant wearily against the edge of the operating table. 'Right, we'll have to give this chap a direct transfusion. Who is type O?'

Freya raised her hand.

'When did you last give blood?'

'A couple of months ago.'

'That'll do.'

In a side room, Freya lay down on a cold, damp camp bed next to the wounded man, and closed her eyes. She tried desperately not to think about the apparatus she could hear being set up at her side. Instead, she forced her mind to linger on the handsome old *palacio* in Madrid where she'd been billeted for a couple of nights on her way to the front, with its beautiful stone staircase, clipped hedges and palm trees. It had been abandoned by a Nationalist supporter at the start of the war, and now nurses and ambulancemen played billiards in the grand rooms with their silk drapes, and flicked through magazines in the library. Each night they ate their bread and chickpeas from the gilded dinner service. It seemed unreal that they were in such peace and luxury only a few miles from the front.

'Right,' a male voice said. 'You'll just feel a little scratch.'

Freya tensed. 'That was very good. I didn't feel a thing.'

'Good. Let's just get you hooked up to this guy's vein.'

'If it's all the same to you, I'd rather not have a blow-by-blow description.' She opened her eyes and looked at the doctor gazing down at her. She could tell from the crinkles at the corners of his eyes he was smiling behind his mask.

'You had your eyes screwed so tight anyone would think you're afraid.'

'I am. I can't stand needles, at least when they are anywhere near me.'

'That's a bit tricky for a nurse, surely?' He glanced over at the wounded soldier. 'I'm sure this guy is going to appreciate it.' The doctor settled her arm, checked the blood was flowing to the patient at her side. 'There, well done. You're kind of busy in here today.'

'Aren't we always?' Freya said. 'At least when this place is crammed full, there's a bit of warmth from all the bodies. We have over two hundred at the moment, even though this unit is designed to cope with only fifty. The men are three to a bed, lying on the floor, everywhere ...' She felt she was talking too much, forced a smile as she flexed her hand. It still ached from the cold. That morning she had helped some of the Spanish nurses wash sheets in the freezing water of a stream that flowed into the Jarama river, scrubbing them clean on the rocks. The air smelt of the battle, but also of thyme, the herbs crushed beneath the boots of thousands of men.

'I love you Brits,' he laughed, 'always looking on the bright side. I'm Tom Henderson by the way.'

'Pleased to meet you, Dr Henderson.'

'Call me Tom.'

Freya looked up at his kind blue eyes. 'I'm Freya.'

'Well, Freya, I reckon after this you've earned yourself a cup of tea,' he said, mimicking an English accent.

'Tea? I wish. I'm not sure the tea *is* tea any more,' Freya said. 'You're too kind. I must get on. The casualties are pouring in.'

'You know what they are calling this battle?'

'I believe they are calling it Suicide Hill.' Freya sighed. 'I heard the 15th Battalion are doing their best, but we've lost virtually every officer, and over half the British men.'

Tom checked the patient. 'Good, his colour's getting better.' He sat on the edge of Freya's bed and pulled down his mask. 'I think the Abraham Lincoln Battalion lost even more. Those poor, brave American guys marched right into the Nationalist lines without any artillery cover. They were cut to shreds.'

Freya shook her head, and sighed. 'At least we've stopped them cutting off Madrid.'

'"They shall not pass"?' Tom looked at her. 'When you see these boys in here, I wonder at what cost.' He smiled sadly. 'Say, when was the last time you had a proper meal?'

'Why? Do I look ghastly?'

'No. A little pale.'

'They gave us some stew last night.' Freya's teeth began chattering. 'Every time I get something with small bones, I tell myself it's rabbit not cat.'

'Me too.' Tom stood and checked the patient. 'I reckon you're about done,' he said. 'A few more minutes.' He settled back beside her. 'Would you like me to hold your hand? You seem a little shaky.'

'Would you mind awfully?'

'Jeez, you're freezing,' he said, rubbing warmth into her fingers.

'I'm fine. I think I'm just rather tired. We've been working non-stop for the last few days. I've only had a couple of hours sleep.' Freya fixed her gaze on his, tried to fight the wooziness she felt.

'Here, give me your other hand.'

'Thank you.' Freya looked at his lowered head, his dark hair falling forward over his brow. 'How long have you been down here?'

'The Canadian Blood Transfusion Service has been going since last November, but I came across in January to join Dr Bethune's unit. We travelled over with a group of Americans from New York. I'm with the Mackenzie-Papineau Battalion.'

'Oh, I assumed ...'

'No, I'm Canadian.' Tom glanced up, grinned at her, dimples forming in his stubble-covered cheeks. 'Toronto born and bred.' He checked his watch. 'It wasn't a great journey – third class all the way across the Atlantic, four bunked up in each cabin and everyone sick as a dog. I spent most of the voyage on deck.'

'Did you stop in Paris?'

'Yeah, what a swell place. I'd love to go back there someday.'

'So would I.' Freya was already imagining strolling arm in arm along the cobbled streets of Montmartre with him. 'Then we hopped a train to Marseilles and a truck to Perpignan, and made it over the Pyrenees. How about you?'

'Our first base was on the Aragon front, near Huesca. Some of us went on to other field stations from there. Eventually I ended up in Madrid, then came here with the Medical Aid ambulances—'

'Did you?' Tom interrupted. 'You mean some lucky guy had you alone in his ambulance all the way here? I'm going to change the way I travel.'

Freya blushed. She wasn't used to someone being so bold. 'It's a beautiful country, don't you think?'

'It's getting better with every moment.'

'The orange trees, the dusty roads ...'

'Maybe you'd like to take a walk later?' Tom stood

and stretched, his white T-shirt pulling taught over his hard stomach.

'That would be …' Freya glanced up at him. 'I'd like that very much.'

He leant down to remove the needle, and Freya turned her head away. 'Listen,' he said. 'They've got us holed up in some swanky house back in Madrid. Apparently it's safer – the fascists won't bomb the wealthy districts. I saw the way you worked today. If you're happy to take your chances with Bethune's temper, we need a new nurse for the unit – one of ours had to go home with typhoid. Would you consider transferring?'

Freya didn't hesitate. 'I'd love to.'

'It's tough work, you'll be out on the front line a lot. Delivering blood, administering it to dying men.'

She rolled her head towards him, and winced as he removed the needle. 'As long as you don't ask me to do another direct transfusion for a while, I think I can handle it.'

Tom pressed some gauze against the inside of her arm. 'There you go. Just keep the pressure on this for a moment or two.'

'I can do it,' she said. 'It just … Well, it's hard, isn't it? So many wounded men everywhere, the awful noise of them crying out.' She shook her head as she thought of the neat, clean wards she had been used to working in at the Nightingale Training School back in London.

As the orderlies lifted the wounded man's stretcher, Tom offered Freya his hand. 'If they are crying out *"Enfermera, curandera, ven aqui! Nurse! Come here!"* they stand a chance. It is the silent ones like this guy you have to watch.' Tom checked the patient's papers, and tucked them under the man's blanket. 'Jordi del Valle. I went against my gut instinct trying to save him, but he is so young.'

'Will he make it?'

'Who knows? Amputations are tough. He almost gave up on the table,' Tom said and sighed. 'There are too many for us to treat, and we're short on resources.' He gazed down at her. 'Look at us, we're working by candlelight half the time.'

'It's rather romantic, if you look at it in the right way.'

'There you go again, looking on the bright side.' Tom checked the dressing on her arm. 'Does it ever bother you, when some of the guys get amorous? I've seen the way they carry on.'

'Not at all. They're like children, most of them. They're lonely. The ones that aren't, well …' Freya pulled a pistol from the pocket of her apron.

Tom held his hands up, laughing. 'Thanks for the warning.'

'I didn't mean …' She fell silent as they heard shouting outside. An explosion shook the room. Freya felt the ground tremble beneath her feet. The blood in her ears sang. Tom pulled her into his arms, shielding her against the wall as plaster dust rained down.

'I thought we were safe here.' The bed where Freya had been lying was littered with plaster. Instinctively they both looked at the ceiling, waiting for more explosions.

'Maybe he got lucky, maybe he had a lousy aim. Are you OK?' Tom shifted back a little, his arm still encircling her waist. They could hear shouting, footsteps running along the corridor.

'I'm fine. Funny, isn't it? How your reflexes kick in.'

Freya looked at him, brushed the dust from his nose. Her heart was beating fast, coursing with adrenalin and the closeness of him. He leant in to kiss her then, his lips brushing hers. 'Do you kiss all your donors, Dr Henderson?'

'Only the cute ones.' He smiled, glanced up as they heard car horns blaring from outside. 'I've got to get back to Madrid, but I'd like to get you that cup of tea sometime.'

Freya held his gaze. 'I'd like that.'

'I'll talk to Beth about getting you out of here too,' Tom said as he stood. 'See you soon.' He paused in the doorway and turned to her. 'Happy Valentine's Day, Freya.'

14

LONDON, SEPTEMBER 2001

'I am glad you're back,' Freya said to Emma. 'I was worried when we couldn't get through to you.'

'I'm afraid I threw my mobile in the sea.' Emma scuffed through a pile of golden leaves on the path. She had listened to Joe's final message one last time: *I've done something really stupid. Listen, I'm going to make this right.* It was unbearable to her. It was too late.

'You're making rather a habit of this,' Charles said as he walked stiffly beside them along the Serpentine. 'Disappearing.'

'Liberty always taught me that you can't rely on anyone except yourself. I just needed some time alone.' A brisk wind chopped at the water as a small boy sent a red sailing boat skimming across the surface.

'Nonsense. You know you can always rely on us.' Charles turned up the collar of his black wool coat. 'We were both worried. You can't cope with all this by yourself, Em.'

Freya shook her head. 'I hate seeing you like this. You look just how you looked when you were a child, determined not to cry when you'd fallen over.'

'I'm fine.' Emma's throat was tight.

'There's been no news of Joe,' Freya said quietly.

'I know.' Emma walked on. 'I asked his mother to let me know if they heard anything.'

'They'll be pleased about the baby …' Freya's voice trailed off.

'I'll tell them, in time. Not yet.' Emma flinched. 'I mean, they have a proper daughter-in-law now.'

'Delilah's on her way home.'

Emma spun around to face her. 'Please don't say anything to her.'

'She'll have to know eventually.'

She shook her head. 'I'm not ready to tell her yet. This baby is the one good thing I have in my life right now, and I'm not going to let her spoil that too.' Emma realised what she had said. 'One of three good things.' She looped her arms with Freya and Charles and they walked on. 'Has the deal gone through? I signed the papers.'

'Yes, I saw you'd dropped them into the office last night.' Freya pointed to a bench. 'Shall we sit down?' Charles dusted off the seat, and offered Freya his hand as she sat. 'The thing is, the Americans have pulled out. Frankly, I had a feeling they might.'

'Because of 9/11?' Emma took a deep breath, gazed across the lake. 'So now what happens? I can't possibly work with Lila. Not now Joe's gone.'

'The package is all there. Delilah thinks she can find another buyer.'

'Let her, then.'

'Are you sure, Emma?' Charles said. 'You don't have to rush into anything. She should be the one to go.'

Emma shook her head. 'I can't possibly buy her out,

not with her and Joe's stake. She holds all the cards, as his wife. She's won. Delilah has all the money she ever wanted. I mean, Joe was always so organised. I bet he changed his will right after the wedding?'

Freya nodded. 'Delilah faxed me a copy, as if I needed proof. It's so unfair.' Freya poked angrily at a crumpled crisp packet with her stick. 'Why should you lose everything?'

Emma looked at her. 'No one said life is fair. Look at Mum.'

'What will you do? There's the studio, of course. You could start again …'

'No.' Emma shook her head. 'I'm going to sell it.'

'Where will you live? You're welcome to come to us, but there's only two bedrooms.'

Emma paused. 'You know, I sat on the beach one night and thought "I can go anywhere". I have you and Charles, and I'll always be there for you, but I have no ties anywhere now, not really. It's amazing how quickly everything that feels solid can fall apart. Joe, Mum, my home, my job, they've all gone.'

'Oh Em, darling.' Freya took her hand.

'I'm not feeling sorry for myself,' she said. 'I'm just …' Emma raked her hand through her hair. 'I went through Mum's will again while I was away. I've decided to move to Valencia permanently.'

'You've what?' Freya's eyes opened wide. 'Using the place as a holiday home is one thing, but why move there?'

'Why not? I want to bring my child up away from here, away from all this. I want to start again.'

'But Liberty said no one has lived in the house for decades, Emma.' Charles dug an old coin out of his pocket, rubbed the face of it with his thumb. 'It's probably falling to pieces.'

'I don't care if it is. I'm going to take the money from selling the studio to do it up. I'm going to make a new life. Of course, I hope you'll come and visit, come and stay as long as you want.'

'No, I don't think so.' Charles looked away.

'Why not? You loved Spain.'

'The country I loved did not survive, nor did many people I loved. Everything has changed.' Charles's fingers worked nervously, turning the coin over and over.

'But surely after all this time? Valencia sounds wonderful.'

'It is.' Freya paused. 'It always was heaven on earth. "The land of flowers, light and love".'

'Really?'

'Oh, that was an old song.' Freya stared out across the lake. 'The mountains, those wonderful blue domes, *Blood and Sand* ...' She sensed Emma's confusion. 'Tyrone Power and Rita Hayworth, darling. It's magical. Did you know the Holy Grail is in the cathedral?'

'You're kidding?' Emma smiled, but it felt strange to her, the muscles of her face unused to it. 'You must come with me.'

'No. No, I don't think so. You must discover the country for yourself. Our memories of the Civil War ... Well, a lot of idealists saw their beliefs broken and destroyed when Franco won.' Freya glanced at Charles. 'If you've made up your mind to go, I don't want our experiences to colour your time there.'

Charles cleared his throat. 'What's that lovely old Majorcan saying?'

'"It was and it was not so",' Freya said. 'That sums

it all up, doesn't it? Two sides to every story. Light and shade,' she murmured. 'I still maintain that there were remarkable acts of individual courage and mercy – they got you through the worst. But the killing was brutal. Who was that ghastly man who said "Death to intelligence, long live death"?'

'Millan Astray.' Charles grimaced. 'He founded the Spanish Foreign Legion. They were nasty when you came up against them, I can tell you. Very fond of their knifework.'

Freya nodded. 'War is always bloody, civil war more than most.'

'Brother turned against brother,' Charles said, shooting a glance at Freya. 'There was such suspicion everywhere. The Republicans tried to rout out the secret Francoists – they called them the "fifth column", the enemy within.'

'But they didn't get all of them,' Freya said quietly. 'Frankly the politics were irrelevant to many of us. People like Charles and I went to Spain because it felt like the only decent, human thing to do.'

'The British government was scared, so were conservatives everywhere,' Charles said. 'All they saw were headlines about Reds raping nuns, massacring priests and landowners. I tell you I never met such a decent crowd as the men and women I fought with in the Brigades. They were just ordinary workers, dockers and miners many of them, who saw that people like them were suffering and democracy was at stake. Now, people think the International Brigades were full of poets with flowers in their caps.'

'Or butterflies,' Freya shot back.

'You were just starting your PhD when you went,

weren't you Uncle Charles?' Emma said 'You had a scholarship, didn't you?'

'Hm – oh yes, I was a grammar school boy. Our parents rather left us in the lurch when they were killed. I managed to scrape together enough to buy the cottages – Chelsea was terribly run-down and boho in those days, and St Ives was a little fishing village. Do you remember, Frey, we had damp running down the walls? We had to hide behind the sofa from the milkman on many an occasion.'

'Is that why you didn't finish your studies?'

'Well, you didn't need to in those days, to teach of course. In some ways it was almost looked down upon – a bit ungentlemanly. Look at Nabokov – one of the finest lepidopterists there ever was, and a complete amateur.'

'You had a correspondence with him for a while, didn't you?' Freya tucked a strand of hair behind her ear, pulled her black beret down. 'Charles was quite the catch in those days,' she said mischievously. 'He was one of the terribly fashionable set. It was such an interesting time. A lot of his contemporaries became quite notorious.'

'I was rather naive, to say the least, about the politics.' He paused. 'About a lot of things.'

'Did you join the Apostles in the end?' Freya said. She leant towards Emma and whispered, 'I've never been able to get a straight answer out of him.'

'Hm? No.' Charles crossed his legs. 'I did get an invitation through my pigeonhole, but I thought it was for some happy-clappy church group, and tossed it out.'

'Poppycock, I don't believe that for a moment!' Freya laughed. 'It was a secret society – chaps from Trinity and King's would meet on a Saturday evening to debate. There was a lifelong bond: people like Lytton Strachey, Rupert Brooke, Burgess and Blunt belonged over the years. Was Cornford ever a member?'

'John? No, he was far too self-effacing.'

'Of course by Charles's time they were recruiting for looks rather than intellect.'

'Oh, shut up, Frey. You're talking about things you know nothing about.'

'I've never understood why he didn't go back to King's, he loved it so there. It was almost like he was punishing himself,' she said to Emma.

'Punishing myself? Do you think so? Perhaps there were too many memories.' Charles frowned. 'I was happy enough at Downing. I went back after 1945 when Wigglesworth took over from Imms. He specialised in butterflies and moths, you see. Marvellous family man, very warm – though you wouldn't think so from Updike's poem about him. It was an exciting time. We really revolutionised the way people looked at insects with the work we did in Cambridge. I was looking into scent scales on butterfly wings at first – you know they release chemicals, pheromones, to attract females?'

Charles had explained his theories a hundred times, but Emma humoured him. 'It sounds fascinating, Uncle Charles.'

'Not bad for little creatures who weigh the same as two rose petals and only live for a matter of days.'

'Did many of your friends go to Spain?'

'Oh yes. There was me, Hugo, John Cornford ...'

'He was a poet, wasn't he?'

'Yes,' Charles said. 'He came back in '36 to persuade us to join the International Brigades. Of course, he was

dead a few months later. I saw him, briefly, in Madrid.'
Charles smiled sadly at the memory. 'He looked like
Byron, terribly dark and romantic with a bandage
around his head. They left by train for the Andújar front
on Christmas Eve. We lost Ralph Fox, and John, the day
after his twenty-first birthday.' He sighed, and looked at
Emma. 'If you're really interested in all those old stories,
I have a going-away present for you. Come and see me in
Cambridge before you leave.'

'Thank you. I will. I hope you'll change your mind
about Valencia. There's no hurry. It will take a few months
to get the place straight.' She waited, hopefully. 'I'm sure
you'll want to come out and see the baby?'

'We'll see.' Freya smiled thinly. 'I hope you know what
you're doing.'

'How will you support yourself?' Charles asked.

'I'll think of something. Perfume, cosmetics, it all seems
so pointless after 9/11.'

'You're wrong,' Freya said. Emma caught the sudden
hardness in her voice. 'People need things like perfume
and poetry, music and art, more than ever during times
like this. People need to remember the simple joys in life.
If you forget, if life loses its colour then they have won.
Those cowardly, heartless bastards have won.'

'Frey,' Charles said.

'I'm sorry. It's talking about the past, it always ...
Well ...' She blinked, lowered her gaze. 'We can't let
them win.'

Emma realised suddenly that she had never seen Freya
cry, not once, not even when Liberty died. She had wanted
to ask her about Liberty's letter, but this didn't seem like
the time. Freya looked tired suddenly.

'I just hope you know what you're doing,' Freya said.

'Don't listen to her,' Charles said. 'She's always been over-cautious …'

Freya scowled at him. 'Nonsense. I've had my moments.'

Charles patted Emma's hand. 'Good luck to you, Em. If this is what you need to do, then do it.' He looked out across the lake. 'It all goes by so fast. We have to enjoy what can be enjoyed.'

15

GUADALAJARA, MARCH 1937

Freya worked with a couple of the Spanish nurses until almost sunset, clearing debris from some of the ruined rooms in the abandoned farmhouse, scrubbing the uneven floors and setting up more beds for the field station to use. She was exhausted, her hands rubbed raw from moving bricks and rocks, her shins bruised and scraped from tripping over metal camp beds. All she wanted now was a stiff drink and to relax with Tom back in Madrid. She longed for a hot bath, for her bed. She felt like a princess waking there in the mornings, surrounded by the luxury of the Nationalist's abandoned home where the Canadian blood transfusion unit had established its headquarters. The contrasts of her life amazed her, the vividness of her days, that in so much horror she had found happiness. She had found Tom. She leant against her mop, and lifted up the tin can of olive oil, its wick sputtering as she surveyed the low-ceilinged, windowless room, the closest they would come to a proper ward.

'Well done, girls,' she said. 'At least now you will be ready for the morning.'

'There you are!' a male voice said.

'Tom?' She spun around. She caught the curious look one of the other nurses shot her. 'This room is ready, Dr Henderson.'

'Good. You didn't have to help out with this, Nurse Temple. You're working hard enough with the transfusion unit as it is.'

'I wanted to,' she said, hand on hip.

'Very well. Are you ready to head back to Madrid?' he asked, looking up from the notes he had been reading. He waited for the Spanish nurses to leave, and tossed the clipboard onto the bed. He took Freya in his arms, kissed her then, his fingers arcing across the small of her back, pulling her to him. 'So this is where you've been hiding. I missed you today,' he said, kissing her neck. They fell back against the wall together, Freya's fingers tangled in his thick, dark hair. 'Christ, I've never wanted anyone so much in my life as you.'

'Tom.' She whispered his name, her lips against his ear. Her head was swimming with tiredness and desire. At the sound of footsteps in the corridor, they both froze, and broke apart. Freya waited, staring at the ruined doorway, her chest rising and falling with her quick breaths.

'Come on.' Tom led her outside once the orderlies had passed with a swaying stretcher. 'We have a little time before the ambulance leaves.'

They walked away from the farmhouse, cut across the fields along a mule track. The sun was low in the sky. It felt to Freya like she was looking at the land through amber, clear golden light spilling around them. Once they were out of sight, Tom took her hand.

Freya pulled the red scarf from her hair and shook out her blonde bob. Her body ached with exertion, but as they walked side by side, she felt it quicken with desire. The warm wind carried the clean scent of him, of cotton, fresh sweat, cologne. She felt the heat rising in her cheeks. In the distance they could hear the boom of the guns on the front line. Freya leant in to him, their shoulders touching.

'Moments like this, it seems impossible that we're at war,' she said.

Tom slung his arm over her shoulder, and she embraced his waist, felt the lean hard muscles of his back working as they climbed away from the field station, away from the war. He pressed his lips to the top of her head. 'This is beautiful. I bet this place is full of poppies in the summertime.' The hillside blushed rose around them, the earth salmon pink, umber, peach, dotted with sage green and silver trees, dusted with white powder like the cheek of a courtesan. 'We could be any young couple, out enjoying the sunset, each other's company ...' He broke off as a sniper bullet zipped past them and embedded itself in a tree. 'Jesus! Get down!' Tom pulled her to the ground, shielded her with his body in the long grass.

'What was that?' Freya shuddered as a second bullet hit the tree in front of them, splintering the bark.

'We must have drifted too close to the lines.' Tom rolled onto his side, looked around. He pointed to a small copse of trees they had passed not far down the hill, and a tumbled-down wall of stones. 'You go first, stay low on your stomach and head for that wall. That guy's a long way off but we don't want to take any chances.'

'Tom, I'm scared.'

'I'll be right behind you.' He kissed her quickly. 'If he's going to get to you, he'll have to go through me first.'

Freya pushed through the grass on her stomach,

panting, rocks and dry earth cutting at her elbows, her knees. The stalks of grass danced above her, dark against the sunset. After what felt like an age, the wall loomed ahead, and she scrambled around, sat with her back against the warm stones, catching her breath. Tom was right behind her, his boots scattering earth and pebbles as he joined her. They looked at one another, and burst out laughing. Tom reached into his pocket and shook out two cigarettes from a crumpled packet. He lit them, and passed one to her.

'This is going to make dates at the cinema seem kind of dull in comparison,' he said, laughing.

Freya exhaled a curl of smoke, and smiled. 'It will take some beating.'

'Still,' Tom said, wiping some dirt from her cheek with his thumb, 'it will be something to tell the grandkids about.'

Freya felt the space between them contract and shift. 'Or perhaps not,' she said quietly. The moment, the possibility was there. 'I want you,' she whispered, her lips fluttering across his cheek, his neck, like the slow-beating wings of a butterfly. He reached over, stubbed out the cigarettes and pulled her into his arms. They fell back against the earth, tangled in one another's arms, in the swaying grass.

Freya stared up at the sky, pinprick stars illuminating one by one. 'I wish we could stay like this forever,' she murmured. Tom raised his head from her stomach, kissed the arc of her ribcage, her breast. He rolled onto his back and took Freya in his arms. She felt the warmth of his chest against her cheek, heard the steady beat of his heart.

'We should be careful,' he said.

'I don't think anyone knows we're seeing one another.'

'I don't mean that. I don't give a damn who knows we're together. I meant that I want to take care of you.' He smoothed her hair back from her brow. 'Maybe we want a little time together alone before ...'

'Oh! You mean ...' Freya blushed. 'I wouldn't worry. I haven't had ... I mean, my ...'

'You know, for a nurse you can be awfully prim,' he said, laughing.

Freya dug him in the ribs. 'They've stopped, anyway. I haven't had one for months so it's very unlikely I'd get pregnant. And if I did ...'

'It would be wonderful,' he said, holding her tight. 'Stay with me tonight,' he said. 'Do you love me, Freya? Could you?'

'Of course.' She sat up, held his dear face in her hands, smiled as she looked at him. 'Of course I love you, Tom.'

He reached up to her. 'Marry me.'

She turned her cheek, kissed the palm of his hand. 'You're crazy. You hardly know me.'

'I know you,' he said, holding her gaze. 'I've never been more sure of anything in my life. Marry me, Freya.'

16

MADRID, SEPTEMBER 2001

Emma raced along the platform, and waved her arm at the guard. Just as the last doors were closing, she jumped onto the packed train. By the time she found her seat in the buffet car, the carriage lurched, and they pulled out of Atocha Station, sunlight blinding her as they clattered along the line. A businessman sitting opposite helped her place her suitcase on the rack, and Emma settled back for the journey to Valencia. She pulled the blind down slightly, and closed her eyes. She had spent the morning exploring the museums in Madrid, and the image of Picasso's *Guernica* danced in her mind as she dozed.

The aroma of lunch cooking in the train kitchen drifted to her – she picked out the scents of garlic and onion, the rich, dull fragrance of saffron. In Spain, Emma felt like she was coming out of hibernation. The night before, she had walked miles, exploring the city streets, stopping for tapas in pavement cafés and watching the elegant natives taking their evening *paseo*. The smells of the city were intoxicating to her – black tobacco, steaming coffee, drains, fresh tomato frying – each one helped her senses come back to life. She had paused outside the door of an old *perfumería*, transfixed by the gilded, coloured bottles in the window. She closed her eyes, and inhaled as the door swung open. *Roses*, she thought. *Mum's perfume.* It was then she was sure she had done the right thing in coming to Spain.

The train clattered out of the city, and Emma took a book from her bag. She ran her fingers over the embossed title on the linen cover – *Butterflies of Andalusia* by Charles St John Temple – flicked it open, and smiled at the studio portrait of Charles. Thick fair hair swept over a smooth brow, a flamboyant tie knotted loosely at the collar of his white shirt. His familiar blue eyes gazed into the distance. *This must have been taken before the war*, Emma thought. *He never looked that unguarded in all the time I've known him.* She turned the pages:

> *Spain. The greatest misery and greatest happiness of my life.*

Emma raised an eyebrow as she read the first line. She had never heard Charles talk in such passionate terms.

> *I felt the wind of change blowing from the south.*
> *I walked the dusty roads, brown as a prophet,*
> *bitten by more than the bugs in the roadside inns.*
> *I travelled through days of searing light and heat.*
> *My Spain was one where chickens pecked the floors*
> *and swallows roosted in the eaves of an old dance*
> *hall strung with carnations. Where black-eyed girls*
> *danced, savage, controlled, terrifying in their beauty,*
> *to a boy singing with the lovely lamentations of Islam*
> *in his voice. My Spain was a land where men who*

were vigorous, independent, undisciplined called you
'hombre'. It was a land that drew you into the heart
of its large, warm families – and yet I have never felt
more alone than in deserted villages shuttered by
shadows, or in vast fields where suddenly a thousand
white butterflies rose like a melody on the wind.

Emma blew a slow whistle under her breath, and shook her head. This was not the Charles she knew. Just as she always did, she then flicked to the last page:

Some said that Spain was an emotional luxury for
a bunch of wet-behind-the-ears idealists, but any man
or woman who loved and fought for the country
would disagree. Spain is Europe in miniature. The
Civil War was an explosion in an armoury, a force
that had been building for centuries. I fought for
this country, and, like many, I paid the price. My
Spain, the land of moonlit walks in the Albaicin and
Alhambra, of the chink of mules' hooves on loose
stone paths, of ochre earth and crushed mint, of
dark parchment faces aged too early, has gone. Life
is a puff of air compared to the moment of truth,
the Spaniards say – and in this beautiful, benighted
country I have seen too many face that moment
when we are all entirely alone.

Emma rifled through the pages, searching for the photographs. She had expected the book to be a dry catalogue of the butterflies Charles had seen in Andalusia, but drawings and notes of these were juxtaposed with images and recollections of the war. *He took all these?*

I didn't know Charles was a professional photographer too. She paused at a photo of a slight, fair woman resting her head against the broken column of a bombed-out building. She read the title: *'Gerda'*. Gerda had a smile on her lips, but she was looking away from the camera, as if she was trying not to laugh. Emma imagined Charles then, pacing the ruined building, his camera trained on the woman. *Gerda*, she thought. *Gerda Taro, she was Robert Capa's partner.* Emma sensed the intensity of Charles's eye. She checked the date – *Cordoba Front, June 1937.* It was a few weeks before the battle at Brunete.

As the train sped along, Emma looked out at the ochre hills sweeping past beneath the watchful gaze of a huge, iconic black Osborne bull billboard. *Poor Charles*, she thought.

Emma flicked on through image after image of the war: soldiers' solemn, defiant faces, broken bodies on the barricades, children with the knowing, exhausted look of old men and women. *The things you and Freya saw.* At the final photograph, she paused, and turned the book sideways. It was a nude – a young woman, modestly draped with a white sheet, a black fan obscuring her features. *Charles!* Emma smiled. *Well I never, you old devil.* She scanned the final paragraph, opposite:

> *If this poor, beleaguered country rises from*
> *the ashes it will be because of her women. What*
> *man fails to appreciate is that societies can move*
> *backwards as well as forwards. We believed in*
> *victory, it was not possible that we would lose. Yet,*
> *we lost. We fought with our women at our side, and*
> *yet Spain returned to the past. Spanish women have*

in them all that is good in Spain. It is alive in their
hearts and their devotion. In Spain I met the most
beautiful women of my life, luminous and fragile,
fleeting and lovely as any butterfly. If Spain rises, free
again, it will be because of them.

Charles had blushed when he'd given her the book. 'It's terribly dated, of course,' he'd said as she unwrapped the brown paper parcel after their tea together at Fitzbillies, near his Cambridge rooms. 'At the time it was eclipsed by Lee's book, and Orwell's. I'm a bit like that chap on the Yellow Pages advert. Whenever I pass a second-hand bookshop, I feel compelled to ask, "Do you have a copy of *Butterflies of Andalusia* by Charles St John Temple?"' Charles laughed. 'The prose leaves something to be desired, but perhaps the photographs have stood the test of time.'

Emma flicked through foxed pages that smelt of mildew. 'You're being modest. They are marvellous! Why did you stop taking pictures?' She could see how proud he was of the little book.

He dabbed at his lips with his napkin. 'I had my moment. There was a little show, at the Club. They still have one of my photos, you know. But, well …' His gaze fell as he nodded at his injured arm. 'This was something of a handicap. Frankly, we needed a steady income when your mother was a child. Freya went back to nursing once Liberty was at school, but when she was a baby we had to make ends meet on my salary.'

Emma took his hand. 'Thank you, I'll treasure it.'

'I can't believe you're going to Spain,' he said quietly. 'You'd visited before the war, hadn't you?'

'Me? Oh, yes. I'd been fannying around chasing butterflies in Andalusia just before war broke out. Hugo and I stayed at Gerald Brenan's old place near Yegen. He was very in with the Bloomsbury Group, you know. Lovely chap, taught me so much about Spanish history.' Charles cleared his throat. 'They have the most marvellous blues down there, and the fritillaries ... oh they are lovely. It's a wonderful place – I remember seeing swarms of ladybirds that turned the rivers blood red.' He paused, leant against the table as he rose, stiffly. At the door, he passed Emma her coat, and retrieved his trilby and scarf.

'Thank you,' she said, and they stepped out onto the cold pavement. Rush-hour traffic swept by in the night, and streetlights gleamed through the bare-branched trees. A crowd of students heading back to their digs drifted past them as Charles and Emma walked slowly, arm in arm.

They paused at the gate of his college, and Charles put his arm around Emma's shoulders and hugged her.

'Take care, Uncle Charles,' Emma said, hugging him tightly. She breathed in his familiar scent – Acqua di Parma, mothballs, Drum tobacco. 'I hope you're not doing too much.'

'Me?' he said. 'I retired officially ages ago but they're good enough to let me pootle around the place. I'm amazed they haven't stuffed me and put me in a glass case along with the other dinosaurs.' He winked at her. 'It's just good to get out of London to be honest. Frey doesn't need me under her feet all the time. I've spent sixty odd years at the university on and off. I belong here.' He tipped his hat to her. 'Take care of yourself, Em. You know we are always here if you need us.'

Emma thought of Liberty's letter: *'In Case of Emergency'*. 'Same here. You know where I'll be if you need me.'

'The land of flowers and love ...?'

17

MADRID, MARCH 1937

Charles and Hugo sat in their usual restaurant on the Gran Via eating lunch. Charles looked around – it seemed that every successful writer in the world was there. He kept expecting someone would take him aside and tell him he had no right to be there. When he had told Capa once how out of his depth he was feeling, Capa had laughed.

'Trust me, Charles,' he said. 'The minute you start to feel like you have a God-given right to be somewhere, it stops being fun. Just enjoy it.'

At the head of the table, Hemingway was holding court, his arm possessively around Martha Gellhorn, his glamorous and intimidatingly smart girlfriend. Charles was so awestruck by her he had barely mustered the courage to say hello. Then there was Ted Allan, the political commissar with Bethune's blood transfusion unit, and Gerda. Charles's eye was drawn to her again and again, as if she were a dazzling butterfly.

'Put your tongue away, Charles,' Hugo whispered as he reached for an ashtray.

'I don't know what you're talking about.' Charles folded his arms.

'You can't take your eyes off her. She will notice if you're not careful.'

Hemingway turned to Ted. 'You know what you need to do, kid? Put your stories away for ten years then come back to them.'

'Papa, you're too tough. Ted's a good writer.' Gerda regarded him levelly.

'Yeah? Well Miss Femme Fatale, maybe in ten years he'll be a great writer. Maybe then he'll write something good and clear and true.'

Charles saw Ted colour. He looked furious, humiliated. Hugo tipped his head towards Charles. 'That's what it looks like when the head of a pride takes a swipe at a cub.' Charles was secretly relieved he hadn't dared to show Hemingway the notes for his book on Spain.

'What's the plan for today – head out again after a good lunch? If you can call it that.' Charles's stomach groaned with hunger as he toyed with the remains of his rice and chickpeas. He still couldn't get used to how normal all the restaurants looked. Everything was in place – the waiters, the china, the white tablecloths. Everything except the food.

'As if Hemingway needs one,' Hugo whispered. 'Do you think he knows how annoying it is for everyone to wake to the smell of his bacon and eggs frying each morning?'

'I shouldn't think he gives a damn.' Charles drained his coffee. 'Perhaps we can persuade the Commies to bring us breakfast in bed as well?'

'Us?' Hugo laughed. 'We're nowhere near important enough.'

Charles glanced at Gerda and wondered how he could become so. What could he do to make her notice him?

When they weren't fighting or filing reports, Charles and Hugo helped out at a battlefield school for the Republican soldiers. The men were being taught to read and write and instructed in the virtues of being faithful to one's wife, of teetotalism, vegetarianism. The earnest study of the uneducated men had moved them both, and as Charles taught them the basics about flora and fauna, Hugo created wonderful illustrations of poppies, butterflies and insects on the old chipped blackboard.

After the class that morning, as they walked among the troops, Charles had seen their students lining up for the mobile *peluquería*, where men were getting shaves and haircuts. The sight of their vulnerable necks, pale skin exposed by the clippers, struck him. He felt such fraternity with the men he was fighting with at that moment, so proud of them, that he felt tears prick his eyes. He knew, suddenly, what it was they were fighting for. If the Nationalists won, everything would go back to the way it had been. These people would be crushed, denied knowledge, beaten back again. He settled down on a warm patch of grass, near a group of new recruits being taught how to strip down and reassemble rifles, and watched their sun-worn peasant faces. In the field, village boys were being drilled, marching backwards and forwards with broomsticks on their shoulders. Charles felt for the first time in his life that he was exactly where he needed to be.

Gunfire had suddenly broken the silence, and Charles scrambled to his feet, looking for his rifle, his camera. Hugo jogged over, and handed him a pair of binoculars. Charles trained them on the figures running towards the hill. He caught sight of a small redheaded woman up ahead, racing across open ground. 'Who is that? She's mad!' Even as

117

he said it, Charles knew who she was. The girl from the photograph. He felt his heart catch in his chest.

'Haven't you met Gerda yet?' Hugo had laughed. 'She's fearless, like Capa. They're gamblers, Charles, gamblers with life. They are like two children in love with each other, and life. All of this is a big game to them.'

Charles watched as Gerda's head disappeared below the line of a foxhole, the sunlight gleaming on her red-blonde hair. He remembered seeing a fox at home, disappearing into the long grass, lithe and bright, vanishing like an extinguished flame.

The little fox. He thought as he looked down the table of men at her. He wished desperately to be the man running at her side.

Charles finally managed to speak to her the next morning. He was striding through the corridor of the Casa de Alianza on the way to the cars, talking to one of the secretaries.

'Can you get this over to the Press Office in the Telefónica Building immediately, please?' Charles said. He made a quick amendment to his report, his pen tearing the thin, translucent paper. 'Damn. This stuff is hopeless.'

The secretary laughed. 'At least you still have paper. I know some girls who are typing on Izal loo roll.'

'Hey! Are you Charles?'

Charles looked up from the draft of his report, and through an open bedroom door saw Ted Allan, typing on a Royal typewriter. 'Thanks,' he said, handing the report to the secretary. He hoped it would get the all-important stamp of approval from the censors. Charles ran his hand through his fair hair, and walked over to Ted.

'Charles Temple. I'm with the *Manchester Guardian*.'

'Good to meet you. I saw you at lunch yesterday. Capa said there was a little Englishman kicking around the place.' He stood and offered Charles his hand. 'I was over at Beth's place last night and your sister asked me to give you this.' He handed Charles a board wrapped in tissue paper.

'Thank you.' Charles unwrapped the board, and turned over a detailed painting of an orange grove, luminous purple mountains in the distance.

Ted looked over his shoulder. 'She's quite the artist, young Freya.' He tilted his head. 'Beth loves art. He's trying to get her to loosen up a bit.'

I bet he is, Charles thought as he glanced into Ted's room. *Little Englishman indeed*. He was easily the same height as this American. Charles froze as he noticed Gerda sitting cross-legged on the bed, her head bent over a camera as she threaded fresh film onto the spool. As she looked up, her close-cropped red-gold hair was a luminous halo in the morning sun. She reminded him of statues of goddesses he had seen in books about the East – self-contained, golden, radiant. Cool eyes observed him from beneath sweeping arched brows – he felt her look at him and through him, like a cat.

'Have you met Gerda?' Ted said.

'No, I'm delighted to meet you.' Charles strode over and offered her his hand. 'You're a photographer as well?'

'Yes. What about you?'

'I'm still learning.'

'Aren't we all.'

'Capa told me it's not enough to have talent – you also have to be Hungarian. I may as well give up.'

Gerda laughed. 'Sounds like him.' She stood and looked

up at Charles. He guessed she was all of five feet tall. 'You know, a camera is only as good as the man – or woman – who uses it.' Her green eyes shone with amusement as she gently placed her fingers on his chest. 'It's an extension of this ...' She touched his heart. 'And this,' she said, touching his forehead, as if in blessing. 'The pictures are there, waiting for you.'

'Oh, I ...' The words hung on Charles's lips.

'Are you coming out to Guadalajara today?'

'I ... Yes. I've just got to send this report through.'

'We'll wait for you. There's room in our car.'

'Thanks.' Charles caught the slight in Ted's expression as he pushed past.

The three young reporters settled into their car as it swung out towards Plaza de Cibeles. Gerda pulled the collar of her coat up around her ears.

'Are you cold?' Ted put his arm around her, held her close.

Charles watched them out of the corner of his eye as he cleaned the lens of his camera.

'How do you like the Contax?' Gerda asked.

'It's good. What do you work with?'

'Rollei,' she said, turning to face the two men, her back against the window of the car. Charles couldn't help noticing the familiar way she tucked her toes under Ted's leg. 'The Contax is too expensive for me. I'm thinking of changing to a Leica though.'

'Gerda's stepping out from the considerable shadow of our Mr Capa,' Ted said.

Charles didn't like the tone of his voice. 'When's Bob due back from Paris?'

'I'm joining him there in a few days,' Gerda said.

'Oh.' Charles tried to hide his disappointment. 'You do get around, you two.'

'You've got to chase the work.' She flashed him a smile. 'We'll be back. Have you seen the shots of the refugees from Málaga I took with him in February?' she asked Charles, pushing her hair behind her ear. 'I've never seen anything like it. It's like a Biblical exodus – there has got to have been 150,000 refugees on the road to Almería. Those bastards just kept coming at them. I saw the planes machine-gunning women, children, the elderly ...' She held Charles's gaze. 'Marvellous, powerful images, of course.'

Later that day, Charles began to understand how those people must have felt. He lay in a shallow foxhole with a couple of the other reporters. The battle raged around him, the Republicans pushing through a victory against Mussolini's Italians. His nails were ragged and bloody from trying to dig down in the hole. It felt like he was sticking out a mile.

'Do you think they are targeting us deliberately?' he asked the man huddled next to him.

The man shook his head as he peered above ground. 'No, they are just— Shit! Get down!' He put his hands over his head and ducked. Nearby, another shell exploded, showering them with earth.

'This isn't funny,' Charles said. Machine-gun bullets danced across the ground around them like hailstones.

'It's not so much the fear of getting shot as wondering where one might be shot,' the man shouted. 'Your whole body bristles with the possibility.'

121

Charles craned around, saw the glint of Gerda's camera lens peeking over the shallow dugout behind him. He sensed the exhilaration among the Republicans. As daylight faded and the fighting became less intense, he lay waiting for the signal to head back to the cars. The knowledge that he had survived another day, that she was nearby, only a few yards away, gave him intense pleasure. Staring out towards the snow-capped peaks of the Sierra, he was stiff with cold, his leg cramping painfully, but for the first time in years, he felt alive.

18

VALENCIA, SEPTEMBER 2001

Emma strolled through Plaza del Ayuntamiento in Valencia, and checked the address of the agent again. She was early, as always, so decided to explore. There was a voluptuousness to the city, a softness in the light that had entranced her immediately. A little further up the street she saw a young woman sluicing the pavement with a tin bucket of water outside a café as a man set out tables and chairs ready for the morning rush. Emma wandered along the square, taking in the baroque architecture and the virile bushy palms. She paused outside a religious icons shop. Serried ranks of identical madonnas gazed out at her, eyes full of melancholy understanding.

The Santa Catalina café looked warm and welcoming, and she settled at the bar. The mirrored walls reflected several Emmas above the ceramic checkerboard floor as she chatted to the barman.

'Have you tried the *horchata*?' he asked her.

'What's that?'

'*Chufas* – tiger-nut milk. Or perhaps the hot chocolate is good for you?'

'When is chocolate ever not good?' Emma cupped her chin in her hand. White bowls were stacked behind the bar, beneath a gilt-framed print of the Valencian Madonna of the Dispossessed, a football trophy and old advertising posters curling at the edges. Doe-eyed flamenco dancers in red-spotted dresses and fringed shawls enticed her to buy Hilo de Oro olive oil, just as they had for decades.

'Are you on holiday?' the barman asked as he placed a dish of *buñuelos* fritters at her side.

'No, this is my home,' she said, testing it out.

Just after nine, Emma pushed open the steel-framed double-glazed door to the estate agent's. The heels of her boots tapped on the ceramic-tile floor.

'*Buenos días.*' A receptionist glanced up listlessly from behind an old manual typewriter. Her long lank hair fell over a nylon frilled shirt and she looked as enthusiastic as the dusty plastic flowers sitting on a doily at her side.

'*Buenos días, Señorita,*' Emma said carefully. 'I am sorry, my Spanish is a little rusty.'

The girl shrugged. 'So is my English.'

'My name is Emma Temple. My assistant said she would call you ...'

From an office next door, Emma heard the sound of metal chair legs scraping on the tiles.

'Fidel! Eh! Fidel!' the girl called. A plume of smoke announced his entrance. A plump man in a home-knitted sweater with a black cigarette clamped between his teeth emerged, sausage fingers extended towards her. Thick grey hair fell over his eyes. Emma guessed he was around her mother's age.

'*Encantado*. Fidel Pons Garcia. Will your husband be joining us?'

'My husband?'

'Eh, none of my business, right?' He glanced at the girl, who was following the conversation agog. 'Maria!' He clapped his hands, and she began to type. From a cupboard he pulled a large hoop of keys.

Emma stepped out onto the pavement. 'It's beautiful here. Do you live in the city?'

'Me? No, I live in my parents' old house in La Pobla, not far from the Villa del Valle.' He ushered her around to a side street. 'My car is over here. You know, I work with my five brothers and our sister. We live in a house on top of one another, work together …' He tossed his cigarette into the gutter as they turned the corner.

'You're lucky,' Emma said. 'To have a large family is wonderful.' Someone shouted from a car, and Fidel stepped out into the traffic. He leant down to the driver's window and chatted amicably for a minute as traffic backed up behind them. No one honked. As the conversation finished, Fidel waved magnanimously at the queue and everyone drove on.

'You're going to live alone in the house?' he said, taking short bouncing steps along the pavement. He stopped by a small, dented Seat and unlocked the door.

'Yes.' Emma's long-legged stroll struggled to keep up.

He shrugged as he opened the door for her. 'You're brave. Half the village think it is haunted.' He swept a pile of papers into the footwell. As Emma settled into the car, the fetid smell of damp dog embraced her. The engine caught on the second turn.

'Really?'

'The other half think it's cursed.'

They drove out of the city a little way, and were soon among orange groves and fields of onions. He pulled off the main road towards a small village, skirting the terracotta-tiled houses on a back road. Emma wound down the window, sniffed the air. She smelt moist earth, the clean green scent of the water cascading down the irrigation ditches. A flock of brown sheep huddled under an old olive tree by the cemetery. Fidel pointed up the hill to a tall pair of wrought-iron gates in a solid whitewashed wall. Above them, Emma could just see a four-square belltower with a Moorish arch.

'There it is,' he said, bringing the car to a sudden stop in a cloud of dust. 'Take your time, I will unlock the gates.'

By the time she caught up with him, Fidel was in the middle of an argument with a Moroccan man who was selling rugs and roses in front of the main gates. Gesticulating, he told the young man to get out of the way.

'No, really, it's OK,' Emma said. She ran her fingers over a chipped ceramic sign: 'Villa del Valle'.

'This is your house now. You don't want this.'

'But the flowers are beautiful.' She reached into her bag, found a banknote and handed it to the man. 'Hello. I'm Emma.'

'Aziz.'

Close to, she could see how young he was. She guessed maybe fifteen, sixteen. 'You can stay, it's fine. This is my house.' Nodding, he handed her an armful of roses.

'Be careful.' The agent scowled at him. 'People like that, they are not welcome here.'

'Moors and Christians? I've read all about the festivals.'

He looked abashed. 'Be careful. He will take advantage.'

'Do you think so? I've always found if you treat people with respect they tend to live up to it.' She leant against the wall, shielding her eyes from the morning sun. An old woman, seeing the gates open for the first time in years, crossed herself and scurried to the other side of the road.

Fidel gave the rusted gates a final shove, and steered her inside. Once the gates closed behind them, the noise of traffic, the village, faded away. Emma found herself in a walled garden. She turned around slowly, a smile breaking out on her lips. *Oh, Mum*, she thought. *It's beautiful.* Thorny bougainvillea with scarlet flowers consumed the walls, and a grove of orange trees filled the lawns. As she walked along the untended path, long grass caressed her bare legs. Insects hummed like paper on a comb. 'I'll need a gardener,' she said.

'You'll need more than that.' Fidel led her towards a side door. She was mesmerised by the tall stucco walls, the shaded terrace at the base of the belltower. All she could see was potential.

'There's no electricity, the water is from the well – and that may be dry – the plumbing hasn't been looked at since the thirties ... I told your mother she was crazy, but she insisted.'

'You met my mother?'

'I ... We helped her with the paperwork.' He pulled the keys from his jacket pocket, searching now for the door key.

'Wait,' Emma said, and fished out the box of letters from her bag. She flicked through the envelopes until she found the one marked 'Villa del Valle', and she tipped the key onto Fidel's palm.

'*Gracias*,' he said, and unlocked the door. 'Once, all the fields at the back belonged to the villa, all the orange groves as far as you can see. Now all there is is this.' He waved his hand dismissively at the tangled mass of the garden.

'It's perfect.' The door's blue paint was peeling. The houses either side were more modern – smart villas with shiny tiles and metal shutters, but the Villa del Valle was clearly far older; parts of it seemed to be Moorish. The windows were tightly closed behind wooden shutters, the heavy wooden doors at the base of the tower bolted shut. Emma looked up at the ornate parapet on the roof and the three wrought-iron balconies on the first floor. 'It's like something from a fairytale.'

The agent raised an eyebrow as he tried the door handle. 'As I said, there's no power, so I don't know how much you'll be able to see.' Emma looked at the black cables snaking over the house next door, and thought starting from scratch would probably be a good thing. '*Joder*!' Fidel swore under his breath. He shouldered the swollen door open with a triumphant '*Vamos*!'

A tabby cat appeared from the long grass, and eyed them warily. 'Ha! You are the same,' the agent said, miming a swollen stomach. He handed her the key, and some papers. 'All the contracts are there.'

'Thank you,' Emma said.

Fidel looked doubtfully into the dark house. 'Are you sure you want to stay here?'

Emma smiled. 'I've never been more sure of anything.'

'Listen, I'll tell my daughter to send up a box of fruit and vegetables for you. She runs the greengrocer's in the market square. If you need anything, ask her, or call me in town. Good luck.'

128

Once they were alone, Emma squatted down and held her hand out to the cat. 'Hello,' she said. It backed away from her, hissing, slunk along the wall into the shadows of the house. 'Not feeling friendly?' She straightened up and watched the cat disappear into the dark hallway, hips swinging, tail high. 'What do you think? Can we be happy here?'

She stepped from room to silent room of shuttered, whitewashed space, her footsteps leaving traces on the dusty terracotta floors. She threw open the windows and light poured in. There was little to see. The last inhabitant had left only old yellowed newspapers, empty bottles of cognac, petrified soap on the basins. The only piece of furniture was a big wooden table in the kitchen. She guessed it had been built in the kitchen, and had been too big to remove, too much effort to saw up and use for firewood.

She stepped out into the back garden and wandered through the knee-high grass. Among the tangled weeds, she found mint, rosemary and lavender growing wild and untended. Emma crushed a stalk of rosemary in her fingers and inhaled. She realised she was looking at the remains of a herb garden. As she paced around the perimeter walls, she plotted out the old raised beds in her mother's notebook. She had always dreamt of creating a scented garden, and had spent hours with Liberty walking the aisles of the Chelsea Gardener, planning the plants that they would choose. She knew instinctively what she wanted to do here, sketched out the planting and new water channels, a small pool at the back of the house. As she stood at the front gate and looked across to the villa, she imagined a tiled fountain, and a low channel of water in the path leading to the house. She would bring the garden back to life. *Maybe*, she thought, *it will do the same for me.* She had no idea how or why Liberty had found this house, but this, she realised, was her last gift to her. 'Thank you, Mum,' she said under her breath.

Emma slept on the kitchen floor of her new home that night, the shutters wide open to the stars. She had bought an inflatable mattress, two blankets and a pillow from the village market, and a cooked chicken from the *Pollos Asados* store. She decided to risk lighting a fire in the hearth, and sat on her bed, eating with her fingers in the firelight. After brushing her teeth with a bottle of Evian, she flung herself down, and bounced straight off the mattress. As she lay in a tangle of blankets, she began to laugh in spite of herself. *So much for the dream*, she thought.

Emma flicked on the torch, reached for her washbag, and pulled out a bottle of almond oil. She sorted through the dark bottles of essential oils and picked out two. Then she measured out a couple of drops of camomile and lavender into the carrier oil, and warmed a small amount in her hands, rubbing them together, inhaling the relaxing scent. She placed her palms on her stomach and massaged gently, felt her baby's answering kick. 'Hey you,' she said, smiling. 'Well, we're here.' She looked uncertainly around the dark shadows of the kitchen. 'Tomorrow we'd better find out about doctors, and hospitals.' It all suddenly felt overwhelming.

She gingerly lay down, and reached for her mother's box of letters. By torchlight, she flicked through them, and selected one. 'On Perfume', she read aloud to her baby. 'Let's see what your grandmother had to say about that.' She tore open the envelope and unfolded the paper. Pressed rose petals cascaded out onto the bed, and Emma laughed.

We are a family of perfumers. It's in our blood, Em, that I'm sure of. Freya says as soon as I could walk I was always picking flowers in the park, making concoctions for her, and you were the same. Perfumers, apothecaries, healers - we all make people feel better.

Emma thought back to Freya's words, her anger by the lake in London: *'People need things like perfume more than ever during times like this.'*

Perfume is the key to our memories. Someone like Kipling said it makes our heartstrings crack. An unexpected smell pulls back the years and lets you glimpse other places, lovers, countries, times. Who doesn't remember the fragrance that their first love wore, or the smell of their mother's dressing room? I always wanted to make perfumes that made people feel how they do when they smell newly cut grass, the scent of a freshly bathed baby's head. Perfume tells us we are here, we are alive.

I remember a Bahraini princess I dined with one night. She carried around a crystal bottle of sandalwood oil and anointed the wrists of her guests. That is what I wanted to do - give perfume as a gift, a blessing. Perfume is sacred - think of the garden in the Song of Songs.

Emma remembered Liberty reading to her as a child, curled up beside her beneath a tree: *'His cheeks are as a bed of spices, as sweet flowers; his lips like lilies, dropping sweet-smelling myrrh.'* It was always Liberty's favourite.

Maybe you've wondered why I always stuck faithfully with rose as my perfume. You know, in the midst of holy war, soldiers returning from the Crusades carried damask roses home with them. I loved that. I like to think they were bringing them to the women they had loved and left behind. You know, perfume is love. Cleopatra drenched the sails of her golden barge in the fragrance of roses, and when she visited Rome, the perfume lingered in the streets long afterwards. Perfume is romance - that is why I fell for the rose.

I travelled for years, as you know, a hunter of fragrances. I loved them all: frangipani in the tropics, coiled incense in the east, roasting coffee and petrol in America. It was never more fun than when I travelled with you - do you remember? I showed you where sandalwood comes from in Mysore, and the iris fields in Tuscany. That's how I learnt my craft, on the road, seeking suppliers in Turkey and Bulgaria, India and Syria, and of course France. Everything I learnt, I passed on to you, Emma, and you have surpassed me. You are an artist of fragrance, the heir of healers, alchemists, apothecaries - you are a magician! Never forget that. It takes time to create a great fragrance, there is no hurry. It took me eight years to create Chérie Farouche for you, but then it took eighteen years for you to become the remarkable woman I made that perfume for. Good things come, with time.

Follow your heart, Emma, follow your nose - listen to the quiet voice inside you. Make people's heartstrings crack. Make perfumes

132

*that remind people how wonderful it is to be
alive. Because it is, Em, to be alive is glorious,
and people need to remember that, and to
stop and smell the flowers.*

Love, Mum x

That night as Emma slept, her dreams inhabited the house, filling it with treasures, secrets, the scents of linen chests and spices, the hushed breath of words once spoken. At daybreak on the first morning in her new home, in the slow dawn of consciousness, she tried to locate herself. Her back ached, and her feet were freezing. She was on the floor. Whose floor? As her eyes adjusted, making out the slim, brilliant cruciform of light breaking through the shutters, she remembered.

She was in Spain. This was her floor, her house, her home. It was a moment she had imagined a thousand times, waking in a new life, in a new country.

Now all she could hear was a buzzing. She wondered at first if it was an alarm clock, somewhere else in the house. Joe had an alarm clock like that when she first met him. She hated it so much that he had thrown it out of the window the first morning she woke alongside him. *What is that?* she thought, rubbing her eyes, her fingers blackening with the kohl she had not been able to remove the night before. Her eyes flickered open.

'Oh. My. God,' she said aloud. Emma wasn't the kind of person given to hysterics, but even she realised how lucky she had been. A few feet above her head, dangling from the beamed roof, was the largest wasps' nest she had ever seen – grey, silvery, like some seething ghost of summers past. Slowly, ever so slowly, Emma crept out of the blankets and closed the door on the room, swatting

133

away a curious wasp that followed her into the hall.

She leant against the wall, breathing deeply, one hand protectively clasped around her stomach. She had hated wasps ever since Freya had told the apocryphal tale of an aunt who had swallowed one in a can of lemonade during a family picnic and promptly died among the scones and jam from asphyxiation. Few things bothered Emma these days. She had travelled around the world alone, but her morbid fear of wasps had endured.

Glancing out of the window, she saw Aziz setting up outside the gates. She called to him, waving him to come inside.

'Are you all right?' He ran towards her.

'Wasps … Or hornets?' Her eyes were wide. 'In there.' She pointed at the kitchen door, pulled her robe around her.

'Do you have any petrol?'

'Maybe. I saw a jerrycan in the workshop.'

'Good.' He ran outside, and Emma heard him dragging the can into the garden. He returned armed with a broom. 'Stay here.' He disappeared into the kitchen, and she heard muffled curses as he knocked down the nest and flung it outside where he set fire to it.

'Did they get you?' she asked when he reappeared.

'A little. But most of them were dead already, as it's nearly winter.' He sucked at the stings.

'Thank you,' she said. 'Come, let me help you.' In the kitchen she searched through the bag of groceries she had bought, and found some vinegar. She sloshed some onto a clean cloth, and dabbed at the welts on his arm.

'You can't live like this,' he said, looking at the tangled mess of her bed. 'You're crazy.'

Emma shrugged. 'Maybe. It's what I want, right now.'

'Crazy woman.' He laughed. 'Stubborn like my mother, my sisters. My mother, she is dead now.'

'Mine too.' Emma looked closely at him. She trusted her instincts. 'How about some coffee? I have a proposal for you.'

The sun cast long shadows on the ochre walls of the Casa de Cultura. It had taken some time for Emma to sort out the paperwork in the village, but finally with Fidel's reluctant help and all the council's stamps in place, she was ready to let Aziz know the good news. He had jumped at her idea to open a proper flower stall in the old shop that fronted the street in the wall of the Villa del Valle. As they had waited for the permits to be stamped, he had told her his story. It turned out he lived with his little sisters on the edge of the village in a run-down chalet. Their parents had died, and at sixteen he was the man of the family, responsible for feeding and clothing everyone.

'Look,' Emma said that morning as she unlocked the street doors of the old shop. Someone had evidently been using it as a garage, but the original shelves were there still. She gazed uneasily up at the sharp hooks hanging from the ceiling. 'What do you think?'

'I think it is a big mess,' he said. 'Like the rest of this place.'

Emma ran her hand across the wooden counter top. 'We could have a till here. If we unblock the windows at the back, there will be natural light, and the double doors at the front will give us a good street display.'

'A till?' He picked up on her excitement.

'A shop, Aziz. We could make a little flower shop here.'

His face clouded. 'But I could never afford ...'

'Listen, this shop is sitting empty, and it would make me happy to help you. I'll pay you the going wage, and a percentage of the profits. What do you think?' She held her hand out to him.

He grinned as he shook her hand. 'How can I ever thank you?' Aziz helped Emma work loose the rusted bolts on the back door leading to the garden. Light flooded the shop from front and back now, and he squinted as they stepped out into the villa's garden. 'I know!' He gestured at the tangled grass and weeds. 'I will make this good for you. Besides, it is bad for business if the garden is a mess.'

Emma laughed. 'It's a deal.'

'I don't know what to say. Why me?'

'I like you. I see how hard you work. You have regular customers already.' She laughed. 'And if I'm going to have the builders in for the next couple of months, I need to use the main gates!'

Aziz looked back into the shop. 'There's a lot to do.'

'So get cracking!' She glanced up at the ceiling again. 'The first things that can go are those horrible hooks.'

'I talked to one of the old women, she told me this was a butcher's shop.'

'Ah, that explains it.' Emma folded her arms. 'I still don't like the feel of it. But we can make it better. We'll need a sign, and some whitewash.' She looked around. 'Some buckets and things too. I'll ask Fidel where to go for them.'

'What shall we call it?'

'We need a good name.' The words in Liberty's letter came into her mind. 'We'll call it the Perfume Garden.'

19

BRUNETE, MAY 1937

'Nurse Temple, where have you been?' Dr Jolly's assistant said, without looking up from his notes. 'You're late.'

'I'm sorry,' Freya said. 'The planes were firing at us as the ambulances drove back from the station.'

He shook his head. 'I think those animals think the red crosses are targets, not symbols of humanitarian work.'

The same thought had crossed Freya's mind as she cowered in a ditch at the side of the road with the precious bottles of blood the men had dragged from the ambulances. Machine-gun bullets strafed the earth a few feet from her face. She could still taste the dust.

'Well, get to work please. I think the battle is only just beginning here. We have five hundred wounded men to cope with tonight.' He glanced up at Freya, concerned. 'Are you all right?'

Freya touched the side of her face, felt the nerve ticking in her eye. 'Yes, of course,' she said. She liked the little Frenchman – he always reminded her more of a pirate than a doctor, with his dark beard and sparkling eyes. She picked up a fresh apron from the nurses' station and smoothed her hair. 'Thank you.'

'Oh, Nurse Temple,' he called after her, 'Dr Henderson was looking for you.'

Freya smiled as she picked her way through the lines of men lying on the floor of the hospital. They had been so busy doing transfusions on the front line, she had volunteered to stay at the hospital for now. She hadn't seen Tom for over a week, and the thought of him now comforted her.

Every floor, every room of the hospital was filled with wounded and dying men. Freya trod gently around the bodies that clogged the dimly lit hall. A doctor was going from man to man with Mimi, one of the French nurses, to see which ones they could help. A spectral bandaged man staggered on crutches ahead of her, stumbling over the legs of beds, of men with broken limbs.

In the station in Madrid, as they were seeing off the wounded on a hospital train on its way to the convalescent homes on the coast, a second train had pulled in to the platform, full of fresh, shining faces, red scarves gleaming in the spring sunlight. *I wonder how long it will be until those soldiers are lying here among these poor souls,* Freya thought now as she passed blood-soaked stretchers lined up by the washroom waiting to be cleaned. She glanced at the empty bottles of blood in a wire basket by the door of her ward and checked the handful of blood-stained bottle tags – each one marked with name, battalion, wound, date. *Thank God we managed to save the fresh supply in the ambulances.*

'Freya!' Tom called to her, as she reached out to open the door.

'Hello, Tom.' She checked to make sure no one was paying them any attention, and kissed him gently on the lips.

'I've been looking everywhere for you.' He pulled her into the shadows of the storeroom.

'We were held up on the Madrid road.'

'Christ, it's been busy. They have three tables working flat out down there.'

He embraced her, sighed as he buried his face in her hair. The scent of ether still clung to him.

'Where have you been? I haven't seen you for days.'

'There have been some problems.' When he looked at her, Freya saw the dark circles under his eyes. 'Darling, there's no easy way to tell you this. They are sending Beth back to Canada, and I must go with him.'

Freya swayed slightly, reached out for the rough wooden shelves. 'You're leaving? I ...'

'Come with me, Freya.'

'Tom, I can't. My work is here.' She shook her head. 'When you see what they did in Guernica ... It's only going to get worse.'

'The bastards are trying to cover it up, you know? They're saying the planes were aiming at a military target, but why the hell were forty-three aircraft from the Condor Legion bombing the town then?' He grimaced. 'They were mowing down civilians with machine-guns as they tried to escape the fires.' He gripped Freya by her arms. 'You're right, it is going to get worse, much worse. The Nazis are using the Spanish cities as testing grounds for what's to come in the rest of Europe, you know that, don't you? It'll be Barcelona, Madrid, Valencia razed to the ground next. I can't bear to leave you here.'

Freya leant her forehead against his lips. 'You know me, I'm bombproof, that's what everyone says.'

'Freya, I'm serious.' Tom took her face in his hands. 'I love you,' he said. 'I want to spend the rest of my life with you. Come with me. We're not leaving until the end of the month. I've got to stick close to Beth, so I may not be around much over the next couple of weeks, but that will give you some time to think.' He kissed her then. 'Please think about it.'

Freya's heart was pulsing an irregular beat as she walked into the ward. She checked the charts, the words swimming before her eyes. All she could think was that Tom was leaving. Her brief moment of happiness was over, just as quickly as it had begun.

'Nurse ...' a man groaned. She looked up, snapped into the moment as she walked towards him. His head was entirely covered with bandages. Where his hands should have been were two bloody, shapeless bundles.

'Hello ... Simon,' she said, checking his notes. 'Let's see if we can't make you more comfortable.' She knew he needed a transfusion, so she took the last bottle from the refrigerator. As it heated to body temperature, she double-checked his blood group, and sterilised the syringe. In a few minutes, she was all done. 'Is that better?'

'Yes, feeling ticketyboo.'

Freya smiled. She was always amazed how the men managed to keep their sense of humour. 'Let's see how you are doing.' She felt for the weak pulse.

'I feel so wretched,' he said, his voice muffled by the bandages. 'I've only been in Spain a couple of days. I've done nothing for the cause.'

'Nothing?' she said. The courage of the man touched her. 'You have done everything.' She tucked the clean sheet in. 'Rest now, if you can. Your pulse is stronger, you're doing well.

Freya wanted nothing more than to lie down on one of the beds and sleep for a week, but as she turned back to the ward and saw two rows of bed after bed stretching into the dim light, some with two men top to tail, each man as desperately wounded as Simon, her heart sank.

Early the next morning, Dr Jolly's assistant found her sitting outside the hospital in the dawn light. Freya had her arms around her knees, and she was rocking gently.

'Freya? What's the matter?'

'I lost five men last night.'

'Oh, God, I'm sorry.' He sat down on the ground beside her, lit a cigarette and handed it to her.

'There were six of them dying, and only me on duty. I had to choose.' She raked her fingers through her hair. 'One by one, they went. I was racing from bed to bed, trying to make them comfortable, trying to ...' She fought the tears welling in her eyes.

'Frey, listen,' he said gently. 'You've been up at the front with the blood unit a long time now. I think it's time you had a break.' He squeezed her arm. 'I'll get Dr Jolly to fill out the papers. Go to the Medical Aid reception centre in Valencia. It will be better for you. Make lots of tea, keep the morale up. The cases are mostly convalescent over there – there will be less loss for you to deal with. Now go back to Madrid and pack your gramophone, your little stove and a bag of tea.'

'This country ...' she said. 'This poor country. They are burning books in Cordoba, thousands of books. Little boys are marching in the streets with wooden rifles. Men are being shot like rabbits – and that man, that Quiepo de Llano, with his broadcasts being shouted out across the country now the Germans have given him a transmitter: What was it he said? "Tonight I shall take a sherry and tomorrow I shall take Málaga." I hate it. I hate this ghastly war. I feel so helpless.'

'That's why Spain needs us,' he said, patting her shoulder as he walked away. 'Take it day by day. There is no tomorrow, no yesterday for many of us now. There is only what we can do, what we can get through today. That is how you can help.'

20

VALENCIA, SEPTEMBER 2001

Beneath the floorboards of Emma's bedroom lay a tiny photograph of a boy with dancing eyes. Sometimes, when the sunlight hit the crack in the shutters just so, a thin bright line broke through, penetrated the floor and illuminated his face. The photograph lay among the dust of decades, alongside dressmaking pins and buttons that had slipped through the boards, and another photo that lay upside down, its edge just touching the boy. It was as if he was waiting.

'I'm fine,' Emma insisted, the phone resting against her shoulder as she fastened a diamond stud into her ear. 'The house? It's not in such a bad state,' she said doubtfully, glancing around as she reached for her other earring on the old dressing table.

'Have you at least got a proper bed now?' Freya asked. 'You must take care of your back, Emma.'

'I'll order one,' she said, distracted. She fumbled for the earring and heard it fall to the floor. She watched it spin on the polished wood, and disappear beneath the crack. 'Damn.'

'What is it?'

'Nothing, don't worry. I just dropped something. An earring that Joe gave me one Christmas.' Emma sighed as she got down on her hands and knees. 'Listen, I'll call you back later. I have a couple of appointments in town.'

'Let me know how you get on at the doctor's, won't you?'

'Will do. Love you, Gammy.'

Emma leant against the board, testing it. It felt loose to her, creaking under the pressure of her hands. *There are some advantages to living in an old wreck*, she thought.

In the woodshed, Emma found a rusted crowbar, and she carried it back towards the house. Aziz looked up from the bonfire where he was burning all the brush he had cleared from the garden. 'Can I help? You must not do heavy things, not with the baby.'

'I need to lift a board in the bedroom. Do you think you can do it?'

It took only a few moments for Aziz to lever the board clear. 'It is no good,' he said, moving it aside. 'These boards are all old. You need a builder.'

'I know,' Emma said, squatting down. She waved her hand, clearing the cloud of dust. 'There it is!' She picked up the earring, and cleaned it off.

'Look at all this,' Aziz said. He reached into the gap between the rafters and picked out the photograph.

'Oh! Isn't that wonderful?' Emma said as he handed it to her. 'There's another one.' She picked up the second photograph, and looked at them, side by side. 'I wonder who they were?' She cleared the dust from their faces with her fingertip.

'Maybe you can ask the agent? Maybe he knows who lived here.'

144

'Good idea. I'll call into the grocer's before I go to the city this afternoon and see if Fidel is around.'

Emma loved the rhythm of her new life. After the weeks of turmoil, seeing the garden coming good gave her real pleasure. At lunchtime as she walked to the gate, she glanced up at the 'whoop-whoop-whoop' of the hoopoe who had taken up residence in the old belltower, and smiled. She had always liked the autumn, and the scent of woodsmoke hanging over the garden from the bonfire made the villa feel more like home.

She strolled out through the gate and down to the village, her arms filled with a bouquet of white Bianca roses. Outside the café a table of buoyant, boisterous old men with one grande dame holding court looked like they had been there for some time. A funeral was holding up the traffic, and cars snaked slowly past. Emma's stomach rumbled with hunger as she saw the woman dishing up paella from a large pan resting on a piece of corrugated cardboard. A man sitting alone eating eels with garlic and peppers dipped bread into a saucer of olive oil and tossed it to a tiny lithe black dog, who skipped off to join his gang of rude little street dogs, cocking his leg on the bottle of water someone had left on the street corner.

Valencian flags snapped in the air outside the town hall as Emma skirted around an old man in a checked shirt, who bent down, cigar in his mouth to squeeze the cheek of a baby in a pram. '*Qué bonita!*' she heard him say. Emma smiled at the mother. She was beginning to recognise faces in La Pobla, to learn its routines. She knew as she reached the end of the street that the old couple would be sitting on upturned orange crates peeling potatoes in the doorway of their crumbling baroque mansion. She knew as she passed Bar Musical that the sound of the Fallas festival band would be drifting out. Emma passed two band members strolling late to practice, autumn sun glinting on their French horn and trombone.

She stopped at the edge of the pavement, and waited to cross. An effigy of a saint in a tiled alcove above her looked down on a *policía local* officer directing the ballet of cars and scooters like a choreographer, his arms arcing, shaping the air. Girls in spandex pants and Puffa jackets clung to their boyfriends on scooters; the boys all had gelled quiffs, cigarettes dangling nonchalantly from the corners of their mouths as they sped through the snarled-up cars. The doorway nearby was strewn with palm leaves and petals for a wedding.

In the market, the smell of polished leather tack greeted her, then the smoky scent of charred meat. A chihuahua ran over the blankets of traders selling Peruvian ponchos and weavings, scurried past her feet. There among the bustle of vendors and villagers strolling to lunch, she saw Fidel's daughter's shop. She knew immediately what it was that his grocer's reminded her of.

When Emma was growing up, Liberty knew a woman whose young daughter had disappeared. The mother ran a tiny shop, a treasure house of hippy jewellery and patchouli oil in a quiet side street off the King's Road. All the local teenagers were drawn there through morbid curiosity. Stepping into the shop from the busy whirl of Chelsea was like stepping into a Victorian parlour laid out for mourning rather than trade. Grief permeated every item. It appealed to their maudlin sensibilities.

As she travelled, Emma came to realise that every town

has a shop like that, a shop that time forgot, suspended in amber. They seem to exist in a customerless limbo, selling single pairs of pants or dusty slippers. It reassured her, to find this constancy across the world. In America she loved the general stores, stocked with bric-a-brac, gasoline and survival rations. In Europe she sought out the marvellous – the shop with a single doll's house in a glass arcade in Paris, an icon store in Florence. The contents varied, but all had the atmosphere of that small shop in her home town, a quasi religious stillness, a sense of surviving loss.

Within days of settling in, she realised there were many shops like that in the backstreets of Valencia, selling fans, *mantillas* combs, but here only Fidel's had survived the modernisation of the village, the encroaching of shiny Mil Objets stores and smart bakers. It stood tucked behind a flight of stone stairs leading up the side of the church. The displays of gleaming tomatoes, plump aubergines and succulent melons lay beside a green doorway, half open, shyly inviting her in. Inside, a neat square of trestle tables covered in red-and-white-checked cloths supported baskets of fresh vegetables. There was, surprisingly, one other customer, an old woman with the look of a gypsy, who balanced a basket of red peppers on her hip as she chatted with Fidel's daughter. She glanced at Emma with dark-eyed curiosity.

'*Buenos días*,' Emma said once the customer had gone. 'Is your father around?'

'*Sí*. He has just got home for lunch – he's out back.' The girl pushed aside a heavy sage curtain, and directed Emma into a courtyard. As Emma glanced around, she remembered Fidel telling her that the family lived here still, above the shop.

'Ah, Emma,' he said, appearing from the workshop. 'How are you? Have you come about the display?' He flicked on the light in the old storeroom. 'You can take whatever you like,' he said, pointing to a rusty wrought-iron flower stand. 'It's seen better days, but if you'd like it …'

'I'd love it! It's beautiful.'

'My wife, before she died, she used to sell flowers at the front of the shop.'

Emma smiled sympathetically, reassured that her instinct had been correct.

'I'm glad that someone is selling flowers in the village again. So much better than the hypermarket's sorry bunches of carnations.'

'You must let me give you something for it.'

'Pah!' He waved his hands. 'You'd be doing me a favour. This place is far too cluttered as it is.' Emma looked around the immaculate whitewashed courtyard with its pots of geraniums and sparkling fountain.

'I don't know what to say.'

'It's a pleasure.' He cocked his head. 'You don't strike me as a florist.'

Emma laughed. 'I'm not. I'm a perfumer by trade.'

'Really? Well you have come to the right place. We love our perfumes in Spain. Every village has its own *perfumería.*'

'Tell me, do you know anything about the history of the house, the Villa del Valle?' Emma fished out the photographs from her wallet and showed them to him. 'I found these under the floorboards this morning.'

'They look very old.' Fidel shook his head, turned away from her. 'No, I know nothing about the house. My

148

agency, we held the contracts for the del Valle family, but that is it. There were a few tenants over the years but it has been empty for a long time.'

'How long have you lived here?'

'My family, we came here in the 1940s. I am sorry, I can't help you.' He thought for a moment. 'You should talk to Immaculada. The de Santangel family have lived in La Pobla for centuries. When she comes into the shop, I'll ask her to drop by and see you.'

'Thank you.' Emma stepped out onto the pavement.

'So, how do you like Valencia?'

'I can't pin it down, yet. I mean, I love it, but it feels quite ...'

'It's hard to get past the surface, perhaps. People are cautious. We are very different from the rest of Spain. We were in Muslim hands for many centuries, and have more of Catalonia than Castilla.'

Emma nodded her head. 'You can see that from the dialect – Valencian seems more like Catalan or French to me.'

'I hope we grow on you. It is a friendly place, a good place, now.'

'I'm hoping to stay,' Emma said. 'I want to make perfume here too, using Spanish ingredients.'

'Ah, you should definitely talk to Immaculada then. The de Santangels are the largest landowners around.' He shook her hand. 'I will ask Macu to visit you.'

Emma had an appointment with an English-speaking doctor in town, so outside the villa she tossed her handbag into the old yellow Land Rover she had bought, and headed for Valencia. As the traffic slowed passing over the dry Turia riverbed, she wound down the window, the breeze blowing in her hair. Her phone vibrated, and Emma hooked in the ear piece.

'Hello, Freya,' she said.

'Just checking you remembered. Your appointment's in ten minutes.'

Emma laughed. 'I'm on my way. Stop worrying.'

'He's good apparently. Your old GP on Sloane Street recommended him.'

'I would have got around to finding a doctor ...'

'You don't want to take any chances, darling. Anyway, I do worry. You're taking on too much, yet again. What on earth you think you are doing opening a flower shop the minute you arrive ...'

Emma indicated to turn into the car park near the bullring. 'I'm just helping out a young Moroccan boy.'

'Oh, Em. Not another good cause? You're as bad as your mother.'

'He's doing very well, actually.' Emma frowned. 'And he's helping me out with the garden.' Emma locked the car, and walked towards a shaded side street. She thought for a moment about asking Freya's advice about finding builders, but had visions of her project-managing the renovations from London. 'I'm coping. I feel better than I have in ages.'

'Good. That's good. Are you eating?'

'Yes,' Emma said, laughing. 'I'm putting some weight back on now. Still not much of a bump, but I'm sure the baby is fine.'

'Libby was tiny when she was having you, right up to the last months.'

'Talking of Mum, I wanted to ask you something.'

150

Emma paused to let a car pass by before crossing the road. 'Gammy?'

'Yes.'

Emma sensed her hesitation. 'Do you know why Mum picked the house?'

'I don't ... Well, you know how impulsive your mother was.'

'I just wondered if you knew anything about it. I found some photos today, some old photos – a boy and a girl. In one of her letters Mum said—'

'Heaven knows, darling. An old place like that, they could be anyone.'

Emma narrowed her eyes. She could tell from Freya's voice that she didn't want to talk. 'I didn't ask if you knew the people, I asked about the house.'

'I don't know anything,' Freya said crossly. 'What is this? The Spanish Inquisition?' They both fell silent, then burst out laughing. 'Oh dear ...' Freya said, catching her breath. 'Your mother always loved Monty Python, didn't she?'

Emma smiled. This obviously wasn't the time to ask Freya about Liberty's letter. 'Is everything OK with you?'

'We're pottering on. Ms Stafford is back,' she said, her voice taking on an edge. 'But I can handle her.'

Emma checked her watch. She didn't want to think about Delilah now. 'Got to go,' she said, walking quickly towards the door with a polished brass plaque on it. 'I'll email you the scan later. Love you.'

An hour later, Emma stepped out into the afternoon sunshine, a hazy image of her child in her hand. She paused in the doorway. 'Look at you!' she said to her baby. She felt like dancing down the street, showing the scan to everyone she met. The blue domes of the city seemed more brilliant today, the sandstone warmer.

Emma strolled through the streets eating a vanilla ice cream, her dark coat swinging loose around her. She found herself in the cathedral square, and curiosity about the Holy Grail drew her towards the cathedral's vast doors.

'*Perdóname*,' a tall, smartly dressed man said as he squeezed by. She caught the scent of Acqua di Parma, leather, starched cotton as he passed. She noticed him immediately, drawn by the familiar citrus scent of Charles's cologne. Emma strolled along the colonnades, and glimpsed him once or twice, walking quickly along the aisles. She paused beside a group of black-clad women praying before a reliquary containing the arm of St Vincent Martyr. The incense-filled silence made her head spin. She walked on, her leather boots tapping on the tiled floor. As she crossed the nave, she felt someone watching her, and she turned quickly. A small boy stood alone beneath the altar, staring at her.

'*Hola*,' she said, squatting down in front of him. 'Are you lost?' The boy shook his head. 'What's your name?'

'Paco!' the man called, and the boy flashed her a quick smile before he ran to his side. Emma stood, looked over at him. The sun came out, and the golden light in the cathedral poured down from the stone windows like honey from the comb. She felt caught in time, for a moment, and he raised his hand in thanks, the boy hugging his leg. As Emma walked, she couldn't help glancing over at him. The man was there again, keeping pace with her, occasionally looking in her direction as he talked to the boy.

Emma finally found the tiny chapel housing the Grail, and read from the guide she'd picked up by the entrance: *'The Santo Caliz is a very ancient work and nothing can be said against the idea that it was utilised by the Lord during the first Eucharistic supper'*. She sat in a pew and looked up at the bejewelled chalice in its glass case.

'Me puedo sentar aquí?' He was at her side suddenly, holding the boy by the hand. 'May I sit here?'

'Sí,' she said, squeezing up to make room for them.

'You are English? American?'

'Both,' she said, laughing. 'Well, half and half.'

'We wanted to say thank you.'

Emma ruffled the boy's hair. 'How old is your son?'

'My son? No, he is my nephew. My sister would kill me if she knew he had run off.' He looked at the Grail. 'It is terrible, no? What they did to this beautiful thing?'

Emma glanced at him. He was well over six foot tall, and his dark hair fell to the collar of his linen suit. His temples were flecked with grey, she noticed, and she tried to guess his age. *Forty, perhaps*, she thought. It was hard to tell. There was an energy about him that made him seem ten years younger than the age the wrinkles at the corners of his eyes suggested.

'Is it really the Grail?'

'Of course, they say it was from Palestine. Two thousand years old.' He offered her his hand. 'I am Luca.'

Luca had folded himself into the cramped pew like an umbrella. There were no other seats in the small chapel, and Emma felt like a seabird sheltering in the shadows of a great cliff among the chattering gaggle of tourists and old women. Luca's knees rose up on either side of him, his back obscuring the view of a dozen gawping tourists. Emma smiled politely as he went on, conspiratorially. 'As if a simple carpenter would have a cup decorated with gold and jewels!' His words washed over her. She watched his hands as his fingertips smoothed the polished wood in front of him. Emma had always found hands more expressive than faces – less easy to disguise. His were perfect, she thought – smooth oval nails, long, tanned fingers, strong, full palms. Gold cufflinks gleamed at his wrists. 'Maybe the little agate cup is authentic,' he said.

A woman with a dark veil turned and pursed her lips, 'Shh.' Emma's reverie broke, and she met his gaze for the first time. She felt like she had come to the end of a long journey.

'Some people will always believe what they want to be the truth,' he whispered as they stood to leave. 'I know you,' he said suddenly, holding open the door for her.

'You just saw me in the cathedral!'

'No, from La Pobla. You are the flower woman?'

She paused and turned to him. 'Yes.'

'Wonderful,' he smiled. 'I wondered ...'

'About?'

'The sign. The "Perfume Garden". You know the old book, Richard Burton?'

Emma laughed. 'I hadn't thought of that. I was thinking of my mother – she always loved the Song of Songs in the Bible.' A smiled played over her lips. 'You mean "The Perfumed Garden"?'

'Exactly, the love text,' he said, evidently pleased she had made the connection.

'Well, there won't be any concubines and aphrodisiacs on offer in La Pobla.' Emma said, laughing.

He leant towards her. 'Too bad. It is just what we need in our lives, a little sensuality.' Luca looked back at the Grail. 'Do you believe in miracles?'

Emma glanced at him. *What if he is some sort of madman, or evangelist?* she thought. *No, he's too well dressed*, she imagined her mother saying. 'Who wouldn't in a place like this?' she said.

'Good. The Virgin – you know the patron of Valencia?'

'Our Lady of the Forsaken?'

'*Sí*, the crazy, the dispossessed.'

'Is she miraculous?'

'Yes. They say she was carved in the fourteenth century by a group of pilgrims who asked for four days' supply of food and a sealed room – the charitable society gave it to them. When the door was opened, the Virgin was there but the pilgrims had gone.'

'How?'

'They were angels of course,' he said. His face was solemn, but as he tilted his head he smiled. 'Ask my mother.'

'Shhh!' The woman turned, hissed again. Emma watched him in profile as he apologised to her. His nose was like a Roman statue, maybe broken. It was only early afternoon, but already his skin was coloured by the blue of stubble.

Luca took hold of Paco's hand, and steered Emma out of the chapel, his other hand resting lightly on the small of her back. Some distant memory stirred in her. *This is how it feels*, she thought. *This is how it feels to be attracted to a stranger again.*

Pigeons rose from the square as they walked outside, towards the Basilica of the Virgin. Luca pulled a packet of cigarettes from his jacket the moment they were outside and past the beggars with their waxed Coca Cola cups. He offered her one.

'I gave up,' she said.

'Too bad,' he shrugged. 'We are a dying breed.'

'That's why I gave up!'

'Then we shall just have to find another vice to share.' His tanned face crinkled as he smiled, the cigarette gripped between even white teeth.

'Well, it was good to meet you both,' Emma said, digging her hands into the pockets of her loose coat.

'Welcome to Valencia,' he said with mock formality. 'I am Luca de Santangel.'

'Emma Temple.'

'Emma,' he murmured. The clock began to chime. He fumbled in his jacket pocket, and pulled out a card. 'If you need anything, call me. We are neighbours now.' She turned the card over between her fingers. 'I am sorry, I must collect my mother.' They walked as far as the Basilica of the Virgin, where hordes of small women dressed in black emerged like ants on a mission.

'A pleasure to meet you, Luca de Santangel.' She glanced at his card. *Santangel?* she thought, remembering her conversation with Fidel.

'And you, Emma Temple.' He held her gaze, and smiled. 'It's a small place – I'm sure we'll bump into one another soon.'

21

VALENCIA, MAY 1937

Freya stopped at the top of the street to catch her breath. The sunset radiating from the lavender mountains was jewel bright, like looking through cranberry glass. The windows glowed orange, golden against the rose sky. She picked up her suitcase, shouldered open the gate of the Villa del Valle, and strode along the neatly tended pathway. She knocked on the newly painted blue door, and heard footsteps coming along the tiled corridor. The door swung open.

'*Sí?*' A young, pretty girl with her hair scraped back from her face popped her head around. A beauty spot between her brows, and dark almond eyes gave her an oriental air.

'Rosa del Valle?' Freya said. The smell of something fragrant cooking enticed her in.

'No, I am Macu. Come, Rosa is in the kitchen.'

Freya followed her along the corridor to the kitchen. A young woman, darker and harder looking than Macu, was pounding herbs in a large stone mortar at the table. She was dressed in black. As she stood and wiped her hands on her apron, Freya saw she was heavily pregnant.

'*Hola, buenas.*' Freya stepped forward and offered her hand. 'I'm Freya Temple – Spanish Medical Aid. There's no room in the nurses' quarters, but they said you might have a room?'

'*Sí, sí.*' Rosa gestured for her to come forward. She went to take the case.

'Oh, no, I couldn't possibly. Not in your ...'

Rosa laughed. 'This? If my husband had his way, I would be out in the garden digging the cabbages.' She took the suitcase. 'Come, I will show you the room, you see if you like it.'

Freya looked at the kitchen counter, saw the piles of fresh herbs. 'Something smells good. What are you cooking?' she asked, pointing at the plants.

'Those?' Rosa shook her head. 'Medicine. It is a good time to pick the plants. Macu and I were busy last night.' She mimed a headache. 'I help people in the village who don't trust the doctor.'

'We are both nurses then?' She followed Rosa to the hall.

Rosa's heels tapped as she led Freya up the stairs. 'Maybe. I help them at the hospital when I can.'

'So we'll be working together?' Freya turned to face her outside the door to her room. She liked Rosa immediately, sensed the humour dancing below the surface of her sad, dark eyes.

'There are only three rooms. Macu sleeps next door to you. This was ... Well, this room is spare now. And I am with Vicente, there.' She pointed down the corridor.

'Rosa!' a man's voice bellowed from downstairs. Freya saw her flinch.

'I'm sorry, I have to go. Vicente is home for his dinner,

158

and he … Well, it's not ready.' She backed away.

'Let me come and help.'

'It's not necessary.'

Freya opened the door, looked around the plainly furnished, clean room. Linen curtains billowed at the open window. 'Perfect.' She handed Rosa the first month's rent and sent her suitcase skidding across the floor to the end of the bed. 'Right, let's cook.' She took Rosa's arm and they walked downstairs.

'I am glad to be here,' Freya said. 'It's so awfully bloody on the front line.'

'I know,' Rosa said. 'I was there, I fought in Madrid.' She paused at the bottom of the stairs. Through the frosted glass window, she could see the bulk of Vicente's torso as he walked back and forth across the kitchen. 'It is changing, now. There was such optimism.' Her face fell. 'Now it is gone.'

'Rosa!' Vicente yelled.

'Come,' Rosa said and beckoned her into the kitchen.

'Where have you been?' Vicente roared as the door opened. 'I've been sweating in the shop all day—' He slammed down a joint of ham on the counter, then caught sight of Freya.

Rosa skirted around him, muttering under her breath. 'This is Freya,' she said. 'She is going to stay here.' Vicente narrowed his eyes. 'She will pay.' Rosa shoved the notes Freya had given her onto the counter. Vicente shrugged and pocketed them.

'*Encantado*,' Freya said, offering her his hand.

Reluctantly, he took it. '*Buenas*.'

'My … husband,' Rosa said, and Freya noticed her hesitation. 'Vicente del Valle. He is *carnicero*.'

'Butcher?'

'Yes, butcher.'

Vicente settled back in his chair at the head of the table, and Freya felt him watching her. His arrogance unnerved her. She rinsed a handful of tomatoes in the sink, and as she chopped she glanced up, catching his eye. He was handsome, certainly, she thought, but there was a weakness to his scarred mouth, a meanness there. Even at rest he looked like he was sucking sherbet.

'In here?' Freya pointed at a glazed earthenware bowl on the counter.

'*Sí, gracias*,' Rosa said. She placed the tomatoes, a loaf of bread fresh from the oven and some cold ham on the table.

'Have you always been a butcher?'

'No, Vicente was a matador,' Rosa said.

'Do you still ...?' Freya mimed waving a bull-fighter's cloak.

'No,' he laughed, leaning forward on the table. His gold teeth gleamed in the light of the oil lamp. 'I am a butcher now. I get my revenge on the bull, eh?'

He scraped back his chair and went to fill his glass with wine in the scullery. Rosa leant towards Freya and whispered, 'He was no good. To be a matador you have to face death squarely.' She pulled a face. 'But his brother, Jordi—'

'Why are you talking about him?' Vicente glared at her. Rosa quickly looked down at her plate. 'My little brother, he was a *recortadore* – a bull leaper.' Freya looked confused. 'It is different. They jump the bulls, but we fight them.' He mimed stabbing a sword into the arched back of a bull with the bread knife.

160

'Jordi was the best bull leaper,' Rosa said quietly.

'You think?' Vicente gripped the knife. 'Maybe he wasn't good enough to jump out of the way of the Nationalists' bullets, eh?'

'Don't.' Rosa shrank into herself.

'If he was the best, why did he knock you up and leave you here, eh? Why did he get himself killed?' Vicente grabbed her hand. 'If he is better than me, then why didn't he marry you?'

'He asked me,' she said quietly, her eyes filling with tears. She glanced at Freya. 'If you are going to live here, maybe it is good you understand. Jordi, Vicente's brother, he was killed in Jarama.' She pointed at a framed photograph of Jordi and Vicente on the sideboard. Freya wondered if two brothers had ever looked more different.

'I'm so sorry.' *Jordi del Valle*, Freya thought. *Why does that name ring a bell?*

'My brother left his woman alone, with a baby, so I take care of her.'

I bet you do, Freya thought, forcing an under-standing smile.

'Rosa, she says she doesn't need a husband, but I made her see sense.'

Freya weighed him up. She could sense Rosa's intense grief, felt her vulnerability beneath the tough front. *You knew when she was weak and just went for her like a predator.*

'Who is your husband now?' he said.

'You are,' Rosa said, her voice barely a whisper.

'I can't hear you!'

'You are, you are my husband,' Rosa said defiantly with tears in her eyes. Satisfied, he grunted and picked up his fork.

161

They ate in silence, Vicente staring resolutely at his plate as he polished off most of the ham and half the loaf of bread. Finally, he pushed away his plate, and strode off outside without a word.

'Is he always so charming?' Freya waited for Rosa to look at her, and they smiled.

'Vicente is not comfortable with women. If you are not a wife, or a mother, or a whore, he doesn't know what to make of you.'

Freya tidied the plates away. 'No, no. You sit down,' she said as Rosa tried to help. 'You should put your feet up when you can.'

'Thank you.' Rosa sank back and rubbed her swollen stomach.

'When are you due?'

'Very soon.'

'Is this your first?' Freya turned to Rosa. 'You must be excited.'

Rosa hesitated. She wanted desperately to talk to someone, and felt instinctively she could trust this English woman. 'Vicente ...' Rosa's face crumpled. 'I have shocked you ...'

'No, no.' Freya sat down at the table, and took Rosa's hand. 'Please don't cry. These are terrible times. You did the best thing for the baby.'

'It is so bad,' she said.

'I'm sure we can sort it out. Now, where do you keep the tea?'

'Tea?'

'Camomile, maybe?' Freya went to the cupboard Rosa indicated. 'I'm going to make us a drink, and you can tell me the whole story. When will your husband be home?'

Rosa laughed bitterly. 'He'll be hours. He's gone to the café to get drunk.'

Freya took down two cups. 'Jolly good. That gives us plenty of time to set the world to rights. Why don't you start at the beginning and tell me how you ended up in this mess?'

Rosa's story poured out as they talked late into the night. 'The strange thing is, I never felt him go,' she said.

'Who? Jordi?' Freya sipped her tea.

'I feel him, here,' she said, bunching her fist over her heart. 'I see things sometimes. But I never saw him die.'

'You mean visions?'

Rosa nodded. 'My mother, and her mother before that were clever women, good with herbs – we call them *curanderas* but some, they call them *hechiceras*, white witches,' Rosa said. 'They taught me to make medicine to cure people. They showed me how to gather herbs and plants at midnight.'

'So you have the gift too?'

'*Sí*. I am one of two – I had a twin sister, she died when we were babies.' Rosa paused. 'And I have this.' She pulled back the sleeves of her black cardigan, showed Freya her fingers, slender as a child's. By the side of the little fingers there were pale scars. 'There were six, one extra on each side. The doctor removed them when I was born.'

Freya raised her eyebrows. 'Six fingers? Well,' she said kindly, 'people are always afraid of wise women.'

'My family were Gitano gypsies. They lived in the caves of Sacromonte, and that is where I grew up.'

'I've heard of Sacromonte. Isn't that where people go to see dancing?'

'*Sí*. We dance all the time, for money, not for money. I can tell you stories of whirling dervishes, and Muslim prophets who came there long, long before the people came to watch us dance. That is where I learnt.'

'Flamenco?'

Rosa pulled a face, waved her hand side to side. 'There is more to it than that. The music, the songs – the *cante jondo* – it is about ...' She gestured to the floor, mimed something rising up. 'It is about life, *duende* ...'

'*Duende*?'

'Spirit. Some say it is evil, a ghost – but it's also magic.' She thumped her heart. 'Passion. You know Lorca? The poet?'

'I've read a little.' Freya looked at her hands. 'I heard about the awful, awful way he died.'

'Federico was a friend of mine,' Rosa said proudly. 'People in my family, they worked for his family. His old housekeeper, she was my cousin. When I visited her, I met him. He came to Sacromonte to see me dance.'

'Really? How wonderful. Did he ever read to you?'

'Yes. He was so kind, such a good man. He gave me one of his books.' Rosa went to the dresser, pulled out a volume hidden behind some old cookery books. 'I never read it, of course. I don't know how.'

Freya flipped open the pages, saw where Lorca had inscribed the book to Rosa. 'I could help you, if you liked, teach you the basics.'

'Would you do that for me?' Rosa's eyes lit up. She took the book from Freya, ran her fingers across the cover before hiding it back among the cookbooks. 'I put him here because Vicente never looks at the cookery books.' She winked at Freya. 'Then, neither do I. I don't want

164

to read cookbooks, but if you teach me to read Lorca, well ...' Her gaze fell. 'They murdered him. Those *hijos de puta* shot him here,' she pointed at her backside. 'All because they said he loved men.' She shook her head. 'Who cares? Love is love. Lorca was a genius.'

'Carry on with your story,' Freya said gently.

Rosa sniffed, tossed her head. 'So, when they started killing my friends, I thought it was time to leave. I went to Madrid, but my family went to Málaga.' She shook her head. 'You heard what they did in Málaga? They were fleeing, hundreds, thousands of them on the roads – women, children – and what did the fascist bastards do?' She shuddered as she recalled her dreams, the planes thundering overhead.

'I heard that the planes strafed the refugees. A friend said he watched as they wove patterns among the people on the roads.'

'Well that was my family, there. Those patterns they wove, the people they killed, that was my family.' She thumped her chest. 'I felt it as they fell.'

'I can't bear it. What kind of a world is this when men in planes, with guns, mow down defenceless women and children?'

'It is not a world, it is hell. We made a hell on earth. Perhaps death is better. Oh, I know some Republicans are not without blame. My comrades kill ... But compared to what the fascists do?' She pulled her shawl around her shoulders.

'You survived, you have the baby. That's something.'

Rosa's face was haunted when she looked at her. 'Survived, for what? Only to lose the man I love, the father of my child.' Her eyes brimmed with unshed tears.

165

'When I met Jordi in Madrid, he made me feel so strong. For the first time in my life, he made me feel free. He told me all about the politics – he made me see for the first time. I wish you could have seen him talk, how he made people feel. Without him,' she said, smiling sadly, 'I don't feel so strong any more. Not so sure. But I feel him, still. Vicente tells me he is dead, he says he saw the papers they took from the body.'

'Why did you marry Vicente? Did he force you, Rosa? He hasn't hurt you, has he? I've met men like him before, you get a sense for them.'

Rosa shook her head. 'He ... Vicente is clever. I was so bad, when he told me Jordi was dead. For days I couldn't eat, sleep. I wanted to die. When I said that to him, he told me to think about the baby.' She looked at Freya. 'These are bad times. I want to give my child the only thing I can. Legitimacy.'

'I understand.'

'It is safe here, for now. I have Macu to help with the house. She is a good girl.' Rosa smiled at Freya. 'And now, we will be friends. You are meant to be here. I feel it.'

22

VALENCIA, OCTOBER 2001

The house drummed with the rhythm of falling water. Emma had run out of pots and pans to catch the drips, and she sat shivering at the kitchen table. When she'd gone to make coffee that morning, the stove had sputtered and died. The gas canister had run out, which meant no breakfast, and no hot water to wash in until the gas man's delivery to the square later that morning. She glanced down as the cat mewed plaintively at the back door.

'Hello, you again?' It blinked at her impassively. 'Are you hungry?' Emma rummaged through the cupboard, and pulled out a tin. 'At least you are all right.' She opened the tuna, and set it down on the back doorstep for the cat. In the weak October light, she watched it eating. 'Where have you hidden your kittens, eh?' She squatted down, tried to stroke its lean back. The cat hissed, ran off across the garden with a chunk of fish in her mouth. 'Don't worry,' Emma called after it. 'No need for thanks.' She leant against the back door and surveyed the rainy garden. It looked worse, in some ways, now that the overgrown plants had been cleared. The lawn was stubbly and dead looking, the perimeter walls in need of fresh paint.

Emma hugged her overcoat around her pyjamas, slipped on a pair of wellingtons and decided to check the outhouse for a spare gas canister. She grabbed the torch, and sploshed across the garden. The old storeroom was dark and silent, dusty cobwebs hanging like old grey knicker elastic from the beams. She swung the torch around. There was little of use in there, just the lawnmower she had bought for Aziz to use, a jerrycan of petrol. She moved the beam of the torch back across the wall, and stepped towards a door at the end she hadn't noticed, partially hidden behind old bamboo canes and rusted rakes. She cleared them aside, tossing them onto the mottled concrete floor. The wood had swollen, and she had to tug hard to open the door. All she saw at first was row upon row of desiccated plants strung from the slatted shelves of a deep cupboard, like a petrified forest. Then she noticed something at the back of the top shelf, a dark shadow. She felt up, her fingers tracing in the dust, and touched stone. Emma clambered up, hoping the shelves would take her weight, and dragged down a heavy stone mortar. *It's beautiful*, she thought. *It must be very old*. She clambered up again, and peered over the shelf, looking for the pestle. It had rolled to the back and was resting on a couple of old books. Emma dragged them down, and staggered out into the garden, coughing with the dust.

At the door of the kitchen, Emma paused. A tiny old woman, dressed in black and as frail as the skeleton of a bird, was wandering around inside, her hand stroking the old kitchen table as she walked. Her white hair was swept back from her high forehead into a bun at the nape of her neck, the widow's peak pointing to a beauty spot between her kohled brows.

'*Buenos días,*' Emma said. 'Can I help you?' She dumped the pestle and mortar on the table. The books slipped to its side.

The old woman paled. '*Madre mia!*'

'Are you all right? I'm sorry if I surprised you.'

She recovered herself. 'I didn't hear you coming.' She held her hard, patent leather handbag in front of her stomach like a shield. 'I am Immaculada. Everyone calls me Macu. Fidel said you wanted to see me.'

'Oh! I'm delighted to meet you. Thank you for coming.' Emma dusted off her hands. 'I would make you a cup of coffee, but I've run out of gas.'

'You are living alone here, like this?' Macu shook her head as she sat on the chair Emma pulled forward for her.

'It's not so bad. I'm going to renovate ...' She could see the concern on the old woman's face. 'It's nice to have a visitor. Most people seem afraid of the house'

'The house?' She clicked her tongue. 'Never fear houses, only people. Ghosts perhaps.' She shrugged, stared at Emma's stomach. 'Are you ...?'

'Yes. The baby's due in January.'

'You need help, especially in your condition. You have family here?'

'No. My mother bought this house, but she died.'

'No family.' She followed Emma's gaze to a framed photo on the windowsill. 'This is your mother?' Emma sensed her surprise. 'What was she called?'

'Liberty.'

'And who was her mother?' Macu asked. Emma detected something in her voice, a tension.

'My grandmother? Her name is Freya Temple.'

169

'Freya?' Macu looked up at her. 'Is she still alive? Well I never …'

'You knew Freya?'

Macu settled back in the chair. 'She was here, a long time ago.'

'In the war?'

She hesitated. 'Yes, in the war.'

'Can I ask you something?' Emma pulled out her wallet, and tipped the two photographs onto her hand. She passed them to Macu. 'Do you know these people?'

Macu breathed in sharply, as if she had been struck. 'These people are my friends. This is Rosa …' Her voice trailed off.

Emma squatted down at her side to look at the photos. 'And the boy?'

'He is Jordi. Jordi del Valle.'

'So this was his house? I'd love to hear all about it. I'm so interested to know about the history of this place.' Emma sensed Macu's reluctance. 'I can't believe you knew Freya, too. Did you work with her in the hospitals?'

Macu handed her the photos, closed her fingers over them. 'I … I am so glad to meet you. To know about Freya, and your mother.' She looked into Emma's eyes. 'We will talk, one day. First, you must speak to your grandmother.' She blinked, looked around her. 'Oh, the things this house has seen. Now, look. It is falling apart.'

'Like me,' Emma said, laughing. She stood awkwardly and leant back against the kitchen table. 'Fidel said I should talk to you about local ingredients, too. I make perfume.'

'Do you?' Macu smiled. 'My friend who lived here, Rosa, was good with herbs too. She made medicine, cures.'

'Really? I'd love to hear more about her.'

'My daughter is waiting in the car, so I have to go. You must come to our home, soon.' Macu heaved herself to her feet. 'We can talk properly then.' She glanced around the dusty hallway. 'In the meantime I will send you one of our housekeeper's daughters to help. Solé, she is good with babies, as well.'

'You don't need to.'

'I want to.' She took her hand. 'You are alone here. It is not right.'

'Thank you. That's one less thing to worry about. Now I just need to find some builders,' Emma said as she opened the door.

'Listen. You go and find my grandson, Luca. After this, go to the bar. He knows all about the farm, and he knows builders.' She kissed Emma's cheeks. 'He will help you put yourself back together again, you'll see.'

'Luca de Santangel is your grandson?' Emma smiled. 'We've already met.'

Emma spotted Luca across the village square, sitting beneath the striped awning of the bar at a pavement table with a group of men. It looked like they had been there some time. Bottles of red wine and cognac littered the table. She waved, and he lifted his chin in greeting, but continued his conversation. A chill wind lifted the awning, splashed rainwater onto the slick pavement in front of the bar. Emma turned up the collar of her coat, and began to walk towards the market. *If he's too rude to come and say hello, I'm damned if I'm going to go over*, she thought.

As she paused outside the *perfumería*, and gazed

with a practised eye at the window displays, she saw his reflection join hers.

'Good morning, Emma Temple.' His face was close to her. She smelt alcohol, tobacco, vetiver soap. Her heart jolted.

'And I thought it was bad in London …' She turned to him and smiled. 'It's not even mid morning!'

He looked at her quizzically. 'What? The wine?'

'It's a bit early.'

'Ah!' He waved a finger. 'Just you wait. You will never see a drunk Spaniard. Not like in England. When I was in London I saw women – women! –staggering drunk and vomiting in the gutter.'

'So now we can't drink?'

'It's not ladylike to get drunk,' he corrected.

'That's so misogynistic!'

'It is the truth,' he shrugged. 'Women like that have no respect for themselves.'

'But what about men?'

'It's different.'

'No it's not!' She stepped aside to let an old woman with a shopping trolley pass her by. She eyed Emma curiously.

'*Señora*,' he said, and nodded at the woman as she passed.

'Your attitudes …' Emma sputtered.

'Old-fashioned, chivalrous …'

'Unreformed, traditional …'

'Stop it, you are flattering me!' he laughed. He leant against the wall with one arm. 'Tell me,' he said quietly. 'What is wrong with a man who provides for you, adores you, makes love to you like you are the only woman in the world …'

172

'I don't need to be made love to,' Emma said, a smile playing on her lips. 'I need a builder. Your grandmother seemed to think you could help.'

Luca shrugged and nodded his head towards the café. 'There are a couple of Polish guys in there looking for work. They are good. You can trust them. They did some work for my sister, Paloma.'

'Thank you.'

Luca folded his arms. 'Maybe they can fix up the basics for you. Like a bathroom?'

Emma touched her hair. It was thick with dust. 'Very amusing. I wanted to talk to you about some business too.'

'Business? I'm disappointed. First builders, now business. I thought you were giving me the eye because you wanted to talk about pleasure.'

'I was not giving you the eye!' She hoped she wasn't blushing.

'Yes you were,' Luca said as he turned to walk away. He glanced back, smiling. 'Look at you. Can't take your eyes off me, can you?'

Emma laughed, folded her arms. 'Are all Spanish men this arrogant?'

'You'll see.' He turned, walked backwards for a few paces. 'Macu called me. She wants you to come to the finca on Saturday. We can talk "business" then.'

In the bar, Emma beckoned to the waitress. 'Are there any builders in here?' she asked the girl.

'Over here.'

Emma turned. Leaning against the jukebox, a slim man in his early twenties was drinking Coca Cola, a rucksack by his chair. To Emma he looked like a neon-lit angel, blonde curls illuminated blue.

'You are a builder?' she asked.

'No, but my friend Borys is. I am a carpenter.'

'Well, I need one of those too,' she said, instinctively smoothing her hair. 'What's your name?'

'Marek.'

'OK, Marek.' Emma jotted down her name and address in her notebook and tore out the sheet. 'I live in the old white house at the top of the hill. If you and your friend can come over today that would be great. Say midday?'

'It's a date,' he said, and pushed open the door of the café for her. Marek leant against the frame, close enough for her to smell soap powder, chewing gum. 'See you then, Emma.'

At midday, Fidel arrived just as Marek and Borys were knocking on the door. Emma was relieved to see they knew each other. She had asked Fidel to help organise the build – she wanted someone on hand who could keep an eye on the job when she was in hospital with the baby.

'They are good workers,' he said to her as they sat around the kitchen table. 'For my brother they worked from dawn till dusk each day.'

'Good,' Borys said. 'I am glad Señor Pons Garcia was pleased. Now, with this job, the garden will be last.' He checked the list, making a couple of notes. 'We will finish with the pool and the terrace. For now, we will set up camp out there with our tents, OK?'

'OK.' Emma laughed.

Fidel looked at the rainwater dripping through the kitchen roof. 'I think maybe you are better off in a tent out there too.'

As they talked through her plans for the house, she discovered Borys was the builder, plumber and electrician. Marek took care of the carpentry, plastering and decorating, as well as the heavy lifting. 'My back, he is not so good now,' Borys said. Emma caught a glimpse of a thick leather belt beneath his waistcoat, and must have looked uncertain. 'But don't worry I work like a superman.'

'I'm sure you do.'

'Together, we make one big man!' Borys ruffled Marek's golden curls. 'I know Marek since he was little boy – my best friend was his father. I promised to take care of him.'

'Eh, I can take care of myself,' Marek said. He glanced at Emma beneath blue-black lashes.

'Well, I am glad to have you both here.' Emma started to clear up the mugs, but Borys stopped her.

'You go rest. We will be very quiet.'

'Don't worry I could sleep through anything.'

As he rinsed the mugs, he said, 'You know you have a hidden room up there?'

'I wondered when I counted the windows outside,' Fidel said. 'Do you think so?'

'In between the main bedroom and the belltower.'

'Maybe there is a body in there?' Marek raised his arms like a zombie. 'People say in the village this house is haunted.'

'Well, I haven't seen anything,' Emma said, laughing. 'How exciting. Can you open it up?'

'For sure.' Borys dried his hands. 'It means breaking

the plaster in the hall upstairs, but we do that anyway for electrics.'

'Wonderful – why don't you start on that soon?'

'Yes soon, but first we make proper plumbing and electricity. You need heat and light for baby, yes?'

'But the secret room sounds far more interesting!'

'It can wait a few more weeks,' Borys said. 'It looks to me like it's been sealed up for years.'

23

VALENCIA, MAY 1937

Rosa walked along the main street, skirting the houses, clinging to the shadows. The baby was kicking hard, pressing against her hip bone, and she winced. It would not be long now, she knew, a week at most. The midday heat shimmered around her, and the blinds were drawn on the streetfront for siesta. Up ahead, a small black dog trotted across the silent road, heading home from the café. She sang quietly to her baby, an old song that her mother had taught her. The silence weighed on her, the blood sang in her ears. *Mamá*, she thought, tried to push away the vision of her mother's broken, bloodied body on the roadside. She tried to remember her at home, rocking in the chair by the fireside, singing songs to her as she sewed. She tried to remember walking on the hillsides in the moonlight with her, gathering fragrant herbs. Still her mother's face, her shocked and agonised face, forced its way into her thoughts.

She wrapped her arm around her stomach and hurried across the road, shifting the weight of her basket. The snatches of conversation she had overheard in the market whirled around her head.

'The anarchists and POUM have staged an uprising in Barcelona,' she heard a woman saying near the fish stall. 'Now what will happen?'

'I hear they are sending Basque children to safety. You watch, Bilbao will fall next,' the fishmonger said to a man as he tucked squid wrapped in newspaper into Rosa's basket. It was all anyone talked about – rumours, fears, speculation about what would happen to them in Valencia.

Sending children to safety, Rosa thought as she leant by the gate to the Villa del Valle. It felt like the war was drawing ever closer. The whitewashed wall at her side radiated heat, the scent of jasmine enveloping her. Rosa shielded her eyes, inhaled the intoxicating smell. She tried to reach up, to gather a few blossoms, but even on tiptoe, she couldn't reach.

She stepped into the cool blue shadows, and smiled sadly. Everything would have been so different if she was coming home to Jordi. The garden was more beautiful than one could imagine from the street. The harsh heat of the pavement fell away, and her feet sank into the gravel pathway. Encircling the house was a meadow, dotted with white flowers and orange trees. Rosa felt as if she was embraced by a scented, silken cloak. Around the walls, bougainvillea climbed to the endless blue sky. Rosa walked along the pathway, entranced, her hand brushing lavender stalks. The beds of herbs were well tended, and had just been watered, cool droplets clinging to their leaves. She was so caught up in the beauty of the place, so intoxicated by the perfumes, she forgot entirely that she was near the back of Vicente's shop, a place she normally avoided. The tang of cold blood on the air caught her by surprise, and she stopped dead. She could hear muffled voices, the laughter of a woman behind the door. Her heart beating fast, she reached out her hand, pulled open the door, held her breath.

Vicente was behind the counter, and a woman with dyed red hair she knew from sight in town was buttoning her dress. She stopped when she saw Rosa, quickly gathered up her bags.

Vicente turned slowly to Rosa. 'Yes?'

'I heard laughter. I was just … I was curious.'

'You know what they say about cats and curiosity.'

Rosa spun around, her face burning with humiliation.

'Now, how can I help you?' Vicente said to the woman.

'I think you've done quite enough for one day …' Rosa heard the woman say. She walked quickly up the path towards the garden. *Jordi*, Rosa thought, willing herself to see something, anything. *Jordi, what happened? Where did you go?*

24

VALENCIA, NOVEMBER 2001

The taxi dropped her by a tall white wall, and Emma walked along the red earth track to the Santangel finca. An orange-wood fire blazed at the side of the road where farmhands warmed themselves and drank cognac, crates of fruit stacked beside them.

A light breeze lifted the hem of her coat, and she pushed a loose tendril of her dark hair away from her face. In the distance, a small dark figure appeared on the path, a little white dog leaping at her heels. As Emma drew closer she could hear the woman chiding the dog. When the woman looked up, the words died on her lips. She skirted around, staring at Emma, her eyes narrowed.

'*Buenos, Señora,*' Emma said uncertainly. '*Luca de Santangel, por favor?*'

With a toss of her head, the woman indicated the sky. '*Qué pasa, chica?*' The woman smiled, but there was steel in her gaze. 'What do you want with my son?'

'Señor de Santangel is your son?' She offered her hand. 'My name is Emma Temple. Fidel suggested I should talk to your family ...'

'Did he?'

'I've just moved into the Villa del Valle.' She saw the woman flinch.

'Come.' She signalled for Emma to follow her. As they walked, Luca's mother pointed upwards. Emma stared at the sky. A small white plane banked above them, and she heard the engine note die down as it began its descent. The *señora* walked on, following the plane's path towards a clearing in the orange groves. By the time they arrived, the plane had landed on the strip and was taxiing towards a shelter. An old man dragged himself to his feet from the shadows, and walked towards the plane, a high-tailed husky as large as a wolf racing ahead of him. The plane door opened, and Emma saw a tan, polished riding boot swing towards the ground. When she turned to talk to the woman, she found she had gone. Emma shielded her eyes from the bright winter sun, and saw the dog obediently lay down at his master's voice. Luca tossed the plane keys to the old man, and strode across the field, his dog at his heels. As he walked towards her, he tilted his head. 'Emma Temple,' he said, extending a hand. His skin was warm to her touch.

'*Buenos*…Hello,SeñordeSantangel,'shesaiduncertainly.

'Luca, please.' He guided her towards the finca.

'Thank you for inviting me.' Emma smiled, pulling her loose coat around her as they walked to the house.

'Are you cold?' Luca shrugged off his jacket, tucked it over her shoulders. The suede leather still held the warmth of his skin.

'Thank you.' Emma inhaled the clean, familiar smell of Acqua di Parma, took in the flawless white cotton of his shirt, tucked into pale riding breeches. 'I'm not used to such chivalry.'

181

'Like I said, Spanish men still believe in *la caballerosidad*.'

'Is that a good thing?'

'I don't know. Why don't you ask my sister?' He called out to a dark, slender woman unloading a Seat in front of the finca's main door, a little girl tucked into the crook of her hip. Emma admired the woman's understated elegance, her well-cut pair of light wool palazzo pants and cashmere wrap cardigan. Her bearing, and her black hair smoothed back into a bun at the nape of her neck reminded Emma of her ballet teacher as a child. 'Eh! Paloma! Do you think Spanish men are old-fashioned?'

'Why do you think I married a Frenchman?' she said.

'Paloma, this is Emma – Fidel sent her to see us.' He kissed her on each cheek, and in turn she kissed Emma.

'Hello,' Emma said, taking the toddler's outstretched, pudgy hand in her fingertips. The child had her mother's Chanel sunglasses in the other hand, and was chewing happily on the frame.

'You are English?' Paloma said.

'Yes. Well, I grew up in the UK, but I was born in America. Mum was a bit of a hippy at that point – Haight-Ashbury, Woodstock.' Emma felt Luca watching her. 'I lived in London … until recently. I don't really know where I'm from.' She felt like she was talking too much. 'Here, let me help,' she said and took a couple of the Carrefour bags from the boot.

'Thank you. Come inside, it's freezing.' Paloma ushered her towards the kitchen as Luca walked away towards the stables. 'Are you just visiting?' The warm scent of woodsmoke greeted them.

'No, I've just moved here. I'm renovating the old Villa del Valle.' Emma hesitated as she saw Luca's mother at the kitchen table, carving serrano ham from a full leg with a glinting knife.

'Really? No one has lived there for years.' Paloma put the groceries on the counter, and eased the little girl into her high chair. 'Mamá, have you met Emma?'

'Yes, we met on the road,' Emma said as the woman raised her chin.

'My mother, Dolores,' Paloma said, a note of apology in her voice.

'I'm dying to find out the history of the place.' Emma smiled hopefully. 'Did you know the del Valles?'

'Me? No. I am too young. Talk to my mother.' She walked out, rubbing her hands clean on a red gingham cloth.

Luca glanced at his mother's retreating figure as he walked into the kitchen. 'Sorry, I wanted to take care of Sasha – my dog.'

'He's beautiful,' Emma said. 'I thought he was a wolf when I first saw him.'

'Here.' Luca directed her towards the fire. 'Warm up. So cold! Can you believe it? Has anyone offered you a drink? Something to eat?' The scent of chicken roasting with lemon and thyme made Emma's stomach growl with hunger.

'I'm fine, really – thank you ...'

'Nonsense! Paloma, who's coming for lunch?' From the room next door, Emma could hear adults chatting, the sound of children running and laughing.

'Just the usual. Olivier will be along once he's finished the lecture.'

'My brother-in-law, the professor.' He leant towards Emma as he tossed a log onto the fire, spoke quietly. 'I adore the man. He can talk the bark off a tree once he gets going.' The fire hissed and cracked. 'Let me take your coat,' he said. 'So you are here with your husband? Boyfriend?' Emma turned and shrugged off his jacket and unbuttoned her coat.

'Luca!' Paloma laughed. 'Excuse my brother. Subtlety is not his strong point.'

'No.' Emma glanced over her shoulder at him. The fire reflected in his dark eyes. 'I'm alone.'

His lips opened to speak, but as she turned back to him his gaze fell to her rounded stomach. The thin silk of her dress clung to her curves.

'*Ay dios mio ...*' Dolores exclaimed from the doorway, staring at Emma. Macu was on her arm. 'This is my mother, Immaculada.'

'Stop fussing,' Macu said, shrugging her daughter off. 'We've met already.' She walked stiffly towards Emma. Her gaze softened as she reached for the gold locket that hung around Emma's neck. 'Beautiful,' she murmured. 'So, how is the house?'

Dolores pursed her lips. 'It is bad blood,' she said. 'That house is—'

'*Callate*! Enough!' Macu said. 'You know nothing.' She embraced Emma, kissed her on both cheeks. 'Don't mind my daughter,' she whispered. 'She hasn't been with a man since 1971 and it shows.' She shuffled past and poured herself a large sherry from a decanter on the kitchen table.

'Tell me, what business do you have with my son?' Dolores interrupted. Luca shrugged as if to say, *It wasn't me.*

Emma pulled herself up proudly. 'Just that. Business. My family owns a company called Liberty Temple—'

'Of course!' Paloma exclaimed. 'You're Emma Temple.

184

I thought I recognised you. I'm a beauty buyer for El Corte Inglés. We aren't lucky enough to sell your range, but I always stock up when I'm in New York or London.'

'Thank you,' Emma said. 'I'm starting a new company. I want to try something different, based on aromatherapy. I need natural ingredients – the best.'

'You're either a genius or crazy,' Paloma said, laughing. 'Some of our produce goes to the perfume manufacturers for sure, but why make your own? Maybe you want to buy essences from one of the big Spanish firms like Destilaciones Bordas Chinchurreta?'

Emma shook her head. 'I want to do it myself, on a small scale at first. If it takes off, then I'll work with the big firms.'

'Tsk.' Dolores interrupted. 'Why do young people make it so difficult, eh?'

Emma held her gaze. 'I just have some new ideas.' The baby danced in her stomach, a hand or foot striking out, sensing her tension. From the yard, a dog howled, a low keening.

'Are you staying for lunch?' she asked.

'Thank you, I'd like that,' Emma said.

'Well, sit down. A woman in your condition needs to rest.' Dolores looked at the clock on the kitchen wall. 'We'll eat when your Frenchman decides to turn up,' she said to Paloma as she flung open the oven door.

'*Ay, Mamá*,' Paloma murmured. 'We have been married twenty years and still she can't say his name without crossing herself,' she whispered to Emma.

As they walked through to the dining room one of Freya's favourite phrases came to Emma's mind: *You could eat off the floor*. The house was immaculately clean, the heavy, dark, wood-panelled doors waxed and polished, the brass candelabras gleaming from the beamed ceilings. The long table was laid for ten – the children sitting with the adults.

The hours passed unnoticed as the family chatted and leisurely ate their way through several courses. Olivier dominated the conversation, reducing them to helpless laughter as he told Emma stories about the scrapes he and Luca had got into as students.

'I was caught, on the drainpipe, climbing out of her room,' he concluded his story. 'Luca had to rescue me, cut my belt free. What was the name of that girl, Luca?' he called down the table.

'I don't remember,' he said, 'you had so many girlfriends.'

'Luca!' Paloma put her arm protectively around her husband, pulled a face.

'Ah, there is only one girl for me, now,' Olivier said, and kissed her forehead. 'But then, well …'

Emma felt Dolores's silent disapproval snaking across the table like barbed wire.

'You are not hungry?' Dolores said to her.

'Thank you, it was delicious. I can't remember the last time I've eaten so much.' The almond tart had finally defeated her, and Emma pushed her pudding plate away, smiling as the children raced outside. Immaculada had nodded off in her chair at the head of the table, and dozed contentedly, her lips working in her sleep. The sun sank low over the orange groves, warm light spilling through the doors to the terrace, gilding the silver candlesticks on the table as Dolores lit the wicks with a long taper. Emma still felt awkward around her, but as she leant over to light the candle in front of Emma, she felt she should say something. 'That was a wonderful meal,' Emma ventured. 'The chicken was perfect, and I've never had such delicious paella.'

'It's not paella,' she corrected her. 'It is *arroz negro* – rice with squid ink.'

'Ah ... that's why it's black.' Emma smiled. 'I'd love the recipe.' She took a sip of her water as one of the girls cleared away the pudding plates. 'So, *Señora*, will your family be able to help me?'

Dolores shook her head as she sat down at her place. 'Impossible.'

'Nothing is impossible,' Olivier said reasonably as he refilled their wine glasses. Emma liked him the moment she met him. He was affable, charming, bulbous-nosed. Clearly he still adored his beautiful wife.

'The thing is, I'm starting over again,' Emma said quietly. 'I want to get rid of all the ... complications. I only want to work with the best suppliers.' She held Dolores's gaze, glanced from her to Luca. 'I heard you are the best. Can you tell me about the orange trees?' Emma said, cupping her chin on her palm as she leant towards him.

'What do you want to know?' Luca said.

'Everything. I adore them. The oranges seem so improbable when you look out at the groves, like something a child would draw, and the smell ...'

'Well, the finest of the flowers are from our groves in the south of Spain. The blossom is best after around ten years, and reaches its peak when the tree is nearly thirty years old.'

Emma resisted the temptation to say 'just like me'.

'From each tree you get maybe five to twenty-five kilogrammes of flowers a year. Each worker can collect maybe eight to twenty kilos a day.'

'What a wonderful job.'

Luca shook his head. 'No, it's hard work, it takes time and it is expensive.'

'You probably know neroli relaxes you. People say walking in the groves is like ...' – Olivier waved his fingers near his temple – '... Zen meditation. Maybe that's why we are so relaxed here.'

'We have many different types,' Luca said, 'all across Spain. In the south, we have land near Seville – those trees are best for fragrance. The flowers are so sweet-smelling, and the neroli is extracted from them. From the leaves and twigs people take petitgrain, and bitter orange oil from the fruits.'

'Perfect. Can I make a small order?' Emma said.

'It's been a good year.' Luca took the wine bottle from Olivier, and refilled his mother's glass, before topping up his own. 'We have more than enough for our regular customers. Where is your lab?'

'Lab?' Emma thought of the sterile laboratories they used in Paris. She laughed. 'I'm working in my kitchen, at home. I haven't got room for all the equipment – distillers, enfleurage frames, presses, so I'll have to outsource ...'

'I know someone who can help you with that,' Paloma said. 'What about Guillermo?' she said to Luca. 'I heard his mother is retiring.'

Luca smiled. 'I'll talk to him.' He looked at his mother. 'What is there to lose if Emma wants to play around?'

'Luca!' Paloma chided him. 'It's hardly "playing" – Emma is one of the best young perfumers in the business.'

'So, Emma,' Olivier said, sensing the tension. 'Is your husband with you here?'

'No, I ... I lost my partner.'

'How careless!'

'We were separated. And then ...' She twisted the locket on its chain. 'He was in New York at the World Trade Center when the attacks happened.'

The table fell silent. 'I am so sorry,' Paloma said. 'Was he killed?'

'He's just disappeared off the face of the earth. It's ...' Emma struggled to explain. 'I think for a while we hoped he'd just turn up. It's still hard to believe.'

Dolores's face softened. 'The baby, did he know?'

Emma shook her head. 'Joe was married to someone else by then.'

'You poor thing, all alone ...' Olivier started to say. At his kindness, tears pricked Emma's eyes. She felt too hot suddenly.

'Olivier.' Paloma kicked him under the table. 'It is none of our business.'

'I'm fine. I can take care of myself. And the baby.' She sensed Luca watching her from his end of the table. He was leaning back in his chair, one elbow resting on the arm, his glass of wine raised. In the candlelight his face had a softness she hadn't noticed before.

'Come,' Olivier said, 'we all need someone.' He put his arm around Paloma's shoulders. 'Maybe in time?'

Emma shook her head. 'No. I was lucky. I had over ten good years with Joe. Now I have the baby, a new home, I am too busy ...'

'Too busy for love?' Olivier laughed, breaking the tension. He covered his ears. 'Stop it! You are killing me.'

Paloma kissed his cheek. 'My husband the old romantic.'

'Where are you staying?' he asked Emma.

'At the Villa del Valle.'

'Really? Are you mad?'

'Everyone seems to think so.' She laughed, relieved to change the subject.

'The place is falling apart. You're not living in the middle of all that?'

'It's not so bad, the builders Luca recommended are very kind. In fact, I enjoy the company.'

Dolores muttered something under her breath. Emma glanced at her watch. 'I should be going, I promised I'd be back to make some decisions on the joinery,' she lied.

'Luca,' Paloma called up the table, 'you'll drive Emma home won't you?'

'It's fine,' Emma said. 'I'll call for a taxi. My car is at the garage.'

'You'll be lucky to get a taxi now,' Luca said. 'It's no trouble. I can drop you off on the way home.'

They drove in silence for a while through the dark night, the headlights picking out orange trees, prickly pear cactuses on the side of the road, sometimes the flash of a wild animal's eyes. The warmth and comfort of the Range Rover relaxed Emma. 'I assumed you lived at the farm,' she said.

'Not all Spanish men live with their mothers.' He glanced at her and smiled. 'No, I have a room there, but my apartment is in El Carmen.'

'I love that part of town. The museum is wonderful.'

'The bars are good, it feels real still.' He flicked on the stereo. Flamenco guitar played softly, round notes falling into the air like stones into still water, hypnotic and sensual. Emma let her head fall back. She felt pleasantly drowsy after the huge meal. The dark sides of the car seemed to shift towards her, to contract. She'd often noticed this feeling when she was tired, how her sense of space seemed to alter, become fluid. Emma glanced at his silhouette. Her eyes settled on his lips – full, and curved. He felt close. She thought of Liberty reciting the Song of Songs like an incantation in the garden: *'Let him kiss me with the kisses of his mouth ... honey and milk are under thy tongue ...'* Emma wondered idly how it would feel to kiss him. He turned and met her gaze.

'I like this music,' she said quickly.

'He is good. He has *duende.*'

'How do you know it is a man playing?'

'All great flamenco guitarists are men.'

'That's outrageous!'

'It's the truth. You have great women dancers ... but men make the music.'

'Nonsense.'

Luca turned slightly to her, gestured with his hand. *'Duende* is ... the dark sounds, a certain magic.'

'Passion?'

'Yes but more than that ... like a ghost.'

'Women can be passionate too.'

'Of course, but it is different. Lorca said *duende* is like roots ...' He sculpted the air with his splayed fingers. 'Roots thrusting into the earth. He said we feel it, here.' He touched his heart. 'We feel *duende.* In the music we feel the touch of the earth and the spirits of those who have lived before.'

They lapsed into silence again. Neither felt the need to

talk. Luca eased the car out of a T-junction. He thought of the first moment he had seen Emma in the cathedral. He had felt a connection. Of all the forgotten moments in his life, he knew he would always remember that. Time had skipped a beat. He glanced across at her now. There was a warmth to her he found irresistible. But now that he knew she was having a child, that made things difficult. Her words, *I want to get rid of all the ... complications,* came back to him. He felt the attraction between them, but knew now why she was holding back.

'I am sorry about my mother,' he said, and nodded at Emma's stomach. 'I think she thought she was going to be a grandmother again.'

'Why? Have you fathered many children around here?'

Luca glanced at her, smiled slowly. 'Not that I know of. I meant Paloma's children. Mamá has her hands full helping her.' He pulled up outside the Villa del Valle. 'Here you are.' He jumped out, came around and opened her door.

'Thank you,' she said as he helped her swing down to the ground. She brushed the hair from her eyes.

'This will be beautiful one day,' he said. 'I've always liked this house.'

'Yes, yes it will.' Emma looked up at him. 'Well, thank you. I look forward to doing business with you, Luca.'

'It's a pleasure.' His eyes wrinkled with amusement. 'I'll talk to some friends. I think we can help with everything you need.'

Emma leant against her gateway and watched the tail-lights of his car disappear up the street. People strolled beneath the street lamps, and lithe caramel-skinned teenagers on mopeds sped past, glossy hair streaming behind them like banners. As she lost track of Luca's car, suddenly she felt very alone. The baby stretched, and she winced, rubbing her stomach. *Lonely*, she thought. *Not alone.* She turned towards her house. 'Come on, little one,' she said aloud to her child. 'Let's get to bed.'

25

VALENCIA, MAY 1937

At nightfall, Rosa lit the lantern above the table. A spring storm rattled the windows of the kitchen, and a black cat seeped into the shadows of the hall. Rosa settled at the head of the table and shuffled the cards, her gold locket gleaming at her neck in the lamplight. 'I don't know if I can do this. Since I've been pregnant, I don't see so clearly.'

'You still haven't felt anything about Jordi?' Freya asked.

'No. I see nothing. It is all my fault. He went off to war to be a hero, to prove he is a better man than his brother. Which he is a hundred times over.' She looked down at the deck. 'If only I had kept him here with me.'

'Jordi did the right thing.' Macu tapped the table. 'Talking of which, I want to know if I should accept Ignacio de Santangel's proposal.'

'He is a good man, even if he is wealthy.' Rosa split the deck a last time.

'Ignacio's mother says I am not good enough for him,' Macu said to Freya. 'He defies her.'

'I thought the Republicans threw most of the landowners out of their homes at the start of the war?' Freya said.

'Or worse,' Rosa said under her breath. 'Ignacio's family survived because they are fair with their workers. You should marry him, Macu. I can tell you that without even looking at the cards.'

'But what if there is no ... boom!' Macu mimed fireworks exploding.

'You look at old couples in the village,' Rosa said, tapping the cards down. 'You think they still have "boom"? How long do you think it lasts?'

Freya thought of Tom. *A lifetime.*

'Boom goes, trust me. Kindness lasts.' Rosa began to deal.

Freya stared, fascinated, at the dog-eared cards decorated with strange images as Rosa dealt them out in a grid. *The Lovers*, she thought. 'Would you read for me sometime?' she asked Rosa. 'I have an important decision to make too.' They heard the church bell start to toll, and she checked her watch. 'Damn, the bus. I'm going to be late for my shift.' She put her arm around Rosa's thin shoulders, kissed the top of her head. 'Don't wait up for me.'

'Stay safe,' Rosa said as she looked up at her. 'The planes will come again tonight. Oh, by the way. Someone was looking for you earlier at the hospital – a young photographer. She said she was a friend of your brother's? Gerda someone?'

'I don't know her.' Freya pulled on her mac.

'She was here taking photos of the People's Army.' Rosa frowned as her gaze roamed over the cards laid out in the lamplight. 'She showed me some of her pictures. It made me think of Madrid, the photos of the children on the barricades.'

'It's surely better that the children have been evacuated now?'

Rosa shrugged. 'I heard they are sending the Basque children away too.' She rubbed her thumb across her lower lip, troubled by the cards. 'Anyway, this Gerda says she will be here for a few days before she meets her partner, Robert someone.'

'Capa?' Freya said. 'He took that marvellous photograph of the falling soldier. If Charles has got to know him, he must be doing well.'

Freya worked through the night as casualties from the bombings were brought in. She felt like she was drowning in the never-ending stream of broken, damaged bodies, but she did what she could to alleviate the suffering of each of them. Early the next morning, she went up to the wards to check on the soldiers convalescing after their operations. The words on the chart she was holding swam before her eyes, and she had to force herself to focus. 'Jim Brown,' she said aloud, and scanned through his notes. *'Chest wound, paralysis of left arm, possible nerve damage?'* one of the doctors had scribbled on his chart. Freya glanced up at his face. The boy had a little more colour than the last time she had seen him. A blood transfusion had brought him back from the edge.

'Now then, Jim,' she said. 'Let's take a look at you. I'm just going to take your pulse.' Jim's left arm shot up in the air, and Freya leapt back in surprise.

'The look on your face!' he said, laughing.

'How long have you been able to move your arm?'

'The pins and needles started a few days ago. I've been practising. Wanted to give you a surprise.'

'Well, you did that.' She laughed, exhaustion and the reproachful stare of the Sister sending her into helpless giggles.

'Now that's a laugh I've missed,' someone said.

Freya spun around to see Tom standing in the doorway, his cap in his hand. 'Tom!' She ran to him, glanced back at the Sister, and pulled him into the nurses' station. 'What a marvellous surprise.'

He lifted her in his arms as he kissed her, her feet dancing above the floor. 'God, I've missed you,' he said, burying his face in her hair, breathing her in. 'How are you?'

'You know how it is. I thought it would be quieter here, but they are bombing the hell out of the city each night.'

'I went to look for you at the house where you're staying.' He paused. 'Frey, I hope I did the right thing. The girl who lives there—'

'Rosa?'

'She had a picture in the kitchen. Her husband and his brother. I was just making conversation while she made some coffee. She told me the brother had been killed. Jordi del Valle ...' Tom frowned. 'I told her that I treated someone by that name, and it sure wasn't the guy in the photograph.'

'That's where I knew the name!' Freya slapped her forehead. 'The transfusion. How did Rosa take it?'

'I don't know. First she laughed, then she cried. I hope I didn't do the wrong thing?'

'It's complicated.' She stroked his face, concerned by how exhausted he looked. 'Are you OK?' Freya took off her nurse's cap, shook out her hair.

'Things are getting kind of tense in Madrid. Beth's gone. He threw a glass ashtray at Culebras, one of the Spanish

197

doctors, the other night. Even I'm in Beth's bad books.'

She pulled on her mac, slipped her arm through his. They passed the young nurse taking over Freya's shift on their way down the stairs. 'Have you crossed over to the "misfits and shits" too?' Freya said quietly.

''Fraid so.'

They walked hand in hand out of the hospital. By the fountain, Tom paused, and turned to her. 'The thing is, Freya, like I said, he's been sent back to Canada. Men like Beth are heroic, they give hope when they are in the right situation, but he was a liability here – all the great work we've done is being compromised. At least at home we can raise money for the Aid Committee.'

'We?' Freya stopped walking. 'You're definitely leaving too?'

'I wanted to tell you face to face. I have to go and help him get straightened out. There was a terrible scene the other day. He hid behind the curtains in the room where they were holding the disciplinary meeting. He heard exactly what everyone thought of him. When Ted Allan called him a "son of a bitch", he stepped out and gave his resignation. They don't even want him to stay on as a surgeon with the Brigades.'

'But you could stay,' Freya pleaded, the palm of her hand against his chest. 'They'll need someone to run the transfusion service now.'

Tom shook his head. 'Culebras has won. It's in Spanish hands now. I'm leaving for Canada tomorrow.'

'Tomorrow? Surely there must be a way for you to stay?'

'Beth needs help, Freya. He's brilliant, but all too human. Every time he falls down, he picks himself up and dusts himself down … but it's getting harder. He's exhausted, demoralised and angry. He needs me.'

'I need you, Tom.' She laid her head against his chest. 'How long do we have?'

'An hour, maybe, until my train.' He raised her chin with his finger, forced her to look into his eyes. 'I came here to persuade you to come with me.'

'I can't. My work counts too.' She thought of all the men and women she had treated, and of all those to come. She thought of Rosa, the baby, of Charles. 'I'm needed here, Tom.' She saw the flickering neon of a 'Hotel' sign, luminous in the morning light, took his hand. 'Come on.'

'Are you sure?'

'I love you, Tom. I don't know if we'll ever see one another again.'

'Don't say that. Please don't say that.'

'I'm tired, Tom. I just want to be with you, even for an hour. Just you and I.'

In the faded luxury of the little hotel room, they undressed one another slowly, memorising each line, each curve, the feel and scent of one another's bodies. They made love with an intensity Freya had never experienced before. Something bound them together forever, now. There would be no one but Tom for her. They lay curled like a shell, her pale back against his stomach, his arms holding her close. She fought sleep, the desperate swirling exhaustion that made her eyelids droop. She didn't want to miss a moment.

'I have to go,' Tom said at last, his lips brushing the back of her neck.

'No,' she said, burying deeper into the sheets, her arms holding his to her.

'I love you, Freya. After all this is over …'

She shook her head, tears coming to her eyes as she felt him slip out of the bed, heard him dress. 'I can't bear it, Tom.'

'I'm not going to lose you, Freya,' he said, swinging his jacket on. 'I wish I had something to give you, a ring …'

'There will be time for us, when this is done.'

He checked his watch. 'Damn, I'm going to be late.' He leant down to her, held her in his arms one last time.

'Be safe. Stay safe,' she whispered, her face buried in his neck.

'I'll come for you,' he said. 'Just as soon as I can, I'll find you. I warn you, I'm not much of a letter writer.'

'Just as well. I've seen your handwriting, I wouldn't be able to read a thing. Typical doctor,' Freya said laughing, blinking back tears as she held him. She couldn't bear for him to see her cry.

'Wait for me. Don't let some other guy sweep you off your feet. Promise?'

Freya felt his arms release her, watched as he backed away from her towards the door. Her lips trembled as she smiled. 'I promise.'

'I'm not going to ask you to come with me again, though you know I want to desperately.' He pulled on his cap, tilted the brim. 'I'm not going to say goodbye …'

'Tom, wait!' Freya sat up in bed. 'I …' Her throat was tight. This was her moment. She could go with him now, run to the station, sail for Canada. She could run, and never look back. *I'm needed here,* she thought. *I can't do it.* 'I love you. I'll wait for you, however long.'

He took one last look at her. 'God, you're beautiful,' he said, smiling, shaking his head.

The door swung closed, and Freya was alone. She looked at herself, reflected in the dressing-table mirror, stretched out in the bed, a white sheet draped over the curve of her hip, her blonde hair mussed up and tangled on the pillow. She touched her lips, swollen and red from their kisses. *Beautiful*, she thought. That was how he had made her feel. *Beautiful*.

The door swung closed, and Freya was alone. She looked at herself, reflected in the dressing-table mirror, stretched out on the bed, a white sheet draped over the curve of her hip, her blonde hair mussed up and tangled on the pillow. She touched her lips, swollen and red from their kisses. Beautiful, she thought. That was how he had made her feel. Beautiful.

26

VALENCIA, DECEMBER 2001

Emma sat on her new bed, propped up by plump goosedown pillows. Empty boxes and carrier bags from El Corte Inglés littered the floor. She closed her eyes, took a speculative bounce and sighed with pleasure, flinging her arms open. Even with the door closed, she could hear the sounds of the builders at work, the whine of the saw and the shuddering of the walls as Borys laid the new wiring. Above her, a cable dangled from the ceiling, waiting for the light fitting. A fire flickered in the grate in her newly painted white room.

She dialled Freya's number, waited for her to pick up. Emma glanced over at the cat, sitting in a patch of warm sunlight on the window ledge. She inspected the fresh red scratches on her wrist. 'Not mellowing much, are you?' she said to the cat. 'You'll come round.' The light outside was clear and wintry. Emma had been studding oranges with cloves that morning, tying them with red gingham ribbons to decorate the little pine tree Marek had dragged back from the market. She hadn't planned to decorate – the thought of her first Christmas without Liberty and Joe was breaking her heart, but when she saw how proudly

Marek and Borys showed her the tree in the corner of the kitchen, she relented. Now, her fingers, holding the phone, were fragrant with spices.

Emma pursed her lips. Freya wasn't picking up. She wanted to talk to her about Liberty's suspicions, to ask her about Macu and Rosa as well. She had tried several times already, but Freya always managed to change the subject. She wanted to talk about Luca, too, she realised. *Not that Freya is the best one to talk to about affairs of the heart*, she thought. *I wonder if she ever loved anyone?* Her thoughts trailed off as the answering machine cut in.

'Hello Gammy, it's Em. Nothing special, just called for a chat. Anyway, love to you and to Charles. Speak soon.'

Emma slumped back on the bed. She realised for the first time that she could no longer see her toes, wriggling in her thick wool socks, beyond the curve of her stomach. She was counting the time till the birth in weeks now, rather than months. She wished her mother was here. She would have the perfect advice for her. She always did. She imagined Liberty sitting at the end of the bed, chattering away, full of ideas and plans.

That wasn't how she was at the end though, Emma thought. She cast her mind back to the last time she had seen her mother alive, how Joe had carried Liberty to her room after the Easter dinner, like a broken bird in his arms. She was almost unrecognisable then, her face hollowed out, her hair gone. And yet she was Liberty to the last, insisting on joining the celebrations. *She always loved the holidays*, Emma thought. Freya had helped Liberty wind a cobalt blue Tuareg scarf into a turban, and slicked crimson lipstick on her pale lips. As everyone ate and drank with forced jollity, Emma had glanced down the table at her mother, propped up with cushions at the end between Charles and Freya, smiling benignly at them, unable to eat, or drink. She seemed to be ebbing away before their eyes. Emma saw Freya nod to Joe as Liberty's eyes closed and he scooped her in his arms.

He had laid her in the bed, and kissed her forehead one last time, walked from the room unable to look at them, tears brimming in his eyes. Emma bathed her mother's face and hands as the nurse topped up her morphine under Freya's watchful eyes. They knew there would not be long now. Charles shuffled into the room and sat with her a while, holding her hand, talking softly to her, telling her the stories he'd told her when she was a child, singing her the old songs.

Freya and Emma lay down beside her that night, keeping vigil, staying with her even as the last breath shook her body. Emma curled against her side, and Freya lay with Liberty's head resting in her arms, stroking her cheek, easing her into sleep as she had on a thousand other nights when storms and monsters had kept her awake.

Sometimes, even now, Emma caught herself thinking 'I must ask Mum where she found that fabric ...' or wanting to share some small, inconsequential thing about the house, or the village. She still found it hard to believe that her mother had gone. Emma blinked, and looked at the black lacquer box on her bedside cabinet. As she lifted the lid off, the orange interior reflected the fire. She flicked through the envelopes until she found the one she wanted: 'On Love'. She tore it open.

Em, what can I tell you about love? I am in no position to lecture you about romantic love, when you and Joe have made more of a

204

success of your relationship than I ever did of
mine.

Emma sighed, read on.

You have always done a wonderful job of loving,
Em. You are the kindest person I know. What
I'm going to ask you is to let yourself be loved.
Let love in. Maybe Freya and I are to blame
- we made you strong and independent. I think
sometimes Joe struggles to keep up. Let him
feel needed, too. I hope you and Joe ride out
whatever it is that's going on and you're not
telling me about.

Emma raised her eyebrows.

Yes, of course I know. I'm your mother. I
know everything. When you were little I
managed to convince you I literally had eyes
in the back of my head. I caught you once,
when I was napping, gently parting my hair,
looking for them.

Thing is, Em, what I've learnt is that
romantic love comes and goes. Sometimes the
people you trust most with your heart are
the least worthy. People are fallible, they
screw up. It's up to you whether you can
bear that, and forgive, or whether you
should walk away. Sometimes life, and love, is
as much about deciding who to let go as who
to take with you on this journey. I hope Joe
is worthy. Never let your capacity for love
be diminished by the actions of others. Stay
true to your heart. You've been so sad
lately, closed yourself off. Maybe it was just
you were hurting too much? Em, please don't

give up. You can live a wonderful life, even
if this love is coming to an end. If Joe's not
the one, there is a man out there who will
keep pace with you, even if you have to run
alone for a time.

Maternal love, however ... well, that's fierce
and boundless, and it forgives everything. As
you know, I never planned to have children.
Freya and I never had the easiest of
relationships; perhaps she put me off the
whole idea. I'll never forget what she said
to me about having a baby. She said that
she would wake in the morning to my cries,
and wonder how she would get through
another day. Perhaps Freya wasn't a
natural mother - some women aren't, I
suppose, and it can't have been easy for
her. When I found out I was expecting you,
though - oh, I was so happy. I was terrified
too, of course, because we ended up alone,
just like Freya. I worried that I wouldn't be
a good enough mother to you. But we muddled
through, I think.

You were, and are, the most wonderful thing
to have happened in my life. I am so sorry
that I won't be there to hold your hand
through that journey. I would give anything
to be a grandmother, to hold a child, and
love again. Oh, when I think of you as a baby
- those gorgeous pudgy arms and legs, those
ageless eyes. You'll see. I didn't know what
love is, in all its terrifying vulnerability and
fierce glory, until I had you. Look at me,
assuming you'll have children! I can't
imagine you not. You will be a wonderful

mother, Em, far more consistent than me.
But promise me you'll spoil them, once in a
while? Let them eat a whole bar of
chocolate in one go, for me.

Love, always.

Mum x

27

VALENCIA, MAY 1937

'Where have you been?' Vicente slammed the door back on its hinges.

'I went into the city with Freya and Macu to hear La Pasionaria talk.' Rosa let down her hair, brushed it through. When Freya was out, she still used Jordi's room to dress, refused to be naked in front of Vicente. He came and stood behind her now.

'You spend too much time with the Englishwoman.'

'I like her. The work we are doing matters …' She could smell the cognac on his hot breath against her neck.

'I matter.' Vicente spun her around, roughly pulled open her dress. He grazed her ear with his lips, cupped her swollen breast. She flinched as she felt the smooth metal of his teeth. 'I am your husband. You did the right thing, Rosa. There is no shame now, for your child. I will take care of you …'

'I could care for myself.'

'No.' He turned her around, forced her backside to his hips, the edge of the dressing table pressing down hard on her stomach so that the baby squirmed. 'You will see. You can see how the war is going. Franco will win, then everything here will return to normal.' His hand gripped

208

her shoulder. 'Valencia is a safe place. A decent place.'

'Please, Vicente,' she begged as he pushed her legs apart. 'Not now ...'

'If you are well enough to go and hear that woman talk, you are well enough to please your husband.'

Rosa tried to distract herself, thought of La Pasionaria's beautiful voice, the warmth of her eyes as she talked of a free, democratic Spain. She had seemed more like a queen to her than a miner's daughter. 'I want to go back to Madrid, to fight.'

'No. This is your home now, and soon women will be at home with the children ...'

'Just like the good old days?'

'Be careful, Rosa. Your Red child is protected now you have married me. I did the decent thing, I married my dead brother's woman. No del Valle will be a bastard.'

'Decent?' Rosa cried. 'You call this decent?'

Vicente tightened his grip on the back of her neck, forcing her head down. 'I am a good man. I will be on the right side. The winning side.' He yanked up her dress, grunted as he forced himself into her. 'Jordi should have known better,' he said, watching himself in the mirror. 'He was so proud of you. He paraded you in front of me like a prize. He should have known the moment I saw you, I would want you ...' His words trailed off as he tensed, gasped, his head rolling back.

Rosa forced him off her. 'You pig.' She went to slap him, and he caught her wrist, squeezed hard until she cried out. 'At least it is over quickly, with you.'

Vicente put his face close to hers. 'You think my dead brother was a better lover, eh? I take you like the bitch you are. Like an animal.'

'He's not dead,' Rosa said. She pulled her dress around her, covered her stomach with her arm.

'I saw the papers, soaked with blood.'

'Whose blood?' Rosa stood up to him, raised her chin. 'You tricked me. I believed you, but he's alive.' She thumped her chest. 'I know he is alive.'

28

VALENCIA, DECEMBER 2001

Luca watched the water in the fountain playing over the voluptuous backside of the reclining statue, lost in thought. He pictured Emma, walking away from him across the square the morning they met, the autumn sun filtered softly through the cotton hem of her dress. He saw the faint outline of her lower thighs, the sway of her hips ...

'Luca, *qué pasa?*'

'*Joder*, Mamá ...' He spun around.

'*Joder?* You say *joder* to your mother? I'll wash your mouth out with soap.' Dolores covered one ear of the girl toddling at her side, pulled her into the silence of her skirts. 'I'll give you *joder* ...'

'You made me jump.' He winced as she punched his arm with her free hand. Luca squatted down and tickled his niece's tummy, pulled a funny face. 'I was just thinking ...' he said as he stood.

'About that woman.' Dolores pursed her lips as she did up the top button of her heavy black coat. 'I know you.'

'Emma is just a friend.'

'And you are just a man.' She clung to his arm as they

walked away through the crowd spilling from the Basilica. 'And that is exactly how these things start.'

'Mamá, I am not looking for love.' He dug his free hand into his pocket. 'Between my work at the finca, the responsibility of caring for our land, you, the families we support, I have no time for love.' He thought of Olivier's laughter at the dinner, and his words sounded hollow even as he uttered them. Luca glanced down at his niece's bouncing brunette ringlets, the tender white parting of her hair. He loved his niece and nephews as his own – any aching hole in his heart was filled by them. There had been a time when he had wanted children, desperately, but that had gone. He had decided not to think about it any more.

'I see how you look at her!' Dolores grumbled. 'I have eyes. Just remember, Luca, she is pregnant with another man's child. And she is living in that house. It will bring nothing but trouble.'

Luca slowed his pace to match his mother's shorter stride. Emma had unsettled him. His days had always seemed full, but now they felt restless and empty. In the evening, there had always been family dinners, or friends to meet at a bar in town. If he was lonely, there were a couple of women he trusted not to expect more than he could give. He enjoyed the peace of living alone – his apartment was comfortable, large enough for his books, a desk, a sofa, a huge TV and a bed big enough to take his six-foot-three frame. He had shaped a life that suited him. He didn't realise he needed anything else, until he met Emma.

Dolores paused on the street to greet an old friend, and in the shop window of a bakery he considered his reflection objectively. His body was slightly heavier than when he was young, but he was at home in it, not running to fat like some of his contemporaries with their self-satisfied bellies pressed up against their desks and café tables. His hair was greying at the temples, but it was not thinning yet, and each morning he could still do two hundred sit-ups before walking Sasha in the orange groves. Each evening he swam at the finca, whatever the weather, his mother watching him from the kitchen window during thunderstorms as he cut through the water, backwards and forwards, oblivious to the lightning in the sky. He was not in bad shape, he thought. He wondered what Emma saw when she looked at him.

He had not meant to drop in to the Perfume Garden that morning, but he had bought the songbird for her on impulse in the market. He knew Emma would like it. That happened a lot to him lately. Several times each day he caught himself thinking that Emma would enjoy something, or he saved up titbits of news or stories to share with her, when they met again. As he ambled along the pavement, he felt his soul lifting, flying ahead of him up the hill to the villa and beyond.

'*Buenos días, Señor*,' Aziz said as Luca pushed open the door, the old bell tinkling.

'*Buenos*.' Luca looked around the shop, disappointed that she was not there. 'Do you have any gardenias?'

Aziz scratched his head. 'I don't know. I'll ask Emma.'

'No, don't disturb …' Luca's voice trailed off. He followed Aziz through the back of the shop into the garden, the bird trilling in its cage.

The house reverberated with the noise of the builders' drills, a cacophony of shuddering and whining.

'Emma,' Aziz said, laughing. 'Emma!' he shouted above the din.

She was dancing in front of the stove to the radio, her chequered men's pyjamas tucked into warm socks and wellingtons, a long blue dressing gown sweeping the floor.

She spun around, spatula in hand. 'Luca? How long have you been standing there? I was just trying to warm up. Come in!' Emma laughed breathlessly. Aziz ushered Luca forward, and walked away towards the shop, smiling. As Emma kissed his cheeks he felt that hers were still cool, newly washed. Her hair hung loose and wet. She was flushed, hurriedly applied mascara smeared beneath one eye.

'You have a little ...' He hesitated, unsure whether to touch her cheek.

'Oh damn,' she said, running a finger beneath her eye. 'I was just trying to make myself presentable. We have a new boiler at last, I can't tell you how exciting it was to have a proper shower.'

'I don't want to disturb you.' Luca offered her the cage. 'I saw this little songbird, and thought maybe he would be a good Christmas present?'

'Thank you.' Emma's eyes lit up. 'What a lovely idea. I did this in Thailand ...' She walked to the door, opened the cage, and the bird flew out into the garden, singing joyfully. The tabby cat tracked its path from the long grass, eyes gleaming.

'I thought it would be a good pet for you?' Luca followed her outside.

Emma realised what she had done. 'Oh dear, I am sorry.'

Luca shrugged, smiling as the bird settled in an orange tree. 'If it stays, then it is meant to be with you.'

She set the cage down on the wall, leaving the door open.

'Have you had breakfast?' she called over her shoulder as they turned back into the kitchen. In the corner of the room, the small tree shone with white lights.

'This is breakfast?' Luca's eyes widened as he looked at the flaming frying pan on the stove. He stepped forward, smothered the fire with a wet cloth.

Emma lifted the teatowel and poked at the peppers. 'Tempted?'

'Of course,' Luca lied. His stomach was full of hot chocolate and *churros* from the café, but he wanted to stay with her.

'Would you mind putting a couple more logs on the fire? I'm hoping they'll get the heating up and running today, but it's still freezing at the moment.' Emma clattered around in the kitchen fetching plates and cutlery. The newly cleaned pestle and mortar sat in pride of place beside the chopping board.

Luca stoked the fire, golden sparks crackling and hissing up the chimney. He held his palms to the flames, felt them warm. He picked up an old book lying on the table, flicked it open.

'I found that out in the store,' Emma said.

'Lorca?' He flicked through the pages.

'I must ask Macu about it. He dedicated it to Rosa. I can't believe she met him. There was a cookbook too, of some sort. I can't make out much of the writing, but I think it belonged to her.'

Somehow in the moments he sat at the table flicking through the poems, Emma conjured alchemy in the kitchen. The burnt offering became chargrilled peppers, succulent, oozing virgin oil, to go with the ham and freshly baked bread.

'You are a magician,' he said as she set the plate before him.

'I think we rescued it. My mother always said that love, dim lighting and good ingredients are ninety per cent of cooking.' She looked away. 'As for the other ten per cent, well you can see how hopeless I am …'

'This box is beautiful.' He pointed at the black lacquer chest on the table.

'It was for perfume.' Emma eased the lid off. 'When Mum died, she filled it with letters for me to read. I've only read a couple so far. I'm trying to make them last.'

'Maybe you are trying to make her last?'

'Maybe.'

'I know,' he said. 'I know how hard it is to let someone go.'

Luca felt his mother tug on his arm, and they walked on along the street. He caught the scent of the gardenias Emma had fashioned into a corsage for him, pinned to Dolores's coat. The heady fragrance made him think of Emma's hands, slender and graceful as they worked. Because of her, everything was different now. His monastic bedroom suddenly seemed like a cell. His wardrobe was full of the same clothes he had worn for years, yet he could no longer find anything to wear that felt right. He still sat at the same table in the bar in El Carmen each Tuesday to play chess and drink with Olivier, yet it seemed changed. He looked the same, as he walked through the city, like any other man watching his niece running among the pigeons. Again and again, the toddler returned to them, arms and hands outstretched, laughter bubbling from her like fresh water from a brook. The

216

world was new, and miraculous to her too. No one could tell to look at him. No one could tell that in his mind he was running across the square, laughing and running like a child with love in his heart.

29

VALENCIA, MAY 1937

'I never thought I would be afraid of the moon,' Freya said. She leant against the window of the storeroom, smoking. As she stubbed out her cigarette she carefully tucked the butt into a metal case in her pocket for later. A single searchlight flickered on, and off.

The clear night sky seemed to darken from the east, to clot with a pulse, a throb, a single note permeating everything. 'Christ, they're coming again,' a voice in the darkness called out.

Freya tensed. She waited calmly, certain of the carnage that was to come. The first bombing raid had terrified her, but now she knew they were powerless to do anything. She mentally tracked the path of the planes as they circled above Plaza la Reina. They were heading towards the hospital, coming closer. There it came, the whine, growing in intensity. The shrill scream of the bombs hurtling down. Would it be them, this time? They huddled against the storeroom's strongest wall. Freya felt as if her body was three times its normal size, large and vulnerable. It seemed like the bombs were aiming directly for her.

'Put out that torch!' she heard someone yell on the

street. 'The militia will think we are signalling the planes.'

Then it came, the crash, the shattering explosions – one, two, three. Close by this time. The wall against her back shook, but held. Above them, the ceiling cracked, plaster fell in slow motion. She glanced down at the man on the stretcher beside her, a white cloth over his face to protect him from glass and debris. Was that it? A fourth explosion, louder than the last tore through the building.

'*Madre mia*!' the Spanish nurse working with Freya cried out. A lightning flash illuminated the room, and as the rush of air knocked Freya to the ground, she saw the nurse's terrified face, caught like a photograph in the brilliance.

Night raids are normally easier, Freya thought as she stumbled to her feet. There was something unreal about watching a raid in the night, the silhouetted figures, the dance of light. It was the ghastly reality of the day raids she couldn't stand, the resigned faces of the adults, the sheer terror of the children. She covered her ears against the hysterical clatter of guns. Another blast. The windows flew open, glass cascading to the ground. Through the gaping holes she saw the star-bright flight of tracers, like silver lace against the sky. The even drone of the fascist fleet continued, unsatisfied.

Outside, she heard the clang of the ambulance bells starting up. Dim, blue-screened headlights washed the road. Silence fell on the city as they waited for the huge bombers to return. She heard the hurried footsteps of people rushing to the *refugios*.

Freya felt hopeless – she thought there was no point hiding in basements. She had seen huge buildings collapse like balsa wood when they took a direct hit. Then what?

A slow, lingering death starved of light, starved of oxygen? Freya grimaced at the thought. The stone-walled storeroom was as good a place as any. It was all a gamble, a hideous lottery. She looked up as she heard someone calling her name.

'Over here!' she shouted. A slight figure scrambled over the debris in the hall, a camera swinging at her neck.

'Freya Temple? I'm Gerda, a friend of your brother's.'

'Pleased to meet you.'

'You'd better hurry. That little Spanish girl, Rosa—'

'Where is she?' Fear coursed like ice through her veins. Rosa hadn't shown up that evening for her shift.

'No, she's fine.' Gerda smiled. 'She's a couple of streets away. The baby is coming.'

The planes dove low, and fast. The next bomb fell, the earth shuddering and jumping. Freya and Gerda cowered in a doorway, waiting for a break in the bombardment. Freya looked down the road and saw a villa appear to rise, intact, from its foundations, then crumple in a cloud of dust and debris, with a sound like the sea crashing against a cliff.

She coughed, the reek of smoke and burnt dust in her lungs. 'How much further?'

'She's in the restaurant on the corner. According to the owner she stopped for a glass of water on the way to work.' Gerda raised her voice as the planes circled overhead again. 'They've bombed the station,' Gerda yelled. 'A trainload of Brigaders have just come in.'

'Were they hit?'

Gerda shook her head. 'But the casualties are bad. I saw women standing out in the open, holding their dead children. There was a doctor on the platform just blaspheming …'

Freya cursed in irritation. 'What good will that do?'

Gerda raised her camera to her eye, took a photo of a plane banking overhead, silhouetted against the flaming sky. 'Let's go.' The girls ran down the street.

'I've been over at the morgue most of the day,' Gerda said, 'photographing people queuing to find out if their missing family members are among the dead. God, these people have guts. When you hear them talk about the bombers it's with dignity and contempt, not fear.'

'They've endured so much. They'll survive this as well.' Freya's shoes slipped on the broken bricks scattered around the tiled entrance to the restaurant as Gerda flung the doors open. They were greeted by the unmistakable keening cry of a woman in labour. 'Rosa!' Freya cried.

'Where have you been?' Rosa yelled. She was on all fours under a solid stone arch beside the dining area, one hand reaching up to the marble column. 'Everyone else has gone! The cowards are hiding in the basement. I said I'd take my chances here …'

'I'm here now,' Freya said. She quickly washed her hands behind the bar. 'Gerda, can you see if there is any hot water in the kitchen? Any towels?'

Rosa swore under her breath. 'I tell you, I will never let a man near me again …' She gripped Freya's hand, as a contraction tore through her. Freya stroked her sweat-streaked brow.

'Listen to me, Rosa. I'm going to check you now, see how far along you are.' Freya positioned herself between Rosa's legs, lifted her skirt.

'Here's the water,' Gerda said, squatting at her side.

'Good grief,' she said, wincing as she caught a glimpse of the baby's head crowning.

'Hold her hand,' Freya said, 'talk to her.' Gerda scurried around to Rosa's side. 'How long have the contractions been coming? You should have told me.'

'A while. I don't want to have the baby in that house, not with him there. I thought I could get to the hospital.' Rosa pursed her lips, panted short breaths.

'You're doing really well. Not long now. I want you to get ready to push. You're fully dilated and this baby is ready to come.' Freya doubled up the towels, laid them on the floor. She rubbed her friend's thigh, soothing her as she would a frightened animal. 'Breathe easily, if you can—'

'Breathe easily? I'd like to see you—'

'Right, push,' Freya said, as Rosa's words twisted into a cry. 'Come on, Rosa!'

The three girls sheltered together in the flickering lamplight through the night, the electricity sputtering, finally plunging them into darkness. The crash of the bombs punctuated Rosa's cries as Gerda lit candles on the restaurant tables, and brought them to her. With each explosion, glasses behind the bar shook and tinkled. Towards dawn, as the last planes turned away from the city, Rosa's final, rending yell tore through the air, joined by the shrill cry of her child.

'It's a girl!' Freya said, placing the baby in Rosa's arms. 'A beautiful, perfect girl.'

'Of course she is perfect,' Rosa said, tears streaking the dust on her cheeks as she slumped back against the column. She gazed into her daughter's dark eyes. 'She looks just like her father.'

222

'You were amazing,' Gerda said, tucking a coat over them.

Rosa looked at the girls. 'Thank you,' she whispered. 'Thank you.'

'I'll never forget this.' Gerda raised her camera to her eye, framing a shot of Rosa with the baby at her breast. 'Damn,' she said, checking her Rolleiflex. 'Out of film.'

'Can I ask you? Will you be godmother for my child?' Rosa asked Freya.

'It would be an honour.'

Gerda kissed her fingers, placed them against the child's cheek. 'May your life be a good one. Make it count,' she said. She looked out through the restaurant window at the dawn sky. 'That is all we can all hope for.' She stood, tucked her camera into her jacket and zipped it up. 'I must get going.'

'Thank you,' Freya said. 'When you see Charles, give him my love?'

'Of course,' Gerda said, grinning. 'I shall give him a kiss from you.'

30

VALENCIA, JANUARY 2002

'I'm fine, it was a false alarm, just some Braxton Hicks,' Emma said, tucking the earpiece of the phone in. She changed gear, and put her foot down, speeding through the orange groves. 'I think the next litter of kittens are due any day now though.'

'Kittens?' Freya said.

'The cat disappeared for a couple of weeks when she had the last lot, and I couldn't catch her quick enough to get her spayed. She's a funny little thing. She'll let me feed her, hangs around the house sometimes, but she still won't let me pick her up.'

'Don't go giving her a name, Em. I know you.'

'Well, the poor little thing's pregnant again, and no sign of the father.'

'I couldn't give a fig about kittens, it's you I'm worried about. You're doing too much. Don't take any risks, Em.' Freya's voice was full of concern. 'When I think of the night your mother was born, she came awfully quickly, and you didn't hang around either.'

Emma slowed at the junction, and indicated right towards the main road. 'Gammy, I wanted to ask you about Mum, and the house. I met—'

'I'd rather hear about you, darling.'

'Please stop worrying. Everything is under control. The house is fine, I have hot water, and electricity—'

'All the luxuries, then?'

'Don't be like that.' Emma heard her sigh. 'What's wrong?'

'Delilah has found out about the baby.'

Emma leant back in the seat. The indicator ticked on as her stomach knotted with anxiety. 'How?'

'I feel so guilty. I've been dreading telling you.'

Emma looked up into the rear-view mirror as the car behind honked. 'I'm sure it wasn't your fault.' She drove on.

'She says she was just looking for a file in my office. Well, we all know what she's like …' Emma heard Freya covering the phone momentarily and closing her office door. 'She found a copy of your scan in my desk.'

'I don't believe it. Now she's sneaking around looking at private papers?'

'Em, I don't want to worry you, but she's flipped out completely. She's put two and two together and figured out you must have slept with Joe after you had split up.'

'Well, let her flip out. After everything she's done to me.' She drove on towards the city. 'Where is she now?'

'She's in Tokyo, trying to salvage the deal. You'd think she'd built Liberty Temple single-handedly the way she is walking around like some kind of martyr to the cause.'

'I don't care any more. Delilah can have it all.' At the thought of her meeting with Luca, Emma smiled. 'I have everything I need here.'

She hadn't seen him since just after New Year, when

she had dropped in to the finca with a poinsettia, a present for Dolores. *A peace offering*, she thought. Emma had found her in the kitchen, plucking a goose for the family's Epiphany dinner. The bird dangled upside down, its beak swinging just above the floor like the stamen of a strange flower among the black folds of Dolores's skirt as her grandchildren and their cousins ran from room to room, whooping with excitement. Paco had rushed past Emma, wearing the gold paper crown from the *Roscón de Reyes* cake.

Glimpsing the warmth of their large family, Emma felt the loneliness of her own solitary Christmas and New Year keenly. She had just wanted to get through the holidays as quickly as possible this year, distracted herself by painting furniture for the nursery and sewing curtains. Paloma had invited her to their party at New Year, but Emma had declined.

'Emma?' Luca had said with surprise as he walked into the kitchen and tossed his keys onto the dresser. 'What a beautiful plant.'

'Your friend brought it for me,' Dolores said. She returned to the goose, tightened the grip of her thighs around its belly, and snatched at the feathers, tossing them to the ground.

The children rushed in, filling the awkward void in the kitchen, and Luca caught the smallest boy, flipping him over and dangling him by the ankles.

'Won't you stay for a drink?' he asked Emma, swinging the giggling toddler back and forth. 'Paloma is around somewhere – I know she'd be glad to see you.'

Emma glanced uncertainly at Dolores as she walked to the door. 'Thanks, but I can see you have a house full.'

'It's traditional for all the family to come together,' he said, scooping the boy up into his arms. 'Now, you are lucky,' he said to the child. 'You have Father Christmas *and* the three wise men.'

Emma smiled, and turned up the collar of her coat against the cold wind as she stepped onto the path. 'Enjoy your party. I've got to get going.'

'I will call you, after the holiday,' Luca called after her. 'I think I have some good news for you.'

I hope so, Emma thought, swinging the Land Rover through the narrow streets of El Carmen. She found a space on Calle Museo near the old convent, and walked around the block to Luca's building. Emma checked the address in her notebook, and pressed the intercom button. Luca buzzed her in through the large, wooden doors that flanked the street. She walked through the shaded courtyard, and as she climbed flight after flight of pale stone steps to the top floor, she stayed close to the wall, trying not to look down through the open arches to the courtyard, vertigo sweeping over her.

Luca answered the door of his apartment wrapped in a white towel. 'Emma, good morning.' He kissed her on both cheeks, then ushered her in. He turned away, shaking the water from his hair. 'I'm sorry, I was expecting Guillermo.'

'Am I early?' She caught her breath. Her beating heart settled as she followed him through the shadows of the hallway to the living room, his bare feet padding across the parquet. His broad shoulders and narrow hips were silhouetted against the light from the terrace, his arms raised like the horns of a bull as he smoothed back his hair. He smelt wonderful to her; the creamy fragrance of almond soap, clean skin made the hair rise at the nape of her neck.

'No, no. I am running behind.' He searched through a bag of freshly ironed clothes from the laundry for a shirt.

'Late night?' she asked. She glanced around his large, high-ceilinged apartment. It seemed monastic to her – dark, modern furniture, a monochrome palette of colours. It felt understated, but luxurious. On his desk, next to a silver paper knife, she glimpsed a photograph of a dark-haired woman.

'It was business,' he said, laughing. 'Would you like some coffee?' The sounds of the street drifted up from the street below. A half-smoked cigar smouldered in a Baccarat crystal ashtray beside a cafetière on the balcony table.

Emma strolled outside through the open French windows, and gazed out across the rooftops and blue domes of the city. She edged cautiously towards the table. 'It's quite a view ...'

'Why thank you.' Luca leant against the doorway, laughing.

'I meant the city.'

'Of course you did.'

Emma blushed, reached for the coffee pot. The buzzer sounded at the front door. 'You're incorrigible.'

'Help yourself. I'll just get the door.'

Emma settled on the wicker sofa, glad to turn away from the dizzying panorama. She heard an exchange, male voices in the hall. It was cold out on the balcony, but exhilarating to be in the fresh morning air. She cupped her mug in her hands, and inhaled the smoky scent.

'Come in, have some coffee.' Luca showed a small,

athletic man to the balcony. 'Emma, this is my friend, Guillermo. I'll just put some clothes on.'

Guillermo shook her hand, and settled back on a chair as Emma poured him a coffee. 'Don't bother dressing on our account, Luca,' he said, raising his eyebrows at Emma. 'Not bad for an old man, eh?'

'Who are you calling an old man?' Luca laughed.

'What do you think, Emma?' Guillermo leant towards her.

Luca glanced back at her as he walked away. 'Are you two checking out my ass?' He smiled as he stepped into the cool shadows of the apartment.

'In your dreams!' She laughed.

'So, Emma,' Guillermo said when they were alone. 'You are a perfumer?'

'I am,' she said. 'I understand from Luca that your mother is too?'

'She is.' Guillermo sipped his coffee. 'Or should I say, she was. My mother, her mother, they have been perfumers for centuries, but now to her great sorrow none of her children wish to carry on.' He glanced at Emma. 'Which is why we may be able to help one another. Concepción, my mother, she will not pass on her work to just anyone, but Luca tells me you are one of the finest noses in the business. And soon to be a mamá?' He leant forwards, rested his hand on her stomach. 'When will the baby come?'

'In a couple of weeks.'

'It's a wonderful thing,' Guillermo said.

'Do you have children?'

'Yes, we are blessed with three.'

Luca joined them, dressed in suede loafers, freshly

229

pressed chinos, a heavy pink shirt rolled at the sleeves. 'Sorry to keep you,' he said.

'You are too late,' Guillermo said, winking at her. 'Emma and I have decided to have an affair. Why are you wasting time with Luca, eh?'

Emma laughed awkwardly. She glanced up to see Luca watching her. 'We are just doing some business. I came to see what was on offer.'

'She was impressed, naturally,' Luca said, smiling. He reached across for his cigar, and sat beside her, his arm over the back of the sofa.

Emma turned to him. 'So?'

He leant towards her. 'Ever since you came to dinner, Paloma has been nagging me. She has always been obsessed with cosmetics, perfume so I didn't take her seriously at first.'

'Women's things?' A smile played over Emma's lips.

'I never understand it,' Guillermo said. 'What is it with women and perfume?'

'It's not just women,' Emma said. 'In some cultures, men buy just as much fragrance as women.'

Guillermo shrugged. 'All you need is a little cologne to feel fresh.'

Emma shook her head. 'No, perfume is more than that. Perfume is ...' She thought of her mother's letter. 'It's love, it's the key to our past ...' She frowned as Guillermo laughed. 'Perfume makes people feel alive.' She struggled to find the right words, motioned in the air with her hands. 'You know, when you're learning to memorise fragrances, they make you keep a notebook of associations. Every perfume is linked to a memory.' She thought of Liberty's last notes in her book: *Jasmine?*

Orange blossom, yes!' 'When you are weaving the top, heart and base notes of a fragrance together, that is how it feels: like you are conjuring a moment in time, like you're transcribing memories in perfume.'

'Ahh ...' Guillermo said. 'You will like my mother. Where did you train?'

Emma sensed that behind his relaxed charm, he was testing her. 'My mother taught me everything she knew, and I studied in Grasse too.'

'You learnt from your mother? That is always best, generation to generation.'

'I looked into your work,' Luca said. 'You didn't tell me you are a genius, Emma.'

Emma felt the heat rising in her cheeks. 'Is that what Paloma said? I don't know about that ...'

'I think the people in your industry would disagree.' He glanced at Guillermo. 'I stayed up half the night reading about Emma's business on the internet.'

Emma glanced at him in surprise. 'It wasn't just me. I worked with my mother. I don't ... I still don't know how I'm supposed to carry on without her.'

'Well, Paloma says you have a great future ahead of you,' he said. 'She said your career is just beginning, whatever happens to your mother's company, and we would be foolish not to help you. She said one day you will be a major customer.' He glanced at Guillermo. 'Between us, we have contacts across Europe, and in time we can introduce you to suppliers, laboratories, whatever you need.' Luca looked at Emma. 'You will make a success of it, I know. Your mother would be proud.'

'Thank you.' At his kindness, she felt her throat tighten. 'It's strange, starting from scratch again. I keep thinking

231

how much fun she would be having with all this.'

Luca sensed her discomfort. 'Tell me something, Emma,' he said to distract her. 'With your expert "nose", how do I smell to you?'

She looked up, surprised, and smiled. 'You?'

'Ha!' Guillermo laughed. 'You smell of late nights and broken hearts.' He grinned as Luca scowled playfully at him.

'You smell of Acqua di Parma. It was one of the first things I noticed about you,' Emma said. 'My great-uncle Charles wears the same cologne.'

'Ay,' Luca ran his hand through his hair, wincing. 'So I smell like an old man to you?'

'I didn't mean that ...'

'No, it is too late now,' Luca said, his hand falling to his heart. 'I am crushed.' He glanced at Emma, and smiled.

Emma nudged him. 'I'll make you a deal. You help me get this all off the ground, and I will create your very own fragrance.' She looked him square in the eye. 'Something unique, like you.'

Guillermo raised his eyebrows. 'Lucky man.'

'Well I need someone to be a guinea pig for my new experiments,' Emma said, tilting her head as she waited for his answer. 'I'm afraid it may take a while.'

'All great art does. I always wanted to be a Muse.' Luca smiled, holding her gaze. 'So, we will help you, and Concepción ...?' He looked at Guillermo, who nodded.

'It will all be arranged,' he said. 'My mother will adore you, Emma. She will expect you in Cuenca as soon as you can get out there. We have sold the house, and my mother needs to sell on her whole stock. She will pass on all her knowledge, her suppliers, and her recipes or formulas or whatever you call them …' He shook his head. 'I am sorry, I am a businessman. I know very little about her work.'

Emma's mind danced with possibilities. She thought of old apothecaries' chests filled with herbs, spices, pictured ranks of gleaming glass flasks with handwritten labels. She thought of the recipe book she had found at the house. 'Wonderful,' she said, excitement brimming over. 'In fact, I have an old book I'd be interested to show Concepción. I think the woman who owned my house made perfumes, or cures, from the herbs she grew in the garden. I'd be interested to try and recreate some of them, but I can't work out the ingredients.'

'I am sure she can help you.'

'Please thank your mother. I'll come as soon as I can.'

'Thank you, Guillermo.' Luca shook his hand. 'You will like Concepción,' he said to Emma. 'She is the best perfumer in the whole of Spain.' He paused. 'Maybe now, the second best.'

31

BRUNETE, JULY 1937

At dawn, Charles woke, sunlight flaring through the open window. Outside on the street he could hear Madrileños going to work. He was – as usual – instantly alert. It had always amazed Freya when they were children how his eyes would flick open like a switch, and he would be up and about. She used to tease him that he was half machine. Today, he hoped to be more human, more alive than he had ever been. Today, he was going to tell Gerda how he felt.

He picked his way through the sleeping men lying on the floor, the bed, the sofa – a soft landscape of gently rising ribcages, a warm blanket of vapours from last night's cigarettes and whiskies drifting over them. In the bathroom, he performed his ablutions quickly, then stood before the mirror. Deliberately, he did not shave – it had taken days to get a semblance of five o'clock shadow, and he hoped it made him seem older, tougher – more like the men asleep next door. He rifled through his sponge bag and found some pomade, slicked it through his fair hair. He tried to make it seem even half as luxuriant and untamed as Capa's. Around his throat, he loosely tied a silk cravat. *Too much?* he wondered. Gerda was so beautifully turned out, even on the front line, he hoped she might appreciate a touch of dandyism, a shot of colour. The men had teased her about wearing lipstick and high heels to the battlefront, and he had been rather disappointed to see that recently she had stuck to rope-soled shoes. She seemed tired since returning from seeing Capa in Paris. At the thought of his friend, Charles felt guilty. He knew Capa loved Gerda. *But so do I*, he thought. *I'll regret it for the rest of my life if I don't tell her.* With Capa out of the way, this was his chance to talk to her. He hadn't thought he stood a chance with Gerda, not until she kissed him.

As he studied his reflection, Charles thought back to that wonderful night at the beginning of June. They had all spent the day on the Navacerrada Pass, finishing up the last shots there, and had dined with General Walter in front of his bunker. Gerda had shown no fear that day. To Charles she had seemed like the spirit of liberty, her fist raised to the sky, yelling 'Forward!', her slight figure, topped with a dark beret, running across the open ground, heat shimmering on the horizon. She captivated every man she met. Walter had joked he had never seen so many men in his unit clean-shaven.

As they sat drinking in a bar on the Gran Via in Madrid later that night, Charles watched Capa and Gerda forlornly. 'What's he got that I haven't?' he said quietly to Hugo.

Hugo looked up from his notebook. 'Capa? Apart from irresistible charm and more talent in his little finger than you'll—'

'All right, all right. I get the picture.' Charles wearily rubbed the heel of his hand between his brows, and took a hit of whisky.

Hugo chewed the end of his pencil thoughtfully. 'Capa is one of life's adventurers. Men want to be him, women can't help loving him.'

'I just wish …'

'The little red fox has got under your skin, eh?'

'Hey, Charles?' Capa called across. 'Do me a favour. I'm playing cards tonight. Can you make sure Gerda gets back to the Alianza safely?'

Charles's heart leapt. 'Of course.'

Gerda slung her camera over her shoulder as she walked towards him. 'Honestly. The way André worries about me. If I can handle myself on a battlefield, I can certainly find my way back to my rooms.'

'Where are you heading tomorrow?' Charles said.

'We're going to hang around in Madrid for a while, then maybe head down to the south again. You should come along.'

'Thanks. I'll think about it,' Charles said, wondering if he could stand the exquisite torture of being around her and Capa all the time.

'I'm going to report from the International Writers' Congress in Valencia next month. They're touring Valencia, Barcelona, Madrid. Everyone will be there – Neruda, Hemingway. Malraux is guiding a group of writers who couldn't get visas down through the Pyrenees.'

'That should be interesting.' Charles felt flustered even talking to her. 'Who are you working for now?'

'*Ce Soir*, and *Life* magazine. I'm hoping the pictures I've taken in Valencia will get me out of Capa's shadow.'

'My sister Freya is in Valencia, with Spanish Medical Aid.'

'Didn't I say? I remembered you mentioned I should

look her up at the hospital. I met her the other night. She was amazing – this little Spanish girl went into labour. Freya delivered the baby.'

'Did she?' Charles smiled at the thought. 'Good old Frey.'

'I ran out of film. I could have kicked myself. It's exactly the kind of shot I want more of, the women and children away from the front line.'

'I got some lovely pictures the other day. There was a memorial in a village a few miles from the front – all the women were dressed in white, carrying flowers up to the cemetery. It was terribly sombre, but when they opened the gates, the entire place was filled with blue flag lilies. It was like the sky had come down to earth. But in the middle was a square, pricked with black crosses for their fallen soldiers. The women scattered white flowers on each grave, on all the pathways. It was quite beautiful.'

'I wish I'd been there.'

I wish you were with me, always, he thought. Charles picked up the heavy Eyemo movie camera from beside the bar door. 'May I help you with this?'

'Thank you.' Gerda smiled up at him. 'Useless thing. Well, not entirely useless. Ted says it's good as a shield from the bullets.'

They walked along the deserted street, the cobbles slick with warm rain. 'Where did you learn to take such good photographs?'

Gerda glanced up at the clouds as the heavens opened. 'André taught me everything I know.'

'André?'

'Bob, as you all call him,' she laughed. 'Capa. Gosh you really are a cherry boy aren't you?' Charles blushed. She

237

looked at him, brushed her wet hair from her face. 'Hey,' she said. 'I'm sorry.' Charles stopped walking, and turned to her. They stood alone, only the sound of the summer rain drumming on the roofs. 'You're very handsome,' she said softly. 'That's why he asked you to look after me, you know.'

'I don't understand.'

'He thinks you're too decent to do anything now you're my protector. He saw the way I looked at you the other night ...'

'But why? You're obviously together, I wouldn't ...'

'André and I are together, that's all – *copains*. Oh sure, he's asked to marry me a hundred times, but I don't know if I want to settle down yet ...' They leapt onto the pavement as a truck thundered past, showering rainwater up in an arc. Gerda skipped into a shop doorway, laughing. Charles thought there was a lightness to her he had never seen in anyone before. He felt, somehow, if he reached out and touched her, his hand would pass right through her, like the shimmering mage of a projector. 'Shall we wait a moment? The rain must stop soon.' She shivered as Charles ducked in beside her.

'Are you saying you believe in free love?'

Gerda laughed. 'You are funny. You English are so formal.' She looked up at him, so close he could feel her breath on his cheek. 'I believe in love, life and the pursuit of happiness.' With her index finger, she touched his right eyelid, the tip brushing his lashes – then his left. She traced the outline of his lips. Desire coursed through him – it was as though her touch had branded him for life.

'Gerda, we can't ...' *Oh God, don't stop, please don't stop*, he thought. 'You're with Capa.'

Gerda laughed. 'Don't you get it? I am Capa – at least half of him. Without me, André wouldn't be Capa.'

'I'm confused.'

'Capa is more than André, more than me. Capa will be a legend.'

'You mean, he's an invention?'

'Precisely. We invented the greatest war photographer in the world, and raised our prices. It worked.' She laughed. 'As for André, you know, I refuse to be one man's woman, just as he is not one woman's man. He can't bear to be alone – I have no illusions about the times we are apart.'

Charles saw a darkness pass across her face, as fleeting as a cloud moving across the sun. 'But you love him?'

'Love?' She laughed. 'Of course I love him. But after the writers' congress, André is going to Paris, and I shall be coming back here to stay at the Alianza.' She hesitated. 'I don't imagine for a moment that he will be lonely in Paris. Why should I be lonely here?' As she moved closer, Charles edged his hip away from her. He didn't want her to feel how aroused he was.

'Gerda ...'

'Do I shock you, Charles?'

'No, I ...'

She kissed him then, and Charles was lost.

Gerda, Gerda, Gerda ... his thoughts were a sigh of longing, he felt himself become aroused even thinking of her, and that kiss, that single, brief, glorious kiss.

'Come on, old chap, there's a queue forming out here,' someone called, thumping on the door. Charles quickly rubbed some toothpaste along his teeth, and unlocked the door. 'Good grief, it smells like a tart's boudoir in here, Temple. What are you hoping to do? Knock the rebel lines out with your aftershave?'

'Shut up,' Charles said as he barged past the older man.

He grabbed his Contax on the way out the door, and jogged down to the lobby. He scooped up a copy of the day's paper, and scanned the headlines – heavy fighting near Brunete. He knew the village had been won and lost twice – the fascists were advancing again. 'Gerda!' he called. He saw her and Ted loading up a car just outside. Gerda was wearing khaki overalls. She seemed more beautiful than ever. *The face of an angel*, he thought. He realised he was staring, and sauntered over, trying to seem casual. 'Where are you two off to? Morning, Ted.'

'Charles.' Ted frowned, put a protective arm around Gerda as he helped her into the car. 'We're heading out to Brunete.'

'Who's up there now?'

'Lister and Walter's divisions, and several others.'

'They need all the men they can get. Franco's troops are pushing in again,' Gerda said. 'I can't bear it. We mustn't let them pass.'

'Is there room for another in the car?' Charles said hopefully.

'Of course—' Gerda started to say.

'Sorry, old boy,' Ted interrupted. 'We'll be full up in here once we get the Eyemo loaded up. Why don't you take the car behind?'

Charles eyeballed him. 'Yes, I understand.' *I understand completely*, he thought, *Capa's away and you're determined to get Gerda alone*. He stalked away to the next car and jumped in alongside some reporters he knew vaguely from the bar.

240

As they bumped along the country roads to Brunete, a glorious July day unfolded. The rising sun bathed the landscape in gold, like silk unfurling from a roll. The entire journey, Charles kept his eyes fixed on the back of Gerda's head. Snatches of their singing drifted back in the shimmering, hot air – 'Los Cuatro Generales'. She always seemed to be laughing, always full of joy. Charles had never envied anyone more than Capa, and now Ted. He wondered if they were lovers. Since that single, marvellous kiss, he had not managed to get Gerda alone. He imagined taking her delicate, fair hand in his, looking into her sea-green eyes. 'I love you, Gerda,' he would say. He wanted her so badly, it was an exquisite pain just looking at her. Let alone imagining holding her, making love to her …

'Christ!' The reporter next to Charles swore as a massive explosion broke Charles's reverie. A billowing cloud of smoke and dust rose on the horizon. 'They've started early.' The car ahead stopped. There was obviously an argument going on. The driver got out of the car and came over to his colleague.

'No further,' their driver said, indicating they should get out.

'What? That's ridiculous! We've paid you to take us to Brunete,' Charles said.

'No.' The driver shook his head obstinately and opened their door.

'Forget it, we'll walk,' Ted called across.

Charles shot out of the car and was at Gerda's side, striding through the golden wheat field. 'May I help with anything?'

'Thanks, Charles,' Ted said quickly and handed him

the heavy Eyemo camera. He walked on ahead at Gerda's side. She looked over her shoulder and gave Charles an apologetic look.

'It will be a good chance for some action shots today,' she called.

'Are you afraid?' Charles shouted.

'Always!' She laughed.

By the time they reached General Walter's offices, sweat was trickling into Charles's eyes, running along his spine. Walter looked up. 'What on earth are you lot doing here? I've just sent a bunch of your fellows packing. It's not safe. Franco's troops could be here any minute.'

'Then we're just in time,' she said, and smiled.

Charles huddled down in the dugout as the biplane swooped low, again the rat-tat-tat of machine guns chopped the air, bullets whizzing overhead. The noise was deafening, the Condor Legion's Stukas and Heinkels thundering through a sky black with smoke and fire, pounding the retreating Republican troops with bombs and gunfire.

'Gerda, it's the camera lens!' Charles shouted. 'The light catches the lens – they are coming straight for us!'

Charles cowered next to Gerda and Ted, horribly aware that his backside was sticking up out of the foxhole. He couldn't bear the thought of being shot there, willed his buttocks to contract, to disappear into the earth.

'We can't lose Brunete ...' Gerda's fists were clenched in fury. They had been shooting film all morning, and she was packing away the last of the rolls. 'Damn it, this is some of the best work I've ever done, but we can't lose this battle.' She leapt to her feet to photograph twelve bombers in formation.

'For God's sake, Gerda, get down!' Ted cried, trying to pull her down beside him. Another explosion blew her back, the earth heaving like the sea before them, fountains of soil pluming into the air.

'*Scheisse*,' she said, spitting earth from her mouth. She ducked down. 'That was close.' She calmly rolled over, and photographed a biplane as it swooped low towards them, spewing bursts of fire between the propeller blades as the bullets rained down on them.

'Don't give up!' she yelled at the retreating Republicans.

Charles checked his watch. It was half past five. Men were streaming around them now, running from the front. He saw a man blown from his feet by the force of the blast. 'We should go ...'

'Fight on, comrades! *No pasarán*! They will not pass!' Gerda's voice was drowned out by the thunderous assault from the sky. 'Oh God,' she said as she slumped down. 'When you think of all the fine people killed in this battle alone, it seems unfair to be alive.'

'Gerda, he's right. We've done all we can. Let's get the hell out of here.' Ted dragged her up, shielding her with his body and slung the camera over his shoulder. He turned to Charles. 'Well? Are you coming?'

Charles sprinted after them, panting for breath. He ran blindly from the front through fields of the dead and dying, stumbling over twisted bodies. It seemed to him they were running through a furnace, a vision of hell far worse than anything Goya had painted. The shouts, the noise of screams and the crashing engines of tanks behind them thundered in his ears. At any moment, he knew it could be his fragile body on the floor, broken and bleeding, feeling life ebb away. He ran faster, and faster, caught up with Ted and Gerda as they reached the Villanueva road. Tanks and jeeps bounced across the rutted ground at high speed, in retreat. One of the tanks slowed to allow the three of them to scramble aboard, and they clung on.

Charles gasped for breath, the vile metallic taste of battle, of smoke and oil, of sweat and fear and death was in his mouth. The tank thundered down the road, and he began to come back to himself. It seemed strangely quiet after the battlefield. His eyes smarted still from the smoke, but here the wheat swayed peacefully in a breeze coming down cool and welcome from the mountains.

'Once we get through here, we'll be clear to Madrid,' Ted yelled.

Charles closed his eyes. He was shaking with adrenalin and fear. He wondered what on earth had compelled him to come to Spain in the first place. This was not the world he remembered. He longed to be in the hills above Yegen again, in the sunlit grass, stalking Mazarine Blues with his net, the clean light and clean linen, the silent air— The tank lurched as it rejoined the main road, dragged him from his daydream.

'Over there!' Gerda cried. 'It's Walter's car.'

They leapt down, and raced past a whitewashed farmhouse towards the retreating car. Charles heard Ted asking if it could take them as far as El Escorial. Clouds drifted lazily in a cobalt sky. Charles could see the car was already loaded down with wounded soldiers. Gerda and Ted were ahead of him, and he saw Gerda bend her head in concentration as she sped towards the car, and made a leap for the running board. Ted leapt onto the other side. They turned to Charles, their faces illuminated with triumph. *My God*, he thought, *they're in their element here*. He realised at that moment he would never be a part of their world.

'Bad luck, Charles!' Ted hollered.

'See you at the hotel, Charles. I must get these pictures wired to Paris,' Gerda called. 'Tonight we'll have a farewell party in Madrid – I've brought champagne!' She waved to him, smiling broadly.

'Gerda!' Charles yelled, waving madly.

She laughed, waved back.

'Gerda!' he screamed. There was nothing he could do. A tank, out of control, careered towards the car, slammed into Gerda. He watched helplessly as she was crushed, thrown aside like a rag doll. Ted flew through the air, limbs dangling, the car mangled and broken like a Dinky Toy, shoved along the road.

A thundering phalanx of aircraft bore down on them. Someone grabbed Charles by the arm, dragged him to the ditch. He hunkered down as ammunition pounded the earth around them, thumping into the soil, the shuddering waves passing through him. Above the noise, he could hear Gerda crying out. And he could not reach her. He could hear Ted calling to her, saying he couldn't move. Charles blinked, his head filled with dancing lights. He curled up in a ball, trying desperately not to pass out, forcing air into his lungs. He wanted to be sick.

People around him began to clamber out of the ditches as the aircraft dispersed. He staggered, shaking, to his feet. He could see a group of men around Ted, pulling him onto a stretcher. His legs dangled helplessly.

'My legs!' Ted cried out. 'I can't move my damn legs. Gerda!' Charles ran over to him. 'Where is she? Charles, find her.' His face was contorted with pain. Charles nodded. Ahead, he saw an ambulance, and on a stretcher a familiar pair of tiny feet beneath a sheet. He ran over, nauseous, afraid of what he might see.

It was Gerda. Her face was pale and her hands were clamped across her stomach, dark blood drenching the sheet. Charles felt the bile rise in his throat as they placed a blanket over her. 'Charles,' she whispered, smiled at him. 'Where are my cameras? Do you know? Are they smashed …'

'I don't know.' He fought back tears as he bent and kissed her forehead. 'Don't worry about them. I'll look for them, I promise.'

'It was my best work, you know,' she said, drifting into unconsciousness.

He looked after her helplessly as they loaded her into the ambulance, and raced off up the road. Charles stood entirely alone as men and vehicles streamed around him, retreating to Madrid.

'Gerda,' he whispered, 'Gerda …'

32

VALENCIA, JANUARY 2002

Luca browsed through the shelves of CDs in FNAC. The store was busy, full of weekend crowds and teenagers flirting, listening to music on the headphones at the end of each aisle. Beyond the pulse of the dance tune blasting from the speakers, he heard Emma's voice.

'He doesn't still live with his mother ...' He heard her laugh. Luca poked his head around the corner, saw Emma rifling through the jazz section, her phone crooked against her shoulder. 'Anyway, it seems the apron strings are wide-ranging here, more like extension leads ... I think it's great, having family around.'

Luca smiled. He heard her voice fading away, so he followed at a distance, careful she didn't spot him. 'Freya, he is not a mummy's boy. I know you said every single Spaniard thinks he is a little god from birth.' He leant against the pillar and folded his arms, an amused smile playing on his lips. Emma picked up a CD and read the back. She was wearing a black swing coat and flat boots, her tan leather bag slung over one shoulder. Her hair was knotted at the nape of her neck, pierced with a red lacquered wooden stick. Luca imagined sliding it out, running his hands through the waves of her glossy dark hair.

'I know, I know. It's the last thing I need right now.' Luca saw her put the CD back. 'I don't want a relationship. Anyway, he's not interested in me. Not in the least. I mean, look at me. Who'd want to get involved with all this? I just ...' He heard her sigh. 'I like him. He makes me feel ...' He saw her rub the side of her head. 'I don't know. It's been a long time.' Emma shifted her bag. 'There's still no news about Joe?' She paused. 'I still can't believe there's no trace of him at all.' Luca's face fell at the mention of 9/11. He sensed the rawness of her grief. 'Keep me posted if you hear anything, anything at all.'

When he was a child, Luca believed absolutely that the world was just an illusion, a magic trick, that it could disappear. This half-digested philosophy settled in him like unripe plums, and even now at times of stress, a part of him would like to believe that if he closed his eyes really tightly for long enough the world and all its troubles would vanish. In bed, alone at night, when the horrors on the late news, the image of Emma's smiling face or his own loneliness threatened to overwhelm him, he still closed his eyes tightly. He knew how she felt.

Luca strode towards her. Emma was bending down now in the English books section, searching the bottom shelf. He reached out, slapped her backside gently. She wheeled around, her angry expression dissolving.

'Sorry, couldn't resist,' he said.

'Well, try!' She smiled in spite of herself as she kissed his cheek. 'This is unexpected.'

Luca shrugged. 'I told you, it is a small place. You bump into people.' He took the book from her hand. '*The*

Diving Bell and the Butterfly? This is very good.'

'You've read it?'

'Olivier is determined my brain won't waste away down here,' he said, smiling. 'He keeps me up to date on what I should be reading. He's forgotten more about literature, philosophy, politics than I'll ever know.'

'I think you're being modest. Paloma said you met Olivier when you were at the Sorbonne.'

'Did she? It was a long time ago.' He slipped his hand in his pocket. 'My father was French. It seemed a good idea to study in Paris.'

'He was French? I was wondering why you use de Santangel.'

'My name?' Luca shrugged. 'In Spain you take the mother and father's names, but here de Santangel means a lot. After my father left, my mother quietly dropped his name from ours.'

'He left? I'm sorry.' Emma paused. 'I know what it's like not to have your father around.'

'It was OK. There has always been a lot of family around – I loved my grandfather, Ignacio. He was a good man, more of a father to me than my own.'

'You're lucky, then.' Emma walked on, gazed at a poster advertising *Jazz in Paris*, a black-and-white image of lovers embracing beneath the Eiffel Tower. 'Wow ... Paris. I'd have loved to have studied there. Mum wanted me to join the family business though. After I trained in Grasse she shipped me off to America. I think she wanted to toughen me up a bit.'

'Did it work?'

'You tell me.' Emma's laugh faded. She had loved Grasse, the steep hills filled with the scent of mimosa.

Sometimes she wondered what would have happened if she had stayed in France. 'Still, I met Joe, and now ...' Her hand caressed her stomach. 'I can't really regret any of it.'

'Olivier and I had a great time.' Luca stepped aside to let a group of teenagers pass. 'We had a tiny apartment overlooking Sacré Cœur. We shared everything ...'

'Wine, bread, women?'

Luca smiled. 'But then Paloma managed to escape Mamá's hawk-like protection of her virginity long enough to board a train to Paris. As luck would have it for Olivier, I was out that night with a girl, and by the time I got back, Olivier had asked her to marry him. With them, it was love at first sight.'

'Paloma said she thinks Olivier wanted to have you as a brother just as much as he wanted her as a wife.'

'She mentioned you had lunch together the other day.' He gestured for her to go ahead through the crowd. 'I am lucky. I love my family. Maybe I am spoilt.' He thought of her words on the phone.

Emma glanced at the CDs in his hand. 'What are you buying?'

'I don't know. Do you think a teenage boy will like these?'

She flipped through them. 'What did you listen to when you were ...?'

'Seventeen. It's for Benito, Paloma's eldest.'

'It's his birthday?' Emma asked.

'Yes – on Saturday. You should come.'

'I don't want to intrude if it's a family thing.'

'I know Paloma would be delighted. The food may not be up to much. Olivier and I are making paella.'

'I'd love to,' Emma said. 'OK, so what did you like at that age?'

'Punk, if I could get away with it.' Luca laughed.

'There we go.' Emma led the way to the Sex Pistols, handed him *Never Mind the Bollocks*. 'Any seventeen-year-old boy would love this. Then get him a gift voucher so he can choose stuff he really likes.'

As they paid, Emma turned to Luca. 'Now you have to help me buy my present for Benito. What do you think he would like from me?'

'I don't know,' Luca said. 'Why don't we have a drink and think about it.'

'How is the flower shop doing?' Luca asked her as they walked among the stalls of the *Mercado Central*. It was bustling, the cool, vaulted halls filled with echoing voices, footsteps, the mingled salty tang of shellfish and sweet fruits. 'There have been so many weddings and funerals lately in the village it must be booming, or blooming.'

Emma laughed. 'The Perfume Garden,' she said, pausing by a fruit stall, 'is doing very well, thank you.' She picked out a melon, inhaled its summery, mouthwatering scent, pressed her fingers into its firm flesh, testing it. 'God, I feel like I've swallowed one of these.' She rubbed her hard, round belly.

'Not long now,' he said, handing some money to the stallholder. 'You look beautiful, anyway.'

'Thank you.' She didn't want him to see how pleased she was, and busied herself tucking the melon in her bag. They walked on to the next stall. 'Did I tell you, I've been experimenting with making some scented candles for the shop? I've found a wonderful old firm to work with, and once I have the scents perfected we'll go into production.'

'I can't keep up with you.' As Luca stepped aside to let a porter pulling crates of fish on ice go past, he caught something in Emma's expression, a fleeting concern. 'I mean, I think it's wonderful, how creative you are. That you see so many opportunities around you.'

'Do you?' Emma's face relaxed. 'Thank you. Mum … well, she said in one of the letters she left for me that maybe I'm too … I don't know. I do too much.'

'No good ever came from someone trying to be less than they are.' He gazed down at her. 'Be everything you should be.'

'You make it sound simple.'

'It is. My grandfather always said do what you love, and do it as well as you can. There's no other way, for me.'

'It's funny, I always thought it would be great to have a flower shop and now I have one on my doorstep.' She thought for a moment. 'After all these years of running a big company, it's been satisfying making a small idea come true.'

'But you will go back to your real work, as a perfumer?'

'Yes, of course,' she said. 'Once everything is tied up in London.' She paused. 'It's fun though, seeing how flowers give people immediate pleasure. With perfume, I was always stuck in the studio, or the lab. Then, once Mum decided I should take over I was on the road seeing our big buyers. I lost touch with the customers, I think.' She shrugged. 'I love it now, watching people coming and going with flowers Aziz has sold them, thinking how happy their friends will be with a spray of gerberas, or how their lovers will feel to get a huge bouquet of roses.'

'You like making people happy, I think.' He nudged

252

her gently. 'But the name – you have a very wicked sense of humour. If only the good little women of the village knew they were buying their carnations for the Virgin from a sensualist.'

'Sensualist?' Emma glanced at him. Luca stepped closer, reached over for a basket of strawberries. He lowered his head to them, inhaled. He offered them to her, and she smelt them, covering his hand with her own.

'Like you said in the cathedral – Song of Songs, Burton's ancient erotic texts …'

'Well, from what I remember from the book, they knew what they were talking about with their aphrodisiacs. You wouldn't believe what you can do with a little ginger and cardamom.' She flashed him a quick smile.

'I'll bear that in mind.'

'It sounds like you've been thinking about this quite enough already,' she said, laughing.

I've thought of little else. He turned to the stallholder and handed over the fruit.

'Let me.' Emma reached for her wallet. 'Is there anything else you want?'

Plenty, he thought as she walked on. *But you are still in love with another man.*

33

MADRID, AUGUST 1937

'Capa?' Charles crooked the telephone against his shoulder, and squeezed the bridge of his nose between his fingertips. His eyes were red-rimmed. On the bar, several French newspapers lay in front of him, each open at the pages covering Gerda's funeral. 'Can you talk? I don't want to disturb you.'

'No, no … it's good to hear your voice, Charlie.'

Sunlight struggled through the blinds, picking out the stooped figures of exhausted men, empty glasses littering the tables. Charles was wearing an old black roll neck, in spite of the stifling heat. 'I'm so sorry about Gerda, Bob. I'm sorry I couldn't get to Paris for the funeral …' He felt his shoulders sag as he gave in to his sorrow.

'What the hell happened?' Capa's voice was thick, choked with grief. 'She never should have been out there. If I'd have been there, I'd have taken care of her.'

Charles hung his head. 'I'm sorry. It all happened so quickly. I tried.'

'I'm not blaming you, Charles. Jesus!' Capa cried. 'No one but me could have made her see sense. I could have saved her.'

Charles picked up a packet of cigarettes. 'Damn,' he said, and threw the empty pack down. He drained his glass, and signalled to the bartender.

'I just feel so … I've been a little crazy since …'

Charles thought of the reports of Gerda's funeral in Paris, how Capa had to be carried from the grave.

'Teddie told me about what happened in the hospital. You know they gave her a blood transfusion, and she said, "Whee, that feels better now." She survived the operation :…' Capa's voice muffled. 'What the hell happened, Charles? I should have been with her. This never would have happened if I had been with her …'

As Capa rambled on, Charles was afraid, he realised, afraid that Capa might lash out, accuse him of trying to seduce the woman he loved. Guilt tightened in Charles's heart like an overwound clock as Capa began to weep.

'She loved you,' Charles said quietly. *I loved her*, he thought, *and she never knew. No one will ever know.*

'Of course she loved me! I don't need anyone to tell me that,' Capa cried. 'She was mine, and I was hers. We belonged together.' Charles waited in silence as Capa tried to compose himself. 'I'm sorry, Charlie. I shouldn't take it out on you.'

'No. You go ahead.' *I deserve it*, Charles thought. He wished Freya was here – she always knew the right thing to say, but he felt tongue-tied.

'Everyone loved Gerda,' Capa said. 'But she chose me. We were going to be married.'

'I know, old man. I'm sorry.'

'The funeral was so beautiful. There were so many flowers.' Capa talked on, telling him everything that had gone on in Paris, but Charles felt like he knew it by heart.

He looked at the photographs in the newspapers laid out before him. Since her death he had tortured himself by reading every detail, every word of the coverage of her life and funeral. He had had no idea how much her work was valued. The Communist Party had declared her an anti-fascist martyr, a latter-day Joan of Arc. Tens of thousands of people lined the streets of Paris when her body was taken to Père Lachaise cemetery on August 1st to the strains of Chopin's funeral march. It would have been her twenty-seventh birthday. In one paper, among the images of the funeral, the crowds, the banners, the flowers, photographs that Gerda had taken were reprinted, including one he knew perfectly well was by Capa. *Does it matter?* he thought. *They were always going to end up together, André and Gerda, Gerda and Capa, two halves of the same coin.* 'We invented the greatest war photographer in the world,' he remembered her saying as they sheltered from the rain, 'Capa will be a legend.' Now, he knew, they would be bound by that legend forever, and he had no part in it. *I never had a part in it.* Charles screwed his eyes tightly shut. *You idiot, you fool. How could I ever have thought I might?* If Gerda had seemed like a goddess to him in life, in death she began to assume a mythical status. Perfect, incorrupt, a single kiss had ruined him for life.

Charles stared down at the newspaper as Capa talked on. In Gerda's photos of the war he saw the bright, hopeful faces of young militiawomen training on the beaches in Barcelona in '36, peasants in Aragon harvesting straw, war orphans in Madrid. *These were the people Gerda cared about*, he thought. *She was always brilliant at capturing the humanity in a situation.* After the initial thrill of seeing his own reports in print had worn off, Charles had realised his work would never have the magic of Gerda's and Capa's images, or the power of Hemingway's words. He felt like a dilettante in comparison. He looked blearily up at the other journalists in the bar. How many of them would be remembered? How many of them would be carried through the streets like martyrs as flowers rained down? Charles's head slumped to his hand. Gerda's photographs pierced your heart, took your breath away. He picked up a page with photos of the People's Army marching in Valencia bullring, revealed an image of an air-raid victim in the newspaper beneath, blood spilling from a blanket onto a chequerboard floor. His mind immediately jumped to Gerda, broken and bleeding on the stretcher. He felt nauseous as he remembered how he had stood helplessly by.

'She was so beautiful,' Charles said quietly as Capa fell silent. He perched on the edge of the stool. 'So beautiful. Her photos ... maybe she gave too much of herself, took too many risks ...'

'Why did no one call me, for Christ's sake? I would have come straight down if I'd have known she was planning to head out to Brunete again ...' Capa's voice was muffled, it sounded like he had his head in his hands. Charles realised he wasn't listening, sensed Capa was in his own hellish world replaying Gerda's death over and over again, just like him. *Always 'what if ...'*, he thought. What if Capa had insisted Gerda stay with him in Paris. What if she hadn't jumped on the car? What if the tank hadn't been out of control, had careered off-course a fraction of a second later? 'I had to read about it, can you believe it? I was in the dentist's waiting-room, Charlie.

I read it in the damn paper. I should never have left her there, never. We were going to be married you know?' he said again.

'I know.' Charles thought guiltily of their kiss, of Ted's closeness to her, and wondered if she would have gone with Capa, tamed her free spirit. He knocked back the shot of whisky the bartender had poured, and motioned for him to leave the bottle.

'You know, in '35 we spent a couple of months on the Île Sainte-Marguerite. It was perfection, Charles, the happiest time of my life.' Capa sighed. 'You know, I shoot a line – happiness is a game of poker, a bottle of Scotch and a pretty girl. But she was my world. I've never known peace and happiness like it. Never will again.'

'I hope, in time, you do, Bob.' Charles stood, and scooped up the papers. 'Listen, when are you coming down?'

'Not for a while. I just want some time alone. I'm going to head to the States and see my family in New York.'

'I understand.' Charles hung his head. 'What then?'

'Who knows. It's all heating up in China. Maybe I'll head out there for a while.' Capa forced a sad laugh. 'You've got to stay close to the story to get a good picture, Charlie.'

'Sure.' *But Gerda got too close,* Charles thought. 'You know where we are if you need anything.'

'I lost the only thing I ever needed,' Capa said. 'It was good of you to call, Charlie.'

'See you around, Capa,' he said. 'Look after yourself.'

'Right back at you, kid. Stay lucky.'

Charles heard Capa hang up the phone. *You're lucky, Bob,* he thought. *She loved you.* He took a last look at the photo of Gerda in the pages of *Ce Soir. Some of us can only dream of love like that.*

34

VALENCIA, JANUARY 2002

'There's no hurry. We can go to Cuenca once the baby has come,' Luca said. To Emma's secret delight, Luca had taken to calling in at the Perfume Garden every few days, sometimes for flowers, sometimes just to chat. 'Concepción is quite happy to wait to talk about selling her business. In spite of Guillermo's encouragement, I get the feeling she is in no hurry to stop work just yet.'

'Good, I'm glad the meeting can wait.' Emma stood from the stool behind the till and stretched, her hand at the small of her back. 'I don't find long car journeys terribly comfortable at the moment.'

'That's new, isn't it?' Luca pointed to the flower stand.

'Fidel gave it to me. I've just finished renovating it.' She ran her fingertips over the newly painted wrought iron.

'His wife used to sell flowers.'

'He told me.'

'Did he? You're certainly getting to know the locals.'

'We have a business to run.' Emma scooped up the

259

trimmed stalks of the flowers she was arranging in iron buckets, and tossed them into the bin.

'Talking of which, where is the boy? You shouldn't be working …'

'It's fine. Aziz needed to take his sister to the doctor. I'm just helping out.'

'Don't let him take advantage of you.'

'I can take care of myself.'

'I know you can.' Luca passed her an iron bucket filled with fragrant freesias.

'Thank you.' She slotted it into one of the hoops on the stand, stepping back to see how the display looked. 'When did Fidel's wife die?'

'Years ago. It was tragic really.'

'What happened?'

'It was Fallas time. You know, the festival in March when everything goes crazy in the city and villages.'

'I've seen pictures. Do they really set fire to those huge figures?'

'Every year,' Luca said.

'It seems rather dangerous.'

Luca shrugged. 'Normally people are careful. They douse all the buildings in water. That year there was an accident in the village …'

'With a firework?'

'No, with one of the bonfires.'

'She burnt? How awful.' Emma imagined the bacchanalian scenes she had read about, the towering fires and crashing explosions, and then, among the revellers, a single figure at a flaming window.

'She was visiting her mother in the old part of the village. I heard they had built one of the fires too close to

260

the house, and the whole lot went up.'

'Her mother died as well?' Emma shivered. 'He seems like such a lovely man, too.'

'He is. They were a devoted couple.'

'He must be lost without her.'

'I guess.'

'You sound uncertain.'

'It always seems to me that the people who have had the best relationships manage to move on somehow. It's the ones who have regrets that get stuck in a mire of grief.'

Emma fell silent for a moment. 'I'd never thought of it like that.'

Marek jogged towards them. 'Emma,' he said. 'Come see. We've knocked through the wall upstairs.'

Emma waddled through the garden to the house and climbed the stairs, followed by the men. Borys stood panting against the broken-down wall, covered from head to foot in dust. Marek took up the sledgehammer. 'Look.' Behind the plaster, the doorway had been roughly boarded up. He anchored the hammer, and pulled hard. Emma couldn't help noticing the powerful curve of his back beneath his white T-shirt as his muscles flexed.

Luca coughed. 'Emma, come. Wait until they are finished. This dust is no good for you.'

'No, it's fine.' She stepped forward. The handle was clear now. Squinting, she reached in, felt the cool brass knob beneath her hand. It turned, and Marek helped her push the door open. In the half light, Emma could make out blue-and-white *azulejos*, tiles with swirling floral patterns running in a frieze around the room. 'It's beautiful!' She supported her stomach with her hand as she ran down the hallway, and returned with a torch. As the light swept the room, she could see a bed still made up, a dressing table, a wardrobe. Then as she swung the beam of light, she made out a face, and cried out.

'What is it?' Luca was at her side instantly, pushing Marek aside. The boy scowled.

Emma's heart was pounding with excitement. 'I don't know …' She peered into the darkness, then began to laugh. 'Oh! It's a poster, an old print.' She stood up, and turned to Borys. 'Well done, both of you. Can you get all of this down? I can't wait to see inside.'

An hour or two later, Marek came to find her. Emma was sitting alone in the flower shop, thinking about her conversation with Luca. She was staring into space, twirling a peony stem in her hand. *I wonder if that's it?* she thought, *Luca's stuck, somehow. Maybe he hasn't been able to move on from whoever he lost?*

'It's done,' Marek said.

Emma jumped. 'The room? Sorry, I was miles away.'

He followed her upstairs. Emma stepped through the ragged doorway and over the pile of rubble just as Borys threw back the shutters and sunlight flooded the room. Emma looked around, a slow smile forming on her lips. The blue-and-white room had been untouched for years, it seemed. The poster on the wall was life-sized – a bullfighter, she thought, judging by the arena in the background, the roses at his feet. She cleared the dust from the paper. 'Jordi del Valle,' she read. 'It's the boy in the photograph under the floorboards! This must have been his house, his room.'

Marek pointed at the dressing table. 'But if it was a man, why are there perfume bottles in here?'

'His wife, perhaps?' Emma picked up one of the glass bottles, uncorked the stopper. When she inhaled, she smelt something dark. *Iris?* 'Would you mind?' she asked Borys. 'I could do with a moment alone in here.'

Once the builders had gone, Emma turned slowly in a circle, taking in the room. 'Why would anyone have sealed this room up?' she said aloud. She stopped in front of the wardrobe, half afraid of what might be inside. Her hand rested on the tasselled key in the lock. The door creaked open, her reflection in the cracked mirror swung away. The clothes inside were simple – dark, understated, all but a red silk dress with a sweeping train. 'Who were you?' Emma whispered.

In the dressing table, she found coral beads, a black paper fan, an embroidered silk shawl. In the central drawer there was an empty tube of red lipstick. As she tried to push the drawer back in, it stuck. Something was jamming it. Emma reached her hand in, felt up into the roof of the drawer. Her fingers ran across the leather cover of a notebook, tucked against the struts.

She turned the book over in her hand, and sat on the bed, a cloud of dust rising in the morning sunlight. 'Rosa Montez', it said, in a childish, slanting hand on the flyleaf. As Emma turned the pages, she realised it was a diary for 1938. Some dates were marked – a cross every four weeks, occasional birthdays and anniversaries. In May she saw 'Loulou, 1st birthday' on the 17th.

Loulou? She gasped. Her mother's birthday. Emma looked around the room, felt like a door had opened in her mind.

35

VALENCIA, AUGUST 1937

Rosa hummed a lullaby, rocking in the lamplight, tracing the sleeping face of her child with her fingertip. 'Little Loulou,' she said. 'He can christen you Lourdes if he wants like his mother, but you are my Loulou.'

Freya leant over them, and smiled. 'How are you feeling?'

'Me?' Rosa said, glancing up at her. 'I am fine. A little tired. She seems to like to be awake all night, and sleep all day. How about you? Is your stomach better?'

'Much better, thank you. The herb tea you made me has really done the trick.'

'Are you sure you're not …' Rosa mimed a rounded stomach.

'Me? Pregnant?' Freya laughed aloud. 'Don't be silly.' As she looked at the baby's face, she was filled with longing. She counted the days. *1st September tomorrow,* she thought. She hadn't had a period for months, but then several of the girls were the same. *Is it crazy to hope I might be, that I might be carrying Tom's child? Then, at least I would have a part of him forever.*

Rosa stood and gave the baby to Freya. 'Will you take her for a while?'

'I'd love to.'

Macu sat at the kitchen table embroidering sheets for the baby, while Rosa pounded herbs with the pestle and mortar. Freya stretched back in the chair, her reading glasses pushed up into her hair. She was exhausted. Every time she closed her eyes, her mind filled with the horrors she had seen at the hospital that day. She was glad to be at home, at peace with the girls, and with the thought of her cool, narrow white bed awaiting her.

'It is nice when Vicente's away,' she murmured as she closed her eyes. She stroked the baby's back as she lay on her chest, loved the warmth of her, the weight of her.

Macu laughed. 'You think it's nice for you? Imagine for poor Rosa, how nice. No beating, no bothering her in the bedroom.'

'Macu,' Rosa chided.

'It's true!' she said. 'So soon after the baby. It's not right ...'

'Enough!' Rosa's cheeks coloured. 'He is my husband, it's his right. I knew what to expect when I married him.'

Freya looked at her. 'Rosa?'

'Mm?' She stopped working away at the mixture.

'I know why you married Vicente – it made sense, for you to have security for your child. Why did he want to marry you?'

Rosa looked down at the bowl, stirred the mixture slowly. 'Jordi had something he couldn't have. Jordi has something, he can never have,' she corrected herself. 'One day—'

A pounding on the front door interrupted her. The girls looked up in surprise. 'Are you expecting anyone?' Freya said.

'No, no one.'

Freya tucked the baby into the woven Moses basket, and strode into the hall, carrying the heavy brass candlestick. 'Stay there.'

'Wait.' Macu grabbed the poker from beside the fireplace. 'I'll come with you.' As Freya unlocked the bolts, she stood ready, the poker raised above her head. 'Leave the chain on.'

Freya inched open the door, and peered out. It was a man, huddled over. Silhouetted against the moonlit sky bright with stars, she couldn't make out his features. She could tell from the blue mono that he was Republican. The cicadas hummed, frenzied in the warm night. '*Qué pasa*?' she said.

'Freya?' The figure stumbled forwards. 'Thank God, they said you were here.' As the man slumped on the doorstep, Freya frantically unhooked the chain.

'Help me,' she said.

Macu dropped the poker with a clatter, and pulled back the door. The man fell backwards onto the floor, his handsome, filthy face illuminated by the moonlight. As she gazed down at him, her lips parted.

'Who is it?' Rosa appeared in the doorway.

'It's my brother,' Freya said, as she knelt beside him, and brushed his hair from his brow. 'It's my brother, Charles.'

Between them, they carried him to bed, stripped him of his filthy, louse-ridden uniform and boots full of holes. In spite of having seen hundreds of men naked and wounded in the last months, Freya felt it would be wrong to see Charles in a state of complete undress, so she left Macu to clean him, while she and Rosa burnt his uniform in the courtyard. Freya wrinkled her nose with distaste as she poked at the smouldering cloth with a stick of orange wood.

'Eugh, that awful smell. Sometimes I think I shall never get rid of it.'

'Blood, sweat and worse. Thank God for perfume, eh?' Rosa nodded in understanding. 'You bathe tonight. I will give you some of my rose bath oil.'

'Oh, no,' Freya turned to her. 'I didn't mean ...'

'Please.' Rosa patted her hand. 'You have had a big shock. It will help you sleep, too. You need to be strong for your brother. He needs you now.'

'God knows where he's been. The last I heard he was stuck in Madrid and couldn't get to Gerda's funeral.' Her face fell. 'It looks like he has been on the road for a month. He must have been through hell.'

Charles lay on the bed in the candlelight, his limbs as loose and guileless as a child's in sleep. Macu stepped forward tentatively with the enamel bowl of steaming water.

'*Señor?*' she said gravely. Charles did not move. She put the bowl down, shook his arm gently. '*Señor?*' She thought for a moment he might be dead, and panicked. She lay her head on his chest, listened to the steady thump of his heart. No, not dead then, but as good as. She added the essences that Rosa had given her to the hot water, and gently she set to work, bathing him. Several times, she returned to the kitchen for fresh water as she washed the filth from his skin. She had helped Rosa and Freya at the hospital caring for the wounded soldiers, but this was the first time she had been alone with a man. When she started on his face, she soaked a fresh towel, and wiped away the dirt from his cheeks, his soft pink lips. Macu paused. He was so young, almost a boy. She rinsed his hair, like spun gold beneath the mud and grease, supported the weight of his head in her hand. At last she stepped back, pulled a clean white sheet up to his shoulders, covering him. He looked like an angel, she thought. Macu crossed herself, ashamed of the thoughts that filled her mind.

'*Cómo está?* How is he?' Rosa appeared at the door.

'He is good,' Macu scooped up the last bowl self-consciously. Rosa blew out the candle.

'Well done. He is to be your special responsibility. If Vicente comes home ...' she paused, thinking quickly, 'we'll tell him Freya's brother is visiting from England. Tell him he was with the conference of writers, that is better. He is sick, and he is staying with us.' Rosa pulled an amber bottle of oil from her apron pocket. 'Every morning, and every night, you are to rub this into his body. Mix a few drops into almond oil, and massage, like this ...' She mimed a circular motion. 'I would do it myself but I have the baby, and Vicente would not like it.'

Macu blushed at the thought. '*Sí*, Rosa. I will do it. I will make him better again.'

'Good girl,' Rosa said, closing the door with a smile on her lips.

36

VALENCIA, JANUARY 2002

Sitting in Plaza la Reina in the heart of Valencia, Emma thought how every single person in that square was there because for one night or one stolen moment their parents loved one another. Sex, pure and simple made the world go round, east and west alike. Every stranger passing by her table had been born as their mother endured the worst pain of her life, had been held up: 'It's a boy!' 'It's a girl!' Their backsides had been wiped and wailing hunger sated, their clothes washed and beds made for years to get them where they were today, busy on the way to work, talking into a mobile, or searching a rubbish bin for a crust of bread.

As her due date drew closer, she had spent the past week in a near frenzy of activity. Paloma had dropped by the evening before to invite her for lunch.

'What on earth do you think you are doing?' Paloma had cried.

Emma teetered on the chair, muslin billowing over her arm. 'You made me jump!'

'Get down from there at once.' Paloma held her hand as she clambered down. 'Don't you have a proper ladder?'

'I was just trying to hang some curtains. I'm hopeless with heights,' Emma said, laughing. 'I thought I could reach …'

'Even more reason why you shouldn't be climbing up there, then. Marek!' she called. 'Borys!' Paloma launched into the builders, told them in no uncertain terms that Emma was not allowed to lift a finger until the baby came.

Instead, Emma focussed her nesting urge on gathering supplies for the weeks after the birth. In the echoing halls of the Mercado Central she stockpiled food for the freezer. The market closed at lunchtime, and the traders cooked paella with the day's leftovers in vast pans outside the door, orange-wood fires sending plumes of smoke up to the sky. Emma stopped to watch them cook. She carried bags of tortoiseshell *mantilla* combs from *Nela*, and fans to send home to Freya as a 'thank you' for holding the fort in London. In Prénatal she couldn't resist buying a tiny babygro with ribbon fastenings, the first part of her baby's wardrobe. As she held it up for inspection now she couldn't believe that soon she would be dressing her child in it.

'Oh!' Paloma cried as she spotted Emma. 'It's so cute! Adorable! You can't believe they are that tiny at first! I have a stack of baby things you can have, I must dig them out for you.'

'That would be wonderful. After everything that's happened in the last few months I haven't wanted to tempt fate by buying too much.' Emma felt embarrassed. 'It's silly. It's not like me to be so superstitious.'

Paloma patted her hand. 'No, I understand. I will make up a bag of clothes for you.'

'What if you have more?'

'Nooo.' She shook her head. 'Three is plenty. Olivier

270

would have a football team, but I have my career to think of now. Benito we had very quickly, but we had to wait for Paco, and the baby. Olivier has his daughter now.' Paloma ordered a glass of wine. 'I'm sorry I'm late. Have you been waiting long?' She rooted around in her handbag for her mobile. 'Mamá … Well. You've met her now. She was meant to be taking care of the children tonight so that Olivier and I could go to the theatre, but we had a falling out.' She mimed a bomb exploding. 'So I asked Luca but he won't be back from Madrid in time. I have to call Olivier and cancel …'

'I'll have them,' Emma said.

'No, I couldn't ask you.'

'Really, I'd love to. Why don't you drop them off at teatime, I can get them ready for bed, then Luca can pick them up later?'

'Are you sure?' Paloma's face brightened. 'It's been so long since we had a night out. I've forgotten what it feels like to be out on a date with my husband.'

'It will be good practice for me.' Emma eased herself back in the chair. 'So, have you managed to find out anything from Macu, about the house? I'd love to know why that room was sealed up.'

Paloma shook her head. 'She wants to talk about it, I can tell, but something's stopping her. Mamá knows too, I'm sure, but she won't tell me.' She leant forward. 'I think there is something shameful, for our family.'

'I don't want to make trouble for you. I've asked Freya, but she won't talk about it either.' Emma swirled the water in her glass, the bubbles sparkling in the sunlight. 'I wish she'd open up. I get the feeling she's carried a burden for a long time.'

'I think a lot of people who lived through the war ...' Paloma hesitated. 'They think memories should stay buried.'

'Which side were your family on?'

Paloma's eyes flickered at the directness of the question. 'It is not as easy as that. Many families just wanted to get by, to live a peaceful life. Ignacio, my grandfather, was a good man, but it was hard for them because ...' She sat back and sighed. 'I think it was known Macu was Red, so was Rosa. I think they were in some kind of trouble. It is a small place, people talk. Mamá ... she likes to do the right thing. She cares a lot about the honour of the Santangel name. Past is past.'

'Is that why your mother dislikes me? Is me living at the house stirring up old memories?' Emma held her gaze. 'So that's why she doesn't like me working with Luca.'

'She tries to protect him, but my brother is a big boy,' Paloma said, smiling. 'It is thanks to him that the Santangels are successful. He has doubled our land, our wealth.'

'Really?'

'My brother the dark horse.' She sipped her wine. 'Maybe in the last few years he has been working too hard.'

I know the feeling, Emma thought. 'Tell me about Luca.'

'What do you want to know?'

Emma blushed, fiddled with the stem of her glass. 'Is he seeing anyone? I mean, I know he's not interested in me ... but why isn't he married with an adoring wife and a troop of kids?'

'You know, he has a lot on his plate. He has a lot of responsibilities.' She looked Emma in the eye. 'Some guys are like that – caught up with work ...'

'But, I mean, he's so … There must have been women?'

'Sex? Of course he's had – has girlfriends. He's just not a family man.'

'No,' Emma shook her head. 'I've seen something in his eyes when he is playing with your kids – it's love, but it's edged with something … grief, maybe. He's been hurt. I know that feeling – I recognise it.'

'Many, many women have hoped to steal his heart and failed. I like you, Emma. Don't set yourself up for more pain. You've been through too much. If you want a relationship, a father for your child, I know heaps of men who would adore you. Just don't pin your hopes on Luca.'

'Of course not. No, I don't need anyone. It's taken me nearly a year to feel strong again. I'm not going to take the risk of …'

Paloma leant back in her chair, her head slumped onto her hand. 'You've fallen for him, haven't you?'

'No!' Emma felt the colour rising to her cheeks. 'I mean, maybe if everything had been different …'

'People grow old waiting for everything to be perfect,' Paloma said. 'My brother is a wonderful man, but he has suffered a lot.' She hesitated. 'He has a lot of ghosts.'

'Don't we all?' Emma stared at the doves rising from the square, wheeling against the blue domes and cerulean sky. 'Would it have made a difference if I wasn't pregnant?'

'No, it's not that. If he trusts you, maybe he will tell you everything when he is ready. It's not my place to talk behind his back. I adore you, Emma, I hope we will become great friends …'

Emma reached forward and took Paloma's hand. 'Same here. I understand.'

'If he hasn't explained why he's alone then I can't, I just can't.'

That night Emma enjoyed the sound of laughter in the house, cartoons on the television, the pounding of small feet up and down the upstairs corridor. *A house like this needs the laughter of children*, she thought. After tea, she bathed the children, dressed them in their cotton pyjamas and brushed their hair as she had watched Paloma do. The warmest room in the house was the kitchen so she tucked them up with blankets on the sofa in front of the fire, and told them a story about magical creatures who lived in the orange groves before humans arrived, about unicorns and lions, talking tigers and snow-white flying horses.

At the end of the story, she sat enjoying the silence, the dozing children, the warmth. A low, mournful cry stirred her, and she struggled to her feet. 'Cat?' she called. She tracked the cries to the kitchen sink, and pulled back the curtains beneath it. There, tucked in the corner on a nest of rags she saw the cat, licking the first kitten. 'Well done!' she said, settling down on her hands and knees. The cat looked at her impassively. 'Good girl,' Emma said. 'You tell me if you need help, OK?' Emma tucked the curtain across and left her in peace. She settled back on the sofa, the wind rattling the French doors to the terrace, and stared at the flickering fire.

She must have nodded off herself, because she woke to find Luca leaning in the doorway watching them, smiling.

'No,' he whispered as she stirred, 'don't move. You all look so peaceful.' He lifted Paco into his arms, squeezed onto the sofa beside them all. As his arm stretched over the sofa, Emma felt his hand brush her shoulder. She smiled sleepily at him. 'Have you had a good day?'

'Yes. But not as much fun as you've had.' He glanced at the piles of paintings on the table and the toys all over the floor.

'It's a mess. I was going to tidy up before you came.' The baby sighed in her sleep, curled up against Emma's side, her arm stretched over her bump. Luca stroked the back of her little hand affectionately. 'Guess what – we have kittens!' she whispered. 'Do you think Paloma would like a couple for the children once they're weaned?'

'I'm sure. In fact, we could do with a couple of cats on the finca. Our old tomcat disappeared.'

'They do that sometimes when they get old.'

'Perhaps, or maybe wild dogs.'

'Let's hope he went peacefully in a sunny spot under an orange tree, eh?' Emma stifled a yawn.

'You're tired. I should get these monkeys home.' He scooped the children into his arms and stood. 'It's a shame to disturb you all. This is what men dream of coming home to.'

'What? Woman with a bun in the oven, a troop of kids, dinner on the table?' Emma laughed as she staggered to her feet.

'No.' He looked hurt. 'You are a businesswoman, I know. Maybe we want different things.'

'Luca,' she caught at his sleeve.

'Thank you, Emma.' The barriers had gone back up again. '*Hasta luego.*'

37

VALENCIA, NOVEMBER 1937

At sunset, Freya dragged herself up the hill to the Villa del Valle. She pulled her coat around her as the chill wind whistled down, bringing the earthy scent of onions from the fields. Every bone in her body ached. All she wanted to do now was sleep.

'*Buenos!*' she called, pushing open the kitchen door. She leant down and kissed the top of the baby's head where she sat in her high wooden chair at the table.

'Busy day?' Rosa asked. She was labelling bottles of essences, rows of amber glass bottles gleaming in the lamplight.

'The hospital is crazy. I wish the Spanish doctors wouldn't give us such a hard time.'

'They have their way of doing things, you have yours. I'll come back soon. Macu can help more with Loulou now she is bigger.'

'Where is Macu?'

Rosa raised her eyes. As they stopped talking, Freya heard the unmistakable squeak of bedsprings overhead. 'They are saying goodbye, I think.'

Freya blushed. Over the last weeks she had seen Charles

transform from a broken shell of a man to his old self. 'Of course. He's leaving for Barcelona tonight.'

'Everyone is leaving for Barcelona,' Rosa said bitterly. 'First the government runs here, now they flee to Barcelona.' She glanced at her child, thought of the children being sent overseas. 'Freya, I want to ask you ...'

'Yes?'

'If anything happens here, anything bad, will you look after Loulou?'

'Of course. But nothing is going to.'

'Who knows? The war is not going well. Every day, I hope that Jordi will walk in that door. Every day, but there is nothing.'

'No word from Vicente either?'

Rosa shook her head. 'Who knows what he is up to. I don't trust him. It is good, I think, that your brother is leaving.'

'I'm glad that Charles and Macu are ...'

'Lovers?' Rosa put down her pen, and gestured at the bottles in front of her. 'Love is the best medicine there is. Macu has experienced her "boum", and your brother is well again. When he goes, I think she will be happy to marry Ignacio now.'

Freya folded her arms and laughed. 'You planned all this, didn't you?'

'I don't know what you mean ...' A smile played on her lips. 'Maybe. I saw how sad he is that Gerda was killed. Maybe he was a little in love with her?'

'Who knows. Being with Macu has made him happy, and I think writing his book is helping.' She glanced down at Rosa's work. 'Your handwriting is really coming on, you know.' Freya peered down at the neat, childish script.

'It's all thanks to you, and your brother.' Rosa pulled over a new notebook. 'Look, I am writing out my recipes. Maybe one day Loulou will make medicine too.'

The thump of the bedstead against the wall upstairs got faster. Freya cleared her throat. 'Shall I make some tea?'

Charles flung himself back against the pillows, and Macu curled in his arms. 'I'm going to miss you,' he murmured into her hair.

'Take me with you, Carlos.'

'I can't. You know that. You're safer here.'

'I would be no trouble, I promise. I can take care of you, I will fight with you as Rosa did with Jordi …'

Charles closed his eyes as he kissed her. 'You have taken care of me, Macu. Without you …' He thought of the weeks he had spent recovering with the girls, the warm last days of autumn. 'You've put me back together again.'

'Only for you to go and fight, maybe be killed?' She held him closer. 'That is what we women do, what Freya and Rosa do in the hospital. They mend the men, only to send them to the front again.'

'That's the way it is,' Charles said. He glanced at the clock. 'I must get ready. The car will be here soon.' He slipped out of bed and packed his few belongings. His hand hesitated over the camera, unused for weeks. 'Macu, may I take your photo, to remember you by?'

'No one has ever taken my picture before.' She lay back in the bed, her dark hair gleaming against the blue-and-white *azulejos* tiles. A white sheet draped across her body, emphasising every curve.

'I want to remember you like this.'

'Wait,' she said, laughing. She reached over to the

bedside table and snapped open a black fan. She held it to her face, gazed steadily at the camera, at Charles standing naked before her.

They walked downstairs arm in arm. 'I will miss you,' she said.

'And I, you.' Charles kissed her forehead. 'Thank you.'

'Don't be silly.'

'No.' He looked into her eyes. 'You may just have saved my life. Take care, Macu.' A car's horn sounded outside. 'I'd better say goodbye to ...' His words trailed off as they heard the terrace door burst open, and Vicente's shout.

'Look at you with your potions!' Vicente yelled. 'Witches the lot of you!'

Charles put his kitbag down. 'Excuse me, Macu.'

Vicente staggered drunkenly across the kitchen towards Rosa, knocked the carefully labelled bottles on the table flying. The baby began to wail with fright.

'Where have you been?' Rosa yelled.

'None of your business.' He pushed her roughly aside.

'Don't you touch her!' Freya cried.

Vicente wheeled on her. 'You? You stuck-up English bitch, you whore ...'

Charles tapped him on the shoulder, and as Vicente turned, thumped him squarely on the nose. Vicente staggered back, fell on to the floor.

'That, sir, is my sister, and that's no way for a gentleman to talk to her.' He flexed his hand. 'Damn, that hurt.'

Rosa calmly stepped over Vicente's prone form and hugged Charles. 'That's no gentleman. That's my husband.' She kissed his cheek. 'You go now. It's better you are not here when he wakes up.'

279

38

VALENCIA, JANUARY 2002

The night was perfectly still. No dogs barked. Moonlight spilled through the muslin drapes, bathing Emma's bed in silvery blue light. She lay awake as the baby turned cartwheels in her stomach. She stroked her tummy, soothing the child with her soft words. 'It's OK.' Her voice faltered as she thought how hurt Luca had looked that evening. 'It's OK.' She rubbed her stomach along the curve of the baby's back, and the child stilled at her touch. It was no use, she was wide awake now and needed to pee – again. She swung her legs out of bed with difficulty and slipped on her Moroccan tan leather slippers, pulling a heavy wool gown around her. The house was cold and silent. She didn't even bother flicking on the bathroom light – she made this night-time journey so often now she could do it in the pitch dark. Tonight, in the moonlight, the house was filled with a strange and beautiful glow. *Tea and toast*, she thought as she washed her hands, her reflection luminous in the mirror.

In the kitchen, she raked the embers of the fire in the stove, and tossed on a few more orange tree branches. The kettle hissed on the range as she stared out across the moonlit mountains. Snowflakes fell hypnotically beyond the window. 'Well look at that,' she said to the baby. 'Snow in Spain, who'd have thought it?' She shivered, and took a mug of tea to sit by the fire. She leant her head against her hand, watching the flames dance, her eyelids heavy, drooping closed. 'Moon River ...' she sang softly to the baby.

'Wider than a mile ...' A male voice joined hers.

She glanced up. Someone was sitting in the shadows by the fire. 'Joe? How did you ...?'

'Who were you talking to?'

'Our baby,' she murmured. 'Joe, how did you find me? I thought you were ... You've been missing for months.'

'I've been busy, baby.' He knelt down before her, placed his hands on her stomach. 'Man, you are huge!' He laid his head against her. 'I can feel him kick.'

'How do you know it's a boy?'

'Of course it is!'

'Could be a girl.'

'Nah! This is little Joe in here, isn't it?' The baby kicked twice in response.

'I missed you so much. I miss our life ...'

'Hey,' he said gently. 'Where's my pal? Where's my buddy? Nothing fazes you, Em. You're tougher than anyone I know.'

'No I'm not.' She bit her lip. 'I don't know how to do this without you.'

Joe sat back on his heels. In the firelight his face seemed softer than she remembered – golden, radiant. 'That doesn't sound like the girl I know. I remember the first time I saw you. You were so confident, striding across the quad in one of those long black coats we all used to wear.'

Emma shifted away. 'That wasn't me, Joe, that was

Lila. She had a long coat, not me.'

'Oh?' He gave her his best little-boy-lost smile. 'You know me and my memory – it's funny, it isn't what it was … Hey, don't cry.' He took her hand.

'Why did you do it, Joe? Why her?'

Joe shrugged. 'I guess I got tired of saying no to her. She needed me … and you, you didn't seem to need me any more.'

'That's not true.'

'If I'm honest, you want to know why I gave in to Lila? Sex …'

'You risked everything we had, for that?' Emma said angrily.

'She'd asked me plenty of times before.'

'So what was different this time?'

'You.'

Emma shook her head. 'You're not going to blame this on me.'

'Well when was the last time we made love?'

Emma glanced down at her stomach. 'Almost nine months ago.'

'You've got to move on, baby. We had a good time …'

'We had a great time. I loved you, Joe.' She felt all the anger well up inside her, everything she had wanted to say. 'You lost faith in me, in us. You took something people search a lifetime for, and threw it away. Even if we had got together again for the sake of the baby, it would never have been what it was.'

'It could have been better.'

'No. Nothing could be better than what we had. I loved you, Joe. I trusted you. You didn't love me enough.'

'Em, people screw up. They can be selfish, impulsive.'

'I'm not just talking about your affair. You lied to me, even when I had all the evidence and gave you chance after chance to confess. You lied and said it was one night. You treated me like an idiot. You didn't have the decency to be honest with me.'

'I hoped you wouldn't find out.'

'You humiliated me.'

'Not everyone is perfect.'

'Meaning what? That I am?'

'No, baby ...'

'That's what Lila said, when I confronted her. That I was Miss Head Girl, too perfect, too closed. Business first. Now look at me, no business, no relationship, just the baby.'

'I'm sorry, Em.' He took her hand. 'But you know, if I knew then, when I met you, what was ahead I wouldn't change a thing.' Tears pooled in his eyes. 'We had some great times. The best. I loved you Em, but we've had our time. You need to find a new life, for you and little Joe.'

'Josephine.'

'Nah!' Joe laughed softly. 'You'll see. It's up to you now. You can do this. I'll be watching, you know. Make sure he grows up to be a better man than his father.' Joe wiped away a tear from her cheek. 'I'm sorry I wasn't the man you deserve, Emma.'

'It was both of us. We took our love for granted.'

'Don't make that mistake next time.'

'Next time?'

'Oh yeah.' Joe smiled. 'Just you wait.' He picked up the blankets from the sofa arm and tucked himself in beside her. 'It's all still to come, and he'll be the luckiest guy in the world.'

'Thanks, Joe.' Emma sighed sleepily.

'For what?'

'For coming all this way.'

Joe kissed the top of her sleeping head. 'You have no idea, baby, you have no idea.'

The sound of a siren on the road swung through the night, and Emma woke with a start. She blinked, confused to find herself alone. 'Joe?' she said. The cat yowled in response from her nest under the sink. 'Wow,' she said, stirring from the sofa. 'That was …' She stared out at the snow drifting by the window. 'That was strange.' Emma wrapped her arms around herself as she gazed out of the window. 'I miss you, Joe,' she said quietly. For the first time, she felt he had really gone. There was no doubt in her heart.

Emma padded across the room, and picked up her mother's box of letters. She settled back on the sofa, and smoothed the lid. It was covered with dust from the builders, and her breath bloomed on the surface as she blew it away, cleared the black lacquer with the sleeve of her pyjamas. As she opened it, the firelight illuminated the orange interior, gilded her face. Emma flicked through the remaining envelopes. 'On Loneliness,' she said, and glanced at the cat. 'That seems right for tonight.'

> Em, let me share something with you which has taken me sixty-four years to learn. I hope it saves you wasting time, as I did.
>
> It's an illusion that we are all alone. We are more connected than we think. It was spending so long in hospitals recently that made me see clearly how much we all need one another. We are all connected at some basic level, but

284

people forget. They forget to connect. They get caught up in the race, in the illusion of 'me' and 'you' when what matters in this life is 'we'. I felt so lucky to go through this last journey with you, with all of you at my side. I saw so many lonely people, Em. I saw the isolation, the fear in their eyes. If the NHS prescribed friendship they would save millions on drugs. I looked at some of the old people who had no visitors day after day, and thought 'when was the last time someone hugged you, or held your hand?' So that's what I did when I was in hospital, I went and talked to them, gave them a hug. And you know what? It helped me feel less afraid and alone too. Loneliness is a blight – we're not meant to go through this life alone.

This is what I learnt. People spend a lifetime looking for this, or that – a place, a house, a person that completes them. But your home is within you, you carry your place in the world. I was always a free spirit, alone in the traditional sense for years – no security, no home, no husband, and I was always searching for something I couldn't name. Then you came, a glorious, wonderful surprise. You taught me something that all the ashrams in India and retreats in California couldn't – you taught me that to give, to love selflessly, fearlessly is the key. You taught me that the only way is to open yourself completely to life. Loneliness closes people off – people get hurt, or scared, and shut down. It comes to us all at some point in our lives – when your father left us, I thought I was broken. I thought I'd never survive. But I did, for you. Times like that are sent to test us, I think. It's your moment of truth. Will you close

down, or will you grow stronger than ever?
As a parent, you wish you could spare your
children this. I hate to think of you alone, Em.
I remember you walking away from me on the
first day of school. You looked so vulnerable, and
uncertain. I just wanted to scoop you up in my
arms and protect you, but I had to let you go.
Every stage of life I've seen you go through
I've felt like that - when your first boyfriend
broke your heart, when you moved to France.
You taught me that love is letting go. I had to
step back. I feel like I am stepping back a
last time, now.

Let go, Em. I know you - you will be missing me
just as much as I miss you already, even thinking
about not being there for you. But take it,
take all the pain, and loss, and loneliness and
send it back to the world as love. Give it wings:
let love shine through you in your work, in your
family, in the home that you make. Transform
your pain, Em, send loneliness flying. Connect with
your life, with the people you meet, the beauty
around you. As you walk through life embrace
the whole magical experience. God knows why we
are here, and what it all means, but at the
end of my life I see we don't have to
understand, we just have to have faith, to feel
it, to embrace the everyday miracle of being
alive. I wish I had known this sooner.

I feel so lucky to have lived, and loved, and to
have been loved by you.

And I do love you, Em, so very, very much.
Mum x

39

TERUEL, JANUARY 1938

Charles cowered in the abandoned tank, writing by candlelight. He glanced up as another explosion shook the earth.

It looks like the pause in the bombardment has ceased, he wrote. As you know, nothing happens during the two to four o'clock siesta. That is one thing I have learnt - if it is hot, you will find the Nationalists in the shade, if it is raining, look under cover. They are predictable in that way at least.

The fighting is bloody here in Teruel, Freya. All the old gang has been here - Capa, Hemingway and Hugo. Each evening we retire to a hotel sixty miles away in Valencia to file our reports. I'm sorry I haven't had a chance to come and see you girls. Do give my love to Rosa and Maru.

Hemingway left for America on Christmas Eve. He plans to raise funds for the Republicans with the film he has made. I fear it may be too late. We are losing this war because of extremists blinded by dogma to the bigger picture. If only the factions supporting the Republican left - the anarchists, the communists and the unions - could put their differences aside. It will destroy me if we lose against fascism because of the petty in-fighting of the political parties.

Thank you for my Christmas parcel of Cadbury's and Players. I was so grateful I almost wept. I thought of you on New Year's Day. I woke early and went out to the courtyard for a cigarette. Snow was falling, and there were pigeons fluttering above. It was like a fairy-tale, the perfect silence. It reminded me of the snow globe you loved so much when you were little. Do you remember, the one I broke? When we go home, I shall buy you another one.

This whole city is like a snow globe. Teruel is a glittering ice city, spiked with turrets, the cathedral spire. When the bombs come, the snow rises up like the ghosts of the dead. We had to use cranes to lift the vehicles up the steep mountain road. The dead are stacked like log piles on the side of the road, frozen stiff, abandoned among broken furniture and burnt-out trucks. God, war is a hideous mess.

At least the line has held, and the city is in our hands. The battle rages on. I have just seen militiamen lead fifty people who have hidden in a basement for two weeks to safety. You never saw a more pitiful sight.

They say the first ten days at the front are the worst. After that, if you have survived, you are an automaton. You have seen too many good men die. Hemingway says there is nothing fitting about modern war - men are dying like dogs for no reason. But when I look at the men around me - the determined, hard faces of the Commies and the weedy intellectuals like me - as each wave of battalions goes forward to face death squarely, it always seems to me there is almost an ecstasy about them. Men who fight together, who hope together, have a nobility and strength they could never achieve alone. War is bloody, but it brings out the truth in man. It seemed like a fairy-tale, a simple case of good versus evil, but honour is dying.

Some time later, Charles returned to his letter, continued in a different pen.

The shelling is getting worse now. It is near the end. We have gone in hand to hand. Freya, I killed a man.

I will never forget his shocked, angry eyes. He was older than me, in his forties maybe, but God he fought back. I was never more alone. It was him or me. The horrid pushing, and shouting, the ghastly gleaming blade of the bayonet. Oh, I have shot at men before, from the safety of dugouts and trenches, but I think many in this war aimed to miss. But this, oh God, this will be on my conscience for all eternity.

I am trying to keep the truth in me, the qualities you know. I have changed, but I will

289

not let it change 'me', if that makes sense. I
want to still see the beauty in the world,
Freya. I need to. I am not Capa - he writes
the poetry of war with his pictures, a tragic
poetry. I feel a dilettante in comparison. He is
haunted, passionate, impulsive - everything I am
not. I wish I were more like him, Frey. I wish I
did not know what it is like to kill a man. Let's
never talk of this again.

Happy New Year.
Your loving brother,

Charles

Charles folded up the letter, and sat for a time with his head in his hands. He scrambled from the tank, the metal cold beneath his blood-caked fingers. He jumped down into the snow, and clicked his lighter. From the flame, he lit his last cigarette, then the corner of the letter. He lifted it to the wind, watched the gold flame lick around the paper, curling, charred as it leapt into the air, the frozen city behind.

40

VALENCIA, JANUARY 2002

Snow fell steadily beyond the window as Emma sat at her desk, Liberty's notebook in front of her. She had spent hours unpacking the vials of fragrance Liberty had collected, arranging them in family groups of citrus, spicy, herbal, floral, woody, leather. The other packing boxes from London littered the house now, unopened. All she had wanted to do was assemble the 'organ', to somehow conjure her mother here with her.

Emma carefully unwrapped the last bottle, a boronia absolute. It joined the hundreds of other vials of essences and absolutes. On one shelf, Emma placed her empty bottles and labels, on another her ingredients. Finally, she centred the scale at the heart of the tiered shelves, and placed an empty glass jar on it, ready to work, but she didn't know where to begin. She knew the fragrance she wanted, like a half-remembered melody she couldn't sing but would know instinctively the moment she heard it. She felt restless, and she snatched up the notebook, paced in front of the window, her warm socks padding on the newly polished floorboards. She read the list she had just written:

Spain – something wonderful:
The seduction of white flowers
Woodsmoke and saffron
Lavender mountains, cranberry sunsets
Blue domes
Lemon trees
Floating bridges
Immense night skies pricked with stars …

Luca's wrists, she thought. *The indentation at the base of his throat. His hair in the wind.* Emma frowned as she selected a few vials from the tiered shelves of her desk. She wanted to transform what she was feeling into fragrance. She closed her eyes, thought of blossom, cedar … When she thought of him, the fragrance deepened, became mixed with earth. With glass pipettes, she measured out a few drops from each vial, replacing them on the shelves as she noted down the amounts she used. Memories, associations danced in her mind – colours, odours, textures – as she inhaled the mix. Since training in Grasse, Emma could imagine in three dimensions the way the molecules of fragrance worked together at a microscopic level, connecting, transforming. She always pictured the fragrance in motion, like a mobile in a chemistry lab.

She needed something else. She selected three more bottles: neroli, bitter orange, petitgrain, sniffing each in turn, clearing her 'nose' by smelling coffee beans in between each. Emma jotted down some notes. The scent relaxed her – she remembered Olivier saying that the smell of orange blossom was associated with meditation, a Zen state. *There's still something missing.*

Emma thought back to walking in the orange groves

with Luca that afternoon, how he had run his hands through the earth. She pulled on her boots, and walked out into the snow. The night air seemed alive, made anew, sparkling. She kicked at the ground. *This is my earth*, she remembered Luca saying, *it made me*. Emma squatted down, scraped the soil with her fingertips, inhaled. What was missing? Emma touched the locket at her neck. What did she need?

The mountains had seemed close that afternoon, sparkling with fresh snow beneath a cobalt sky. She had felt like she could reach out and touch them. Luca had offered her his hand. A fresh gust of cold wind ravished her as she stepped down off the road into the grove.

'What a day.' She felt the Morse code of her heart pulsing strong in her. Luca whistled for Sasha, and Olivier and Paloma walked arm in arm ahead, the children throwing snowballs.

'That dog has a mind of his own,' Luca said. 'He is a real Spaniard. Hates getting up in the morning, won't eat much before lunch, but once he's been out for his evening *paseo*, he's like a different animal.'

'I've never seen a dog who can look so exhausted.' Emma buried her cold nose down into her soft pink scarf.

'It's like he has a hangover every morning,' Luca laughed. 'When he wakes up, he has bags under his eyes.'

'You can imagine him rubbing his chin in front of the mirror, getting ready to have a shave.' Emma laughed.

'Or ordering strong black coffee at the same little café each day to ease himself into the morning.' Oblivious, the dog criss-crossed between the trees ahead of them, nose to the ground, tail high, tracking the course of something. 'Are you all right? You're not too tired?'

'No, I'm fine.' Her hips were aching painfully but she wasn't going to let anything spoil this glorious afternoon. 'I'm bored of sitting at home, waiting for this baby to come. It's wonderful to be out, exploring.' She glanced at Luca. 'You've never thought of leaving here, of travelling?'

'I've travelled all over the world. At least enough to know that I always want to return here.' He smiled, squatted down on his heels, raked through the snow to the ochre soil. 'This is my earth. It made me. When I die, I want to be here.' Sasha ran over, sniffed his face, and Luca laughed. He tossed a snowball off into the groves and the dog chased away. 'We belong here.'

'You're lucky.' Emma pushed a branch out of her path as they walked on. 'I wish I felt like that. Sometimes I don't know who I am, especially now Mum has gone.'

'Is your father alive?'

'Dad? Yes, but he has a whole other family now. I spent some time with him recently, but we're not close. He just … Well, the birthday cards stopped when I was about nine, put it that way.'

'Perhaps now is the time to choose your own life?'

Emma glanced at him. 'A clean slate? Maybe you are right.'

'Have you managed to find out anything more about the house?' he asked as they walked on.

Emma shook her head. 'Freya won't talk to me, and I don't want to push Macu too much.' She dug her hands into her pockets. 'I'd just love to know the truth about what went on.'

'The truth?' Luca smiled and shook his head. 'Sometimes there are many truths. It depends on how you look at something.' He scuffed the snow with his boot. 'You are

294

happy here?' he asked her after a while.

'In Valencia? Yes, yes I am.'

'I am glad. I thought, perhaps, you would not stay long.'

'Looks like I'm here for the duration.' Emma spoke quietly, sensing that he was trying to say something important.

'I would have been sorry, if you had left.' Luca hesitated. 'Emma, I know ...' Sasha barked suddenly, a low, mournful cry more like the howl of a wolf, and another dog's bark snapped in the cold air. 'Sasha!' Luca called, running into the grove. Emma followed at a distance, struggling through the snow, the green branches of the trees catching at her. The cries of the dogs grew fiercer.

In a clearing, Emma came upon them. A muscular black Alsatian stalked around Sasha, its teeth bared and ears hard against its head. Sasha reared up, his silver hackles raised, and brought his front legs down on the dog. They locked, snarling, striking at one another. Luca leapt towards them, pulling Sasha clear. The Alsatian snapped at him, catching the flesh of his hand in its teeth. Luca roared, and kicked out at the dog, which ran off into the trees.

'Let me see,' Emma said, taking his hand. He shook a white handkerchief from his pocket as she inspected the bite.

'It's nothing,' he said, stemming the blood with the handkerchief.

'You should have it checked,' she said. Luca snorted and shook his head. 'The dog might have rabies.' Emma tied the handkerchief tightly around his hand and Luca winced.

'No, it was tagged,' he said. 'They are always fighting, these two.' He looked over to where Sasha lay, head on the ground, waiting to see what would happen next. 'You ...' he growled, and the dog rolled over on its back.

'Men,' Emma sighed. 'Just don't know when to let it go, do you?' She winced, caught her breath as her stomach hardened with a contraction.

'Emma?' He touched her arm.

She exhaled, smiled. 'Don't worry. It's just Braxton Hicks – the baby isn't due for a couple of weeks yet. Just a false alarm.'

Emma stood now, wincing as another contraction set in. She exhaled slowly, her breath a cloud of white, and looked out across the sleeping garden. She imagined the summer to come, and all the summers after as the garden came back to life. In her mind, she conjured the perfume of flowers, the dappled shade of the trees on fresh grass, the sound of running water in the fountain. *Perhaps now is the time to choose your own life*, she remembered Luca saying. She looked up at the moon, said a silent 'thank you' to her mother. *I choose this*, she thought. *I choose this place, this life.*

41

VALENCIA, JULY 1938

Rosa swung in a hammock in the garden, the July sun beating down through the leaves where she lay, her child asleep in her arms. The village was quiet at siesta time, and all she could hear was the water dancing in the fountain. It seemed impossible that the war was drawing ever closer, at the Ebro river now. She closed her eyes, felt the steady rise and fall of the child's ribcage beneath her hand, brushed the damp curls from her hot brow. She felt afraid now, not for herself, but for her daughter. Rosa jumped as the latch on the gate clicked. She raised her hand to her eyes, shielding them from the sun.

'*Quién está ahí?* Who's there?' she said. She heard the crunch of gravel beneath boots, and struggled to her feet, laying the child down to sleep. As she turned, the man took her in his arms, pulled her to him.

Rosa fought back, pushing him away. As she struggled, she saw his filthy beard, smelt the stink of his ragged clothes.

'Rosa,' he said. 'Don't you recognise me?'

At the sound of his voice, she stilled, her heart thundering beneath her ribs. 'Jordi?' she cried. 'Jordi?' She started to shake, to weep. She took his face in her hands, and looked into his eyes. 'Oh God, you're alive. I knew you were alive!' They clung to one another in the dappled light, as their child slept on beside them.

Macu came around the side of the house, carrying a tray of peaches. When she saw them, her hand slipped, the fruit tumbled to the floor.

'It's like you saw a ghost, Macu.' Jordi turned to the sleeping baby.

Rosa watched his face. 'She is your daughter,' she said, a tear trickling down her cheek.

He stepped forward, reached out his hand, dark against Loulou's pale cheek, her white dress. He hesitated, his hand trembling. 'I can't ...' he whispered, his voice tight with tears. 'She is too perfect.'

Rosa lifted the child into his arms. 'She is yours, ours.' Jordi buried his face in her hair. 'She is beautiful,' he said, and kissed the top of Rosa's head. 'You haven't changed.'

'You have.' Rosa tugged his beard. She thumped his chest. 'Where have you been? They told me you were dead. They showed me your papers.'

Jordi thought back through the months of combat, hazy memories rolling into one another. 'I lost my papers. I gave my jacket to a comrade who was badly injured.'

'You're alive. That's all that matters.' She thought of Vicente. 'Jordi, there's something you need to know ...'

The shutters upstairs rattled open, and Vicente appeared on the balcony in his pink dressing gown, stretching and yawning after his siesta. 'Rosa!' he bellowed. 'Rosa!'

Jordi looked from her anxious face to his brother and knew.

'They told me you were dead,' she said, clutching at his shirt.

Jordi thrust the baby into her arms and pushed her away. 'You, and him? How could you?'

'Please, he told me it would be best for our daughter, for Loulou.'

Vicente leant on the balcony, looked down into the garden. 'Who's there?' Jordi gazed up at him, his eyes full of anger and pain. Vicente began to laugh. 'Well look, it's the prodigal son.'

'Do you love him?' Jordi said to her. His eyes scared her. He looked like the man she loved, sounded like him, but his eyes were dead. He had the look of an animal that has been beaten, its spirit broken.

'Are you mad?' she said. 'I love you, Jordi, I have always loved you. He told me I had to marry him, to protect our child.'

'You married him?' Jordi took a step back.

'*Sí*,' Vicente said, folding his arms.

Jordi stuck his cap on his head. 'Then there is nothing to be done.'

'I will divorce him!' Rosa whispered, clutched at his hand. 'Jordi, I have heard nothing from you, nothing, for over a year. If you had written ...'

'I can't write. You know that.'

'You could have got a message to me.'

'I have been fighting, Rosa, all over Spain,' he said, his voice cracking with anger. 'And now, not far from here, the bodies of my friends are on the banks of the Ebro.' He flinched as he thought of the swollen bodies washed up along the river, buzzing with flies.

She saw the madness in his eyes flare then, the damage the war had done.

'We have been trapped in the bottom of a valley for

days.' He wiped his mouth with the back of his hand. His throat thickened again at the thought of the heat, the dust. 'Marco's brother was killed trying to cross the river. We brought him home.'

'You're going back?' she said incredulously.

'Of course, the battle is just beginning there. To resist is to win.' He clenched his fist. 'We may lose five thousand, but they will lose four times that many.'

'It is too much. There is too much loss,' Rosa said, weeping. 'I can't take any more.'

They sat in silence around the kitchen table at nightfall. Jordi had bathed for the first time in months, changed into fresh clothes. His hair hung wild and dark to the collar of his white shirt, and where he had shaved his beard, his skin was a lighter caramel against the dark angles of his sunken cheeks. The child slept in his arms at the head of the table. At the opposite end, Vicente cleaned his nails with the tip of a knife.

'Would you like some wine, Jordi?' Freya asked, offering him the jug.

'I don't drink,' he said. He looked at her, as if seeing her for the first time. 'Your nurses are wonderful,' he said to Freya. 'So brave. They work in a train in a tunnel near the front, they work in caves near the river where you cannot stand up. It was dark where they tried to save Marco's brother. That is where my friend died, in a cave. An English woman held his hand, right to the end.'

'We never let a boy die alone,' Freya said quietly.

'Then your nurses will hold a lot of dead men's hands in the next months.' Vicente folded his arms and stared at his brother.

300

Jordi scraped back his chair, walked around to Rosa and handed her the child. 'It is time for me to go.'

'So soon?' She looked up at him, her gaze pleading with him to stay.

'Be safe, little brother,' Vicente said, without getting up from the table.

Jordi snatched up his jacket, and marched towards the door. Rosa bundled the child into Macu's arms and ran after him.

'Wait,' she cried out, running along the path after him. 'You can't just leave.'

'There is nothing here for me now.'

She caught his arm, forced him to look at her. 'Jordi, I am here. Your child is here.'

In the moonlight he looked younger to her again, the scars of the war softened on his face. 'I thought you would wait.'

'If it had just been me …' She took his face in her hands. 'I told you, I married him only so our child would be safe.'

'The thought of you, with him …'

'He does not have me.' She held him tight. 'Only you, Jordi. Only you.' She felt him breathing hard, the beat of his heart against her face.

'Come, tomorrow, to Sagunto. We have a camp in the ruins. I will wait for you before I return to the front.'

'Tomorrow?'

'Are you scared?'

'With you, never.' She kissed him then, felt life rising up in her again.

The front door banged open, and Jordi looked up to see Vicente standing there.

'Rosa,' he yelled. 'Come back inside.'

Rosa hesitated. Every fibre of her body told her to run with Jordi now, run and keep going. Then she saw Vicente had the child in his arms. On the street she could hear Marco's mother crying, begging him to stay. She lowered her voice. 'I will come, tomorrow.'

Jordi hugged her, whispered in her ear. 'Better the lover of a hero than a coward's wife.'

'Come with me,' he said. Jordi held her close to him beneath the rough blanket, her cheek against his smooth chest. She felt his heart steadying as they lay, limbs entwined, sated. Beneath them, in the moonlight, the ruins of Sagunto slept.

'I can't, you know I can't.' She buried her face in his neck. 'If I go with you, he will never rest. He will come after me, and I can't leave our child.'

'I won't let you do this.' He cupped her face in his hand. 'The thought of you with him ...'

'It's the only way, for now.' As her gaze searched his face, her eyes filled with tears. 'I love you, Jordi. I will always love you.'

'I'd rather die than be without you.' Jordi screwed his eyes shut. 'Promise me, if I don't come back, you will never love him.' His voice broke, and when she looked at him, she suddenly saw him for the boy he still was. He was not a soldier, she was not the great dancer he had fallen for. They were just a boy and girl in love.

'Never.'

'I can't bear it. My own brother, how could he ...'

'He said he was doing the decent thing.'

'Decent?' Jordi's voice was low, angry. 'I should kill

him. I trusted him. It was always the same, when I was a child. If I made something, he would break it.'

'He can't touch us,' she said. She lifted his hand to her heart. 'When it is safe, send word to me, and I will come to you.'

'What about the child?'

'If I can, I will bring her. If not …' Rosa's voice trailed away. 'Children are being sent to safety all the time. Freya tells me she is being sent home soon. She will go to a hospital at the border. If I have to, I will take Loulou there.' Her chest tightened as she thought of being separated from her child. She forced down her tears. 'There is no good here, for her now. If we lose the war, no child of ours will be safe.'

'Can you trust the English woman?'

Rosa looked at him. 'Yes. Yes, I can. Freya will take care of her until we are free. We can escape, together. There's still time.'

He reached between her breasts. In the firelight, the gold locket swung from a fine gold chain.

'See?' she said. 'I wore it tonight. Me and you. I will always be with you.' He kissed her eyes as she began to cry, her lashes darkening into points. 'Always.'

'We will leave in a few days, go north. We will fight to the end.'

'If we only have days, we must make them last a lifetime.'

He leant down and kissed her breastbone near the locket as she lay back on the earth. 'I love you, Rosa,' he murmured as he fell into an exhausted sleep.

Rosa lay awake all night, into the cold grey dawn. She did not want to miss a moment with him. She thought of the Lorca poem that Freya had read to her, and she understood as she looked at Jordi, his skin dark against the earth. *We are the same,* she thought, *we are all of this earth.* She stroked his sleeping face, remembered Jordi's words: '*We have hours, not years together, perhaps – but they are full hours, full of you, and me, and our love.*' He rolled over in his sleep, his muscles twitching from exertion. She breathed in the scent of crushed pine branches beneath them, and her face stilled as she remembered what else he said. '*I face death head on. I am not afraid any more, now I have you in my arms again.*'

42

LONDON, JANUARY 2002

Freya swirled her brush in white spirit, wiped the bristles clean. *Woman's Hour* was on the radio, and she listened to the discussion about Afghanistan as she sorted through the tubes of oil paint at her side. She squeezed a bright, ultramarine blue onto her glass palette, and turned to the large canvas on her easel.

Charles tapped on the door. 'Do you want anything from Waitrose? I'm just popping out for a paper.' He shuffled over to her, peered down his nose through his half-moon glasses. 'Oh, I like that. It's coming on really well.' He laid his hand on her shoulder.

'Thank you.' Freya tilted her head, looked at the mountainous landscape taking shape on the canvas. 'I haven't felt like painting Spain for years.'

'I remember that view,' he said. 'It was from your room, in the villa, wasn't it?'

'I'm surprised you remember the view.' Freya raised an eyebrow. 'As I recall, the view was the last thing on your mind when you were recovering in that room.' She patted Charles's hand. 'Can you get a couple of yellow peppers? I thought I'd make gazpacho tonight.'

Charles buttoned up his winter coat, tucked the empty sleeve in. 'Any word from Em?'

'She's fine. A few contractions,' Freya said. 'It won't be long now.'

'Good.' Charles hesitated by the door, looked at the dog-eared photograph of Rosa with Liberty as a baby Freya had recently framed and hung on the wall. 'I remember taking that.'

'It feels like yesterday.'

'You know she's going to want to know the whole story, don't you?'

Freya's brush hovered over the canvas. 'I know. It's time she knew.' She thought of the mountains, the luminous light. She flexed her hand and winced.

'Rheumatism playing up?'

Freya nodded. 'I think it was washing all those sheets in freezing streams. I've never been the same since Spain.'

'You want to go back, don't you?'

'Could we?' She turned to him.

'I don't know.'

'Think of the baby, Charles. We could help Emma.'

'Get under her feet more like.' He coughed, caught his breath.

'She has no idea what to expect, how exhausted you are at first. Do you remember Libby, with Em?' Her eyes took on a softness. 'She didn't think she needed us either, but she didn't have a clue, bless her.'

'Liberty never thought she needed anyone, always charging through life trying to control everything. Look at that box of letters she left for Em. She couldn't let go even from beyond the grave.'

'I think they are bringing Emma some comfort.'

306

Charles laughed through his nose. 'Lord knows what words of wisdom she's doling out. She was always a wilful girl.'

'She was that.' Freya sat back and looked at her painting. 'Maybe I tried too hard to protect her.'

'Libby loved you. She soon came running once she was knocked up and Mr Free Love didn't want to know. You put her back together again, just like you always did.' Charles raised his chin. 'We did our best for her. I'd do the same again in a heartbeat.'

'Same here.' Freya picked up her walking stick. She shuffled over to Charles, smoothed down his collar. 'No regrets?'

'Regret is a useless emotion.'

Freya thought of the nights she had found him, head slumped on his desk, surrounded by photographs of Gerda, Hugo, and their friends. 'It's time, Charles. Think about Spain, at least.'

'Spain? I think of little else.'

She kissed his dry, wrinkled cheek. 'You and me both.'

43

BARCELONA ROAD, JANUARY 1939

'Well, we made it. The last of the last-ditchers, eh?'
Charles rolled his head towards Hugo as the planes dove
down towards them again. 'Who would have thought
it, a couple of cherry boys like us, staying at the Hotel
Florida with Hemingway and Capa ...'

His voice was drowned out by the rat-tat-tat of
machine guns, the frenzy of feet and screams from the
road. Four hundred thousand people snaking along the
road towards the French border, diving for cover like a
column of dominoes, falling.

'You were right. It's time to go home, old boy. I'm sick
of orange-peel chips and lettuce tobacco. When you think
all this time the cities in the Nationalist zones haven't
changed a bit. The rich are well dressed, their stomachs,
the churches and bullrings are full. Life is as it ever was.
What was it all for?' He took Hugo's hand in his, laced
their fingers together. Charles forced down a sob. 'I
remember you joking when we joined up – "perhaps we
should just shoot ourselves in the foot now?" Maybe we
should have done just that. Maybe we should.'

Charles shook as the scenes they'd just witnessed in

Barcelona crowded into his head: the wounded crawling from the hospitals, the young in tears and the old cursing. He screwed his eyes shut as he remembered seeing a woman, wild with grief, clutching a blanket, shielding what remained of her child from further harm.

'How could Mussolini's bastards drop those packets marked "Chocolate" onto the streets, knowing innocent children would pick them up, never dreaming they'd be bombs?' His head sank forward as he sobbed. Through tear-filled eyes he watched as children with bloody rags tied around their arms and feet struggled by, crying from pain and hunger. Some clung to their parents. Many were alone. Across from him huddled a woman with a new-born child at her exposed breast. Next to her, an old woman who had given up hope lay down by the side of the road to wait for death. The people on the road stepped aside, pulled their donkeys and mules to the verge as trucks thundered past, taking the Prado's Goyas, El Grecos and Velázquezs to safety.

'Look at that, Hugo,' he said. 'They're saving the bloody paintings, but what about these poor people, eh?'

Charles's thoughts drifted back to October, when the International Brigades had marched through Barcelona on their way home. Thousands of Catalans had lined the Diagonal, waiting for the men to come. The city crackled with fear and suspicion, and Assault Guards ordered up from Valencia by the government kept the peace with a sheer display of force. Everyone knew the end was near now; all trust, all hope had gone.

Just after 4.30 p.m., he heard them coming, the sound of boots marching through the flowers and ticker tape raining down from the balconies. His hackles rose, goosebumps peppered his skin. First came an honour guard of Republican soldiers, then hundreds of sailors singing at the top of their voices.

'It can't be over, Hugo,' he had said, raising his camera to his eye.

'It is, for us. The International Brigades are being sent home.' Hugo raised his fist in the air as the first of the Internationals marched by, a German brigade. Petals ankle deep on the road were crushed beneath their boots.

'What the hell the Non-Intervention Committee is thinking of, I don't know,' Charles said in despair. 'They're ordering the Spanish to send us all home, but what about all the Nazis and Italian fascists who are fighting for Franco? Will they go too? Will they hell. This is the end. What chance do the Republicans stand against him now?'

Charles choked back tears as two hundred of the Abraham Lincoln Brigade marched past. As he photographed them, he was there again in Jarama. Had it really been only a year and a half, just over? He blinked as he remembered the carnage. 'I find it hard to recall what life was like before all this.' His voice shook. 'So much of me is caught up in Spain.'

Capa was wearing a huge camel-hair coat with wide lapels and pearl buttons.

'Pull yourself together, man.' He handed Charles a handkerchief.

'I'm sorry. I just can't believe it's over.' He blew his nose.

'It's not – for them.' Capa pointed at a small boy being hoisted onto his father's shoulders. 'Nor for us. We have a job to do, still. We have to tell the world.' Capa turned down Charles's collar, brushed some dust from his shoulder. 'Smarten yourself up, Charlie. Gerda taught me about presentation, you know. Because of her, my hair is short, I wear a tie, my shoes are shined. Because of her ...' His eyes grew sad as he watched the men marching past. 'Gerda would have loved this.'

The Republican politician, Dolores Ibárruri, took to the stage.

'La Pasionaria,' Charles said under his breath as her voice rang out across the crowd. Even the tinny loudspeakers couldn't hide the strength and warmth of her voice:

'These men reached our country as crusaders for freedom, to fight and die for Spain's liberty and independence threatened by German and Italian fascism. They gave up everything – their loves, their country, home and fortune ...' Charles looked at Hugo, remembered clowning around on the River Cam with him that day. It had seemed like such an adventure, coming to Spain. '... They came and they told us: "We are here. Your cause, Spain's cause is ours. It is the cause of all advanced and progressive mankind."'

The thousands gathered on the street cheered as one. Charles looked at the unsmiling, sorrowful face of the child on his father's shoulders.

'You can go proudly. You are history. You are legend,' La Pasionaria cried.

'I'm not going,' Charles said. 'Look at these people. We can't just leave the Catalans – it's going to be a catastrophe. The conditions in Barcelona are only going to get worse.'

'I heard that some Brigaders are staying, unofficially,' Hugo said. 'They are joining up with the Republican troops.'

'Then we must go with them.' Charles leant his head against Hugo's, as children do, sharing a secret. 'Together to the end?'

Hugo squeezed his shoulder. 'To the end.'

'It's over, Hugo,' Charles said, cowering in the ditch beside the Barcelona road as the planes swooped low again. He screwed up his eyes as he heard the planes come closer, closer. The last wave had caught them. He had been running at Hugo's side, saw the plane bank down, head directly at them. The line of people ahead of them parted like a dark tide, bodies and carts lurching to the side of the road, screams mingling with the metallic rat-tat-tat of the machine guns, bullets weaving a deathly path through them.

'Over here!' Hugo had cried, dragging Charles towards a shallow ditch.

'Wait!' Charles spotted a small boy of two or three over his shoulder. The child was standing in the middle of the road, wailing, open-mouthed with distress, separated from his mother. A woman was running up the road towards him, screaming. Charles ran back, Hugo at his heels. The plane was so close now, he could feel the thud, the vibration of the bullets hitting the earth. Charles grabbed the child, and Hugo dragged the woman to safety, diving for the ditch as the planes swept over.

The mother and child sheltered next to him now, rocking in silence, pale with shock. The woman could not look at Charles. He remembered landing in the ditch, the thud of the earth against his chest, a seeping wetness through his coat from the slush and mud. He remembered Hugo, falling on top of him. 'It's over,' he mumbled. 'Now

312

the Nationalists have marched down the Ramblas, the reprisals will begin.' His words slurred as he slipped in and out of consciousness. A numb, throbbing pain began to register in his left arm. He tried to move it, and found he could not. 'This was our war, wasn't it? Hugo? Such a picturesque war – a savage, bloody mess, but God the country … so glorious. And the women … I miss women, Hugo. God muddled with men, but the women he got right. Is there anything so perfect?' He drifted for a moment, the image of Macu, naked, floated to the surface as darkness descended on him. He felt like he was underwater, the sound of the assault raging around him muffled and far away.

He remembered hiding in a barn near the Ebro in November. It was like he was there again, with Hugo. The animals had gone long ago, and now the stable sheltered men, huddled together in the straw for warmth, survivors of the last great battle of the war. Hemingway had a thick wool blanket tucked over his head, only his beard and glasses showing. 'So we found four peasants, lean and hungry-looking men …' he was saying.

Aren't they all, Charles had thought as he shivered next to Hugo.

'One hundred thousand casualties they reckon, so when Lister told us to get back, I wasn't going to argue. We pitched into this flat-bottomed boat, one man at each corner,' Hemingway went on. 'All the bridges were down, so the only way out of there was to brave the rapids …'

Will you please shut up, for mercy's sake, Charles thought. Hemingway's voice grated on his nerves.

'Two of the rowers deserted, so I seized an oar.' Hemingway mimed heaving down. 'It was a fight. My hands were stiff with cold. We were plunging downstream towards the Mora bridge. It was bombed, and broken ...'

Charles tucked his head down. *Good old Papa, saves the day* ... He jumped as a rat scuttled by in the shadows.

Capa laughed quietly as he slumped at Charles's side. The wind and snow was beating at the door of the stable, the old wood creaking. 'He can sure shoot a line, can't he? You can see the cogs working, turning everything into a great story even as we watch.' He glanced at Charles. 'Are you OK?'

'Me? Fine. I just want to get the hell out of here.'

'Are you still annoyed you missed that shot?'

They had been out by the Segre River, following one last battalion of do-or-die Republicans. They were a rag-tag lot in camouflage uniforms, armed with old Russian rifles. As they pushed fearlessly on, there had been a deafening explosion. A soldier staggered forward, his face full of terror as earth and rock cascaded down. Capa had calmly raised his camera, caught the moment.

'You'll smell the powder in that one,' he'd said under his breath.

It was then that Charles discovered he had forgotten to load any film in his own camera.

'You have a death wish, Capa,' Charles said, huddling down in the straw as the wind wailed through.

Capa laughed, closed his eyes. 'Maybe. Say, we're going on to Barcelona. Are you going to come?'

Charles laced his fingers behind his head, settled down to sleep. 'Wouldn't miss it for the world.'

A Republican soldier squatted down in front of Charles. '*Disculpe, compañero*, excuse me, comrade, can you write?'

Charles opened an eye, saw a young boy with thick dark hair squatting in front of him. '*Sí.*'

'Our friend …' He pointed at a heavily bandaged man lying on a stretcher in the corner. Another boy was holding his hand. 'He wants to dictate a message for his wife.'

'Of course.' Charles scrambled up, and made his way over, treading carefully between the men stretched out on the floor. He pulled a notebook and pencil from his back pocket.

'Thank you,' the boy said, and shook his hand. 'Come, Marco,' he said to the boy kneeling by the wounded man. They turned to go.

'You two aren't going out in this weather, surely?' Charles said. 'At least wait till morning.'

'Jordi, he is right,' Marco said. 'It's crazy. Let's wait, then go home.'

Jordi forced open the door. His eyes were gleaming, crazed. 'It's not over yet. We will fight till the end. I'm not going home.'

'Home,' Charles mumbled as he returned to consciousness, the throbbing in his arm making him wince as he tried to move. 'I want to go home … to my butterflies. They are wonderful. God was having a good day when he invented butterflies …' His eyes rolled. 'I think perhaps it's possible to know the truth of the world to be ghastly, and yet still see the wonder in being alive. What do you think, Hugo?'

'This one's alive!' he heard someone call. Then the scramble of feet.

'How will they report this one, eh, Hugo?' he said. 'What to do when you and I have seen so much, and seen the truth, and they tell something different? I hope to God this is the end of double-speak. Imagine a world built on lies, and nonsense ... is that what we have fought for?'

'Wait! I know him,' a man shouted from the road. 'Get a stretcher over here!'

Charles felt someone reaching down to him, dragging something away at his side. Pain, sudden and sickening flooded in from Charles's arm.

'It's time, Charlie,' Capa said.

'Wait ...' Charles mumbled, delirious with pain. 'Hugo ...'

'He's gone, Charlie.' Capa leant over him. 'I've been looking all over for you.'

Charles glanced at Hugo, gulped back a sob. 'I got the shot, Capa.'

Capa looked into Charles's eyes, compassion on his face. 'I think this time, Charlie, you got too close.' He helped the ambulance driver heave him onto the stretcher. 'Let's get you out of here. I'll see you in France.'

'Yes ... France.' Lights danced before Charles's eyes. 'Wait ...'

Capa turned. Charles tried to unhook his camera, and he helped him. 'Would you like me to send the film on to your newspaper?'

'Yes. Then take it. I have no use for it now.'

'I can't ...'

'No, really. I'd like you to have it. It's a Contax. Should have bought a car, like Hugo said.'

'Thank you.' Capa squeezed his right hand.

'Take extraordinary pictures with it. Show the world.'

The medic tucked Charles in on the stretcher, gently covering his bullet-shattered left arm. 'Come on, laddie, let's get you out of here.'

'Wait.' Charles's head rolled to the side as he was lifted away, and he gazed for the last time into Hugo's unseeing eyes.

44

VALENCIA, JANUARY 2002

After walking the length of the village, Emma was out of breath. She dipped her hand in the fountain near the church, cooled her wrists. Doves swooped down into the square, white against the ochre paintwork and the dazzling blue sky, already streaked with the gold of sunset. She sat down on the low white wall, and rummaged through her basket for a bottle of water. She sipped at it, and wiped her lips. From the basket, she took the picture she had just picked up from the framer's. The gilding gleamed in the evening sun as she tore back the bubblewrap. The photographs of Rosa and Jordi were mounted together now, safe behind glass.

'Who were you?' Emma said quietly. She gazed at Jordi's face, so proud and strong, and Rosa. She looked up as an elegantly dressed woman emerged through the church door. The woman turned to talk to a waiter at the café next door, and Emma waved as she recognised Macu. She wore a white silk shirt beneath her winter coat, loose dark wool trousers and loafers. As Emma swung her bag over her shoulder and began to walk towards her, Macu's eyes opened wide in surprise.

'What are you doing out here in the cold? You should

be resting before the baby comes.'

'I'm so bored, sitting around the house.' Emma kissed her. 'I just walked to the framer to pick this up.'

'These are the photographs that you found?'

Emma realised Macu wasn't looking at her, she was looking at the locket. 'Yes. They were under the floorboards, in the house.'

She looked Emma in the eye finally. 'I was hoping I would bump into you. Let's get a drink,' she said, and they walked arm in arm to the café, her cane tapping against the pavement.

They sat at a table near the counter, and Macu sipped at her cognac before reaching for her handbag. She slid an envelope across the table to Emma. 'I wanted you to have this. You'll have to get another frame.'

The sounds of the café, the hiss of the coffee machine, the chatter of the customers seemed to fall away as Emma lifted open the flap. Inside, there was a photograph. She recognised Rosa immediately. 'When was this taken?'

'The autumn of 1937. Not long after Loulou was born.'

'The baby?' Emma gazed at the battered photo. Rosa sat in the garden of the Villa del Valle, a child in her arms.

'Oh, Emma,' Macu said, taking her hand. 'Look at Rosa closely, do you not see?'

Emma squinted, searched the grainy image of Rosa's face. Then she saw it. 'The locket,' she said. Her hand flew to her neck. 'She's wearing my locket.'

Macu touched Emma's hand, her face full of compassion. 'Jordi gave it to your grandmother.'

'To Freya?'

'No, *cariño*, he gave it to Rosa.'

319

45

VALENCIA, FEBRUARY 1939

Oleander, jacaranda, oleander, jacaranda ... Freya thought as she strolled up the hill to the Villa del Valle, running her hand along the railings. Glossy dark leaves waited for the brilliant pink and white flowers to come. The light was falling, and as she reached the wall of the villa, Freya sighed wearily. It was to be her last night in the house, and her bags were packed ready to leave for the Spanish hospital on the border. The thought of all that lay ahead, the desperate plight of the refugees, of grey, rainy London depressed her. She was going to miss Spain, in spite of all she had lived through. She noticed a chink of light coming from Vicente's shop, and heard the sound of male voices talking low and fast. She glanced around the street to check she was alone, and sidled over to the door.

'It's over,' a man said. She could hear the arrogance, the boastfulness in his voice. 'The Reds are fleeing like rats. Soon Madrid and Valencia will fall.'

'And we will be ready to welcome the great Generalissimo.' Freya recognised Vicente's voice. 'Our time is coming, my friend.'

'I'll be fine,' Rosa had said when Freya had told her that afternoon it was time for her to leave. Behind her defiance, Freya sensed her uncertainty. Rosa stroked the child's head as she slept in her arms, a tiny hand grasping the lace at the collar of her blouse. 'Would you mind giving me some water?' Freya took the beaded net from the pitcher, and poured a glass for her. 'Thank you,' she said. She felt Freya watching her. 'Really, I'll be fine.'

Freya looked her in the eye. 'This ...' she indicated the scar on Rosa's cheekbone. 'It will get worse, you know.'

Rosa turned her head to the fire, stared into the flames. 'He hasn't hit me since. He was angry that I disappeared. I told him I was with Macu, helping with her wedding trousseau, but he didn't believe me. He would kill me if he knew I had been with Jordi. Vicente has promised ...' She frowned as Freya snorted with disbelief.

'Vicente is a thug, a bully.'

And now, Freya thought, *it turns out he's Fifth Column. I must warn Rosa.*

'What have we here?' A strong hand shot from the shadows of the alleyway, gripped Freya's arm, dragged her into the shop. 'Look, Vicente, these Red nurses are making house calls now.' The man threw her forward towards the counter, blocked the door.

Vicente had his back to her, arranging his knives on the wooden board. Freya recognised the man at his side from the village. There was a plate of almonds and Manchego cheese on the counter, and the man was chewing, dark eyes watching her. The muscles beneath Vicente's tight white shirt rippled as he turned to Freya, the knives gleaming in the light of the oil lamp. 'Well. I hear you are leaving us?'

'Yes, that's right.' Freya pulled herself up to her full height. Her heart was thundering.

'She was listening outside,' the man said from the doorway.

Vicente clicked his tongue. 'Silly girl. What did you hear?'

'Nothing. I heard nothing. I just came to say goodbye.'

He stepped towards her, slowly. His nostrils flared, sniffing the air. 'You know, when you fight the bulls you learn to smell fear.'

'Fear?' She glared at him. 'Why would I be afraid of you?'

'You should be.' The light caught the blade of a short knife Vicente still had in his hand.

'As I said, I came to say goodbye.'

'You know, only liars tell the same story each time.'

'I didn't hear—'

Vicente pushed her back against the counter, forced his thighs between her legs. She felt his breath, hot against her neck, and then the blade. 'I think maybe before I kill you, we will have some fun.'

The man by the door laughed. She heard the sound of the street door closing, the bolt sliding in.

'Please don't,' Freya begged, struggling. He forced his tongue, thick and bitter with almonds into her mouth. They held her down then, and Freya screwed her eyes closed and tried not to cry.

'Vicente!' Rosa rattled the back door of the shop. 'Vicente!'

He grunted, turned his head to look at the door. Freya felt his weight shift, and she reared up, bit down hard on

322

his ear. Vicente roared, stepped back, clutching the side of his head.

'Let me go,' Freya said, her voice shaking, but firm. She pushed her skirt down. 'Let me go now and I will tell no one. I'll leave, immediately.' She raised her sleeve, wiped the blood from her split lip.

Vicente buttoned his trousers and nodded to the man by the counter to undo the door. Rosa marched into the shop with the child on her hip and looked in disgust at the men. She took Freya's arm and led her to the house. 'I am so sorry. I saw,' she whispered. 'I saw in my head what he did to you.'

'Rosa!' they heard Vicente bellow, not far behind.

'Come with me.' Freya was shaking violently. 'I can't leave you with that … that monster. The Medical Aid convoy is leaving tonight.'

'No,' Rosa said as they ran upstairs.

'But why?'

'Freya …' Rosa shook her head. She locked the bedroom door behind them. 'I have nothing.' She cradled Loulou's head. 'This was Jordi's home, and it is hers.'

'So you would stay here, for the sake of a house?' Freya said incredulously.

'It is more than that. You wouldn't understand. Her life will be different from mine. My child *tiene ángel* – she has grace.' Rosa put her fingertips to the side of her head. 'It is not just a house. I have seen it, seen that the future of our family is here. A woman of our blood will be here, long after that bastard Vicente is gone.'

'How can you possibly trust him?' Her face contorted with disgust. 'He could turn on you at any time, tell them you fought for the Republicans …'

'I know!' Rosa cried. 'I know,' she said, lowering her voice. 'But I must wait for Jordi to come ...' She hesitated. 'I am pregnant again.'

'Oh God, Rosa,' Freya said. She rolled her eyes, and her shoulders sank. 'I wondered why you were dressing like that. Hasn't he noticed?'

'Vicente? No, I am careful – it is like with Loulou, I didn't show much till the end with her either. He said I am getting fat and I agreed with him.'

'Surely you could have taken precautions?'

'Precautions?' Rosa laughed bitterly. 'It is Jordi's child, not Vicente's.' She shifted the child on her hip. 'It's not his, I know this. I tell him I have my period when I am most fertile. For a butcher he is very squeamish about blood if you see what I am saying. Other times he is too drunk to notice – I am careful, tell him he is such a big man he make me bleed a little ...' She turned her pale, tired face to Freya.

'Rosa!' Vicente bellowed up the stairs.

'I'm coming!' she called. Freya followed her as she raced downstairs. In the doorway to the kitchen, she stopped dead. Vicente was on a chair, hanging a photograph of Franco above the fireplace. As he stepped down and turned, he looked at her, his eyes narrowed in defiance. Blood caked his wounded ear.

'There, everything will soon be as it should.' He put his arm around Rosa, pulled her roughly to him. 'Barcelona has already fallen, and we are ready, for when they come. I'd like to say I will miss you ...' he said to Freya.

'But you can't?'

'It's only because you are a friend of Rosa's that I do not kill you now.'

'You can't scare me,' Freya said quietly, walking over to him. Rosa's eyes warned her off. 'I'm a nurse, not a soldier.'

'How do we know that, eh?' He sneered. 'You could be a spy. We have ways of finding out, you know.'

'You'd like that, wouldn't you?' she goaded him. 'Do you get a kick out of hurting women, Vicente? Is it more fun than taunting bulls?'

'Why you ...!' He raised his hand.

'*Señor*!' Macu interrupted. She strode through the door carrying a huge pan of steaming paella from the oven outside. Beyond her, in the garden, the flames leapt, the orange wood gleaming, cracking, smoke rising.

'Vicente,' Rosa said. 'We must eat.'

'To hell with that.' He kicked out, knocked the paella pan to the floor. Saffron-tinted rice scattered, and Macu fell to her knees, cowering.

Vicente turned on Freya. 'Look at you,' he hissed, his face close to hers. 'What man would want you? Skinny whore ...'

'Vicente!' Rosa pulled at his arm. He swung around with his free arm, knocked her against the counter.

'Get off me, woman. You are no better.'

Rosa doubled over, panting.

'You animal!' Freya cried. 'How can you hit her when she is carrying a child—' The words died on her lips as Rosa looked at her frantically.

A sly look crept over Vicente's face. 'Is this true?' He pulled Rosa to him, crushed his lips against hers. 'Ha!' His pelvis thrust against hers. 'Ha!' His chest puffed out, his head slanting back with the arrogance of the matador. 'Now you really are mine,' he murmured. Loulou began to cry.

'I must see to her,' Rosa said.

'Leave her,' Vicente said. 'Leave the little bastard.' He grabbed her wrist as she started to walk away. Rosa flinched.

'You're hurting her!' Freya cried.

'This?' He leered. 'This is just the beginning.' His knuckles were white as he squeezed her arm. 'Every day, you will pay ... and when she is old enough,' his mouth twisted cruelly, 'then she will pay too.'

The bile rose in Freya's mouth. 'No,' she said. 'I won't let you.'

'You?' He pushed Rosa aside. 'What can you do? You are nothing. Get out of here.' He picked up Freya's suitcase, threw it out onto the path. 'I do what I want.' He leered. 'This is my house.'

'It is the del Valle's house – Jordi's as much as yours by right,' Rosa said quietly. She stepped forward, hugged Freya. 'I am sorry. So sorry, for what he did to you. Forget it. Forget all of us.'

'No.' Freya screwed her eyes closed, hugged Rosa tightly. 'I will never forget you, and Loulou. I'll wait for you. There is a hospital at Cerbère, that's where I'll be,' she whispered. 'I'll wait for you.'

46

VALENCIA, JANUARY 2002

Macu settled back in her chair, cupped her empty glass with her hands. Beyond the café windows, the lights of the village square sparkled like jewels in the night. 'That is the last time I saw Freya.'

Emma sat with her head in her hands. 'I had no idea.'

Macu looked tired to Emma. She seemed to be far away in her thoughts. 'She was a good woman, a brave woman. I understand why she spared you all this.'

'Poor, poor Freya. I still don't understand how she and Mum escaped. What happened to Rosa?'

'She ended up in Mexico.'

Emma's eyes widened in surprise. 'Mexico?'

'I have no idea about Freya and your mother's story, you will have to ask her, but in prison I asked Rosa—'

'Prison?' Emma cried.

'*Sí.*' Macu glanced at her watch as they heard Dolores's voice on the street. 'I will tell you another time. My daughter has come to pick me up now.'

'But wait, why was Rosa in Mexico?' Emma's mind whirled with questions as Macu heaved herself to her feet.

'She cared for the refugee children there, taught them

to read and write.' Macu paused. 'She died in a nunnery. She was not old.'

Emma looked down at the photograph of Rosa and Liberty. 'A nunnery? I thought Republicans didn't believe in the Church?'

'The Church supported Franco, and many Republicans were atheists, but it was a big mistake taking on God. Simple, working people like Rosa and me grew up with God's love in our hearts. We could not let go.' Macu looked at Emma. 'When Rosa lost her faith in man, maybe …' She paused. 'Maybe God was all she had to turn to.'

'Mamá!' Dolores bustled through the café. 'Why are you here?' She glanced at Emma and grudgingly nodded.

'I was talking to Emma. I was telling her about her family.'

'I'm sorry,' Emma said as Dolores scowled. 'It's getting late for you.'

'We will talk another time.' Macu patted her hand.

'Please, there's still so much I don't understand. Tell me what happened when Valencia fell.'

'It was a bad time, a very bad time. When Catalonia fell, and Madrid, and our own Valencia …' Macu took a deep breath. 'I remember it like yesterday. It was cold, but sunny. As the tanks rolled into town, I remember the sun glinting on the Nationalists' bayonets. There were thousands running ahead of them, trying to get away.' She paused. 'Those who stayed welcomed Franco. There was no choice.'

'Macu, did you stay?'

'Me? Yes, I stayed. I married Ignacio shortly before the Nationalists arrived.'

'And Jordi, what about him?'

'I don't know. Jordi came back from the front, just as he had promised.' Macu hesitated. 'But Rosa had gone north with the child, your mother, to take her to Freya. I heard Jordi and his brother arguing one night in the kitchen. Vicente said he would make sure he and his comrades got away safely if he left Vicente and Rosa in peace. If not, he would betray them to the Nationalists.'

'I don't understand. I thought Vicente was just a butcher …'

'A butcher? Ha! He was that all right. He was Fifth Column, the enemy within. All along he had been for Franco and the fascists. All along.'

'What happened?'

Dolores took her mother's arm. 'We have to go. Now.'

Macu stepped awkwardly from the table, the chair scraping on the terrazzo floor. 'I can't talk about this now. My daughter, she is bossing me around.'

Emma suddenly realised something. 'Wait! You said you spoke to Rosa in prison?'

Macu spoke quickly, angrily to her daughter. 'Yes,' she said to Emma. 'Yes, I saw Rosa.' She paused. 'I was with her in prison. I will come and see you soon. I will tell you everything I know.' She took Emma's hand. 'I understand why Freya didn't want to talk about this. After what that *hijo de puta* did to her before she left for the border …'

'Mamá!' Dolores cried.

Macu embraced Emma. 'Before we talk more, call Freya. She is a good woman. Do not blame her for hiding all this from you.'

47

CERBERE, MARCH 1939

Still they came. For weeks the refugees had poured down from the Pyrenees to the French border, an endless stream of grey, broken figures materialising like spirits from the mist and the sleet, huddled in blankets, stooped by the cold wind blowing in from the sea. Freya did what she could for them as they passed through. She exchanged bread for the guns that the soldiers dropped at the border. She wrapped blankets around the shoulders of shivering mothers clutching silent, dark-eyed children in their arms. She bathed their cold and bleeding feet with freezing water from the stream. And she waited, day after day for that one precious face among the masses; she waited for Rosa.

As she walked along the corridor of the old chateau they were using as a field hospital, the sole of her shoe flapped. She had gone forty-eight hours without sleep, and the babble of voices seemed muffled to her. She pressed her hand against the cold stone wall, swayed slightly. She hesitated by the hall, searched the crowd in case she had missed her. People clustered around the great stone fireplace, spooning thin soup from tin cups into their mouths. A father held his young child closer to the crackling brush fire, trying to warm her feet, his hand dark and rough against the pale skin of her calf. Everywhere that smell, that awful smell that she thought would never leave her skin, her memory. The smell of blood, and filth, and smoke – the smell of defeat. As she blinked, she felt the world falling away, the corridor shifting around her.

'I hope you're on your way to bed, Nurse?'

Freya turned to the woman who had spoken. 'Yes, Sister ... I ...'

'You're exhausted,' she said. 'You're no good to me in the theatre if you don't get some rest.'

'But ...'

'I know you're worried about your friend, but you can't spend every waking moment looking for her.'

Freya nodded, stumbled to the dormitory. Another nurse was dressing, the paraffin lamp illuminating the cathedral arch of her ribcage as she pulled a white vest over her head. Freya's old gramophone played quietly, a Casals cello suite bubbling from the shadows.

'I hope you don't mind?' the girl said. 'I just couldn't bear the silence.'

Freya collapsed on her bed fully clothed. 'It's funny, isn't it,' she murmured, 'how used you become to the noise.' Her eyes drooped. 'Mimi?'

'Mm?' The girl turned, hairpins in her mouth as she fastened dark tendrils of hair.

'You'll wake me, if you see her? She has a child, a baby with her.'

'Show me the picture of them again.' She took the dog-eared black-and-white photograph of Rosa in the garden with the baby. 'Who is she? A friend?'

'I am going now.' Rosa blinked back tears as she looked at her daughter's face. 'I only brought her to you. I must find Jordi. If he is alive ...'

'No,' Freya pleaded. 'If he's alive, he can take care of himself. Think of your baby ...'

'I am thinking of her. How can I let her think her mother just left her father behind? Negrín demanded that Franco make no reprisals, but we cannot trust that man.'

'I know. But what if they catch you?'

'What more can they do to me?' She breathed in the scent of her baby, pressed her lips to her head. 'Be safe, *cariño*,' she whispered, and handed the child to Freya.

'Please don't. I can't ...'

Rosa shook her head. 'You told me, you would do anything for me. Well, I have nothing.' She pounded her fist in her palm. 'They took everything from me, my home, my life, my love. All I have is my child.'

'Please stay. I've been posted to the maternity hospital at Elne, you'll be safe there, you can help me until the baby comes ...'

'No. Promise me you will take her away from here. Go, soon. Never let them catch her. Take her to England with you.'

'I can't! I'm not married, I ...' Freya could see tears welling in Rosa's defiant eyes

'You must! This is why I came. You told me, you would help us ...'

'I meant both of you – there are boats leaving for Mexico. You could have a new life. You can't just abandon her.'

'Abandon?' she snapped. 'I love this child more than life, so I brought her to you.' Rosa wiped at her cheek.

48

VALENCIA, JANUARY 2002

Luca leant against the kitchen table, his arms folded across his chest. 'How are you?'

'I'm ... I'm fine.' Emma's eyes were red and puffy. 'I just didn't sleep very well last night, after I spoke with Freya.'

'Macu told me she spoke to you. She's worried about you.' Luca waited for her to look at him. He reached out and took her hand. 'I'm worried about you.'

Emma blinked away fresh tears. 'She told me. She told me how Rosa left Mum at the French border with her.' She put her arm around her stomach protectively. 'How could anyone do that? How could you leave your child?'

Luca sighed. 'They were terrible times. Macu can maybe help you understand. She is coming here after the market. She wants to explain everything.' Luca squeezed her hand, and settled back. 'Were you working?' He nodded towards the notebooks scattered across the counter, the chemical formulas and diagrams.

'Just experimenting, trying to distract myself.' Emma pointed at the old recipe book on the table. 'I think it was Rosa's. I thought at first it was a cookbook, but when I started looking through they seem to be instructions.'

'They look like spells,' Luca said, laughing uneasily. 'Maybe she was a healer? These must be recipes for simples. You should ask my grandmother.' He paused at a page with a drawing of a flowering plant. 'I hope you are not making this?'

Emma peered over his shoulder. 'Poison? What plant is that?'

'Oleander.' He stirred the large pestle and mortar. 'This smells wonderful. Is it mint?'

'Massage for tired feet,' Emma said. 'Mine are killing me.'

His face softened. 'It gets better, after the baby comes. I remember Paloma was tired too.' Luca rolled up his sleeves. 'Here, let me try for you.'

Emma blushed. 'No, I couldn't ...'

'It's fine. Macu will be a while.'

Luca guided her to the old armchair by the fire, and pulled over a stool. He draped a towel over his knee and lifted her foot onto his lap. Emma wiggled her foot out of its sheepskin Ugg boot. 'No wellies today?' he said as he eased her foot free.

'No, too cold. Oh, that feels good.' Emma's head fell back against the chair as warm oil dribbled between her toes.

'Soon you will feel like you are walking on air,' he said. 'Does that feel better?' He cupped her foot in his hands. 'It will all be OK, you know.'

'Do you think so?'

'It is a big shock, I imagine?'

'I don't know who I am any more.' Emma frowned as she thought of her conversation with Freya, how upset she had been. 'I feel terrible, I think I took it out on my grandmother … on Freya.' She paused. 'I can't believe she lied to us all these years.'

'Perhaps she was protecting you the best way she knew how?'

'Perhaps.' Emma gazed at him, his head bent in concentration as he massaged her foot, working the sole with his thumbs. 'I could get used to this.'

Marek breezed in. 'I'm sorry, am I interrupting?' He dumped their tea mugs in the sink.

'Not at all, Marek,' Emma said, rolling her head to look at him. 'Luca was just helping me try out a new potion.'

Luca glared at him, wiped his hands self-consciously. 'I should go and check on Macu.'

'If you want the other foot doing later, just ask!' Marek winked at Emma on the way past.

'Show some respect!' Luca snapped.

'Eh, eh …' Marek backed away, hands in the air. Luca glared after him, until they heard the sound of the digger starting up.

'When are they leaving?' Luca said.

'Soon, there's just the garden now.' Emma's head lolled against the chair.

'He treats this house like it's his own.'

She rubbed her foot dry, and slipped it into her boot. 'It's OK, really,' she said, putting her hand on Luca's arm.

He glanced down at her. 'No. It's not. None of it is "OK",' he said, stressing an English accent.

'I'll just get dressed.' She looked at him uncertainly. 'I don't want to keep Macu waiting.'

49

VALENCIA, MARCH 1939

Rosa ran, her breath catching fast in her throat, a sharp pain in her side. The truck had dropped her on the road, and she ran through the orange groves as fast as she could, an electrical storm chasing down from the mountains, lightning forking up into the charged air. The rusted back gate of the Villa del Valle banged in the wind, and she wrenched it open, gasping.

'Thank God, you are here! Vicente is coming!' Macu ran to her, took her weight. 'The Nationalists are having a victory party in town. He expects you to dance.'

'To dance? Is he crazy?'

'It would be good to keep him happy, for now.' Macu looked her in the eye. 'Where have you been?'

'It took longer than I thought to get back. The roads are blocked with refugees heading north. I had to come cross country a lot of the way, hitch lifts where I could.'

'Jordi was here. He has been looking for you.'

'He was here?' Rosa said frantically. 'Where is he? I must go to him.'

Macu shook her head. 'He has gone to the coast.'

She sat Rosa on the stone bench beneath the tower,

and filled a bowl of water from the pump. She washed the blood and umber dust from Rosa's feet, all the time praying to St Vincent under her breath that they would be saved.

'Come.' She dragged Rosa upstairs, undressed her, combed her hair. Rosa's limbs were loose and unresisting, like a rag doll, like a child. 'I heard him arguing with Jordi. He said if you stay with him, he will let Jordi go. Vicente arranged for a boat, out on the beaches near the Albufera. They will take Jordi and Marco to safety.' She tugged at a tangle in Rosa's hair. 'I can't believe Valencia has fallen.'

'We lost, Macu. We lost it all.'

'But Loulou?'

'She is safe. She is with Freya.'

'Good. We will never give up.' Macu took a deep breath, and raised her chin. 'We will fight them from within. I am married to a good man now.' She guided Rosa to the dressing table, her hands on her shoulders. 'Get ready. Vicente will not be happy if you make him wait.' She kissed the top of her head, closed her eyes tight shut. 'Remember what they say – we Spaniards die dancing. Never let him break you, Rosa. Never.'

As the candle guttered, her reflection in the mirror darkened. Rosa watched herself disappear. She twisted the gold tube of lipstick, scraped the last crimson traces out with her thumbnail and rubbed them slowly across her mouth, a split in her nail catching at her lip. She traced the scratch with her tongue as the light died. Her hand shook as she placed the lipstick on the dressing table, the metal clicking on the glass. She thought of the day she had bought it in Madrid – her first and last luxury, how it had made her feel like a woman. *The great Rosa Montez, muse of Lorca, the greatest dancer in all of Andalusia,* she thought. *Who am I now? Nobody. A shadow.* In silhouette against the light from the hall, as she pinned up her hair, she saw the familiar shape of her profile, arms, breasts, the dark sheen of her red dress, but her heart, her soul had gone. She screwed up her eyes, wished herself gone, wished she was with Jordi.

'Rosa!' Macu called from downstairs. 'Come on! You can't be late for him!' Then she heard Macu's footsteps clattering up the staircase. As her friend reached the doorway, she blinked, once, twice. 'Aren't you ready yet?' Her voice was strained with fear. She strode across the room. 'It's time,' she insisted. 'They will be suspicious if you are late. Let me help you.' She picked up the tall tortoiseshell *mantilla* comb, and eased it into Rosa's hair. The teeth dug into her skin, pulled taught against her scalp. In silhouette she looked like a queen. 'Are you all right?' Rosa nodded, afraid that if she spoke, Macu's kindness would bring on the tears that threatened to spill from her eyes. 'Remember, this is for Jordi. You dance for all of us,' she said quietly. She jumped as a car door slammed outside the gate. Rosa listened, her heart beating fast as they heard the gravel path crunch beneath boots marching towards the house.

'Macu!' Vicente yelled from downstairs. 'Where are you?' Rosa stiffened. This was it. There was still time to run. Her fingers instinctively searched for the gold filigree locket around her neck. It had gone.

'Tell him I'm coming.' She squeezed her hand. 'It will be all right.'

'Macu!' he roared. 'Ignacio is waiting for you.'

Alone again, Rosa opened the shutters wide, looked out across the garden she had grown to love. She reached into the pocket of her old black dress, pulled out the photographs of Jordi and her. She had looked at the camera with a passion and defiance she felt no trace of now. This was the only picture she had of him. Jordi smiled, his eyes dancing, full of love. She smoothed it with her thumb, remembered how it had felt to run her fingers through the warm dark curls that hung down to his shoulders the last time she saw him, remembered how his eyelashes had brushed her jaw as he kissed her neck. *I love you*, she thought. *I will always love you.* She did not know what to do with the photographs now they were not safely in the locket. Vicente would destroy them. She crouched down, searching for a crack in the floorboards. She remembered the loose board by the bed in her room, and ran through the house silently. She stooped by the side of the bed and slipped them through, letting them fall softly into the darkness. She could rescue them later.

At the sound of her heels, clicking lightly on the staircase, Vicente turned. His irritation thawed as he walked towards her, desire pumping through his veins, molten and unstoppable. 'Rosa, Rosa ...' he whispered, caressing the gentle swell of her stomach through the full red skirt of the dress. 'So my little dove has flown home. You got here just in time. The General has sent a car,' he said proudly. 'Where have you been this time? It's been days.'

'None of your business.'

'I think you took the child to the English woman, didn't

you, Rosa? Who cares. Soon we will have our own child.'
He stepped back. 'Well? What do you think?' His hand
swept over his new uniform.

'You look like a fascist pig.'

He wavered, no longer the hero, just the awkward
elder son of a Valencian landowner. But like all predators
he smelt fear, and as he saw her eyes flicker uncertainly,
his snapped back hungrily to hers. He was in charge now.
His firm hand at the base of her spine guided her to the
door where Macu waited, his fingers spreading, feeling
the roll of her hip as she walked. The women exchanged
a last look, full of everything they had not said, all the
dreams that had come to nothing. Rosa lifted her chin,
and walked on into the night.

As they drove through the darkness towards the city,
Rosa wondered, *Is this how it feels when you are on your
last journey?* She thought of all the men who had 'taken
a walk' this way. They passed houses dark in the night
where she was used to seeing warm light spilling out,
the sound of music, voices. All gone. The people fled, or
disappeared. The closer they came to the city, the stronger
the smell of burning, of carnage.

'Close the window, Rosa, it's not—'

'No. I want to remember this.'

At the first checkpoint, the car slowed. Soldiers checked
their papers, scanned the passengers. Vicente leant over.
'Hurry up,' he barked. 'Move these people out of the way.
The General is expecting us.' Rosa saw the young soldier's
eyes open in surprise.

'Yes, sir.'

Rosa touched the cool glass as they passed streams

of people pale with exhaustion and fear. Her heart beat harder – what if she saw him among them? What if Jordi hadn't made it to the coast in time?

The beautiful blue domes of the city gleamed in the half light as they always had, the Turia river flowed on. But all around them, everything had changed. As they joined a convoy of military vehicles, Rosa saw a man being dragged from an apartment building, his wife clinging, screaming, to his leg. Soldiers bundled her back inside the courtyard, pushed back terrified children who hovered in the shadows of the doorway. As they drove by, Rosa craned her head, caught the woman's cries of 'No, no, no!', saw a dark-uniformed soldier raise the butt of his rifle and bring it crashing down on the side of the man's head. He crumpled to the gutter. Rosa swore under her breath.

'This is just the beginning,' Vicente said. 'They are going to rout out the rot.'

'Are you threatening me?'

'You, my dear?' He cupped her face. 'No. You are mine. And Macu? Well, if your little friend keeps her head down then she will be safe with de Santangel too.' He patted his pocket, pulled out a leather case. 'Can't you drive any faster?' he said irritably to the driver as he lit a cigar.

'I'm sorry.' The driver indicated the trucks and tanks ahead.

He checked his watch. 'We will walk from here. Pull over.'

'Are you sure it is safe, sir?'

'Are you questioning me?'

'No, sir.' The driver looked straight ahead as he drove slowly to the side of the road.

Vicente walked around to Rosa's door. As he checked the street, she gazed at the holster at his waist. *I could shoot him*, part of her thought. She imagined them walking the back streets to the palace, turning, kissing him, falling into the shadows of one of the patios – and then, a single shot. She saw herself running barefoot through the streets, taking a simple cotton shift from a washing line. She imagined walking through the night, hiding from patrols, then reaching the coast at dawn just as the boats arrived, racing down the beach to Jordi, embracing, laughing in the surf. Vicente opened the door, and she blinked, stepped mechanically from the car. She glanced around: four soldiers stepped out from a car behind them. Of course, they had an escort.

Glancing down the street, Vicente pulled his pistol ostentatiously from its holster, and took her arm. He guided her along the familiar back streets and alleyways to the Palacio del Marqués de Dos Aguas. At this time of night, she thought, the cafés should be open, the children playing on the street with the little dogs racing and yapping as the parents sit talking under the stars, eating tapas and drinking. But the streets were eerily silent. The smell of burning hung heavily on the air. Shops and cafés were shuttered. All Rosa heard was the sound of the soldiers marching behind her, and her own breath catching in her throat.

'Is he safe?' she said quietly.

'Not now ...'

She yanked her arm from his. 'Is Jordi safe?'

His eyes hardened. 'I made a deal, didn't I?'

'If I ever find out you betrayed him ...'

'You'll what?'

Rosa stumbled deliberately, bent down to check her shoe. Slowly he squatted down beside her, the snout of his pistol grazing the cobbles. Without looking at him, she said quietly, 'I will make you pay.' She raised her eyes to his. 'You have me now. You have my word. I am buying his freedom with my body. But you will never, ever have my soul.'

Vicente clasped her wrist, hard. 'Stupid woman.' He leant close to her. She felt his hot breath on her ear, smelt the scent of stale tobacco. 'It's not your soul, or your heart, or your love – whatever it is that you prize so highly – that I've ever been interested in.' She struggled but he held her firm. 'Tonight, and every night, you will be in my bed. I will make you forget my brother ever existed.' Her stomach lurched with nausea as his gold teeth caught at her earlobe, his tongue traced the dip against her neck. 'I have you. And you have our child.' He released her, and she shivered as she stepped away.

'Are you cold?' he said, loud enough for the soldiers to hear.

She glanced back at them, shook her head. As they walked on, they passed a courtyard lit with flares. The heavy double doors were open and Rosa glimpsed Nationalist soldiers laughing and smoking around a fire, and beyond them, a body lay, bare and grimy feet emerging from the shadows of a wall scarred with bullet holes. She swallowed hard as Vicente slipped his arm around her waist, guided her to the street.

'You're a sensible woman, Rosa. You may think you are doing this for love, but my brother was a fool, a young fool. You're smarter than him. You're a survivor.'

'No.' She shook her head.

345

'Yes you are.' His fingers dug into her hip bone as he pulled her closer. 'It's a new era, Rosa, and it pays to be on the winning side.' His arm swept out across the city. 'All of this will be ours. Our great city will rise again, and this time we will be in charge. We will have status, riches.'

Rosa gazed up at the elaborate carvings of the palace door, the twisting bodies and writhing plasterwork like the icing on a demented wedding cake. Her stomach tightened with fear.

'What's this, del Valle?' An officer laughed. 'No car?'

'It's a beautiful evening for a stroll with my wife.'

'Your wife?' He eyed her with a mixture of curiosity and lust. 'Congratulations. Where have you kept this beauty hidden?' He bowed low, kissed her hand.

'A wise man keeps his treasure at home,' Vicente said.

Rosa blinked as the doors swung open and they left the dark street behind. The light was dazzling, glittering from chandeliers, sparkling in the fountain as they crossed the tiled courtyard. She lifted the hem of her gown and they swept up the staircase to the state rooms, passing soldier after soldier.

'The General is in the *fumoir*,' the soldier said, leading them through to a side room. 'Come, pay your respects.' Rosa heard the sound of male voices, harsh laughter drifting out on the cigar smoke. She raised the back of her hands to her lips, inhaled the fresh scent of orange blossom.

'Say nothing unless you are spoken to,' Vicente hissed as the noise swelled. The room made Rosa think of a chess set; everything was black and white – the tiled floor, the ebony furniture inlaid with ivory, the muted uniforms of the soldiers. There at the heart of the room sat the conquering General holding court. He glanced over as Vicente guided Rosa towards him.

'General.' The officer clicked his heels. 'May I introduce Vicente del Valle, and his wife. They were most helpful with the war effort from behind the lines.'

Rosa flinched. It was unbearable to be included in Vicente's double-dealing.

The General eyed her as he flicked ash from his cigar into a marble ashtray at his side. 'I was just wondering what had happened to our dancer.'

Rosa glared at the man. She could see him coolly assessing her. He could tell, she knew it. He could tell she was descended from gypsies, that she was a Republican. She imagined them dragging Jordi from a side room, throwing him down on the floor before her, bloodied and broken. She saw herself clinging to him, kissing his dear face, unafraid of dying as long as they were together. Rosa raised her chin defiantly.

'My wife is a famous dancer, General.' Vicente bowed low. 'Of course Rosa would be delighted to dance for you.'

'I must congratulate you, del Valle. It looks like you have tamed a wild one here. Very beautiful, but perhaps you should clip her wings? Pull her claws?' The men around him laughed indulgently. Rosa felt their ambition and desire ebb around her like black oil on water.

'Thank you, General.' Vicente flushed with pleasure.

The General slowly exhaled a plume of grey smoke. 'You will dance for us tonight.'

'I will dance,' Rosa said, 'but for Spain.'

The General's eyes narrowed at the slight. Vicente's palms grew clammy with sweat. It was over before it had begun. He could have risen through the ranks, earned untold riches – but this, he could tell from the expression on the men's faces, this would never be forgotten. They would be lucky if they were not soon 'taken for a ride'. Rosa swept out to the ballroom where the women already sat at chairs arranged around the dance floor.

As she strode through the room, silence fell. Her heels clicked on the wooden floor. She scanned the faces, recognised many of them. Landowners' wives, bankers' wives, women she knew from the church and the market. Ordinary local women, showing their true colours now, she thought. Or were they just afraid, like everyone else? Their gazes followed her, some sad and fearful, others jealous and vicious, snapping at her as she walked. They were the ones who would betray their neighbours, even incriminate the innocent for old debts or slights. Then there, at the edge of the circle, she saw Macu. Don Ignacio de Santangel was helping her settle into a chair. He had not collaborated with the General, she knew, not joined the Nationalists like Vicente, but he had kept his head down and enough of his wealth would survive. The men and soldiers filed in behind Rosa like a black stream, flowing in to join the women until the room was full. As the General took his seat, Rosa noticed Vicente had been taken aside, guided to a chair further away. *Good*, she thought, *it has begun*. She glanced at Vicente's wounded, furious face, and knew she would be punished that night. *Do what you will. I am stronger than you. You will never break me.*

Rosa paced, centre stage, eyes closed, barely listening as someone introduced her, told the crowd that there would be an addition to the programme tonight. Beneath her, she could hear a guitarist tuning up. The notes drifted to her through vents in the ballroom floor, from a hidden room below. In decades past an orchestra would have been secreted down there, playing for the dancers above. *Who is playing?* she wondered. *One of ours, no doubt. Perhaps he had bought his life, or his family's by agreeing to perform like a circus animal for the great General too?* Each note rose up in her like a fragile bubble, surging through her legs, her torso, her arms, her neck, as she rolled her head, loosening up, freeing her spirit. She paced like a caged animal, her blood quickening to the vibrations of the notes, sensed the eyes in the darkness watching her. As the guitarist stopped tuning up, she stood still, waiting. Breathing. Her eyes rolled back, lips parted, and with a stamp of her foot it began.

She recognised the singer immediately. The woman's husband had been taken the moment the troops rolled into town. The keening pain of the woman's voice gave Rosa's movements edge and precision. *Duende* rose from the bowels of the earth, forked like electricity through the notes, the voice, her limbs. As the music flowed, she lost herself. It was always like this. This was a dance that was in her blood, her bones. She had performed so many times, in the caves with her family. She had danced in the shadow of the Alhambra for Lorca. Her hand snaked above her like vines. She remembered him reciting, an incantation, how even the wind seemed green, how the branches came alive. Her feet pounded like thunder, her dress whipping through the air. She danced as she had for Picasso in the Albaicin, as she had for Jordi, in the firelight, on their last night together in the ruins at Sagunto. There she had felt the warmth of the ancient stones answer the

349

life in her limbs. That had been her greatest dance, she knew, her passion, her love, drawing the spirits of the earth, the ghosts from the ruins. She would never dance like that again for anyone, and this, tonight, was only an echo of that, an aftershock. This would be her last dance.

The music gathered pace now. Rosa sensed the pain, the passion in the melody. She wondered if they could hear her feet dancing above them, the answering staccato stamps and beats. As she turned, she fixed first the General, then Vicente with her eyes. They would never take her spirit. She danced for the man and the country she loved.

On and on, faster and faster the music and dance welled up. Her limbs melted into the air. She was not there. She saw Jordi, running for the coast. They were behind him now. Vicente had betrayed his brother, she was sure of it. The dogs and soldiers were close by. She saw Jordi and Marco racing through the rice fields to an old Barraca farmhouse, hiding out in the steeply pitched roof as the farmer's wife said, 'No, I haven't seen anyone here.' She saw them, lying on the dusty floorboards, gazing down at the soldiers as they dragged the woman outside.

'We can't let them take her,' she heard Jordi whisper to his friend.

'They'll kill her anyway.' She saw Marco shake his head. 'Everyone knows the family are anarchists.'

She saw Jordi check his pistol. 'Would you rather die like a hero or live like a coward?'

'If they just shot me, I wouldn't mind so much,' she heard Marco reply. 'I just don't want to be taken alive.'

'Come on then.' Jordi embraced his friend. 'What are we waiting for?'

350

The music was in her now, racing and swirling in her blood. Somewhere in the room, she was aware of cries – 'Olé! Olé!' – the clapping of hands. But she was not there. She was flying above the earth now, running like the wind behind Jordi, willing him on to the sea. The bullets were flying with her, past her, as she tried to shield him. Marco fell. Jordi ran back.

'Go,' Marco cried, clamping his hand to his side, blood seeping through his fingers to the sand.

'No! I'll not leave you.' Rosa watched Jordi glance up, catch sight of a small fishing boat on the horizon. 'I'll carry you.'

Marco cried out as Jordi tried to lift him. 'Leave me!' There were shouts nearby. 'But leave your pistol too. Go, now,' he whispered as Rosa saw Jordi press the gun into his hand.

Rosa's feet beat an impossible rhythm, staccato, quick-fire, raining down like sparks as the music reached its crescendo. In the heat and the fire, she saw Marco lift the pistol to his temple. Crack, went the heel of her shoe. She was running again then, running at Jordi's side to the boat.

'*We are Spaniards,*' he had said to her when they were last together. '*Life is a tragedy to us.*' They had shared one last, desperate kiss. '*Salud, Rosa!*' he'd cried. '*We despise death, our love defies it!*' Faster and faster, she danced on, the dance of her life, her thundering feet, one, two beats more and it stopped, suddenly. His arms flung into the air. She raised hers as he raised his, twisting above her. She felt herself losing him. As he fell, she fell, and the spirit drained from her. She lay panting on the floor as the applause thundered around her. She closed her eyes tight and searched for him. Was he diving? Swimming to the boat she had seen on the horizon? Had he outrun them? She breathed hard, lights flashing behind her eyes as she came back to herself. Or had they shot him down? Were his arms flung upwards to heaven as he died, or in victory as he escaped to freedom? As she lay still in the pool of light from the chandelier above her, her red dress spilled out around her. The applause raged on, and her body sank against the floor, willing it to swallow her up. 'Jordi,' she murmured, her ribs pressed down, her knee pushed hard against her stomach. And in response, a tiny foot pressed back, flexed, kicked out to freedom.

50

VALENCIA, JANUARY 2002

Emma struggled into a loose grey jumper, sprayed 'Chérie Farouche' on her brush. Just as she ran it through her hair, her mobile rang.

'Freya?' Her face set hard.

'Em, darling.' Emma could hear the panic in her voice. 'I saw your message. Are you all right? Is the baby all right?'

'No, I'm not all right,' she said. 'How could I be after our conversation?' she cried out. 'Of all the people I thought I could trust ...'

'Emma, please.'

'I can't believe it's all a lie. You lied to me! Who am I, Freya? Who am I?'

'Darling, please calm down. Let me explain ...'

'No. No more lies.' Emma heard voices downstairs. 'I'm going to talk to Macu. I'm going to find out what happened to Rosa. Did you know that she was in prison?'

'Prison? Oh God, no.' Freya's voice shook. 'I was always afraid of that.'

'I have so many questions just running around and around in my mind.' Emma's chest was tight, and she was breathing heavily as she staggered downstairs. 'How did you and Mum get home, to England?'

'I'd told Rosa where I would be, at Cerbère, and I'd managed to get a post at a maternity unit they had set up in an old mansion in Elne. I hoped she'd come with me there.' She paused. 'But when she went back for Jordi, I stayed at the border, and managed to track down Charles. It was chaos. They were machine-gunning the refugees, the bastards. That's how Hugo was killed, and Charles lost his arm. By the time they reached the medical centre with him, gangrene had set in. Poor Charles. Eventually, once he was strong enough to travel, we left together.'

'With Mum?'

'Yes.'

'And nobody stopped you? You just took a child from Spain to England, and raised her as your daughter?'

Freya hesitated. 'It wasn't quite as simple as that.'

'How could Rosa just abandon Mum?'

Freya sighed. 'I've never understood it myself, how anyone could give up their child. She said she had no choice, but she did. She chose Jordi.'

'She knew Mum would be safe with you.'

'Perhaps. Those militiawomen were incredibly strong. I remember one girl saying to me she would kill her own child rather than be unable to fight at her husband's side.'

Emma glanced up as she heard Luca calling. 'I've got to go.'

'Emma, please understand, I had my reasons …' She paused. 'Very good reasons for hiding the truth. I was only trying to protect Liberty, and you.'

'Did Mum know?'

'Not until very near the end.' Freya's voice was thick

354

with emotion. 'She forced it out of me finally.'

'Is that why she came to Spain? Is that why she bought this house?'

'Yes. She made me promise that I would tell you, eventually. It never seemed like the right time, and now …' She sighed. 'It's funny. Rosa said to me once that her female descendents would live in the Villa del Valle, and she was right. I think Liberty wanted to give you something she felt she never had.'

Roots and wings; Emma thought of her mother's words. She grimaced as her stomach hardened with a contraction. 'I have to go. I'll speak to you later.'

'Love you, Em. You will take care—' Freya's words cut off as Emma hung up.

'Emma!' Luca yelled from the kitchen.

'I'm coming.' She winced, her hand against her side. 'What on earth's the matter?'

'You need to come and see this.'

Luca led her through the kitchen, and pointed at the pit Marek was digging for the pool in the garden.

'*O mój Boże* …' Marek said. 'My God!' He yanked the lever back on the digger and stopped the engine. 'Borys!' He yelled.

'What is it?' Borys ambled around the side of the house carrying boxes of deep blue tesserae ready for tiling the pool.

Marek scrambled up onto the digger scoop, and dug his hand into the ochre earth. Borys put down the boxes with a grunt, dust flaring at their base. He turned to Marek muttering under his breath in Polish. His mouth fell open, and he crossed himself. Silhouetted against the sunlight,

Marek was holding up a skull – a human skull. He turned towards the house, and saw Emma standing with Luca at the door, staring at him. Marek lifted the skull to show them, the morning sun glinting on its gold teeth.

51

VALENCIA, APRIL 1939

'Where have you been? He has gone mad!' Macu wrung her hands. The oil lamp in the kitchen swung in the breeze as the back door banged open, light swinging around the shadows. Rosa calmly placed a woven basket full of glossy green leaves on the kitchen table, and the wind rolling down from the mountains lifted her hair.

'He has sealed up Jordi's room!' Macu cried. 'All your things, your dresses, your perfume, they are all still inside.'

Rosa thought of the photographs hidden beneath the floorboards in her bedroom. At least they were safe. *Together forever*, she thought. She dragged the heavy black cauldron from the fire, and checked the boiling water.

'I don't need them,' she said quietly, shovelling in the leaves.

'It's like he's trying to wipe out his brother entirely. It's like Jordi never existed.'

'He is guilty,' Rosa said as she wiped down the pestle and mortar.

'Guilty? Who is guilty?' Vicente said, barging into the kitchen. He was stripped to the waist, his muscular, scarred body gleaming with sweat. He marched over to Rosa. 'Where have you been?'

'Gathering food and snails for dinner, Vicente.' When she looked at him, her eyes were black pools. 'I am cooking your favourite.' She pointed at the skinned rabbit in her basket.

'Good.' He grunted, and strode outside. They could hear him shovelling plaster into a bucket. When he walked through, rain slicked his face, and he left muddy footprints through the house.

'Aren't you going to say anything?' Macu whispered to her.

Rosa shook her head as she pounded the leaves. 'All in good time.'

Macu checked the paella, testing the crispy layer of *socarrat* at the bottom of the pan. She stepped back from the fire. 'It is ready,' she said. 'Shall I call him?'

'Yes.' Rosa tipped most of a bottle of cognac down the drain, then placed it on the table. She was breathing slowly, though her heart leapt in her chest. She listened to the dull thump of his feet across the landing above her head, followed his path as he walked down the wooden stairs. Rosa poured herself a small glass of cognac, and sat down to wait for him.

'About time.' Vicente strode through the kitchen. He washed his hands in the basin of water at the sink, ran them over his sweating face.

'Macu, would you mind serving my husband?' Rosa said calmly. Macu scraped the paella pan with a large metal spoon, filled a bowl with the steaming rice. He started to eat without acknowledging her.

Rosa sipped her drink. 'Vicente?'

'Nngh?' he grunted, without looking up from his food.

'Why have you sealed Jordi's room?'

'Jordi?' Vicente sucked a snail, tossed the empty shell aside. 'He has no use of a bed where he is now.'

Rosa's face was pale as she looked at him. 'What do you mean?'

'Jordi is gone.' Rice clung to his glistening lips as a cruel smile formed. 'Haven't you heard? The Republicans surrendered formally at eleven o'clock this morning. Franco is victorious. This is all mine now.'

'You said you would help him. You said you would make sure he reached the boats.'

Vicente laughed. 'The docks are crowded with fifty thousand people trying to escape. Maybe he was lucky, maybe he wasn't.'

'Vicente.' Her voice was low, her fists clenched under the table. 'What have you heard?'

He shrugged, his face full of conceit. 'A little bird told me they were running for the boats off the beaches near the Albufera.' He lunged at the bottle, poured out what was left. 'There are thousands and thousands,' he repeated, draining his glass, 'jamming the coast like rats. Marco was shot.'

'Oh God, no,' Macu said, her hand on her face.

'And Jordi?' He pulled a face. 'Who knows … What do you think? The two of them against the great Generalissimo's troops.' He turned on his wife, his face colouring with anger again. 'Who cares, anyway? That is the past. This is the future, you, and me.' He pushed back his chair, strode around to her. Vicente placed his hand on her stomach. 'Our child.'

Rosa glanced at Macu. She saw her fighting to compose herself. 'Of course, Vicente,' she said calmly.

'Jordi got what he deserved. Never forget I could have the troops here like that, if I wanted.' He clicked his fingers in Macu's face.

'Why don't you then?' she said.

'Maybe a few of your friends got away but most are being rounded up for the prisons and the bullrings.' He mimed cocking a gun, pointed his index finger at Macu. 'You? You're not worth the effort it would take me to go into town.' He waved his hand, dismissing her. 'Goodbye and good riddance to you. This is a great day. The flag of Old Spain flies again from our balcony.' He pointed his glass at Rosa. 'And you, my love, my little dove, are my wife again. No more of this "*mi compañero*" nonsense.'

'Let me get you some more cognac.' Rosa dragged Macu into the pantry, and closed the door.

'How can you stay here? The man is an animal! The things he has done to Jordi, and Freya, and me ...' Macu was shaking with emotion, trying hard to control herself. Rosa calmly unlocked the corner cabinet and sorted through the glass bottles, selecting a blue one. 'Rosa, what is that?'

'Just a little sedative. I don't want him to touch me tonight.'

'I wish I'd had some when he came for me.'

Rosa turned to the counter, and steadied herself. When she looked up, her eyes were dark and determined. 'Macu,' she said, taking her old friend's hand. 'I am sorry. If I had known ...'

Macu's face fell. 'It is nothing. Compared to what he

does to you, it is nothing. But you can't let him get away with this.'

'I have no intention of doing that,' Rosa said steadily. 'He threatened my daughter, he betrayed the man I loved, his brother, and …' she said, uncorking a bottle of cognac, 'he hangs a picture of that man, that man in my kitchen! Fascist pig!' A stream of expletives fell like a curse as she poured away some of the cognac. 'Enough,' she said. Macu watched in silence as Rosa picked up the dark blue bottle and turned it to the light. She came and stood at her side. 'For what he has done to me, to Freya, to you, to Jordi, he will pay. Will the world be a better or worse place for one less fascist?' She tipped the entire contents of the bottle into the cognac. She took the cloth from the white bowl she had left steeping on the side, ladled in the mixture through a funnel.

'Rosa, what is that?'

'No, don't let it touch you. It is the leaves I cooked earlier. Oleander,' she said simply. 'A few drops would kill most men. For Vicente, I use more.'

'I can't let you do this,' Macu said quietly.

'It's nothing to do with you,' Rosa said. 'This is my decision. Vicente will never stop, he will never let me go.' She clenched her fist. 'You go now, if you want. The sooner you go, the safer you will be. It won't be long until the troops come to search the village. It is safer if you are at home, with Ignacio. You must never come back, never see me again.'

'No.' Macu hugged her tightly. 'I will stay. I will help you.'

Vicente's head lurched up as Rosa carried the bottle over to him, the firelight gleaming through the dark amber liquid. '*Joder*! You took your time.' He thumped the table, threw down the newspaper.

Rosa looked down at the headline: '*La conquista de Valencia y Alicante ha puesto definitivo termino la peste roja*'. *Peste roja*, she thought. *Red plague – exterminated.*

'Well, what are you waiting for, eh?' He shoved his empty glass towards her. In the bloodshot eyes, the flaccid face, Rosa glimpsed what he would become, how his looks would desert him as his true character etched itself on his face. She filled his glass, and placed the bottle on the counter.

Rosa dished out more of the paella into the earthenware bowl and carried it to him. He drunkenly scooped mouth after mouthful. Rosa knitted quietly in the lamplight as he ate. He struggled to his feet, staggered across the kitchen like a bull at the end of a long fight, ribboned *banderillas* streaming from its bleeding flanks. He refilled his glass, sat down, and knocked back the drink. As his eyes drooped, Rosa put down her knitting, and waited.

The minutes ticked by, only the crack and hiss of the fire, and the thunder rolling overhead breaking the silence. Macu finally crept across to the table. 'Rosa?' she whispered. 'Is he …?'

'He should be,' Rosa said. Her face was set hard with bitterness. They heard rain begin to fall harder, drumming down on the roof of the house.

'Is he breathing?' Macu tiptoed towards him. 'I'll check.' She stepped forward, her hand reaching to touch his neck. Just as she reached him, Vicente snorted, reeled forwards. The women cried out as he stumbled to his feet.

'What have you done to me?' He clutched his stomach, grimacing. His words were thick and heavy. 'You witches!

I curse you!' Rosa backed away, but he grabbed Macu by the neck. The storm raged outside, the wind screaming through the garden, through the open door. Macu began to choke, her feet dangling above the floor. She clawed frantically at his huge hand.

'Help!' she rasped. 'I can't—'

Rosa tried to drag him off her, but Vicente's hands were clamped tight, his muscles contorted, bulging in his back. She wheeled around, seized the heavy stone mortar in her hands, raised it high, and brought it crashing down on the side of his head. He released Macu with a gasp, and by the time he hit the floor, dark blood was flowing from his temple into the shadows. '*Hijo de puta.*' She spat on him. 'You son of a bitch.'

The women stood in silence above him, shaking, catching their breath. They both jumped as lightning cracked across the sky. 'You must go,' Rosa said, turning to Macu.

The girl shook her head. 'No, I will stay. You are my friend, for good or bad.' She took Rosa's hand. 'I'll stay, I'll help you.' She looked down at Vicente. 'What do we do with him?' she said finally.

Rosa looked out at the dark garden. The lightning illuminated the pile of plaster where Vicente had been working, the shovel stuck into the earth. 'First we dig a hole,' she said. 'I will go and find another shovel in the shed.' She gathered up the cookbook, Lorca's book of poetry and the heavy mortar, and staggered out into the garden with them, the rain streaming down her face. She shouldered open the storeroom and heaved the mortar and pestle onto the top shelf. As she crossed the garden, she pulled the gold ring from her finger, and tossed it into

363

the well. She gazed down into the dark water, and the shimmering image of a woman she no longer recognised looked back. The ring fell, in slow motion, turning and gleaming, down to the smooth rocks and the silence below. *It is like I was never here*, she thought.

Macu ran out to join her, and the two women dug the ochre earth, the storm raging around them. 'It's taking too long!' Macu cried. After half an hour, the pit was only a few feet deep. 'He is too big!'

Rosa looked back into the kitchen, saw Vicente's twisted body lying on the floor. She glanced at the pile of lime plaster beneath the awning of the shed, waiting to finish the wall. 'No. It will be fine. I can do this.' She put down the shovel. 'Macu, help me drag him to the shop. I can take care of it from there.'

'The shop?' Macu grimaced. 'Rosa, what are you going to do?'

Rosa marched up the path to the kitchen. 'I am going to tidy up. By the time I have finished, you would never know we have been here.' She thought again of the photographs, beneath the floor upstairs. 'The house will go to sleep for a long, long, time, like in a fairy tale.' The girls grabbed a leg each, and heaved Vicente out of the kitchen, his head bumping down the stone step. His arms dragged behind him as they pulled him through the orange trees, across the grass slick with cold rain.

Rosa caught her breath as she opened up the back door to the shop. She turned to Macu. 'I can manage now. I want you to go.' Lightning cracked the sky again, and Macu glanced into the dark room, saw the rows of silver knives illuminated, gleaming darkly. Rosa took her shoulders. 'Macu, forget all about me. Forget all of this.'

'I can't. You are my friend.'

Rosa hugged her, felt her shaking in her arms. 'Go, and make a good life with Ignacio. You can have everything, Macu – a home, a life, a family.' She squeezed her tightly. 'Be safe.' She kissed her on both cheeks. 'Forget all of this. Forget me.'

Rosa heard Macu's feet running away through the garden, waited until she heard the back gate swing closed. She looked back at the house, the wind blowing through the orange trees. Bile rose up in her throat as she thought of what she had to do, and her fingers trembled, reaching across the cold tiles of the counter. 'It's time, Vicente,' she said quietly. 'It's time.'

52

VALENCIA, JANUARY 2002

'Not those ones, these,' Macu said, pointing towards the white lilies at the back of Aziz's display.

'*Sí, Señora.*' Aziz eased the stems from the steel bucket, heads nodding in the breeze. The heady scent of incense licked the air from their white tongue-like petals.

'*Buenos días*, Macu,' Emma said, stopping to kiss her cheeks. 'Those are beautiful, Aziz. Are they for something special?'

'I'm taking them to the cemetery for my Ignacio,' Macu said.

'Morning,' Fidel said. He carried a wooden crate of fresh vegetables into the shop. 'I have your order here. My daughter asked me to drop it by for you.'

'Thank you. What do I owe you?' Emma reached for her wallet.

Fidel patted her hand. 'Nothing. It's a pleasure. You need all the fresh fruit and vegetables you can eat. It is good for the baby.'

'Are you all right?' Macu said. 'You are very pale.'

'I'm fine.' Emma leant against the counter. 'I've just …

I've had a bit of a shock. They've unearthed a skeleton in the back garden.'

'A skeleton?' Macu staggered back.

'It's the strangest thing – it has gold teeth.'

'I tell you, this house has *mala sombra* – bad energy,' Aziz said as he handed Macu the bouquet of flowers.

'Rubbish,' Emma said. The sun was shining, but she felt suddenly cold. 'Luca's called the police. I think they are going to bring an undertaker to deal with the remains.'

'Come,' Macu said. 'It will be a while until they are here. We need to talk.' She took Emma's arm. 'Let's walk to the cemetery together. You too, Fidel.'

They ambled along the dusty pavement, in silence except for the tap of Macu's walking stick. Fidel pushed open the squeaking iron gates of the cemetery and ushered the women inside. Emma pulled down her sunglasses against the glare of the white walls, the fierce light glinting off the polished headstones and gilt vases. On each neatly tended grave there were fresh flowers. *I can see why Aziz is doing well*, she thought, panting as her stomach contracted.

Macu walked along the gravel path, and stopped at a large marble tomb. 'Can you help me?' she asked Emma, pointing to the wilting carnations in the vase at its base. Emma leant down awkwardly, emptied the vase. She looked at the list of names inscribed in the marble. Beneath Ignacio's, she saw: *'Alejandra Ramirez Villanueva 1971–1999'*. *She was the same age as me, whoever she was*, Emma realised. Beneath that, there was a simple *'Xavier de Santangel Ramirez 1999'*.

'Here,' Fidel said, and passed her a penknife to trim the base of the lilies.

'It's lovely here,' Emma said. 'Very peaceful.'

'I like to come here each week and talk to Ignacio.' Macu stepped back and sat on the stone bench against the wall with Fidel. She let her head rest back and raised her face to the sun. 'So, ask me whatever you want.'

Emma slid the last of the lilies into the vase, and settled down on the bench beside them. 'Why will no one tell me the truth? Please tell me what happened here, after the war, I mean.'

'They were very bad times,' Macu said quietly. 'I was lucky. The Santangels, they were a big family, they protected me. I tried to help Rosa, but when she came back after leaving your mother with Freya …'

'She was trying to reach Jordi? What happened to him?'

'Nobody knows. So many people disappeared.'

'And Rosa?'

'She was rounded up with the people at the docks. She was sent to prison.' Macu paused. 'There were rescue vessels in the harbour, some of them even took women and children on board. But those bastards broke their agreement. The Nationalists said they would give safe passage to the refugees, but Franco's men made every last one of the refugees disembark. It was a trap, a hideous trap. They caught them like butterflies in a net.' Macu's breath shuddered. 'There were men, brave men like Jordi and Marco, embracing on the docks and shooting each other's brains out rather than fall into fascist hands. Rosa told me she saw men do it, saying, "On three: *uno, dos, tres* …" Boom. Can you imagine? What a way to die.'

'Macu,' Fidel said, 'maybe we should wait. It is not good for Emma, for the baby.'

'No. Emma wants to know. If she is to make a new

368

life here, she must know the truth about our families.'
She closed her eyes. 'The people who had no bullets to
kill themselves with were herded into the bullrings and
prisons. There was no food, nothing for the children,
only the clothes on their backs.'

'They took the women and children too?' Emma said.

Fidel nodded. 'Just being the wife or girlfriend of a Red
after the war was enough. After Barcelona and Valencia
fell, they rounded up thousands, hundreds of thousands
in the prisons.'

'No one talks about what went on in the prisons,'
Macu said, 'or the concentration camps.'

'You mean like in Nazi Germany?' Emma said.

Macu nodded. 'It was horrific. People were treated
like animals, in Spain, in their own homeland, and in
France.' She looked out across the graveyard. 'You know,
they swept aside the abuses of Franco's regime when he
died in 1975 – everyone wanted an easy transition to
democracy. There have been no trials. No one wants to
break this unwritten pact of silence. They think if they
don't remember it is better.' Macu sighed. 'But even the
dead have rights. We must talk, we must make sure this
never happens again.'

Fidel wrung his hands in his lap. 'There is no peace here.
So many families destroyed, so many children without
their parents. People look at Spain and see the land of
sun, the holiday homes, but underneath … It is not so
bad here you think, but there are still people who will not
buy from me because my family were Reds.' He paused.
'Sometimes I wonder if the fire that killed my wife, her
mother … I wonder if it was an accident.'

'Surely not?' Emma said.

Fidel shrugged. 'My mother was in prison too. She was one of the people rounded up at the docks, just like Rosa.' He hung his head. 'You know, so many children died.'

'They kept the children with the women?' Emma's stomach twisted.

'Yes. They gave the women maybe one herring a day, a few noodles in seawater. Mothers, their milk dried up, their babies died. It was terrible, terrible,' Macu said. 'A warder told Rosa: We don't want to convince you we are right, we want to punish you.' She looked at Emma. 'They treated the women like animals.'

'You know, they said we were mentally deficient,' Fidel said, 'that to be Red was an abnormality. The scientists, they experimented on our men – the International Brigades, they were among the first.'

Emma thought of Charles, felt nausea welling up in her. 'I understand,' she said, her voice a whisper. 'I understand why people want to close this away. I feel like I've opened Pandora's box.'

'No. It is right that you know the truth.' Macu hesitated. 'I want you to know that your grandmother, she was very brave.' She took Emma's hand. 'You know, I managed to see Rosa. By then they had sent her to Ventas prison, in Madrid. They were moving prisoners back to their point of origin. Rosa was from the south, but her last address was Madrid, so they took her there. It was built for five hundred women, but they held over five thousand, mothers with small children. Oh, they were cruel.'

'Where I was, they believed children should be removed from the parents,' Fidel said. 'They took me from my mother.' He screwed his eyes shut. 'I remember walking in the yard, that freezing yard, with the other children,

370

looking up at the bars – all the mothers would gather there, pushed against the windows, trying desperately to see their child. I was maybe four, five years old. I missed my mother so much.'

'You have to remember, most of these women had done nothing,' Macu said. 'They were the daughters, the wives of Republicans. That was their only "crime". That is why they were dragged naked through the streets with their heads shaved, humiliated, tortured, imprisoned.'

Emma felt her head swimming. 'Tell me what happened to Rosa.'

'I only managed to see her because they thought she might die, after losing the baby.'

Emma turned to her. 'The baby?'

'*Sí.*' Macu nodded. 'She had fallen pregnant again, with Jordi's child. They had been together, before he went to fight in the last battles of the war.' She looked at Emma. 'I remember the sound of the doors locking behind me. I was terrified I might not be allowed out. The toilets were overflowing with excrement – God, the stench. All you could hear was the sound of children weeping. Rosa told me five, six children a day were dying. Dysentery, meningitis – measles was a death sentence.'

'What about the baby?'

Macu slowly shook her head. 'She gave birth in prison. Can you imagine, bringing a life into the world in that place? Rosa said they took the baby away to clean him up – they told her it was a boy. So my friend, my dear, brave Rosa waited, and waited, lying there cold and alone and bleeding. Finally they came back and told her the child was dead.' Macu's voice caught, a tear trickled down her cheek. 'He had been still-born.' She pulled a lace handkerchief from her pocket and wiped at her face. 'She asked to see the body but they said they had already buried him, with the other children.'

'Oh God,' Emma said, her hand across her stomach. 'Poor Rosa.'

'Maybe they lied. They took children all the time,' Fidel said. 'They gave them to "good" Nationalist couples who raised them to salute the Generalissimo.'

Macu clenched her fist around the handkerchief. 'It happened too much. Rosa thought she would be executed now that her baby had gone – that happened to a woman she knew. The girl had been raped by nine policemen, and sentenced to death. They waited for her to give birth, and shot her two days later. Rosa said it was the worst thing she had seen in all the war. They tore the child from her arms, and the woman was dragged away, screaming for her baby. Rosa was broken by the time I saw her.'

There was a tight knot in Emma's throat. 'Oh God, this is too much to take in. How did she get out? How did Rosa get to Mexico?'

'I helped her,' Macu said quietly. 'When I saw what they did to her … She told me the priests said to them, "You are worse than whores. You have destroyed your children even as they are born." Rosa still believed, her faith never deserted her. When the priest said that, she was destroyed. She thought her child died because of her. She was broken, broken.' Macu twisted the handkerchief in her hands. 'I knew she would die if she stayed there. So, we switched clothes, papers. Rosa walked out of Ventas in a fox-fur coat, to the waiting car. My driver took her to the coast. I lay low long enough for her to get away, then pretended she knocked me out. I banged my head against the wall to make a bruise, and cuts.' Macu's frail fingers traced her hairline. 'Ignacio came and saved me. He knew, I think, what I did. But we never talked about it.'

'He was a good man,' Fidel said.

'Rosa was right about him,' Macu said to Emma. 'He defied his parents, and he married me. He loved me, and I grew to love him. For sixty years, we had a long and happy marriage. Neither of us were "Red" or "fascist", we just loved one another, and loved our country. He had powerful friends and he got a pardon for Rosa.'

Emma hugged Macu. 'Thank you.' She held the old woman in her arms. 'Because of you, my grandmother escaped.'

Macu patted her back. 'She was my friend. There is not a family in Spain, I think, without a grief to nurse. Fidel's generation are the lost children,' she said. 'We will bear this anguish until the day we die.'

'What is worse,' Fidel said, 'is that even those who escaped, the children who were adopted in Russia, Mexico, England – Franco would not let them rest. He killed their parents, then he went after them. The Falange foreign service hunted the children down. Even with new names, new families, they were not safe.'

Emma thought of Liberty, of Freya's uncharacteristic panic every time Emma wandered off as a child, and understood at last.

'Tell me about when my mother came here,' she said to Fidel.

'It was a long time ago, now,' he said. 'February last year?'

Emma thought for a moment. 'I had to go to New York.'

She frowned. 'Mum said she was going to Cornwall, one last time. It wasn't long before she died.'

Fidel's face softened. 'She wanted the house to be a surprise for you. I am sorry that I could not tell you when we first met.'

As Emma looked up at him, he saw tears pool in her eyes. 'No, that's fine. Mum always loved surprises. Tell me about her visit.'

'I took her up into the mountains, so she could see the land of her fathers. I showed her the village, and the Villa del Valle.' He smiled at the memory. 'She said, "This is it, this is it! My whole life, I've felt I was homesick for somewhere I'd never known." She told me that in Britain, where she grew up, the Celts called it "*hiraeth*" – a longing for home.'

Emma smiled. 'I'm so glad, that she was happy here.'

'That is what she wanted, for you. She said that she hoped this would be a new beginning for you.'

'It is what Rosa would have wanted too,' Macu said softly. 'You know, she escaped to Mexico on a boat, the SS *Sinaia*, from Sète in the end. Nancy Mitford and her husband had set up an office in Perpignan to help refugee mothers escape. Rosa worked with her.' Macu smiled. 'Can you imagine your grandmother in the middle of that chaos? All these people with cardboard suitcases, donkeys, goats and dogs all over the place. It must have been bedlam.' She shook her head. 'I had one letter from her, once she got to Mexico. Rosa went on the boat as a nurse to help the children. She never came back.' Macu gazed out across the cemetery. 'After she died, a nun sent me the photograph of her that I gave you the other day. Our friend Carlos took it in the autumn of 1937, and she treasured it.' Macu glanced at Emma's necklace. 'We did not have many photographs in those days.' She smiled at the thought of her old friend. 'Rosa loved that garden. I know she would be so happy that you are making it good again.'

Emma squeezed her hand. 'Thank you. I know how hard talking about all this must be.'

'Not being able to talk is hard,' Fidel said. 'People think the old wounds have healed. Well, not for our families.' He offered Macu his hand. 'My father, he was taken.' Emma was shocked to see him wipe away a tear as they walked through the cemetery. 'So many Republican families have nowhere to go still, nowhere to grieve. On 1st November, where do they take their flowers to honour their dead?' The temperature dropped as they stepped into the shade. He ran his hand over the pockmarked plaster of the far wall. 'See here? These are bullet holes. They rounded up the men of the village who had supported the Republicans, and made them dig a big hole. They shot them, and threw their bodies in. My father is here, somewhere.' He opened his palms, swept them over the green, green grass. 'All I want is to find him. He should be buried properly, over there, like Franco's men,' he said, pointing at the neat rows of well-tended graves beneath a war memorial. 'It is all I want.'

'There are graves like this all over the country,' Macu said. 'People were thrown down wells, cliffs, ditches. Maybe one day Spain will open its eyes. We are a democracy now. Some people say the past should stay buried, but until people like Fidel's father are laid to rest, the old wounds will not heal.'

'I wonder who was buried at the house,' Emma said, frowning.

'Him?' Macu said. 'That was your grandmother's husband.'

'Jordi?'

'No, not Jordi,' she said with anger in her voice. 'That son of a bitch, Vicente.'

Emma's face contorted. She placed her hand against the wall, gasped.

'Emma,' Fidel said. 'Are you all right?'

Macu looked at her, full of concern. 'We have upset you. I did not want to tell you all this, not at the moment.'

Emma pursed her lips, exhaled slowly. 'No. I'm glad I know. But I think …' She gritted her teeth as another contraction began. 'I think I need to get to the hospital.'

53

LONDON, MAY 1939

A red Triumph Dolomite careered down Pond Place, past the workers' cottages, showering Freya and the pram with filthy water. 'Damn you,' she said under her breath as she slicked back her rain-drenched hair, fumbling for the key with her cold fingers. 'Shh …' She rocked the pram with her foot as she opened the door to the cottage. She hoped Charles was in a better mood. Since his return from the convalescent home, he had been unable to see or speak to anyone. Freya readied herself. She remembered the words of the matron in Spain: *Just when you think you can't take it any more, smile. Always smile, girls.* The door was grimy with soot, and from each chimney, a thick plume of grey smoke rose into the darkening sky. Freya coughed, her chest aching. She hadn't been able to shake her cold. The door bumped open, sticking on the damp carpet where it had swollen. She was greeted by the sound of Billie Holiday on the gramophone, and a haze of cigarette smoke.

'There you are. Where have you been? It started tipping down hours ago,' Charles said. He heaved himself up from the sofa. The house was freezing, and he wore a couple of jumpers and a scarf. Freya dragged the heavy pram into the room.

'You look—'

'I look dreadful.' She glanced at the coffee table littered with empty bottles, glimmering weakly in the light of the coal fire.

'Can I get you a drink, old girl?' Charles inspected a glass dubiously and set it back down on the table. His hand shook as he reached for the bottle of brandy and the glass careered off the table, smashing on the hearth. 'Oh ruddy hell,' he mumbled, and tried to kneel to pick up the shards of glass.

'Just leave it,' Freya snapped. The baby's shrill wail increased in pitch.

'No, no. I can do it,' Charles slurred. 'I'm still getting used to doing things with one hand.'

'Leave it!' she yelled. 'For God's sake, Charles …' She burst into tears.

He stubbed out his cigarette and stepped cautiously towards her. From his jacket pocket he pulled a clean handkerchief, waving it like a flag of surrender.

'Thank you,' she said, wiping her eyes. 'I am sorry. I don't normally … I don't know what's wrong with me.'

He put his arm around her shoulders. Freya looked up at him forlornly, tears pouring down her cheeks. 'Can I get you anything? A cup of tea?'

Freya shook her head, fighting to compose herself. 'No, thank you. I'm just so terribly tired. I've walked miles, trying to get her to sleep. She won't stop crying, I just don't know what I'm doing wrong.'

'May I?' He untucked the blankets from the pram. Liberty's lips were pale, her legs drawn up to her stomach

378

as she cried. 'She has colic, I think.'

'I know. I've tried everything. I don't know if it's the food, or ...' Freya began to sob again. 'I didn't know it was going to be so hard. It just never stops. Day and night.'

'There, there.' Charles patted her on the shoulder. 'It will get easier, I'm sure.'

'Oh God, I hope so. I don't think I can handle much more.'

'Listen, I have an idea,' he said. 'Why don't you have an early night? I'm quite sure I can cope.'

'No, it wouldn't be right.' Freya eyed the table of glasses.

'Nonsense. I'm not paralytic, Frey. Now,' he said, crooking the child on his hip as he gazed into her eyes. 'Young lady, you have one of England's finest young lepidopterists taking care of you. I know nothing about rusks, but I can bore you silly about butterflies.' Charles winked at Freya as she laughed through her tears. 'Go to bed.'

That night, as Freya had her first unbroken night's sleep in weeks, Charles paced the living room. He had a muslin draped over his waistcoat, and jiggled Liberty up and down on his shoulder as he walked.

'Gosh, you have amazing stamina,' he said. He paused, his eyes turning towards the child. 'Oh dear, I think you've ...' He pulled a face. 'I do hope you're in a nappy?' Charles walked wearily to the kitchen. 'Let's see. I think Freya has a bunch drying over the range.'

He laid the child down on a clean towel on the kitchen table, and she gazed at him, sucking her thumb. 'I think you're feeling better after that?' he said quietly. 'Now. How does one ...?' Charles scratched his head. 'I've seen

379

Freya do it. It can't be that hard.' He looked around. 'Some warm water? Cotton wool or something?'

Charles rummaged around under the sink, and filled a bowl with water from the kettle, mixing it with cold. He scratched his head. 'I know! I have some cotton wool in the study.' He returned clutching a glass jar. 'Messier work than chloroforming butterflies, but there you go.' He gingerly unbuttoned Liberty's vest. 'Oh Lord, it's ...' He grimaced. Charles felt hysterical laughter bubbling inside him. He pulled down some clean nightclothes from the airer. 'Shall we try these?' He pursed his lips. 'Eugh. Lord, how can such a small person make all this?' He turned his face away as he cleaned her. 'I say, can you give me a hand here? You just put your foot in it.'

He finally managed to get a clean nappy and pyjamas on the child. 'There, not too bad, and we didn't impale you with the nappy pin.' He stepped back to admire his work. The clean nappy bulged down to her knees. 'It doesn't look terribly smart but hopefully it will hold until morning.' He carried her through to the living room, and stretched out on the sofa with her resting on his stomach.

Freya woke to the sound of milk bottles being placed on the doorstep below her bedroom window. As always, her first thoughts were of Tom. She had heard nothing from him as the months dragged on, and finally, yesterday, she had told herself it was hopeless. He had forgotten about her. *'Smile girls,'* her matron's voice came to her now. *'No tears, be strong.'* She sighed and stretched. *What a blissful night's sleep.* Her eyes flew open. 'Liberty!' she cried aloud, and sat bolt upright. The cot at the foot of her bed was empty. 'Charles!' she yelled, dragging her old blue flannelette dressing gown on. She shot out of bed, ran downstairs. 'Charles, where's—' She stopped dead, and began to smile. There, on the sofa, Charles lay snoring, the child tucked safely beside him, reaching up to play with a mobile of multicoloured paper butterflies that he had made for her.

Bamoleiro dressing gown on she shot out of bed, ran downstairs, Charles, where's — She stopped dead, and began to smile. There, on the sofa, Charles lay snoring the child tucked safely beside him, reaching up to play with a mobile of multicoloured paper butterflies that he had made for her.

54

LONDON, JANUARY 2002

'Freya!' Charles stumbled through the conservatory. 'Freya!'

'I'm in the kitchen,' she called. The theme tune from *The Archers* drifted through the cottage. Freya looked up from the heart-shaped tarts she was making.

'She's in labour, Frey. A chap called Luca something just rang.'

'Luca de Santangel. He's Macu's grandson.' Freya dusted off her hands.

'Good Lord, Macu has grandchildren?' Charles slumped down at the kitchen table.

'Charles, she has great-grandchildren. How old do you think we still are? Twenty?' She carried on spooning strawberry jam into the cases.

'Yes, I suppose I do, sometimes,' he said. 'I can't believe our Em is going to be a mother.'

'Have you decided?'

'About what?'

'Spain, Charles. If you won't come, I'm going to go by myself. Em has some young nanny sorted out to help her through the first weeks, so she doesn't need us straight away. I thought maybe in a month or two, when the weather is better?'

'I'll see. It would do you good, I think. A little break in the sun after all the problems you've been having with Delilah.'

'I can handle her.' Freya looked down at the neat rows of hearts. 'I'm just worried about Emma. I couldn't bear it if all this came between us, not after all this time.'

'Secrets have a nasty habit of revealing themselves.' Charles traced his finger in the flour on the table. 'I said we should have told them the truth years ago.'

'You did not!' Freya said. 'You were the one who started it. Because of you, our whole life was built on a lie.'

'Frey, I remember clearly telling you when Libby turned eighteen we should ...'

'Poppycock.' She staggered to her feet, leaning heavily on her cane. 'If we'd have told her, the first thing she would have done was race off to Spain to try and find Jordi and Rosa, and it still wasn't safe. The reprisals went on for years.' Freya tugged on the old oven door. 'Damn,' she said, the handle coming off in her hand.

Charles muttered under his breath. 'Leave it to me.' He took the handle from her, and wiggled it into place.

'You said you'd get this fixed.'

'Another lie?'

'Don't start, Charles, just don't.' Freya swung around with the tray of tarts, and stumbled. The tray clattered to the floor. 'Look what you made me do!' she cried, looking at the broken cases and jam oozing onto the old wooden floor.

'Bugger. Sorry, Frey,' he said. Ming stalked over and took a speculative sniff of a tart, before turning tail. 'Still, even the cat thinks your pastry looked a bit dry.' Freya laughed, in spite of herself as she reached for the broom. 'What are you doing baking hearts anyway? It's not Valentine's day for a couple of weeks.'

'I was going to post a box to Em,' she said as she swept up the mess. 'Don't you remember? We used to make them every year.' Freya blinked quickly.

Charles caught the tremble in her voice, and shuffled forwards, put his arm around her. 'Come on old girl ...'

'Don't you dare say "stiff upper lip".'

He turned off the oven. 'I was going to ask you if you fancied a Bloody Mary at the Club, wet the baby's head.'

Freya tossed the broom aside, and took his arm. 'Now that is a good idea. Do you think Em will ever forgive us?' she said as they hobbled through the house. 'She sounded so angry when I spoke to her earlier.'

'She's had a big shock.' Charles lifted down her grey wool cape from the pegs by the front door, and handed it to her. 'We'll soon know.'

'I can't bear it. I've been afraid this day would come.' She smoothed down Charles's scarf. 'I've been afraid of losing them my whole life.'

'Will you tell her?' Charles couldn't look at her. 'Will you tell her what I did?'

'What *we* did.' Freya reassured him. 'No, not unless I have to. Emma's been through enough.'

55

LONDON, MAY 1941

Freya lay tangled in the sheets, Liberty sleeping peacefully beside her. She was dreaming of Valencia, the day an enemy squadron shelled the harbour. It was a children's fête day. She had been touched that even though the war was raging, they staged this celebration for the children, just like any year. She had given Rosa a break, taken Liberty to see the parades of papier mâché figures. The faces of Mickey Mouse, Felix the Cat, Donald Duck, Sancho Panza and Don Quixote loomed in her mind now, swaying, huge and macabre. The clouds had opened, and the crowds of children had sheltered under the vast Mickey Mouse.

Freya thrashed out in her dream. She was running now, pushing the pram through the rain, through the dark orange groves. The pram was growing larger and larger, careering through the trees, roots tangling the wheels. Up ahead in the moonlight, she could see Tom, waiting for her.

'Freya,' he called, beckoning her. 'Freya …'

'Mmm?' She blinked, the grey light of a London dawn breaking in. The spring rain ran down the old sash window, which rattled in the wind.

'Freya.' Charles shook her awake.

She pushed herself up on her elbows, careful not to wake the child sleeping at her side. 'What is it?'

'You were calling out in your sleep.'

'I was just dreaming, I think ...' Freya pushed the thoughts of Tom from her mind. As the months turned into years, she had accepted his loss as just one among the many of the war. 'I was remembering when they brought you in to the hospital, at the border,' she lied.

'You were very brave.' Charles sat on the edge of the bed. 'I'd never seen you cry before.' He thought for a moment. 'Even I cried, a little, when they took my arm off.' He smiled sadly. 'One gets rather fond of one's limbs. Still, at least I didn't end up with the sleepers in the wash house, eh, even with you nursing me.'

Freya nudged him. She looked down at Liberty as she stirred in her sleep. 'Just as well. We're all she has, now. I so want her to have a real family, as we did, growing up. Even when we lost Mummy and Daddy, we had all those happy memories to fall back on.' She stroked the child's sleeping head. 'We always knew who we were, where we came from in the world.' Freya looked at Charles. 'We have to make sure she's safe. What if I adopted her formally ...'

'Frey, you mustn't worry.'

'But I was talking to one of the girls on the Basque Children's committee. The damned fascists are coming after the refugee children, Charles. What will we do? What if they come for Liberty?'

'What can we do?' Charles frowned.

'I was thinking – the cottage in Cornwall ...'

'It's hardly habitable, Frey. Don't you remember how

run-down it is? It was the only place we could afford with that last bit of our inheritance. I bought it thinking of our future, but we haven't had any money to do it up yet.'

'Charles, after the conditions we lived in in Spain, it will seem like a palace.'

'You mean, you're thinking of leaving?'

Freya caught the hurt in his voice. 'It wouldn't be forever, Charles. And you could come too.'

'No, one of us has to work, and I'd not be much use as a fisherman with this.' He nodded at his missing arm. He thought for a moment. 'I shall go back to my butterflies. At least you only need one arm for the net, and I'm sure my old college would take me back to teach. I'll write to Imms.' He looked at Freya. 'You've been so terribly brave, Frey. I promise you, everything will be all right. I'm going to take care of you both.'

56

VALENCIA, JANUARY 2002

The trolley wheeled through to the operating theatre, wheels squeaking on the linoleum. Emma watched the lights flickering above her. The room was dark when they pushed her in. As the fluorescent tubes buzzed, illuminated, the sound of a radio drifted in, playing eighties pop.

'Now, Emma,' the anaesthetist said kindly, 'relax.' He took her arms, strapped them cruciform to a plank of wood across the operating table. Emma closed her eyes.

The hours had rolled into one another as Emma lay in the hospital room. 'Please, can't I walk around?'

'No.' The nurse looked up from between her legs. 'It is no good. Your waters have broken, but you are still only two fingers ...'

Emma groaned. The contractions were coming hard and fast now, and the pain tore through her.

'Be quiet,' the nurse said.

Emma thought, *What? Be quiet? You bitch, you have no*— and another tidal wave of pain ripped through her. '*Necesito control ... dolor*,' she gasped, the correct vocabulary abandoning her.

'No, impossible.' The nurse shook her head.

'Epidural.' Emma gritted her teeth and forced her head up. She glared at the nurse. 'Now!'

The nurse pursed her lips. 'I will ask your husband.'

Husband? Emma thought as she followed the nurse's green figure retreating down the corridor. Her vision blurred as the pain returned. She breathed through it, but it felt like every atom of her body was contracting then expanding at lightning speed. She heard voices. Luca. He had stayed.

'If you are not her husband, you cannot sign the papers,' the nurse said.

'I am as good as her husband,' Luca took Emma's hand. She gripped hard as the next contraction came. 'Oh God. What can I do?'

'Epidural, now,' she gasped.

'Get her an epidural,' Luca said to the nurse. 'Get the doctor. Now! I will sign whatever you want. I am with Emma, we are lovers, the baby is mine.' He glanced at her for confirmation.

'Yes.' She cried out again.

'Do I have to get the doctor myself?' Luca turned to the nurse.

He held her hand as they administered the injection. Ice cold, numb relief flooded through her. She came back to herself, breathed easily. 'Thank you,' she whispered. Luca stroked her hair. 'Thank you for staying. I don't know what I would have done …' She was suddenly aware that she was wearing a blue surgical gown, and her backside was hanging out.

'When I saw them take you away, you looked so lost …

389

and so brave.' His eyes were red rimmed, dark circles beneath them. 'It reminded me—' He shook his head. 'It doesn't matter. I hope you don't mind, what I said? That I am with you, and the baby …' He took Emma's hand. 'I spoke to the doctor.' He lowered his eyes. 'The reason you have such bad pain. The baby, he is stuck.'

'Oh.' Tears welled in Emma's eyes as she looked at the monitor tracking her baby's heartbeat. 'Is … Everything is going to be OK isn't it?' The room filled with doctors and nurses.

'Yes of course it is. Emma, I—'

'Emma,' a man in scrubs interrupted, leant down so she could see him, 'your baby is in distress. We have to get him out as quickly as possible.'

'Oh God. Please, save my baby.' Tears rolled down her cheeks. She turned to Luca. 'If anything happens to me …'

'Don't.' Luca kissed her forehead as they prepared to lift her onto the trolley. 'Everything will be fine. I'll wait for you.'

She could hear the sound of metal on metal now. Behind the screen hiding her stomach, she felt nothing but a tugging push and pull. Then he was there. A cry. Startled, she opened her eyes as the anaesthetist dropped the screen slightly. 'Look, Emma,' he said. 'Your son.' She glimpsed a curved back, narrow vernix-covered hips lifting clear of her body. Her head shook with the effort of holding it up to look at him. The screen went back, and she slumped down, grinning. She wanted desperately to hold him. As they worked on her, she listened to her baby, a stranger suddenly, crying in an adjacent room. She tried to turn her head towards him, drifting in and out of consciousness.

'*Eh, Mamá!*' she heard a nurse say. '*Rubio! Qué bonito!*' The woman lowered the baby to her side. He looked just like Joe in miniature. Fathomless dark eyes returned her stare. She tried to lift an arm to touch his hand, the soft blonde hair on his head, but she was still strapped down. She longed to hold him, but all she could do was move her head a little.

'Hello, baby,' she whispered. He blinked at her. She felt as if he knew everything, the secrets of the universe and the meaning of life. The baby was lifted away, and Emma closed her eyes, exhausted.

When she awoke she was in a room on the maternity ward. The sound of other babies crooning and crying disturbed her. It was dark. *Where am I? How long have I been asleep?* she thought. Her body ached, icy pins and needles coursing through her. She was tucked up to her chin in blankets. She licked her lips. She had never been so thirsty in her life. *Oh God, the baby! Where's the baby?* She still couldn't move. She rolled her head to the side, and found Luca dozing in a chair, the baby curled up in a blanket sleeping peacefully on his chest.

'Luca,' she whispered.

'Hey, you're awake.' He cradled the baby as he leant forward and kissed her forehead. 'Look what you have done.' He held the baby so she could see him. 'He's perfect, beautiful.'

Emma lifted her arms clear, trailing drips. Gently, Luca placed the sleeping child in her arms. She kissed his tiny fingers, inhaled his soft, clean scent.

'So, there you are.' She smiled wearily at her child. The baby stirred at her voice, dark eyes blinking reflectively. A knitted hat covered the blonde fuzz of his hair.

Luca stroked her hair. 'You were incredible.'

'I thought …' Her eyes filled with tears.

'You are both fine, you'll recover. And he has ten fingers, ten toes – and a great set of lungs.'

'Ah! You're awake,' a nurse bustled in. 'Let's check a few things.'

'Water …' Emma murmured. 'Please can I have some water?'

'No, no liquids for a few hours.'

'You're kidding?'

'No liquids, then *dieta blanda*.' She checked the morphine drip, and tidied the sheets. 'When he wakes, you can feed him, OK? Your husband is staying with you?'

'I don't … Do you have to go?'

'Not if you don't want me to. Paloma is coming to see you in the morning.'

'Stay, I'd like that.'

The nurse glanced curiously from Emma to Luca. 'Good. Get some rest.'

Luca stooped and took the baby from her arms, settled back into the armchair at her side, murmuring softly in Spanish to him. 'What will you call him?'

Emma looked at them together. The baby seemed tiny in Luca's large, tanned hands. 'Joseph Luca Temple,' she said quietly.

'Really?' A smile broke across Luca's face, his teeth white and even against the dark stubble of his chin. 'Hello, Joseph Luca.' He kissed the baby's head. 'You won't give him your partner's family name?'

'We were never married. Now he's gone, I want the baby to feel connected to my family at least.'

'Do you still miss him?'

'No.' In that moment, Emma realised it was true. 'Not any more. I did ... I mean, you can't be with someone for years and just stop loving them, can you?'

'No.' Luca looked very tired suddenly. 'No, you can't. Even when someone leaves you, once the pain dies down, the love is still there.'

'Is that what happened to you? Did you lose someone too?'

'Yes,' Luca glanced at her. 'I loved someone very much, and they were taken away from me. My wife, Alejandra. A couple of years ago, she lost a baby, lost her life giving birth.'

'Oh Luca, I'm so sorry.' Emma reached for his hand.

'There was nothing I could do. Nothing I could do to help her.'

'And there's been no one since? Haven't you been lonely?'

He shrugged. 'Sometimes, but I am busy, and there are Paloma's children – they are like my own.'

Emma looked at him, compassion filling her heart. 'Would you be Joseph's godfather?'

'Thank you,' he said, smiling. 'It would be an honour.' Luca reached over, stroked a strand of hair away from her cheek. 'Get some sleep.'

At dawn she woke to Joseph's cries. Overnight she seemed to have grown a new body. She laughed with disbelief as she looked down at her breasts. At least at first it seemed funny. The baby wailed with hunger, and yet he couldn't feed. Luca left to shower and have breakfast and a steady stream of visitors for the girl in the next-door bed stared impassively at her. Sore and bloodied, too proud to ask for help, she finally broke down and sobbed.

'Emma!' Paloma arrived bearing a huge arrangement of birds of paradise. 'Oh you poor girl, what you've been through! Luca told me all about it!' She kissed her on both cheeks, glanced at the family next door '*Buenos*,' she acknowledged them. 'Why have they got no bloody curtains in this place?' She rearranged the chairs to try and give them some privacy. 'Now, who's this making all the noise? Joseph Luca? Eh, *cariño* ...' She soothed him, laid the baby along the flat of her arm, rubbing his back. 'Colic, eh?'

'Is it? I don't know. I'm not very good at all this.' She gestured at her breasts. 'I can't get him to feed.'

Paloma perched on the side of the bed. 'Don't worry. I hadn't a clue either,' she said gently. 'Can I help you?'

'Oh please, I'd ... we'd be so grateful.'

Paloma glanced over at an elderly uncle who was staring at the spectacle. 'Eh!' she chided him. He looked away, picked up a magazine. 'Sometimes I think they should paint a sign above the door of every maternity ward: "Leave Your Dignity Here".' She laughed. 'Now then, show me what you have been doing.' Gently, she helped Emma get the baby into position.

'Oh!' Emma's eyes widened in surprise as the baby latched on. The relief was instantaneous. 'It's working! You did it!'

'*Hola*.' Luca stood shyly at the door, with an armful of dusky pink roses. 'I can come back ...'

'No, it's fine, I'm getting used to an audience,' Emma said, laughing. 'Your sister has worked miracles.'

Luca slumped into the armchair. He had shaved,

and she caught the reassuring scent of Acqua di Parma. 'Olivier's just parking the car. You look better.'

'Nurse Ratched finally let me have a glass of water,' she said.

'Oh God, I remember that,' Paloma said. 'And it's like a greenhouse in here. *Dieta blanda*?' Emma nodded. 'They'll have you on gruel for days, then noodle soup if you are lucky. I tell you, by the end of the week you'll think *natillas* pudding has never tasted so good.'

'How long will you be in for?' Luca asked.

'A week at least.' Emma winced as she moved.

'I'll come as often as I can.' He caught Paloma watching him.

'I don't know what I would have done without you,' Emma said.

'It was very brave of you,' Paloma said to him. He blinked and looked down. Emma looked from brother to sister, aware now of the secrets that Luca held.

'It's helped, I think.' He reached out for the baby's hand, stroked it with his index finger. 'For years I was afraid ... Then to see this little man, my godson ...'

'Oh!' Paloma cried. 'That's wonderful! We must have the christening party at the finca.'

'I couldn't impose—' Emma began to say.

'It would be our pleasure,' Luca said. 'Joseph Luca is family now.' He smiled at Emma. 'Can I get you anything?'

'A cold bottle of water would be wonderful.'

After Luca had gone, Emma gingerly edged out of the bed with Paloma's help. Her breath was tight and short. 'It will get easier,' Paloma said. 'The anaesthetic makes it hard to breathe. Can you manage?'

'I'll be fine,' Emma said, taking tiny steps. 'I just need

the bathroom.' She stepped noiselessly to the en suite, and heard the sound of Luca and Olivier talking in the corridor.

'Look at you, like a proud father,' she overheard Olivier say.

'Godfather,' Luca corrected him.

'Paloma tells me you stayed with her in the hospital?'

'I couldn't leave Emma alone.'

'Be careful, Luca. You're playing with fire.'

'I don't know what you mean.'

'Luca, it has taken ages for you to put yourself back together again after Alejandra. You've only just recovered.'

'Emma is a friend.'

Emma frowned, looked down at her hand resting on the door handle. *What was I expecting?* she thought. *I've been kidding myself.*

'Do you really know what you are doing? It's too complicated – she doesn't belong here, she has another man's child.'

'I told you,' Luca said. 'Emma is just a friend. That is all. I felt sorry for her, here alone.' Emma heard the defensiveness in his voice.

He felt sorry for me.

'Good, good,' Olivier said. 'I was just worried.'

'Well don't. There's nothing to worry about.'

Just a friend, she thought, hope fleeing. *I'm just a friend.*

396

57

LONDON, MAY 1941

Freya unlocked the door of the cottage and threw her medical bag down. She kicked off her shoes at the door and sighed. It was quiet, but she could hear Charles in the kitchen, laying out the dinner plates on the old table.

'Hiho,' she said, stopping to check Liberty, who was lying curled up asleep on the sofa by the fire with her friend.

'You're late,' Charles said as she walked into the kitchen.

'It was a long delivery.' Freya yawned. 'Poor girl was a child herself.' She looked at Charles. 'Has everything been OK here? Did Libby and Matie play nicely?'

'They've been fine. I picked Matie up this afternoon. They said they will collect her tomorrow morning.'

'Did you do their tea?'

'Yes, they're ready for bed.' He tossed the cloth onto the wooden draining board, and frowned. 'Listen, we had a visit this morning. I think you'd better sit down, Freya.'

'What is it, Charles?' She perched on the edge of the old pine table.

'You know I've been keeping an eye on what the Falange are up to in England?'

'Yes?'

'They've been getting a lot of help from the English fascists. There are Falange cells all over the country now – London, Bristol, Glasgow … The thing is, they are stepping up their efforts to repatriate children. You've heard of the Special Delegation for the Repatriation of Minors?' Freya nodded. She was dreading what was coming. 'Well, responsibility for rounding up the children has been transferred to the Falange's Foreign Service. Pius XII has even issued a papal edict saying that the children must go back to Spain or face being accused of apostasy.'

'What? They'll throw them out of the Church? Oh, good grief.'

'A papal envoy has approached the children's committee.' Charles raked his fingers through his hair. 'The fascists are being clever – much of the repatriation is being done through diplomatic channels. The British press aren't helping – all the cockamamie stories they are printing about the children stealing.'

'It was the same in France, with the refugees. They thought they were criminals. There is such small-minded, bigoted …' Freya wrung her hands in frustration. 'When you look at those beautiful, innocent children in the refugee colonies at Hammersmith and Barnes. Do you remember how beautifully Matie and the Basque children sang at that fundraiser? How can anyone look at them and call them criminals? We can't let the fascists kidnap them.'

'I don't think the Falange are going door to door snatching children.'

Freya snorted. 'You want to bet? After what we saw in the war, I wouldn't be surprised by anything they did. What does this mean for us?'

'I spoke to one of the chaps in Hammersmith this afternoon. The relief organisations are sending many of the children home.'

'To Spain?' Freya looked through the kitchen doorway to where Liberty lay sleeping quietly on the sofa, firelight dancing over her face. Her blood chilled. 'No. No, they can't take her.'

'The thing is, a chap *did* arrive on the doorstep today. He gave me this.' Charles slid an envelope across the table to her.

'And you say they aren't hunting down children? How did they find us? I don't understand.'

'They are saying the Republicans committed an atrocity sending children overseas.'

'An atrocity? Taking children out of a war zone is an atrocity?'

'Their country isn't at war any more, ours is. Frey, they're evacuating children from London at the moment.' Charles tapped the headline of *The Times*. 'Children are being killed every night in the bombings.' He lit a cigarette. 'The chap who came today, well, he said the children deserve to be brought up as Spaniards.'

'As good fascists, he means. I—' Freya stared at the envelope. Her words faded as she recognised Rosa's childish handwriting.

'Not all Nationalists are fascists.' Charles waited. 'Frey?'

She closed her eyes, rubbed the bridge of her nose. 'Like not all Republicans are Commies? Tell that to the bitch of a matron who got me fired from my night job when she found out I'd been in Spain – "We can't have Red nurses on our ward, Miss Temple." It's unbelievable.

I went as a humanitarian! I went because I wanted to help ordinary, working people like us. Not only are the veterans from the Brigades not getting a pension, we are *still* being persecuted.'

'Maybe it's no bad thing, losing that job. You're doing too much, Frey. Volunteering at the colonies with the refugee children, working as a midwife, taking care of Libby.'

'What choice is there? The children need help, and we need to eat.'

'I told you. We'll be all right. They're finding me a position in Cambridge. We'll get by.'

'What about the men who can't? The dockers and builders who lost arms and legs?' Freya put her head in her hands. 'We're broke, Charles.' She was close to tears. 'It's never going to stop, is it? Not while Franco is in charge. They are going to keep coming after the Republicans and their families.'

'We have to face it. Children are being sent back from the USSR, from France ...'

'From England?'

'Yes, from England. I spoke to a lovely woman who was working with the Quakers. They took a group of children down to the Spanish border, and handed them over. She said it was one of the worst things she has ever had to do. But the parents of the children had written asking for them to be returned to Spain.'

'Like Rosa?' Freya tapped the envelope on her thumb. 'I don't believe it. It terrifies me, the thought of whatever they did to her to make her write this.' Freya ripped it open and scanned the letter. 'Look at this, it was written just after the end of the war. Why has it taken so long to get here, eh?' She read on and began to laugh. 'Good old Rosa. Listen to this: "Send Lourdes home to the bosom of her family to be raised as a good Spaniard. Remember how Vicente doted on her? There will be plenty more of that."' Freya ran her finger over Rosa's signature. 'What did they do to her to even get our address?' she said quietly. 'The letter is a warning, Charles. We mustn't let them get Liberty, whatever happens.'

'The thing is, Frey, they've found her now. They know she's here.' He took her hand. 'They're coming for Matie in the morning, and they want to take Libby too.'

A wave of nausea swept over her, and Freya shook her head. 'No, no, no. I promised Rosa she would be safe. To hell with them if they think we are morally unfit to raise a Spanish child.' She got to her feet, pacing the kitchen as she thought. 'Nothing, no scheme thought up by fat, rich, frightened men is going to beat us. We can't let them win, Charles.'

'It will never stop.'

'Then neither will we. They can be as devious and cruel as they want, but they will never destroy truth, and courage.'

'But what about the agents? They are coming back.'

'Then I'll have to run, with Libby.' Freya looked at her brother, his pale unshaven face. 'I'll adopt her, change her name.' She walked through to the living room, and Charles followed. 'Do you think ...' she whispered. 'Libby and Matie get on so well. Couldn't we take her too?'

'No, Frey! They're not like kittens. You can't save every Spanish child, you know.' Charles took Freya's hand. 'Matie will be fine, the committee will make sure of that. I promised you, I will take care of you and Liberty.'

401

He looked at the girls sleeping on the sofa. 'Whatever it takes.'

'I'll leave for Cornwall in the morning.'

58

VALENCIA, MARCH 2002

Just before the Fallas party, Emma tossed the last of the empty boxes into the skip. Padding barefoot through the rooms, she enjoyed the peace. Over the last few weeks, the house had come together. In Emma's room, Joseph slept quietly, a fire crackling in the stove, split logs piled ready at its side. Down the corridor, she could hear guitar music drifting from Solé's room, the sound of her shower. It was taking some time to get used to having her around the house, but Macu had been right, Emma had underestimated how exhausting the first few weeks with a new baby would be, and she needed all the help she could get. Solé was a kind girl, if a little too trusting. Borys and Marek enjoyed teasing her – so far she believed that Polos were Poland's main national export, and Borys's 'Chopin' vodka was bottled directly from an underground stream at his house. Emma smiled as she flopped back on her bed, stretched out her arms, luxuriated in her new white covers. It felt, finally, like everything had come right.

Emma rolled her head to the side as her mobile beeped. It was a text from Freya: *'Em, didn't want to disturb as you are at party. Warning: Delilah on her way.'* Emma's stomach lurched as she read on. *'Japanese won't sign without you. She's coming to persuade you face to face. You hold all the cards. Love to you and little man. F x'*

Emma bit her lip, punched in a text. *'Thanks Frey, Delilah can go to hell. Love you. Em x'*

She dressed slowly, taking time with her hair and make-up. It was the first time in a month she had managed anything more than sweatpants and her old jumper. *If Delilah's on her way, it's just as well I'm re-entering the land of the living*, Emma thought. She had been dreading the time when she would have to face her old friend, had pictured it a thousand times. Delilah would be dressed in her favourite grey silk shirt, pencil skirt, Louboutin heels, smoking in the shadows like a Veronica Lake heroine. Emma would no doubt be in a milk-stained T-shirt, with unwashed hair and saggy leggings.

The thought of Delilah had thrown her. Emma hadn't spoken to Freya since their argument, but now, she realised, she wished she was there to help her deal with Delilah. *I'll call her in the morning*, she thought. *We can't carry on the way things are.* Emma pulled a couple of dresses from her wardrobe. Nothing seemed quite right. She padded through to the blue bedroom, and flicked on the light. From the wardrobe, she lifted the red dress. She was the same height and build as Rosa, and with the extra curves pregnancy had given her, it was like it had been tailored for her. With a pair of delicate heels, and a spritz of her new jasmine perfume, she was ready for the night. Emma raised her wrist to her nose, and inhaled. The balance of neroli in the top notes was not quite right yet, but the heart of it, the creamy, carnal indole scent of the jasmine, made the hair rise at the nape of her neck. She was getting close. *There's no hurry ...* She thought of her mother's letter on perfume. *It takes time to create a great fragrance.*

Marek let out a low whistle as she walked downstairs. '*Mi amor ...*' he said under his breath.

'Emma, you look so beautiful,' Borys said, clutching his old cap in his hands. 'We came now, to say goodbye. We will stay in the inn near the bus station tonight.'

'Are you leaving already? Won't you come to the dance?'

'I am too old to dance,' Borys said, easing his back.

'I may come along later.' Marek stepped forward, pointed at the chimney breast. 'We hung the picture for you. Who are they? The girl is very beautiful. Almost as beautiful as you.'

'It's Rosa, my grandmother,' Emma said, the heat rising in her cheeks. 'Of course, she was a lot younger than me.' She pretended to concentrate on the photos, felt Marek still watching her. 'Thank you,' she said. 'What a lovely surprise. I'd been meaning to get around to it.' She tilted her head and smiled at Rosa's beautiful, defiant face. The house felt complete now, somehow. 'I can't believe it is your last night,' she said, turning to Borys and Marek. 'I'm going to miss you.' She caught Marek's eye. 'I'm going to miss you both,' she said carefully. 'Where will you go now?'

'To Sopot,' Marek said. 'We are going home now.'

'I'm glad for you. Are you happy?'

He shrugged. 'It's a nice resort, near Gdansk. Maybe you will come one day?' He held out his hand. 'We have a last surprise for you.' He led her out to the courtyard.

'OK!' he called. Borys flicked a switch in the belltower, and the pool illuminated, the new blue mosaic gleaming.

'Oh! It's beautiful! I didn't think you'd have time to do this! I'll think of you every time I swim here with Joseph. He'll love it!' She hugged Borys, then Marek, who held her close. She sensed his reluctance to let go. 'Thank you so much! Really, thank you for everything.' Emma stepped away, Marek following her with his gaze. 'We should celebrate. Do you like cava?'

'Cava? Yes, of course.'

'Well, let's open a bottle. Joseph is staying with Solé at Macu's tonight, so for once I can relax,' Emma called over her shoulder as she went to the kitchen. She came back with three glasses and handed the bottle to Borys. The cork exploded, shot across the pool.

'To our last night,' she toasted. 'To coming home.'

Salsa pulsed along the streets of La Pobla, the rhythm like a heartbeat in the night. Emma felt young, and alive. Walking with Paloma towards the market square they drew cries of '*Guapa*!' and '*Mi amor*!' The night sky was like blue velvet, stars sparkling above the white lights hung in the plane trees.

'Is it always like this?' Emma asked, laughing as Paloma pushed through a group of men. The dark streets thronged with people, the cool night air laced with the smell of woodsmoke, roasting meat, the sharp explosions of *traca* firecrackers. Children dressed in traditional black smocks and blue-and-white-checked Fallas neckscarves wove between the legs of the adults as they embraced and danced. Music pulsed from the open doorways of bars. The night felt full of possibility.

'Tonight, anything goes.' Paloma waved to Luca over by the bar. 'It is Fallas, the feast of St Joseph.' They weaved through the crowd. 'By the way, everything is ready for the christening party tomorrow.'

'Thank you. It's so kind of you all.'

'It seemed like an appropriate time to celebrate little Joseph's arrival, and we are family now. Joseph is Luca's godson.' Paloma glanced at Marek, who was leaning against a table, surrounded by a group of teenagers. 'Is he really going home?'

'Who?' Emma smoothed down the red silk of her dress. She was feeling self-conscious, aware of the dark looks of the older women in the village.

'Who? Your gorgeous builder of course!' she said, laughing. 'Half the girls in the village are crazy about him.'

'Really, I hadn't noticed,' she lied.

Paloma saw him watching Emma. 'But tonight he has eyes only for you.'

'Oh, nonsense!' Emma glanced at him.

'No, really! I know that look.'

'He's too young.'

'Rubbish. What is he, twenty-two, twenty-three?'

'Yes, and I'm an old crone of thirty!'

'Listen, you should have some fun,' Paloma said. She could see the expression on Luca's face as he walked towards them too. 'You don't need something complicated. Not yet.' She turned to Emma. 'For heaven's sake, you're not going to spend the rest of your life with him! You need some fun, a wonderful, crazy night.'

Luca pushed through the crowd. 'Emma, would you like to dance?'

'Go, shoo …' Paloma pushed them towards the dance

floor as she took Luca's glass of wine. 'I am going to find my husband.'

Luca took her in his arms, and the music lifted her. Emma gave in to the rhythm, her hips loosening, moving easily with his. She lost herself, swept away by the melody, the closeness of him, the crush of the crowd. *Just friends*, she told herself. She closed her eyes, remembered seeing him for the first time, the way time seemed to stop. He held her closer. She smelt his familiar, clean scent of leather, cologne, warm skin. She remembered how she felt the first time, sitting with him in the cathedral. She wished she could stay like this forever.

The beat picked up, and as she spun away, their fingertips parted. A girl in a tight black dress cut in, dancing hard and close to Luca. He looked for Emma in the darkness, but when the girl kissed him, forced her lips to his, Emma backed away. She glanced back over her shoulder as she walked, crestfallen, to the bar.

'Where's Luca?' Olivier asked. Emma nodded towards the dance floor. She was trying not to show how upset she was.

'Not her again,' Paloma said.

'Again? Who is she?' Emma tried to sound casual.

'No one. Just one of his girlfriends.'

'One of the many, eh?' Emma picked up her bag. 'Listen, I've had a wonderful time, but I'm tired.'

'No, wait …' Paloma reached for her hand.

'Really.' She glanced quickly at the dance floor. The girl was grinding against him, Luca laughing as she swung her leg to his hip.

The music ended, and Luca walked to the bar, followed by the girl. 'Maybe I'll join you for one, Luca, for old time's sake?'

'Suit yourself.' He shrugged as he lit a cigarette, and looked around for Emma. As he glanced down the girl took it from his lips. Annoyed, he reached for another one.

The girl inhaled deeply, blew a long plume of smoke from pursed lips. She leant on the bar, pushing her breasts into a deep cleavage. 'I don't have to work tonight,' she murmured. 'We could ...'

'No,' Luca said. He knocked back his glass of cognac, poured another.

'Hey, we always have fun, don't we?' She traced the back of his hand with a scarlet nail.

'I said no.'

'No strings ... just like always.'

Luca stuck the cigarette into the corner of his mouth, and reached into his pocket. He tossed a wad of notes onto the counter, and picked up the bottle of cognac.

'You're leaving? What's changed?' Her brow furrowed. 'Ah,' she sneered. 'The perfume woman?'

'I don't know what you're talking about.'

The girl leant towards him. 'I love perfume. You know what you smell of, Luca,' she whispered in his ear. 'Sex. Always, since we were children. It's such a waste. You saved yourself for Alejandra, your childhood sweetheart, now you keep yourself for her ...'

'Go to hell.'

'You need to remember who your friends are, Luca,' she whispered, dipping her finger in the cognac, running it over his lips. 'You were glad of a friend when Alejandra—'

'Don't talk about my wife.'

'Does your girlfriend know about her, eh?' she called after him. 'Does she know her rival is a ghost?'

Marek jogged after Emma as she walked away from the square. 'Emma!' he called. 'You're not leaving?' He caught up with her. 'I hoped you would dance with me.'

'I'm tired,' she said. She pulled the clip from her hair, let it fall loose around her shoulders.

'God, you look beautiful,' Marek said. The lights in the square illuminated his blonde curls, soft and golden against his smooth skin.

Emma looked back at the square, watched the couples turning around and around beneath the strings of lights in the night. The music crept into her, rising from the soles of her feet, pulsing in her blood. 'You want to dance?' she asked without looking at him. 'Let's dance.'

He took her hand. They walked together back to the dance floor. As he took her in his arms, they were eye to eye. It felt good to her, his lean, hard body moving with hers, guiding her around and around. They leant into one another, foreheads touching, lips close, his arm pulling her closer, closer to him. 'Let me be with you tonight,' he whispered, 'let me have one night with you before I leave.'

'No, I ...'

'I'm crazy about you. All these weeks, every night I've thought about being with you.' His lips brushed her temple. 'I know you've thought about it too.' He led her to the shadows at the edge of the square, pushed her gently back against the warm bark of a plane tree. He kissed her then, the softest, sweetest kiss.

What am I doing? she thought. His hands were in her hair now, holding her head as their kisses tumbled one

410

into another. He pulled her to him, the breath caught in her throat. She ached for the feel of another body against hers again. She didn't want to be alone any more. When he led her from the dance floor, she had already made up her mind.

The song had not ended by the time Luca strode back to the dance floor. He scanned the crowds, looking for Emma.

'Hey, you.' The girl in the black dress followed him.

'Go away, I'm not interested.'

'Are you looking for your perfume woman?' She inspected her nails. 'I just saw her leave with that hot little builder of hers. They were all over one another. If I wasn't so crazy about you I'd have gone for him myself.'

'No, you're wrong.'

'I bet he's screwing her right now.'

Luca backed away from her and pushed his way through the crowd towards the Villa del Valle.

Paloma ran after him. 'Luca? Luca! What the hell is wrong with you?'

'She, Emma …' His face contorted. 'Has she gone with that boy?'

Paloma put her hands on her hips. 'Yes. I told her to.'

'You did what? *Joder*! How could you?' He felt like he was choking, unspoken words thick in his throat.

'What do you expect?' she said calmly. 'Do you think she will wait forever for you?'

Luca drove for hours through the mountains, flicking the lights on and off, daring fate to take him. He saw them in his mind; he saw Marek slipping the crimson fabric from her shoulder, kissing her neck. He saw Emma

411

unbuttoning his shirt, running her hands through his hair. He pictured them again and again, tortured by his thoughts. Luca thumped the steering wheel, roaring with jealousy as he drove through the night.

At dawn he found himself back in the village. He parked up and strode through the deserted streets towards her house.

Emma and Marek had not made it as far as the bed. They awoke on the rug by the fire in the kitchen at the sound of the key in the front door.

'Solé is back! Quick!' Emma giggled.

'You go up.' Marek tossed her the dress and pulled his jeans on. 'I'll take care of the baby until you come down.'

He chatted with Solé for a minute, mentally tracing Emma's steps to the bathroom, hearing the shower switch on. She handed him the baby, and went out to get the bags from the car. He turned his back, popped Joseph on his shoulder as he began to cry.

'Hey, no crying.' He rocked the baby as he made coffee. 'No crying.' At the sound of the door latch, he called over his shoulder, 'Do you want some coffee?' When Solé didn't answer, he glanced around to find Luca glowering on the doorstep. 'What are you doing here?' Marek jiggled the baby up and down. Joseph's eyes opened momentarily, then screwed closed as his wailing intensified.

Luca strode towards them. 'Not like that.' He took the baby. Marek folded his arms, leant back against the stove. 'He hates being bounced around. Eh, *cariño*?' he murmured gently, his lips on the soft down of his hair. Joseph grasped the cotton of his shirt and his cries shuddered then stopped as Luca held him firmly, gently. The baby closed his eyes, his ear against Luca's heart.

412

'Why are you still here?' Luca glared at the boy.

'Why do you think?'

'You little shit, you're nothing ...'

They heard Emma walking down the creaking staircase. 'I may be nothing but I'm the one who spent the night with her,' Marek said quietly as she walked towards them. 'Remember that.'

'Luca?' Emma pushed her hair back from her face, still damp from the shower. She was barefoot, dressed in a simple white sundress. Her skin was luminous, her lips swollen from kissing. Luca had never wanted her more. 'You look awful,' she said gently. 'Do you want some coffee?'

He grabbed her arm, dragged her into the hall. 'Did you sleep with him?'

'I beg your pardon?' Emma pulled the door to the kitchen closed. 'That's none of your—'

'Did you sleep with him?' Luca shifted the baby in his arms.

'So what if I did? So what, Luca? What do you care? We are just friends.' She held his gaze. 'That's right, isn't it? That's what you said to Olivier.'

'He's a boy! A child!' He tried to control his anger, glanced at the sleeping baby. 'How could you choose him when—'

'When what?' She stepped towards him, lowered her voice. 'When what, Luca? What am I supposed to do, live like a nun? Don't be such a hypocrite. I know all about you and that ... that woman from last night.'

Luca shifted defensively. 'What about her? It was only ever about sex.'

'And that's supposed to make it better? You'll have sex

413

with someone like her, but every time we get close you—'

'Why? Why him?'

'Because I'm lonely. Because I haven't felt wanted, for so long. Not since Joe left me, not since you—'

'Not since I what?'

'That's just it,' she said, exasperated. 'You haven't. You must have felt it … what we have.' She willed him to look at her. 'I don't know where I am with you. With Marek … it was simple. He made me feel good about myself. I felt young, and alive, and I needed that. I need that.' Emma touched his arm, and he flinched. 'What is it? Is it your wife?'

'Alejandra has been gone a long time.'

'But I'm here, Luca. And I'm real. And I don't want to be alone any more.' She stepped back as the front door opened.

'*Hola*,' Solé said. She glanced quickly from Luca to Emma, and took the baby from him.

Emma could hear the girl chatting with Marek in the kitchen. She looked up at Luca as she heard Marek's footsteps coming towards them. 'I don't want to be alone.'

Luca looked at Marek. 'You need to go now,' he said, his voice shaking with anger. He turned to Emma. 'I'll see you at the christening.'

'Please don't …' Emma said.

'Thank you, Emma. For everything.' Marek took her hand, kissed it, raised his gaze to Luca's.

Luca marched through the village towards the café. Unfortunately, Marek's bus was late. 'Eh, old man,' he heckled from across the street. 'She kicked you out? Couldn't give her what she wanted?' He laughed, reached

414

into his pocket for a cigarette. He glanced down as Luca stepped out into the traffic, striding towards him. By the time he'd lit the cigarette and looked up again, Luca was in front of him. Luca grabbed his collar, swung his arm back.

'Don't you talk about Emma like that,' he said, bunching his fist.

'What are you going to do? Hit me?' Marek sneered. He reeled backwards as Luca pushed him away.

'You're not worth it.' Luca looked at Marek sprawled in the gutter and saw him for what he was – a gauche kid who had got lucky. He sighed, and held out his hand. 'Here.'

Marek scrambled to his feet. 'I don't get it. Why didn't you hit me?'

'Because you are a kid, and you are a long way from home. And I was like you once.' He dusted off Marek's arm.

'I'm sorry.'

'Remember.' Luca prodded him in the chest. 'Remember how lucky you are. Emma is an extraordinary woman.'

'You love her, don't you?'

'It's complicated.'

'I think she loves you too.'

'Why?'

Marek shrugged. 'In the night, she said your name.'

'Really?' Luca fought a smile.

'Maybe you're the lucky one.' The bus rumbled up the village high street.

As Marek swung his bag into the bus and clambered up the steps, he turned. 'Don't hang around, you know. She's too good. If you don't make your move someone else will.'

415

59

LONDON, MAY 1941

'One, two, three ...' Charles began to count to one hundred as Matie and Liberty ran giggling through the cottage to the garden, looking for somewhere to hide. Once they were out of earshot, he slumped down in the armchair by the window, and rubbed the bridge of his nose. He had just taken a phone call from a friend at the Barnes colony. It was time for the children to return to Spain, and they would be coming to get the girls soon.

Charles gazed out of the grimy window at the empty street. They had been lucky, so far. The bombs were falling nightly on London. Unlike many who cowered in shelters and the underground during the attacks, he and Freya carried on as normal during the bombing raids. Freya had joked that morning that they were 'bombproof', but he wondered if life would ever seem simple and safe again. He thought of the girls' conversation at breakfast.

'I am going home,' Matie had lisped, spooning up her porridge.

'Home? Where is home?' Liberty swung her legs on the chair.

'My home is Spain. I am going to Spain.'

'Uncle Charles, where is my home? Is my home Spain?'

Charles had looked up from his newspaper. 'No. Your home is here, Libby, with your Mummy – Freya, and me.'

Spain, he thought now, his stomach tight with emotion. He bit at a piece of loose skin beside his thumbnail as images kaleidoscoped in his mind. He was no good alone with himself these days, unable to rest, to shake the memories, the ghosts in the back of his head. Charles covered his face with the palm of his hand, raked his hair as if he were trying to push them away. 'Ninety-nine, one hundred,' he called. He strode through the house, making straight for the conservatory. But for a pair of dusty old Lloyd Loom chairs, it was empty now – he hoped that one day it would be full of plants and butterflies. His footsteps echoed across the cracked tiles. 'Coming, ready or not!' He knew that Liberty always hid in the little alcove in the corner, and he scraped back the door.

'Not fair!' Liberty pouted.

'Right, Libby,' Charles said, his heart racing. 'Let's play another game. I won't tell Matie where you are hiding. I want you to stay here, do you understand?' The child nodded. 'I want you to be very, very quiet.'

'Like a mouse!'

'Yes, like a mouse.' Charles glanced at his watch. They would be here any minute. 'Stay here until I come and get you.'

He pushed the cupboard door closed, and locked it.

'Matie!' he called as he went out into the garden. 'Matie!' He heard giggling from behind the potting shed. 'Found you!' He picked her up and hugged her, a lump forming in his throat. Charles carried her into the house, and she clung to his neck. 'Now, Matie, some nice people from the committee will be here soon, with some other people, from Spain.'

'From home?'

'Yes, Matie, from home. Libby is hiding,' he said. 'She's hiding very, very well. So these people mustn't find her, Matie. If they ask you where Libby is, you say she has gone away. You say you were playing last night and Libby went away.'

'Yes, Uncle Charles.'

'It's a game,' he said quietly. 'Just a game.' There was a knock at the door as he walked through the house. 'It's time to go home,' he said as he opened the door. His face set grimly as he looked at the men on the doorstep. A woman from the rescue committee stepped forward and took Matie's hand.

'Goodbye, Matie,' he said, screwing his eyes closed as he kissed the top of her head. 'God bless.'

'You have the children's papers?'

'Yes. One moment.' Charles reached into his pocket, and handed them to the man.

'Where is the other child?'

'Didn't they tell you?' Charles held his gaze. 'There was an accident. Lourdes del Valle was killed in a bombing raid.'

'I'm sorry. We will of course investigate.' The man shook his hand. His eyes narrowed, glancing at Charles's missing arm. 'This must be very difficult for you. I can assure you the child's future is in Spain.'

Charles looked at Matie's bright, hopeful face in the back of the car. She waved at him. 'Take care of her,' he said quietly, and closed the door.

Charles leant against the wall, listening to the car pull away. His heart was thumping, and he stumbled as he walked towards the kitchen. He poured a large whisky from the bottle on the dresser, and picked up the phone.

'Hello,' he said, his hand shaking as he held the receiver. 'Is that the children's committee? This is Charles Temple. I'm afraid I have some bad news. The little girl staying with us, Lourdes del Valle. Yes …' He listened as the woman sorted through her paperwork. 'We were caught out last night during the bombing raid.' He listened as the woman at the other end of the phone talked. 'I'm afraid she was killed. Yes, the rest of us are unharmed, a few bruises. No, they haven't been able to recover a body yet. Yes, of course. I'll come in and sign any paperwork you need. Thank you. Yes, we are all devastated.'

'Charles?' Freya said. He wheeled around, saw her standing in the kitchen behind him, her face ashen. She was carrying a basket of groceries ready for the journey to Cornwall.

'Goodbye,' he said and hung up the phone.

'Charles, what have you done?'

'Freya, I had no choice. They came for Liberty.'

'What did you do?' she yelled.

'Matie has gone home, but Libby is safe.'

'What are you talking about? Have you gone mad? How could you pretend she's dead? I wanted to adopt her, legally.' Freya walked to the telephone. 'I'm going to call the committee, tell them you'd been drinking, tell them you'd lost your senses.'

Charles pressed down on the phone, disconnected the line. 'They will take her. They will take Liberty from you, just like they took Matie. Do you understand?' He gripped Freya by the shoulder. 'I promised you I would protect you and Liberty.'

'So what are we supposed to do? Run, and hide all our lives?' Freya shook her head in disbelief. 'You're insane!' She rubbed the back of her hand over her lips.

'From now on, Spain never existed,' Charles said. 'Rosa, Jordi, they are gone. Lourdes del Valle is dead.' He hugged her, whispered into her hair, 'Liberty Temple is your daughter, Freya. No one must ever know the truth.'

'I can't do it, Charles. I can't build our whole life on a lie.'

'Well you have no choice. They will take her, if they find out, Frey. They have the letter from Rosa and that's all the authority they need. We can do it, Frey, we have to, for Libby. I don't know if they are going to fall for it. Children are being killed every single day in the raids, but they'll be suspicious. They'll be watching us.' He turned to Freya. 'I think it is best if you and Liberty leave for Cornwall immediately. It's not safe here, the Falange have spies everywhere.'

'The suitcases are almost packed.'

'Good. I'll bring the car around and take you straight to the station.' He thought for a moment. 'In case they are watching the house, we can hide Libby in one of the cases, tell her it's part of the game.'

'Part of the game?' Freya cried, cupped her hands over her face, rubbed wearily at her eyes. 'I can't—'

'You can, Frey. We can do this, for her.' His voice shook. 'If we save one child, just one child from … from, *that*,' he said, screwing his eyes shut as images of the war powered into his mind. He shook his head, and looked at Freya. 'One child, one precious child makes a difference.'

'We'll never get away with it.'

'We will. We're at war – people disappear all the time. The authorities are overworked, people slip through the cracks.' Charles thought for a moment. 'Once you get to Cornwall, just tell them we lost everything during the Blitz, all our paperwork, her birth certificate. Tell them she's your illegitimate daughter, that you had her in Spain.' He took her hand. 'Liberty is your daughter now, Freya.'

'Where is she?'

'She's hiding in the conservatory.' As Freya ran through, Charles drained his drink, listened to her talking calmly to the child. Freya pushed past him, holding her, Liberty's legs wrapped around her waist.

'Where is Matie, Uncle Charles?' Liberty said over Freya's shoulder.

'She had to go home.' Charles held Freya's gaze, his eyes hard and determined. 'Now, darling, we are going to play a game. Let's pretend …'

60

VALENCIA, MARCH 2002

Emma had not missed hangovers. She searched through the new cupboards in her bathroom, but couldn't find any paracetamol. She squeezed two sachets of Calpol into her mouth and grimaced.

'Solé,' she called down the stairs, hopping as she zipped up her boot. 'It's time to go.' She could hear voices in the kitchen, and furrowed her brow. She grabbed her favourite Nicole Farhi jacket and ran downstairs.

'The service starts in quarter of an hour,' she said, looking down as she fastened Rosa's locket around her neck.

'Well, look at you, stranger,' Delilah drawled.

Emma's head shot up. Delilah was standing in the middle of the kitchen, with Joseph in her arms.

'Your nanny tells me you're on the way to Joe's christening.' She looked down at the baby. 'I feel like the bad fairy, turning up without an invite.'

'How did you get in here?' Emma saw Solé flush.

'I told her I'm an old friend.' Delilah stepped towards her. 'He's beautiful, Em. He looks just like his Daddy.' She waved her hand around the room. 'And all this. It's

422

perfect. But then you always do everything to perfection.'

'I'm not perfect. I've never tried to be perfect.'

Delilah rolled her eyes 'You don't have to try to be anything – you just *are* perfect. Face of a successful company, homemaker, beauty, loyal friend … you had it all, and now you're the mother of his child.' She leant in to Emma. 'Congratulations.'

'This wasn't to get back at you, if that's what you think.'

'You fucked him, after he was with me,' she said under her breath. 'You have his baby. It's not fair, you still have part of Joe.'

'We're both grieving,' Emma whispered, glancing at Solé.

'Yeah, except I'm not allowed to. I was the bitch who broke you up.'

'Play the victim if you want to, Lila, you were always very good at that.'

'He loved me. He married me.'

'He loved us both, and nothing is ever going to change that.' She looked at the clock. 'Solé, would you mind taking Joseph on to the church? I'll see you there in a few minutes. Luca is waiting for you.'

'Luca? Who's Luca?' Delilah asked as she handed the baby to Solé. Emma tried not to show her relief.

'Joseph's godfather. A friend.'

'How nice. Just like me.'

Emma waited until she heard the front door close. She rounded on Delilah. 'You gave up any rights to my friendship the first time you slept with Joe.'

Delilah held up her hands. 'Forgive me.'

'Give me one good reason why I should.' Emma glared at her.

'Because I'm sorry from the bottom of my heart.' She tilted her head. 'Because I bet you haven't stayed up all night talking and listening to James Taylor with anyone else. Do you remember?' She began to sing 'You've got a friend ...'

'Stop it!' Emma picked up her handbag and slung it over her shoulder. 'For the love of God, don't start singing at me,' she said walking away.

'Yeah, I could never hold a tune.' Delilah followed her outside, slipped on a pair of sunglasses, the gilt tips catching the sunlight.

'Listen, this is a bad time.'

'I'm not going to stay long. I just want you to sign the papers.'

'I'm going to need to think about that.' Emma said as she locked the front door behind them. 'Where are you staying?'

'Here.'

'You've got to be joking?'

'What are you going to do, throw me out? We need to go over the Japanese deal. No need to thank me by the way ...'

'Thank you?' Emma cried.

'Without me, the entire sale would have fallen through. You want a clean break? Fine. That's what I'm giving you.' The women strode out through the gate and headed towards the village. Delilah glanced at Emma. 'You look too good for a woman who has just had a baby.'

'Flattery will get you nowhere.' Her headache was still thumping, and she winced in the bright sun. 'Do you know, Lila, when I first knew for sure you and Joe were having an affair? I was driving to the office, and saw you

424

walking along the King's Road. I waved at you, slowed down to give you a lift – I know you saw me, and you walked away.'

'I don't remember.'

'You were so guilty, you couldn't look at me.'

'That was after the first time,' she said quietly.

'So where did this happen?'

'What?'

'When did your affair begin?'

'Don't, Em ...'

'No!' she yelled, stopping dead. 'I want to know. How many nights do you think I cried myself to sleep, Lila? Wondering how and where it started.'

'Brighton,' she said quietly.

'Brighton?'

'We'd been working late. It was a beautiful evening. I said to Joe, why don't we drive down to the coast just for fun, like we all used to in the old days.'

Emma remembered the three of them in Joe's convertible, Lila normally hung-over and asleep in the back seat, the wind lashing her face as they raced towards the coast.

'It should have been me,' Delilah said quietly.

'What?'

'I waited all that time for him. He'd been dating that girl at home ...'

'Clare?'

'Yeah, that's right. Square Clare. All through the first year at Columbia, he stayed faithful to her. I tried my best ...'

'I'm sure you did.'

'Then I heard he'd split up with her. That first night

of our last semester, I was going to tell him I was in love with him.' Delilah laughed bitterly. 'But there you were, pitching up for your stupid little course like a breath of fresh air, vibrant, beautiful.' She sighed. 'Joe confided in me that night – can you believe it? I could see you had both fallen in love at first sight.' She looked Emma in the eye. 'I'd missed my one chance. You stole my moment. I hated you.'

Emma held her gaze. 'You hid it well.' She turned and walked on to the church.

'I didn't want to lose him. If I showed you how I felt, I'd have lost Joe too. They always say love is just a different way of looking at a friend. I had to learn to make my love for Joe look like friendship.'

'So none of it ... *Our* friendship, it was all a sham?'

'At first. But you – you're just so damn lovable. I think it was when I had flu that winter I first started to warm to you.'

'Me, or my ginger chicken soup?' Emma remembered spending hours taking care of her. Endless hot water bottles, hours spent poring through old copies of *Vanity Fair* and *Vogue* on her bed, surrounded by tissues. 'I don't know how I never caught it.'

'You? You're never sick. You have the immune system of a hippopotamus.'

'Are they healthy?'

'God knows.' Delilah rifled through her handbag and lit a cigarette. 'Oh, what a mess, Em. I'm sorry.'

Emma stopped on the steps of the church, and looked at Delilah. This was the woman who had deliberately destroyed her life. *But she's hurting too*, she thought. Reluctantly, Emma hugged her. 'I forgive you.'

'Really?'

'What else can I do? We both …' She hesitated. 'We both lost him.'

Delilah held her close. 'Thank you. Life's too short, Em, that's what your Mum said to me once.' Emma stiffened at the mention of Liberty, but Delilah held on. 'She was right, as always. Let's put the past behind us.'

'As you said, I just want a clean break.' Emma stepped back as Luca walked towards her with Joseph in his arms. 'Stay if you want to, or go. I don't care. There's nothing for you here.'

As Delilah watched her walk into the church, her face set hard and she whispered, 'I wouldn't count on it.'

Uprooted tree stumps ready for the bonfires towered in a pile on the outskirts of the village like a funeral pyre, roots crusted with balls of red earth. Beyond them, figures walked across the open land, like the souls of the dispossessed in the grey light of the late afternoon, eyes to the ground.

'What are they doing, the people out there?' Delilah said as she swung the car past, tyres squealing.

'They're gathering snails,' Emma said from the back seat. She tucked Joseph into his car seat with a blanket. 'It's Fallas. Everyone is cooking paella.'

'What do they do with them?'

'Put them in a bag with herbs, clean them, and eat them. You should try them.'

'Eugh, sounds disgusting.' Delilah's hire car bumped along the road. 'Damn,' she muttered as they hit a pothole. 'Maybe we should have brought yours. This is going to bugger up my tracking. I don't know how you can live

427

here. I mean look at this shithole – the whole country is like a building site. Mangy dogs everywhere. Look at that …' She gesticulated towards a flock of brown sheep grazing the dusty earth in the shade of an olive tree. 'It's like the fricking Biblical times.'

'I like it here.'

'Oh don't get defensive, darling. I'm just worried about you, Em, that's all. This is hardly what you're used to.' She ran her hand through her glossy blonde waves. Emma was always surprised by how small Lila's fingers were, like a child's, tapering to tiny red nails from a soft, round palm. 'You do seem awfully on edge.'

I wonder why, Emma thought. She couldn't believe Delilah had charmed an invitation to the party out of Dolores.

'Have you spoken to anyone? I mean a lot of women get depressed after having a baby.' Delilah glanced in the rear-view mirror.

'I'm not depressed!'

'Come on, darling, look at you. You've let yourself go a bit, haven't you? When was the last time you had your hair done?'

Emma took a deep breath. Up ahead at a farm a furnace glimmered darkly. A group of six or seven men were bent intently over a stone plinth. Four dark legs thrashed above them.

'What the hell is going on there?' Delilah cried.

'Don't look,' Emma said, remembering the effect blood had on her. She winced at the piercing shrieks of the animal. 'They're killing a pig.'

'What is this? Lord of the fucking Flies?' Delilah raised her fist as the car roared past. 'Bastards!'

'You eat bacon. Where do you think it comes from?'

'I don't want to know!' Delilah checked her reflection in the rear-view mirror, ran her tongue over her teeth.

'Turn here.' Emma indicated the long drive to the de Santangel finca.

'Well ...' Delilah said as they swept up to the front of the house. 'This is impressive. Your friend has looks and money. Quite a package.'

'*Hola*,' Luca said, opening the door for Emma. She could feel how angry he still was with her, but he was hiding it well. He kissed Joseph's head, then Emma on both cheeks. 'It was a lovely service. Come on inside.'

Delilah climbed out. 'Hello everyone, what a beautiful place. I ...' She strolled around, her voice trailing off as she saw the caterers carrying a freshly slaughtered lamb to the fire pit for roasting. 'Oh God!' she gasped and fainted. Luca lunged forward and caught her in his arms.

'Not again,' Emma said. 'She always does this at the sight of blood.'

Luca carried her to a bench, reached into the fountain and splashed water on her brow. Delilah fluttered her eyes.

'Slap her,' Emma muttered. 'That helps sometimes.'

'I apologise, Delilah,' he said.

'I could forgive you anything.' She gazed up at him. 'Do call me Lila, all my friends do.'

'Delighted to meet you, Lila.'

Emma stalked towards the house as Paloma came out to greet her, arms open wide in greeting. 'Here's the guest of honour!' She took Joseph in her arms. 'Where's your friend?'

Emma nodded towards the fountain. 'Draped over your brother.'

Paloma's eyes narrowed. 'Ah. I know her kind.' She leant in to Emma. 'My guess is she doesn't have many girlfriends?'

Emma realised suddenly she hadn't. Emma still had people she'd known since schooldays in her life. *Loyal friends*, she thought. *Delilah had only me.*

'Luca's no fool.'

Unlike me. Emma frowned. She wasn't going to let Delilah spoil the day. She looped her arm through Paloma's. 'Thank you, this is so beautiful,' she said as they walked through to the party.

'It's our pleasure. How about a drink? Let me get you some juice.'

'Juice? No thanks – I'd love a glass of wine.'

'Wine? Welcome back to the land of the living!'

As the guests mingled, Joseph was passed from person to person, old ladies cooing over him, giving Emma advice she hadn't sought but accepted with good grace. On the terrace, Paloma had set a table with white linen, strung lanterns from the shady tree overhead. The meal was simple, but delicious. Luca sat at the head of the table. Emma noticed Delilah made sure she was sitting at his side. She had always tolerated Delilah's flirtatiousness towards every attractive man she came across, but now her every move, her voice, her laughter grated on her nerves. Emma selected a fig from the bowl on the table, inhaled its clear green notes, and woody, earthy scent. She picked up a small, sharp silver knife, sliced it open. *I think what I am feeling is close to hate.* Emma's senses were acute. She felt like she was seeing clearly for the first time in months. Her teeth sank into the sweet fruit, soft on her tongue. She looked up, felt Luca watching her.

Night fell, and the adults sat talking while children ran, laughing, across the lawns. Benito dragged the stereo outside, and in the courtyard people began to dance.

'He's been very good.' Luca squatted down beside Emma's chair. He stroked the baby's face as he slept in her arms.

'Joseph? I think he's enjoyed the attention. He gets that from his father,' Emma said coolly. Luca's free arm draped over the back of her chair as he sipped his wine.

'Is your friend OK?'

'How do I know? She was sitting on your lap last time I saw her.'

Luca's lips twitched, amused. 'Is she pregnant too?'

'The fainting? No she's always been like that.' She glanced at him. 'Why, are you interested?'

He shrugged. 'I said I would show her Valencia tomorrow. Why don't you come along?'

Emma glared at his back as he walked over to talk to Delilah.

'Don't make it so obvious,' Paloma whispered to Emma, evidently reading her thoughts. She squeezed her shoulder, and leant down to her. 'No one here knows the history. As far as they know she is your best friend, come over from England for the christening. You will come off badly. Someone like her is very good at charming everyone – like Machiavelli, a semblance of goodness, no? When underneath, I'm guessing ...'

'Thank God you're here.' Emma patted her hand. 'No one would believe it anyway, would they? Look at how easy and charming she is. No one would believe she stole the love of my life.'

'Was he?'

'Joe?' Emma hesitated. 'I ... I don't know. He was the first man I ever loved. I was practically a kid when I met him.'

'Then don't speak too soon.' Paloma rested her head against Emma's. 'Perhaps the love of your life is still to come.' She was not surprised to see that Luca's gaze rested on Emma, not on Delilah at all.

61

LONDON, MARCH 2002

Charles sat at a picnic table sipping a Styrofoam cup of tea in the courtyard beside the Chelsea Gardener. He was reading the newsletter from the International Brigade Memorial Trust, waiting for Freya. An obituary for one of the doctors who had worked with Bethune's blood transfusion service caught his eye. *What was the name of that chap?* he thought, casting his mind all the way back to a day in 1942.

He had been lolling around in the cottage one afternoon, trying to get the nerve up to call Freya down in Cornwall. It took several thuds of the doorknocker to rouse him.

'Who the hell is that now?' Charles had staggered to his feet, knocking over an empty bottle. The kitchen table was littered with glasses and dirty plates, and the cat stood in the middle of it, licking a bowl. He stumbled through the living room, tripping on a pile of books and newspapers. There was another knock on the door. 'I'm coming!' he yelled, wrenched open the door, and peered out. The light was fading as evening fell, and he squinted at the man standing on the doorstep. 'Can I help you?'

Tom took off his trilby, and tucked it under his arm.

'Hello,' he said, and offered Charles his hand. He folded up the piece of paper with the address written on it.

Charles glimpsed Freya's handwriting. He looked suspiciously at the bouquet of white roses in his hand. 'Do I know you?'

Tom laughed. 'No, we've never met. I'm Tom Henderson. I'm a friend of Freya's. You must be her brother, Charles.'

'I'm afraid she doesn't live here, any more.' Charles leant against the doorway. His head was spinning, and Tom's face swayed before him.

'It's been a while. I've been in China, with Bethune's blood unit.'

'Bethune? I remember him.'

'He died in '39, sadly, but we've been carrying on his work.'

Charles had the horrible sensation that he was about to be sick. 'She's gone,' he said brusquely.

'Do you have a forwarding address? I wrote to Freya a couple of times, but never heard back. I'm going home to Canada, but I hoped ...'

'She married some time ago,' Charles lied, thinking guiltily of the letters he'd destroyed. 'She has a daughter.' He saw Tom's face fall with disappointment. But he wasn't going to risk anyone connected with Spain being a part of their life. The only way they could be safe was to cut off from their past entirely. 'She's not coming back.'

Charles heaved himself to his feet now, and tossed his cup into the bin. He shuffled through to the garden centre, and spotted Freya up ahead, choosing bedding plants.

'Frey!' he called. She looked up, and smiled. *Still beautiful*, he thought, walking towards her. It was like a painting: the dazzling flowers in the fading light setting off the angular lines of her white bob and her stooped, slender body in its trademark black polo neck.

'I'm not done,' she snapped. 'You know I don't like to be rushed. I told you to have some tea and wait for me.'

'Stop ruddy bossing me around, woman.' He tapped the newsletter sticking out of his jacket pocket. 'Another one gone – some chap who ran the blood transfusion units.'

Freya's face fell. 'Not Tom Henderson?'

'No, but that's the name I was searching for. Who was he?'

'Tom?' Freya touched the petals of the deep-blue pansy she was holding. Charles noticed how her face softened, the sadness in her eyes. 'Tom was …' She shrugged and put the plant down. 'We were in love. I hoped …' She sighed. 'Well, it didn't work out. The last I heard, he went off to China with Bethune. He forgot all about me.' She hugged herself. 'I never forgot him though. Maybe that's why I never married. None of the other men could hold a candle to Tom.'

'For heaven's sake, woman, all this time? Why didn't you tell me about him?'

'I don't know why I'm telling you now.' She walked on through the Chelsea Gardener, gazing at the rows of multicoloured plants laid out for the spring. 'I think it's Emma, having the baby. It feels like a new beginning for us all. After Liberty, and poor Matie …' Her voice trailed off. 'My own problems didn't seem to matter any more. I buried myself down in Cornwall, made a new life.' Freya followed him with her gaze as he walked on. 'You know, it's the christening this weekend, and Fallas.'

'Oh Frey, I still haven't made up my mind.'

'I'd like to be there, for Emma. Delilah is on her way,

and I don't trust her one bit. Not one bit.'

They shuffled home along the teeming streets, headlights starting to illuminate as night fell. Cars beeped in frustration as they took too long to cross the road, and Charles flicked a white van the V-sign once they were safely on the pavement. He was puffing for breath as he pulled out the front-door keys.

'Why didn't you tell me all this years ago?' he said as the door closed behind them. 'The Canadian chap turned up in London, you know.'

'Tom?' Her jaw dropped. 'Tom came back for me?' Freya felt behind her, lowered herself onto a chair by the front window.

'Yes, very pleasant fellow. I told him you were married, had a child.'

'Oh, Charles.' She shook her head as she flicked on the lamp. 'Why?'

'Well, you still weren't talking to me, and it was so soon after they tried to take Libby. I thought it was safer if we cut off all links with Spain. I was trying to protect you both.' He squeezed her shoulder. 'There were letters too …' Charles winced as Freya cried out. 'If I'm honest, I didn't think it was important, just some wartime romance.'

'Why didn't you tell me?'

'Christ, I'm sorry, Frey, if I'd known …' Charles pulled his glasses from his top pocket. 'If he mattered so much, why did you never try to contact him?'

'I was scared.' Freya looked at her hands. 'When I heard nothing, I was scared he'd found someone else, or that what we had would have changed. I was scared I loved more than I was loved.' She glanced at Charles.

'Ridiculous. I've never known you to be scared of

436

anything.' He shuffled over to his laptop. 'I always thought you could have done more with your life. Perhaps because of this Tom chap you never took the risk.'

'More than what, Charles? I worked, I raised a family. Has it ever occurred to you that I have done everything I always wanted. I lived, Charles—'

'And loved?'

'Yes, I loved. I loved Tom, very much, very passionately even though we were together a short time.' She rubbed her eyes. 'Anyway, you're a fine one to talk, Casanova,' Freya said. 'You were so caught up with the impossible dream of Gerda, you missed what was right in front of you. Whatever you say, you wasted your life on regret, too, Charles.'

Charles slumped down into the desk chair. 'You're talking about Immaculada, aren't you?'

'You missed your chance, Charles. She adored you. If you had asked, she would have gone with you.'

'Do you think I haven't been over this a thousand times in my mind? What if I had taken her with me? What if Hugo and I had just left after the Brigades disbanded?' He raked his hand through his hair and glanced at the sideboard. 'Is there any Scotch left?'

'No. And you know you're not supposed to – the doctor warned you about your liver.'

'Frey, I am eighty-six. Let me live a little.' He polished his glasses. 'She was a beautiful girl,' he said, his face growing wistful. 'I expect she married that sensible boy who followed her around like a puppy. What was his name?'

'Ignacio.'

'Yes, Ignacio.' Charles pressed his lips together, and shrugged. 'Maybe we both missed our chances. But it's not too late.' He flexed his fingers over Freya's laptop. 'There's no time like the present.'

'What are you doing?' Freya struggled to her feet, looked over his shoulder. Charles typed 'Dr Thomas Henderson, Canada' into Google. Seconds later, an address appeared. 'Oh, I don't know. I can't …'

'Too late now.' Charles dialled through the number on screen, and handed her the reciever.

'Good morning, Dr Henderson's office.'

'I can't do this, Charles …' Freya began to say. 'Ah, good morning. Is that Dr Tom Henderson?'

'Yes, good morning, ma'am. How can we help?'

'Is it possible to have a word with him?'

'I'll put you through. May I ask who is calling?'

'Freya Temple.'

'One moment please.'

Freya was shaking, and Charles stood to let her sit down. She heard the sound of a phone being picked up. 'Good morning. Tom Henderson.' Her heart was beating hard.

'Tom? Is that you?' He sounded the same to her, exactly the same. It couldn't be possible. She felt the years fall away, remembered how it felt to hold him, how his eyes crinkled when he smiled, how she loved him.

The man laughed. 'Yes, it's me. Who is this?'

'It's Freya.' Perhaps he had forgotten her, after all this time? 'You may not remember … we worked together with Beth.'

'Beth?' She heard him pause. 'Dr Bethune? Oh, I get it. You must want my dad? Tom Henderson Senior?'

Freya clapped her hand to her head. 'Of course.'

'Say, are you *the* Freya? The one he always talked

438

about after Mom died?'

The Freya, she thought. 'I hope so.'

He laughed. 'Oh man, he would have loved this.'

Her heart sank. 'Do you mean Tom's …?'

'I'm afraid Dad died last spring.'

'I'm so sorry.' Freya felt tears coming to her eyes. 'I'm so terribly sorry for your loss.'

'Hell …' He sighed. 'I miss Dad every day. But, you know, my son is the spitting image of him.'

'Did he … did you all have a good life?'

'The best,' he said. 'After Dad came back from China in '42, he married my Mom. They had six kids—'

'Six?' Freya laughed through her tears.

'You know what Dad was like, he always loved kids.'

Freya thought of him playing with the children on the street in Madrid, clowning around, handing out sweets. 'I expect he was a wonderful father.'

'Mom and Dad had fifty good years together. Lived to see his grandkids, that's what he always wanted.'

Freya pictured him, the patriarch of a brood of dark-haired children. 'I'm so glad to hear he was happy.'

'He never forgot you, Freya,' he said. He fell silent for a moment. 'Man, you guys saw some times.'

'We did,' she said, and stemmed a tear. 'We certainly did.'

'He wondered … I don't know if I should even ask you this. Dad talked a lot about you, after Mom died. He wondered sometimes whether you regretted not coming with him.'

Freya thought of his handsome, open face, how she loved him. 'I have had a wonderful life too.' She hesitated. 'But yes, every day I've thought of him. Every single day of my life.'

62

VALENCIA, MARCH 2002

'Open your mouth,' Luca said, looking at his watch.

'Why?' Delilah said.

'Trust me! The Mascletà fireworks ...' There was a huge explosion. The air shook, and cheers erupted from the packed city square.

Emma's eyes widened with shock. It felt to her like the air was shimmering, disintegrating – the noise was like a physical blow, the acrid smoke overwhelmed her. 'Why do they do this?' she shouted.

'It makes you feel alive!' Luca laughed, guided them through the festival crowds to where they had parked near Plaza la Reina. An effigy of the Virgin as tall as the cathedral towered over them beneath blue-and-white awnings. Fallas Queens bearing carnations passed the flowers up to men who clambered around the scaffolding, threading the stems in, weaving the Virgin's robes. As the crush thinned out, he turned to them. 'What would you like to do now? See the coast, or eat? The bullfight perhaps?'

'Oh, the bullfight!' Delilah took his arm.

'Are you sure? We don't want you fainting again,' Emma said.

'I'm sure Luca will take care of me, and you should try everything once.' Delilah lowered her sunglasses and stared at him from beneath sooty lashes. 'Or twice, if you enjoy it.'

Emma fought the temptation to punch Luca in the arm as he laughed. Her eyes bored into Delilah's slender back as they walked on, striding ahead of her. Her shoulders were thrust back, outlining the blades, her spine a sinuous indentation above her backside, undulating like an inverted heart. She was wearing pink. Emma knew this meant she wanted to appear feminine, vulnerable. Emma glanced nervously at Luca. *Oh God, he can't take his eyes off her. I feel like I'm wearing a tent.* The breeze lifted the loose white cotton dress that Emma wore.

Emma hadn't wanted to risk leaving Delilah alone with Luca, so she had joined them, leaving Joseph at home with Solé.

'Shotgun!' Delilah cried, jumping into the front seat of Luca's car. He opened the door for Emma, and she slipped into the back.

Luca edged through the back streets and pulled out into the swirling traffic on Guillem de Castro. 'So this is your first time in Valencia, Lila?'

'It is. I think it's marvellous.' She leant forward, gazed up at the twin towers of the Torres de Quart. 'Look at that gorgeous castle! It's like something from a fairy tale. Like Rapunzel.'

'It's not a castle. They are part of the old wall. I think it was a women's prison for a while.'

'When was that?' Emma looked at the huge Gothic towers, and thought of Rosa. *Was she imprisoned there, before Ventas?* She imagined all the women crammed in the cold stone rooms with their children.

'I don't know. A long time ago. You know the story of El Cid?' Luca drove on. 'Charlton Heston rode from that tower, strapped to his horse.'

'How romantic!' Delilah said, gazing up at the huge stone towers, pocked with the marks of cannonballs. Through the archway she glimpsed several huge papier mâché figures. 'God, they're a bit macabre, aren't they? Were you serious when you said they are going to burn all those things tomorrow night?'

'Of course,' he said. 'It's the last night of the Fallas festival, la Cremà. The whole city will be ablaze.'

Delilah craned around to look at the towers. 'Look, there are people up there – we should go up later.' She glanced back at Emma, and pulled a face. 'Oh, of course we can't. I'd forgotten about your vertigo, Em.'

Emma folded her arms. 'Don't let me stop you.'

'You should be careful,' Luca said. 'The keepers of the tower are forever locking visitors inside in their rush to go home. It took ages to find the keyholder the other night. Some poor family had been locked in there for hours.' He glanced at his watch and turned to Delilah. 'You like architecture? We have a little time before the bullfight. I'll show you the new City of Arts and Sciences.'

Luca drove out over the Calatrava Bridge. Emma gazed up at the white ribs arched against the cobalt sky. They seemed like bleached bones to her. The dazzling white buildings, set in shimmering tesserae pools, reminded her of vertebrae, ribs, eyes. She thought of Vicente's fractured bones, scattered beneath the lime. 'It must have been during the war,' the policeman had said. 'There were so many atrocities ... this man had been cut limb from limb.' Emma leant her head against the window. At least his remains were now safely interred in the del Valle family grave. She was not superstitious, but she had definitely felt the atmosphere in the house change. Emma was so lost in her thoughts that when the car stopped near the bullring after circling the city, she looked up in surprise. Luca came around and opened the door for her.

'Thank you,' Emma said.

'You're very quiet. Are you enjoying yourself?'

'It's very entertaining.' Emma folded her arms. 'The way you've been flirting with Delilah.'

'Flirting? I was being kind to your friend, that's all.'

'Very kind.'

'Now you're being unreasonable.'

'Unreasonable?' She couldn't stop herself now. 'I'm always reasonable, Luca. Good old reasonable Emma. Don't you think you've punished me enough?'

'What is wrong with you today?'

'Nothing. I told you, I'm just tired.'

'Would you like to go home?'

'Yes.'

'We're not leaving are we?' Delilah joined them. 'Come on, don't be so boring, Em!'

Emma bit the inside of her cheek. The thought of spending any more time with Delilah didn't appeal. She checked her watch. 'You two go ahead. I should get back for Joseph.'

'Are you sure?' Luca said.

She backed away from them. 'Have fun. I'll get a cab and see you back at the house.' She caught the triumphant look on Delilah's face as she turned away.

In Plaza de Toros, a searing blue disk of sky looked down on the churned ochre earth.

'I hope these seats are all right?' Luca ushered Delilah in ahead of him.

'I'm sure they are perfect.'

'I like the sun. When you buy tickets for the *corrida* you choose, *sol* or *sombra*. Sun or shade.'

'Fascinating.' Delilah gazed around the arena. 'Does Em enjoy this?'

'I don't know. We've never been.'

'I doubt she would. Bless her, she can be very moody.' Delilah pulled a red lipstick from her bag, pouted her lips. 'So, tell me what happens.'

'The matadors go to the *capilla*—'

'The what?'

'The chapel. Before they fight, they ask the Virgin for protection.' The crowd roared. 'Now, this is the *paseíllo* – the parade.'

Delilah yawned. The heat made her feel languorous. 'Who sits up there?'

'That is the box for the President, or the most important person here. Today it is the mayor, and with him a vet and an artistic consultant.'

'Art?' She laughed through her nose. 'They call butchering bulls art?'

'It is.'

'Oh come on, it's a funny little man in a shiny suit—'

'It is the suit of lights, the silk is strong, like armour.'

'... goading a great big bull.'

'If you saw the matador's bodies, there is nothing funny about it. Each one is a mass of scars.' He folded his arms. 'You don't understand. We identify with the bull and the

444

matador. It is the intensity of the relationship—'

Delilah cried out, burying her head on Luca's shoulder as the bull staggered under a blow, deadly bright *banderillas* sticks fluttering, hooked in its back. When she raised her head, lipstick had smeared across his shirt. 'I am sorry …' As she went in to kiss him, Luca stood abruptly.

'No, I am sorry. You have made a mistake.'

He pushed his way out of the bullring, and reached for his mobile phone as it buzzed. He looked at the message: *'Cuenca, tomorrow? Emma.'*

Emma sat on the terrace, watching the flaming sunset, the phone at her side. She mulled over her conversation with Freya. She had told her about Delilah's arrival in Spain, and Freya told her the story of her affair with Tom.

'Fight for him, Emma,' Freya said, her voice catching. 'If you think you have a chance of happiness with this man, don't let Delilah ruin everything before it's even started.'

Emma was surrounded by the last of Liberty's letters, the empty box gleaming. She sipped her wine, and gazed out across the mountains, bats looping lazily above the orange trees. In her hand lay the final envelope: 'In Case of an Emergency'. She picked up the silver knife, gilded by the last rays of the sun. She hesitated for a moment, then slit the envelope open.

> Darling Emma,
> First off, whatever it is is nowhere near as
> bad as you think. If you have reached one of
> those moments in life where you are at a
> crossroads, stop and think. Change is the one
> sure thing in life. As much as we cling to the
> familiar, everything is transient. Life can be

*beautiful or dreadful - often simultaneously.
When it is dreadful, it is good to remember
that everything changes. It will pass. Think of
the possibilities ahead - seek out the beautiful.*

*Stop, and listen to yourself. The answer is
within you. Make your decision, then act. It
really doesn't matter much whether you have
made the perfect choice. You have made a
choice. You are determining your own fate, not
buffeted around by chance. This is why so many
dreams remain just that - people fail to follow
their gut instinct, Em. Trust yourself. Take
that step. If life knocks you down, get back up.
If it knocks you down again, get back on your
feet and look it in the eye - every time.*

*There will always be something or someone to
battle against. Most often, that battle is with
yourself. Choose your fights carefully, and your
friends. Life is short, and trust me it goes by
too fast. Don't waste time on people who sap
your energy, Em - surround yourself with
people who give you strength. Don't let idiots
push you around. Be strong. Fight back. Don't
let them pass the line you have drawn. If your
heart and soul is strong, you win - every time.*

*You are stronger than you can ever realise,
and I am always, always covering your back.
I love you, Emma. You can do it.*

Mum xxx

Emma smiled. This was the advice she had been
looking for. *Thanks, Mum.* She looked at the letters
scattered across the table. All the other advice, about

business, family, friendships, each letter would have its day. She picked up her mobile and fired off a text to Luca. Next, she unscrewed the lid of her Montblanc and flipped through the Japanese contracts for Liberty Temple. She initialled each page, and paused when she reached the final one. For a moment, she imagined going back to London, staging a buyout, forcing Delilah out of the company. Emma looked out across her garden at the sunset, the lavender mountains. *Seek out the beautiful.* This was where she belonged. This was worth fighting for.

With a flourish, she signed her name next to Delilah's signatures, and tossed the contracts aside. She kicked off her flip-flops and padded barefoot into the garden, breathing in the green scent of the cold grass beneath her feet, the spice of the herbs. It felt like an enormous weight had lifted from her. She walked around the perimeter walls, her head held high. Her fingertips brushed the leaves of the plants, and she imagined the flowers to come. Rosa's garden was coming back to life, and aromatic basil, mint, rosemary scented the air. In her mind she conjured the perfumes, imagined a whirlwind of petals raining down. 'Awake, O north wind,' she said quietly, reciting the Song of Songs as Liberty had so many times to her as a child. 'And come, thou south; blow upon my garden, that the spices thereof may flow out. Let my beloved come into his garden.'

After checking Joseph in his cot, and lighting the fire in the kitchen, Emma came back outside. She wrapped a thick wool cardigan over her dress, and settled down to wait for Delilah, watching the sun sink low.

The garden door flung open. 'The next time I go to a bloody bullfight remind me to buy *sombra* not *sol*, OK?' Delilah stalked out to the terrace. Her face was sunburnt, her eyes halos of white. 'You could have told me how strong the sun is here. Why are my suitcases in the hallway?'

Emma turned to her. 'Because you are leaving.' She calmly packed up her mother's letters into the lacquer box, and tucked it under her arm.

'What?'

'I said,' Emma repeated, striding towards her, scooping up the contracts on the way, 'you are leaving.'

'I can't leave now! Night's falling – you know I can't drive in the dark.'

'Fine.' Emma pushed past. 'Go in the morning, then. Luca and I have a meeting to go to first thing. When I get back, I want you gone.'

'Hold on, Em, what's he told you?' Delilah's eyes glinted.

'Don't start, Lila.' Emma rounded on her. 'Don't even think of trying to twist this around. It's over.' She tossed down the contracts. 'I've signed the papers. Sell the company, take the money and get out of my life.'

'Is that it?' Delilah cried after her. 'After all these years?'

'I wish I had never met you.'

'You can't just walk away from me. How can you?'

Emma paused, shot a glance over her shoulder. 'It's easy. Watch.'

63

VALENCIA, MARCH 2002

The seatbelt sign went on. Freya looked down at the sparkling carpet of lights below them, the roundabouts and roads that hadn't been there sixty years ago. The roads glowed orange, pulsed like synapses in the early morning light. 'We're here, Charles. We're back.'

Charles opened his eyes, gazed out of the airplane window at the rose light refracting in the glass as the plane banked into Valencia airport.

'I was just thinking, Frey. Do you remember? When they tried to take Liberty from us?'

'I'll never forget it. Never.'

'I thought you'd never forgive me for saying she'd been killed.'

Freya took his hand. She remembered how Charles had appeared one day in Cornwall. She had ignored his letters, his calls. He walked towards her along Bamaluz Beach, broken and dishevelled, buffeted by the wind. They had stood and looked at one another as Liberty played, splashing in the surf, oblivious to everything that had gone on. Freya had taken the first step, and they had clung to one another, their strange little family reunited beneath a soaring, dazzling sky. 'It was a long time ago.' She looked down at the Spanish coast, the sea glittering in the distance.

'I sat there, thinking about the christening last night, and Delilah showing up. I thought about Rosa, how the worst thing that can happen to a mother is losing her child.'

Freya shook her head. 'Come on, Charles. You're losing your marbles.' She squeezed his hand. 'The curse of the del Valles – is that what you think? You are far too sensible for that.'

He looked at his sister. 'You know how unstable she is. The last attempt failed, but ...' Charles frowned. 'Maybe we should have told Emma.'

'I didn't want to worry her. She's had so much on her plate.' Freya gazed out of the window as the plane touched down. 'I didn't think Delilah would have the nerve to show up here, but after I spoke to Em last night, I just got the most awful feeling ...'

Charles sensed her concern, and patted her hand. 'Don't worry. It's too late for us, but it's not too late for Emma.' Charles lay his head back against the seat, looked out at the familiar mountain ranges. He thought of Gerda, of Hugo.

'Where did all the years go, Charles?' Freya said, a wistfulness in her voice. 'If only we'd—'

'If only? You can waste a lifetime thinking of all the "if onlys". There is no happily ever after. There's contentment if you are lucky. But happiness – true happiness – it's like one of my butterflies. It's dazzling, and unlikely, and you find it when you least expect it.' He blinked quickly, looked at Freya. 'It goes too soon.'

Freya squeezed his hand. 'Not if you catch it on the wing.'

Delilah dragged her last suitcase to the car. She heard the telephone ringing in the house, and she strode back inside and closed the front door.

'Temple residence,' she said.

'Delilah, is that you?'

'Well, Frey, how nice to hear from you.'

'What are you doing there?'

'Just leaving actually. Emma signed the contracts.'

'Is Emma there?'

Delilah turned her head as she heard the key in the lock. 'No, she left early for some meeting.'

Solé pushed the pram through the door. 'Sorry, madam. I forgot his bottle and he was hungry.'

'You are a parasite, Delilah! You always have been. You've sucked everyone and everything dry.'

'Yada-yada, you sound like a scratched record, Freya.'

Delilah motioned to Solé to hand her the baby. Joseph began to cry.

'Is that Joseph?' Freya said. 'Why has Emma left you alone with him?'

Delilah smiled as she heard the panic in her voice.

'Just go. You have everything you want now,' Freya said.

'For once, you know, you are absolutely right.'

'She hung up on me.' Freya and Charles shuffled out of the arrivals hall into the bright sunlight.

'Emma's phone is off.' Charles squinted, looked at his phone.

'I wish she'd stop doing that. How many times have I

told her? Well, keep trying. We have to warn her.' Freya glanced back impatiently. 'Charles, come on,' Freya said, hailing a taxi with her walking stick. 'The barbarians are at the door.' She swung her cape over her shoulder. 'Our girl needs us. We have to stop Delilah. I couldn't bear it if anything happened to Emma's child.'

64

CUENCA, MARCH 2002

The road to Cuenca cut through rolling hills, climbing into the mountains. The earth was red and ochre against the blue sky, like the blood and sand of the bullring. The drive unfurled the tension in her. She was happy just to be with Luca, to travel in silence knowing that a whole morning lay ahead of them. They parked outside the town, and walked across the stone bridge to the cliffs. Above them, the houses clung to the rock, their wooden balconies jutting out into the abyss.

'In the summer the fields around here are full of sunflowers,' Luca said. 'Each face is raised to the sun in perfect formation, the heads turning through the day.'

'I'd love to see it. And I'd love to stay in this *parador*.' She glanced in at the beautiful old hotel.

'There is a lovely one in the grounds of the Alhambra too, in Granada.' Luca guided her towards the bridge. 'I've never stayed there, but every time I go to the gardens, I see people ...' He hesitated. 'Couples. It always seems so ...'

'Romantic?'

'Yes.'

Luca guided her to a narrow alleyway behind Cuenca's cathedral. 'It is quite different from Valencia, no?'

'Completely.' Emma gazed up at the dark, ancient walls, sensed the shadows, the relics inside. She shivered. 'I still haven't got to grips with this feeling in Spain, the dark and the light.'

'*Sol y sombra*. It is what we are all about.'

'I have to be honest, I find the dark rather frightening still.'

'Perhaps you are meant to.' They paused outside a studded wooden door, and he knocked. Emma heard footsteps coming towards them along a stone floor, and the door creaked open. 'Concepción,' Luca said as he leant down to embrace a tiny woman dressed in black.

'Luca, Luca,' she said, cupping his face in her hands. 'Look at you. You are working too hard still? When are you going to settle down and have some sons who can work for you, eh?'

'Concepción, this is my friend Emma. Emma, Concepción Santos.'

'Come in.' She stepped aside to let them enter her atelier. The door closed behind them, and the shadows, the scent of sandalwood, spices embraced them. A black cat wound its way around Emma's ankles like a skein of silk around fingertips.

'So, you are a perfumer too?' she said to Emma.

'Emma's family is from Valencia,' Luca jumped in. 'Her grandmother was from Granada, Sacromonte. She was a friend of my grandmother's.'

The old woman folded her arms. 'And what are you going to make? My son showed me your company on his computer. It seems very modern, all about packaging.'

454

'That's all gone,' Emma said. 'I've shipped over my mum's organ of fragrances, but I want to build one of my own for the first time. I want natural essences that are rooted here.' Emma thought of *duende*, something rising from the ground, a spirit, a passion. That was the magic she wanted in her work.

'It will not be easy.' She pursed her lips. 'People will tell you using natural ingredients is too hard.'

'I'll start with simple formulas, perhaps colognes using the blossoms.'

Concepción clicked her tongue. 'Valencia is not the place for blossom. The best are from Sicily, and Andalusia.'

'Emma knows that. We can help her with some of ours from the south,' Luca interrupted.

'Of course, I will have to use ingredients from all over the world – that is how perfumery has always been – and eventually, if it all works, production will need to be on a big scale. But I want the company to have its roots here. For now, I'm going to concentrate on making bespoke fragrances.'

'That is how it was in the old days,' Concepción said, 'before all the synthetics came along. I am glad that perfume is returning to nature. Perhaps it will become more holistic again.'

'And when it takes off, will you travel again so much?' Luca asked Emma.

'No,' Emma said. 'The balance was all wrong, before. I'll employ someone young, who wants to be on the road all the time. I'm going to stay home, and do what I'm good at.'

'Making perfume, love and babies.' Concepción laughed. 'Well, look at me. I am nearly ninety and I have spent my life doing what I love.' She beckoned Emma closer, and whispered. 'You know, in the Alhambra the concubines in the harems would eat musk so that when they made love their sweat was perfumed. I can show you some old recipes.' She patted her hand, and beckoned for them to follow. Emma sensed she had passed some kind of test. As they walked along the dimly lit hallway, Emma felt the temperature dropping. It was like walking into the hillside, into a cave. Concepción unlocked a side door, and flicked on dim candle lights.

'I appreciate you letting me see your studio ...' Emma began to say, her words trailing off as she stepped into the room. It was windowless, hung with deep-red velvet curtains. Before her stood a massive mahogany table, the tiers of shelves filled with tiny glass bottles, each with a hand-written label, some with worn gilding around the stoppers. 'Oh, this is remarkable.' She felt like a child again, remembered going to the corner shop each Saturday with Charles to select a quarter of sweets from the glass jars of gobstoppers and rainbow crystals. Hundreds of vials of pure perfume, extracts, absolutes, essences and attars glittered around her.

'I've never seen ... do you call it an "organ" in Spanish too? It makes my desk look amateurish.' As she turned, and her eyes adjusted to the light, she saw the back wall was stacked with shelves of jars, each filled with herbs and gleaming liquids.

'My family have worked with fragrance for centuries,' Concepción said. 'My ancestors came from Arabia – they created scents for Boabdil, the sultan, at the Alhambra.'

'I think some of these bottles have been around since Boabdil's time,' Luca said, laughing.

Concepción ran her hand affectionately over the worn wood of the work table. 'I think "organ" is a good word. When you make a great perfume, it is like hearing a melody become a symphony. You compose a scent, it is like music.'

'I've still so much to learn,' Emma said, turning slowly on the spot.

'There is no hurry. All the best perfumes take years.'

'That's what my mum used to say.'

Concepción's face fell. 'Now there is no one left in my family who is interested. I am the last.' She waved her hand towards the far wall. 'Some of these ingredients have been macerating for years. Like wine, some crops and some years are better than others. See what you think,' she said and left them alone.

'This is amazing,' Emma said as she leant down to examine the labels. *Ambergris*, she thought. *Of course.* 'Some of these bottles look like they are hundreds of years old. This glass looks Venetian.'

'Concepción is like my grandmother, they never throw anything away,' Luca said. 'Since the war, I think they like to feel they have enough put away.'

'You know, when I trained in Grasse, I learnt to memorise three thousand smells,' she said. 'I think there are some here I've never even thought of.' She opened a vial, and inhaled. 'There are only a few hundred naturals. That's what I'm interested in now.'

'Won't that limit you?'

Emma shook her head. 'Perfume's rooted in nature, and the combinations are almost infinite. I love that. Mum always said the oil is the soul of the plant, the flower. To her, perfume was sacred.'

'And you agree?' Luca smiled as he saw the excitement in her eyes. He settled back on the high wood stool by the table. 'What is that one?'

'Close your eyes.' As she approached him, his knee brushing against her thigh, he peeked through one eye. She put the bottle down and unwound the red pashmina scarf from her neck. She covered his nose, his lips. 'Breathe,' she said. 'This will clear your nose, your palette.' Luca's fingertips jumped on his thighs as she blindfolded him. 'No cheating,' she whispered, her breath against his ear. 'Trust me.' Emma lifted the bottle towards him. 'Now, what do you smell?'

'Sandalwood,' he said. 'That's easy.' He laughed uncertainly.

'Very good.' Emma took a clean flask from the table, and measured out a small amount, dropping it into perfume alcohol. She turned, and Luca sensed her hips shifting close to him. Every noise, every smell intensified as the blood swelled in his veins. 'Now, what's this?'

He inhaled. 'Spice.' A warm, woody scent intoxicated him. 'Cinnamon, or clove?' He reached out blindly for her, found her waist.

'Excellent,' she murmured. Emma worked quickly now. He heard the delicate chink of the glass bottles as she sorted through the vials, felt the shift and curve of her back as she conjured the fragrance.

'What are you doing?' He reached for her again. He was aware of his breath, the beat of his own heart. Snatches of fragrance came to him like the notes of a melody – lavender, orange wood, neroli, leather ... something he couldn't name, like earth after rain.

'Patience!' she said, laughing.

He heard the glass dropper chink a final time, and his lips parted as the fragrance came to him: warm skin, summer air, sex. 'All I can smell is ...'

'You,' Emma said. She took his hand, dropped a little of the mix against the inside of his wrist, and massaged it in with her thumb. 'What do you think?'

Luca lifted his hand, still in hers, breathed in. His senses swam, he felt like he was waking up after a long sleep. Emma loosened the scarf, he felt it fall away against his cheek. 'I think you are a magician.' He took her face in his hands, closed his eyes as he kissed her then. The air around them seemed to dilate as their lips touched. The scarf fell to the floor, to the shadows as they held one another. He murmured her name as he kissed her neck, his hands in her hair, hers tracing the curve of his shoulders, his back.

'What did you put in that?' He smiled as he caught his breath.

'A secret.' She could hear Concepción's footsteps tapping along the corridor. Emma turned to the desk again and wrote out a label, attaching it to the vial. Emma eased in the stopper as Luca pulled her to him. He kissed her, a kiss like he had never known. He felt himself falling, fearlessly. The door creaked open, and he stepped away, breathless.

'*Oh, me gusta.*' Concepción tottered towards them carrying a tea tray with a decanter of sherry, cut glass twinkling in the dim light. 'Very masculine. Very ...' She looked at them both, her eyes dancing. 'It reminds me a little of Peau d'Espagne.'

'I'm glad. That's exactly what I was aiming for.'

'But there is something extra ... it is not musk?'

'Ambergris,' Emma said.

'Ah, interesting.' Concepción put the sherry down, and glanced at them, knowingly. 'I like the balance. Very aphrodisiac. You have the start of something here, I think. What will you call it?'

Emma smiled. There could only be one name. '*Duende*.' She turned to the old woman. 'You must let me pay for the ingredients,' she said, reaching for her bag.

'I won't hear of it.' Concepción clapped her hands. 'So, what do you think?' She poured them all a glass of sherry, offered around a plate of salted almonds.

Emma looked at Luca, and he saw his desire echoed in her gaze. 'It would be an honour to continue your work. I'd love you to teach me everything you know.'

'What will you do, Concepción?' Luca asked her. He licked the salt from his lips, felt the sherry coursing warm down his throat.

'I shall retire. My sister lives in Málaga. She has been asking me to come and live with them. This house has already sold. They are going to turn it into some kind of tourist attraction.' She waved her hand at the perfumes. 'All I care is that this goes on.'

'I think,' Emma said, looking at Luca, 'it is only just beginning.'

65

VALENCIA, MARCH 2002

Luca buried his face in Emma's hair as she unlocked the front door of the Villa del Valle. 'You smell wonderful.'

'I smell of sex,' she whispered as she turned to him. The sunset was dazzling, the sky flaming amber and rose above them.

'Precisely.' He kissed her. 'You should forget orange blossom. If you could create a fragrance that makes men feel how I feel at this moment ...'

'We could do that, something aphrodisiac.'

'More than that.' He traced her jaw line with his fingertips. '*Duende* ... magic ... love.'

'You love me? You. Love. Me ...' She laughed quietly.

'I've loved you from the moment I first saw you.'

The moment she pushed open the front door to silence, Emma knew there was something wrong. Normally, she would hear the sound of Solé's radio as she ironed, or Joseph's *Tellytubbies* DVD. Her heels clicked on the tiles as she walked through the dark house. Delilah's bags had gone, she noticed. She called Solé's mobile from the kitchen phone.

'*Digame*,' the girl answered. Emma could hear laughter in the background.

'Solé? Where are you?'

'Me? I'm at the village park. The Cremà celebrations are starting.'

'Come home. How's Joseph?'

'Joe? Isn't he with you?'

A wave of panic flooded through her. 'No. I left him with you. I told you—'

'But she said it would be all right.'

'Who? Who said it would be all right?'

'Your friend said she'd take him for a walk. She said you would be home soon, that she would wait for you.'

'She's not here,' Emma cried. 'Delilah has gone, and she has taken my baby!'

'Oh my dear, dear girl, it's worse than I thought.' Freya dumped a leather holdall in the doorway.

'Freya? Charles?' Emma spun around. 'What are you doing here?'

'We thought you might need a hand with Delilah,' Charles said. 'It seems we are too late. Where have you been? We've been sitting in the café all day. Your phone was off.'

Emma's hand shook as she hung up the kitchen phone. 'She's taken the baby.'

Freya held her in her arms for a moment before snapping into action. 'I knew she was capable of a lot but this takes the biscuit. Right. Have you called the police?'

'The police?' Luca said. 'Do you think that is necessary?'

'Yes,' Freya said firmly. 'We haven't wanted to worry you about what's been going on with Delilah. She's not very stable.' Luca pulled out his mobile.

'When has she ever been?' Charles muttered as he

462

lowered himself onto a chair. He looked around the kitchen. 'Remarkable. It hasn't changed at all.'

'What do you mean, not very stable?' Emma's heart was pounding.

'I'm sure it will be fine,' Freya said as Luca spoke to the police.

'Right, they're on their way,' he said.

'Listen, sit down Emma, and I'll make some tea,' Freya said.

'Tea? I don't want tea!' she cried, but Freya had already reached into the cupboard by the stove.

'Same place Rosa used to keep it.' She lit the gas under the kettle, and measured out some leaves into the pot. 'There's nothing we can do until the police get here. You can fill me in on what's been going on.'

'I am going to fetch the family. We need all the help we can get,' Luca said. He bent his head to Emma's, kissed her tenderly. 'It will be all right. We will find Joseph, I know it.'

Freya followed him with her gaze as he left. 'Luca?' she asked Emma.

'Yes, I'm sorry, I should have introduced you.'

'There's plenty of time for that. Now, you need to think clearly,' she said. 'Look, sit down for God's sake, you're making me dizzy. You need to keep your energy up. Have you eaten?'

'No, not since this morning.'

'Right.' She rummaged through the cupboards until she found the bread. 'Sweet tea and toast. I'll make enough for everyone.'

Emma knew better than to argue. In a crisis, this was always Freya's first response. 'I'm glad you're both here.'

463

Emma took Charles's hand. 'I understand. I know what happened in Spain.' She buried her face on Charles's shoulder as he hugged her. 'Thank you. I understand what you did, for Mum.'

'We did what we had to, to keep her safe.' He glanced at Freya. 'We'd do it again in a heartbeat.'

The kitchen clock ticked away the minutes. 'I see some things don't change.' Charles drained his cup, staring out across the garden. The sky had darkened outside, and he jumped at the sound of the first firework. 'Where the hell are the police?'

'Everything takes time out here.' Emma glanced up as the door swung open and Dolores strode into the room.

'Luca called me,' she said. 'We were on the way to the celebrations, but we have come to help.' Solé appeared from behind her, red-eyed.

'It is my fault. I trusted your friend,' she said.

Emma hugged her. 'No, it's not your fault. You didn't know.'

Outside, they heard the sound of car doors slamming, and feet marching up the pathway. Freya turned to intercept the police. 'Where would she go?' She glanced at the notebook by the phone, saw Delilah's writing. 'Hotel Ad Hoc?'

'It's near the cathedral,' Dolores said. 'She has gone to the city.'

'Lila's too smart to leave an address lying around,' Emma said.

'At least it's a start.'

Emma spoke quickly with the police officers. 'Here, this is the most recent photograph I have of her.' She handed them a copy of Liberty Temple's latest corporate brochure. She looked up as Luca appeared with Paloma and Olivier.

'Hello,' Charles said, stepping forward. He offered his hand. 'This is Freya, and I'm—'

'Carlos?' Immaculada stepped out of the shadows.

'Macu?'

Freya laughed, clapped her hands together. 'I don't believe it.' She hobbled forwards, embraced her old friend. She glanced at Charles, saw the colour had risen in his cheeks.

'You all know one another?' Luca said, confusion on his face.

'It's a long story,' Immaculada said. 'A very long story. In the meantime, let us find the child.'

'This…' Emma said, pulling a photograph of Joseph from her wallet, 'this is my son.'

'We will circulate these immediately,' the policeman said. 'Is there anything else we need to know?'

'She's capable of anything,' Freya said. 'She tried to kill herself a couple of months ago.' Emma looked up in surprise. 'I didn't want to worry you …'

'And now she has my baby!' Emma raked her hand through her hair.

Luca put his arm around her shoulders. 'What are you waiting for? Go, find them,' he said to the policeman. As they trooped out, he turned to Emma. 'What do you want to do?'

'I can't just stay here. The number of times I've thought if I had just gone to New York, I would have found Joe …' She rubbed her eyes. 'I can't just wait this time. Will you drive me?'

'Of course,' Luca grabbed his keys.

'We'll be right behind,' Olivier said, guiding Paloma and Dolores out.

'We will stay here,' Freya said, and Macu took her arm. 'Do you have your mobile?' Emma nodded. 'Make sure it's on. If we hear anything, I'll call you.'

'Isn't it the Cremà, St Joseph's Day, today?' Charles said, watching them leave. 'By tonight the whole city will be blazing.' He picked up a photo of baby Joe from the mantelpiece. He could see the similarity, see Liberty as a baby in the child. He thought of everything they had done to protect her. *All the lies, all the lives lost, that's what we were fighting for*, he thought, *so that future generations could just be children, innocent and safe.* His stomach coiled with helpless fear as he thought of Emma's child.

66

VALENCIA, MARCH 2002

Luca slammed down his hand on the horn, gesticulating at the car in front to move out of the way. Tail lights snaked red into the city. 'It's no good,' he said. 'It will take too long to drive into the centre. Everyone is coming in from miles around for Fallas.'

Emma sat on the edge of the seat, her hands clutching the dashboard. 'Stop here. It will be quicker to run.' Luca swerved to the side of the road, Olivier's car close behind.

They abandoned the cars on the outskirts of the dry Turia riverbed, ran over the Trinidad Bridge and weaved through the crowds towards Plaza de la Virgen. The deeper they ran into the narrowing, dark streets, the heavier the air grew with woodsmoke, the smell of cordite, the flash and noise of *traca* firecrackers. The night sky pulsed with a sinister glow.

'They will burn the Fallas figures soon,' Luca shouted, checking his watch. 'Everything goes crazy then, we must try and find her before …'

'Before it's too late?' Emma said. While Olivier, Paloma and Dolores searched the square, Emma and Luca ran to the hotel. The receptionist told them Delilah had stayed only a few hours, checked out earlier that evening with her child.

'Her child!' Emma cried as they ran through the crowded streets. They found Olivier near the Basilica.

'Any luck?' he shouted above the noise as Dolores and Paloma joined them.

Emma shook her head. 'She could be anywhere by now.'

Luca's phone rang, and he spoke quickly, covering his ear against the thump of the fireworks and the shouts of the crowd. 'The police say she has not been at the airport,' he said, 'and they are watching the train station. Her car?'

'She wouldn't drive, not in the dark.' Emma's mind was whirling, trying to make sense of what was happening.

'So she is in the city. If she was planning to drive, she would wait for the morning. We still have a chance …'

Emma felt panic overwhelm her as countless people surged around them. 'But look at this place – it's hopeless!'

'Can you think of anything Delilah said? Anything at all?' Paloma asked her.

'Do not worry, *cariño*,' Dolores said. 'We will search the whole city if we have to. Try and think calmly. You know this woman. Where would she go?'

They pushed through the crowds into the narrow back streets. 'Wait!' Emma called out to Luca. He reached back to her, took her hand. The macabre papier mâché figures of dragons, princesses, knights loomed over them, the size of houses. Fireworks fountained into the sky, sparkling gold raining down on the city. Emma's heart thundered in her chest, the blood singing in her ears. Then it came to her. *It's like a fairy tale*, Emma remembered Delilah saying. As soon as they hit clear road on Calle Caballeros, she began to run again. 'I know where she is!' Emma pointed ahead. 'The towers! She'd go to the towers.'

Emma and Luca raced through the old streets side by side, snaking through the crowds of revellers. The Torres de Quart loomed ahead of them, massive and dark, dwarfing the houses either side on the narrow street. The back of the tower had been cut away long ago, and the open vaulted halls gaped dark like hungry mouths. It did not take long for Luca to spot Delilah at one of the terraces, Joseph swaddled in her arms. 'There!' he cried.

'Delilah!' Emma yelled above the crashing fireworks, and ran forward just as she turned and spotted her. Delilah backed away from the edge into the shadows.

The crowds roared as the vast Fallas figures ignited across the city. Emma and Luca forced their way along the pavement, pushing people aside, smoke choking them, blinding their eyes. A woman grabbed Emma's shoulder. 'Is that your friend stuck in the tower? She was calling for help. Don't worry, someone has phoned for the keyholder.'

'Calling for help?' Emma shielded her eyes, looked up. Her head swam with the scale of the huge stone walls.

'It happens sometimes,' the woman yelled above the noise. 'People get locked in by accident.'

Accident? Emma thought. *I don't believe that for a moment.*

'The gate is this way!' Luca yelled.

Emma ran to the iron railings, and grabbed the bars. She rattled them, banged her hand flat against them in frustration. 'It's locked.' She gazed up the first flight of stone steps to the arched wooden door. 'We have to get inside.'

'God knows how long it will take the keyholder to come, especially now.' Luca put his arm protectively around Emma as they were jostled by the crowd. 'I will call the police again,' he said.

Emma gazed up at the towers soaring above them. 'That bitch knows I hate heights,' she said under her breath as she rolled up her sleeves. She swung her leg up onto the iron bar on the gate.

'What are you doing? Be careful!' Luca cried, glancing up from the phone.

'It will take too long if we wait for the police. There has to be a way in.' She looked back at him. 'This is between Delilah and me.' Emma scrambled up, heaving herself to the top. She winced with the effort, her stomach muscles still weak from the birth.

'Watch the spikes!' he yelled, and climbed up behind her. 'Put your feet on my shoulders. You can jump over then.' A crowd had gathered around them. A couple of men stepped forward to help, climbing the railings themselves to help Emma over. She swung clear, and dropped to the other side. She cried out in pain.

'Emma!' Luca called. 'Are you OK?'

'I'm fine,' she said, straightening up. 'My ankle ...' She looked up at the tower, saw a flash of blonde hair on the top terrace as Delilah looked down on them.

Luca reached through the bars to her. 'Wait for us.'

'No. She has my child. I have to get him, now.'

'Be careful. I'll be right behind you.'

Emma ran up the stone steps outside the tower, and tried the first door. It was locked. She flung her shoulder against it, but the heavy, studded door didn't budge. She sprinted down again, sweat trickling along her spine.

There has to be a way in, she thought, frantically searching in the shadows for a door, a window left open a crack.

'Emma!' She heard Luca shouting above the crowd. She ran back to him, and saw an old man sorting through a hoop of keys. 'It was lucky, he was in town for the Cremà.'

'Give it to me!' she yelled, her hand stretching through the bars. The man unclipped an old iron key, and passed it to her. She ran back up the steps, stumbling. The key shook in her hand, and she missed the lock the first time. At last, it turned, the door creaked open and she plunged into the darkness of the first hall, her footsteps echoing. She felt like she was in a nightmare, sprinting up the flights of stone stairs, round and round, steps cantilevered out into the air, the sound of her baby's plaintive cries driving her on. She stumbled as she heard Joseph scream in fear above her. Her ankle gave way and she slipped back down the stairs, dangling over the sheer drop to the vaulted hall. Vertigo swept over her, and her fingers clutched at the smooth stone. She caught herself, scrambled to her feet, grasping the thin metal balustrade. She ran faster, her heart thumping, her lungs bursting.

The night sky unfolded before her as she sped out onto the top terrace, a grey blanket of smoke rising to the stars from across the city. Beneath her she saw the blazing Fallas figures. Blue flashing lights were forcing their way through the crowds packing the roads.

Emma ducked as a metal bar flew past her head.

'Don't come any closer!' Delilah yelled.

'You took my baby.' Emma glared at her.

'I didn't take him,' she said. 'I got locked in.'

'Rubbish. You knew exactly what you were doing. You

figured it would be a good place to hide out through the night, that I'd never look for you here.'

'Yeah, you and your vertigo,' Delilah sneered. 'Does it scare you, Em? Being up here?' She leant over the edge. 'We're very, very high.'

Emma inched forwards. 'What is this? Another cry for help? What did you want, Delilah? Attention?'

'Cry for help?' Delilah said quietly.

'Don't hurt my baby.'

'Your baby? He should have been our baby, mine and Joe's.' Delilah brushed the top of his head with her lips. 'I just wanted … I wanted …'

Emma strode forwards. Delilah was on the edge of the battlements now, her hair lifting in the breeze, sparks rising up from below, illuminated by the fires. 'Joseph is my baby.'

'No! He should have been mine.' She took a step back, held the child closer. 'I told him all about Joe. I told him all about his father.'

Emma's voice strained. 'Please, just get down from there.'

'Why? What have I got to live for?'

Emma thought fast. 'The money, Delilah. You'll be a rich woman, that's what you've always wanted. Take it all, I don't care.' The baby's pitiful wails clawed at her heart. 'I just want my child.'

'Money? I just want him, I want Joe.' Delilah wiped her wild eyes with the back of her hand, mascara smearing black across her face. The baby swung perilously from one arm. Emma held her breath, ready to leap for him. She edged closer. 'I loved Joe from the moment I met him, but you had to come along and spoil it all.'

'I didn't know.'

472

'It's not fair.'

'We don't know Joe's gone.'

'We do!' Delilah began to cry, her mouth a ragged hole. 'He's dead!'

'We'll never know for sure. Perhaps he'll come for you.' She was within touching distance of the baby.

'For me?' Delilah wept uncontrollably.

Emma shielded her eyes from the smoke and sparks. Behind Delilah she saw a figure edging along the parapet.

'You could have had anyone,' Delilah sobbed, 'but you took him. Just like I'm going to take your baby.'

'No!'

As Delilah jumped to the edge, Luca grabbed her.

'Give Emma the baby,' he said quietly.

'Let go of me!' Delilah struggled, thrashing out at him.

Emma grasped Joseph around his waist. 'Let him go,' she begged. 'He's a baby, an innocent baby.'

Delilah looked Emma in the eye, her face wild with grief.

'I'm here,' Luca said quietly.

'Let him go,' Emma whispered, her voice hoarse and desperate. 'Please, my baby ...' She felt Delilah release her grip, and she pulled Joseph into her arms.

Delilah looked at Emma and the child, tears coursing down her cheeks. 'You have it all. You have everything I ever wanted.'

Luca jumped down onto the terrace. 'I'll take him,' he said, lifting Joseph to safety. 'See if you can make her see sense.'

'He's so beautiful,' Delilah said under her breath. 'So beautiful.'

'Thank you,' Emma said to Luca. She turned back to Delilah just at the moment she swung her legs over

473

the edge. Their gazes locked. Emma would never forget the absolute calm on Delilah's face as she fell. 'No! Lila!' Emma lunged forwards, and caught her wrist as she jumped. The stone dug hard against Emma's arms, scraping her skin as she struggled to hold on.

'Let me go!' Delilah screamed, her legs dangling in the air, her free arm flailing. One of her shoes tumbled away into the darkness, bouncing down the stone steps to the street below.

'I can't hold you!' Emma cried. 'Lila, reach up to me!'

Emma's grip on her wrist slipped. Delilah's eyes opened wide, her last words drifting up to Emma as she fell away: 'We almost made it, Joe, we almost made it,' she cried as she plunged into the flame-filled streets below.

'Lila!' Emma screamed. A horrified roar went up from the crowd. Across Valencia seven hundred Fallas figures burst into flame. Emma covered her eyes with her hands, and turned to Luca. He was cradling the baby against his chest, and reached out for her with his free arm.

'Thank God you are all right. I'm sorry I didn't get here in time.' He kissed her temple. The sound of sirens cut through the night.

'You did. You saved my child.'

They held fast to one another, and Emma looked out across the city. Above the flames the night sky shone with thousands of stars. She thought of her mother. She thought of Rosa, dancing for Jordi in her red dress in the firelight, of Freya and Tom, walking through the Spanish hills arm in arm. She thought of all the lives cut short by war, all the years that might have been. She thought of Joe, reading her message as he reached the Twin Towers and the shadow of a plane passed overhead. She thought of the falling man in New York, and the falling soldier in Capa's photograph. She saw all their lives written out across the night sky. She saw the past, the present, the future fall away as one.

'She's gone.' Luca held her and the baby tight. 'You are safe, now.'

'We saved him,' she said as she kissed Joseph, looked up at Luca. They turned and walked away into the night, and Emma reached up, clutched the gold locket in her hand. 'Maybe now it's time to save one another.'

AUTHOR'S NOTE

In July 1936, conservative generals led by Francisco Franco staged a military rebellion against the democratically elected government of the Second Spanish Republic. It is estimated the Spanish Civil War of 1936–9 that ensued cost the lives of half a million people. Another half a million Spaniards fled as refugees.

This battle was the prelude to World War II. Franco's rebel Nationalists gained support from Hitler's Nazi troops and Mussolini's Italian fascists. Nearly 60,000 volunteers from over fifty countries joined the International Brigades as combatants and non-combatants to fight the Nationalists and their supporters alongside the Republican Army. Among the volunteers were many women, who mostly worked with medical units.

Some 200,000 people died in combat – 4,900 of them from the Brigades. The other 300,000 who lost their lives during the war and the reprisals that followed the Nationalist victory were murdered, executed, or killed in bombing raids. Many of these victims were women and children. Valencia held out against the Nationalists until the end. It was the last major city to fall in Spain. Veterans from the International Brigades and Republican exiles went on to fight fascism in Europe in World War II.

The Spanish Civil War divided the country, and individual families. Until 2007 there was a national *pacto de olvido*, a pact of forgetting. The Spanish writer George Santayana said 'those who cannot remember the past are condemned to repeat it'. Now, thanks to the Law of Historical Memory, the history of the war is being rewritten. This account of women at war, and their families, blends fiction with the real events of that time. The true memories of those involved bear witness to the extraordinary sacrifices ordinary people make for freedom.

ACKNOWLEDGEMENTS

Many people have generously shared their knowledge and experience during the research for this book. Particular thanks goes to Professor Paul Preston, Jim Jump of the International Brigades Memorial Trust, Emilio Silva of the Association for the Recovery of Historical Memory and Cynthia Jackson of the Robert Capa Archive at the International Center of Photography for their extensive help and research suggestions. I would also like to thank Stuart Christie, Angela Jackson, Natalia Benjamin of the Basque Children of '37 Association, James Cronan of the National Archives, Mónica Moreira, Harriet Batchelor Patrizi, Reverend Alison Craven of St Luke's and Christ Church, Tim Birch, Susana Gil, Pilar Ballesteros, Ivan Llanza Ortiz, David Barros, Jorge Garzón, John Muddeman, Julian Donohue of the Lepidopterists' Society, Mark Ritchie of the Royal Borough of Kensington and Chelsea, and Lisa Wood of John Rylands University Archive. Thanks also to Drs Rookmaaker, Foster, Friday and Asher of Cambridge University, Elaine Oliver, Jonathan Smith of Trinity College Library and Tracy Wilkinson of King's College Archive. Isabelle Gellé and Luca Turin were generous with their inspiring advice about perfumes.

I would like to thank Peter Stanford, and David Whiting of the Cecil Day-Lewis Estate for permission to quote the beautiful extract from 'Walking Away'.

My thanks go to Leila Aboulela, to Sherry Ashworth, Nicholas Royle, my MA group at MMU and the maniacs of Moniack Mhor for their help with the story.

Thank you to my wonderful agent, Sheila Crowley, and all at Curtis Brown. The team at Corvus is remarkable – particular thanks to my exceptional editor Laura Palmer, Lucy Ridout, Nicole Muir, Rina Gill, and Becci Sharpe.

To paraphrase Marcel Proust, the 'charming gardeners' who make my soul blossom have supported me with great patience in the writing of this book – to my husband and children, and to my family, with love and thanks - always. Don't forget to smell the flowers.

Paula
Amazon
June 2023